The PULSE of HIS SOUL

The Story of
John Lothropp
a Forgotten Forefather

ORA SMITH

LIGHTEN PRESS

Praise for The Pulse of His Soul

"Intriguing. Exciting. Difficult to put down. *The Pulse of His Soul* is a must-read history of John Lothropp, a devout Anglican minister, who challenged the beliefs of the early Church of England."
— Richard W. Price, MA, Accredited Genealogist, owner and president of Price Genealogy

"A love story for the ages begins this journey of the Reverend John Lothropp and Hannah Howse. Love, despair, faith, courage in early 1600's England . . . This saga rivals that of the Mayflower Pilgrims and chronicles the founding of what became the Congregational Church in the United States."
—Marla Mountz Vincent, 9th great-granddaughter of Reverend John, former Director at Large Board of Trustees and former Chairperson, Update to Huntington's 1884 Genealogy of Reverend John Lothropp for the Lothropp Family Foundation

"I could not put it down. I found I was racing through it, wanting to know what happened next. There was more than one heart-stopping moment, and on other occasions I had tears in my eyes. I highly recommend it, and I think it is well worth all of five stars."
— Evelyn Tidman, author of *One Small Candle: The Story of William Bradford and the Pilgrim Fathers*

"*The Pulse of His Soul* is beautifully told and rich in historical detail. The America we know exists in part because of John Lothropp. Ora Smith is a master storyteller."
— Sarah Hinze, author of *A Pawn for a King: Ada de Warenne 1123-1178, Queen Mother to the Kings of Scots*

The PULSE of HIS SOUL

The Story of
John Lothropp
a Forgotten Forefather

ORA SMITH

LIGHTEN PRESS

Copyright © 2020 by Ora Smith

Published by Lighten Press
www.lightenpress.com

Printed in the United States of America

This is a work of fiction.

All rights reserved. No part of this publication can be reproduced, stored in a retrieval system, or transmitted in any form or by any means—for example, electronic, photocopy, recording—without the prior written permission of the publisher. The only exception is brief quotations and printed reviews.

ISBN:
978-0-9980410-3-2

All scriptures quoted in this novel by Reverend John Lothropp are from the Bishops' Bible. Prayers and catechisms are cited from *The Book of Common Prayer*. Both are taken from 1604 editions.

This story is a work of fiction. With the exception of recognized historical figures and events, all characters and events are the product of the author's imagination. Any resemblance to any person, living or dead, is purely coincidental.

Cover design by
Adrienne Quintana, Pink Umbrella Books
Cover photo iStock.com/cyno66

BISAC Subject Headings
FIC014000   FICTION / Historical / General
FIC042030   FICTION / Christian / Historical
FIC041000   FICTION / Biographical
FIC019000   FICTION / Literary
FIC026000   FICTION / Religious
ET030   CULTURAL HERITAGE / British
TP028   TOPICAL / Christian Interest

Dedication

Because ancestors can help us know who we are, this book is dedicated to all those who descend from Reverend John Lothropp. On this 400th Anniversary of our Pilgrim Fathers, let's remember one more Separatist who came to America to make Her great.

The author chose to use the surname spelling *Lothropp* because this spelling was used by John Lothropp's own hand. It appears his children in America and his brother Thomas used the spelling *Lothrop* and *Lathrop* with *Lathrop* now the most common form.

For a Glossary of Terms relating to the 17th century and Church of England, see page 346.

Contents

Joan Didion Quote	i
Map	ii
Part I	1
Chapter One	1
Chapter Two	9
Chapter Three	17
Chapter Four	23
Chapter Five	30
Chapter Six	37
Chapter Seven	43
Chapter Eight	48
Chapter Nine	57
Chapter Ten	64
Chapter Eleven	73
Chapter Twelve	82
Chapter Thirteen	93
Chapter Fourteen	102
PART II	110
Chapter Fifteen	110
Chapter Sixteen	118
Chapter Seventeen	125
Chapter Eighteen	136
Chapter Nineteen	146
Chapter Twenty	157
Chapter Twenty-One	168
PART III	173
Chapter Twenty-Two	173
Chapter Twenty-Three	180
Chapter Twenty-Four	192
Chapter Twenty-Five	198
Chapter Twenty-Six	208

Chapter Twenty-Seven	214
Chapter Twenty-Eight	221
Chapter Twenty-Nine	229
Chapter Thirty	234
Chapter Thirty-One	242
Chapter Thirty-Two	249
Chapter Thirty-Three	262
Chapter Thirty-Four	270
Chapter Thirty-Five	276
Chapter Thirty-Six	283
PART IV	288
Chapter Thirty-Seven	288
Chapter Thirty-Eight	294
Chapter Thirty-Nine	302
Author's Notes	309
Factual Notes of Historical Figures	315
Independents Arrested	334
Trial and Imprisonment	334
The *Griffin*	336
Men of Kent	336
John Lothropp's Compatriots	337
Famous Decendents of John Lothropp	339
Decendancy Chart	345
Glossary of Terms	346
Reformation Timeline	354
Bibliography	356
Acknowledgements	364
Also by the Author	365
The John Lothropp Foundation	367

"The past could be jettisoned . . . but seeds got carried."
—Joan Didion, *Where I Was From*

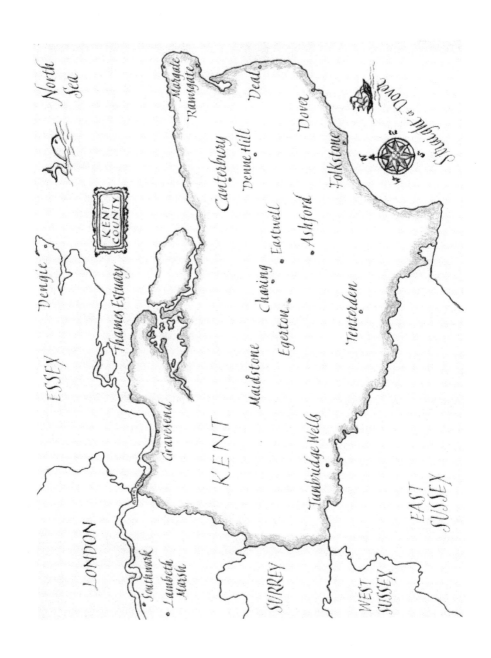

Part I

Chapter One

January 1589
Etton Village in the East Riding of Yorkshire, England

Icy wind blew against John's ears until they burned. Clutching his hat, he ran to catch up with his eleven brothers and sisters as they followed their father into the old stone Church of Saint Mary. Often forgotten now, he would have no-one to care for him since Mother had died. The last one into the church, the large door banged shut behind him. He didn't know what made him feel most scared—the wail of the wind moaning to get in or the sound of crying that made him want to run out.

The men wore dark colors and the women wore black with white veils, collars, and headdresses. But like him and his siblings, some of the young women wore all white. Thom, John's older brother, told him 'twas because they weren't married. Thom was smart because he was seven—two years older than John.

Everyone stood while his family filed into the ancient Lothropp pew, youngest to oldest. He huddled between Thom and William, who sat on Nursemaid's lap. Father sat near the aisle, his face as hard as the stone statues outside.

Dressed in white robes and a ridiculously high wig, the vicar stood before the congregation. "We've gathered to honor Maude

Lothropp, a woman who knew her duty as wife and mother, dying in her efforts to follow the commandment to multiply and replenish the earth." His words echoed off the recently whitewashed walls where there used to be papal murals.

John's mother had said that white purification pleased the monarch, Queen Elizabeth, so now the colorful paintings were hidden.

The vicar's voice grew louder. "Although a creature intellectually and physically inferior to man, she, a servant to God, shall rest with Him forever."

John squirmed. His mother wasn't *inferior*. She was kind and soft and made him feel safe. Those words welled inside him, pushing him to stand up and shout, but William's nursemaid laid a hand on John's shoulder before he could open his mouth. She nodded toward his father.

Brow lowered, Father glared directly down the row at John.

John sat. Attracting Father's attention was worse than being locked in the dark clothes cupboard by his brothers. John clasped his hands. But it was hard to stay still while the mean man in the robes talked nonsense about Mother. Rather than listen, he thought about how she sang him songs when he was sad and laughed when he rolled down the big hill near home and how she kissed him goodnight. Her good night kisses had been gone for days now. Sniffling, he swiped away a tear with his sleeve and leaned on Thom's shoulder.

Someone behind him waved a handkerchief next to his face.

He wiped his nose and cheeks, the cloth soft like Mother's.

The vicar droned on, raising his voice and banging on the pulpit until it hurt John's ears worse than the cold wind.

Why did he have to yell? He was supposed to be honoring Mother. If John was a preacher, he'd say words like "peace" and "love" and "all will be well."

He tried hard to ignore the vicar's horrible words. The only thing that made John's tears stop for a moment was when the vicar lurched forward and talcum puffed out of his wig. Then John wanted to snicker. But a quick look at Father changed his mind.

After it felt like John had missed dinner and supper, the vicar finally stopped talking and the congregation stood and shuffled just outside the entrance.

Last night, John had overheard Father say they couldn't afford a vault inside the church, but they were wealthy enough for his mother to be buried near the porch door. John didn't want her to be buried anywhere. He wanted her to tuck him in bed and listen to his catechism.

At Father's command, he and his brothers and sisters lined up along the trench that held their mother's casket with a white cloth draped over it. He tried not to think about her being in that dark, small space. 'Twas too much like the cupboard. And that made his chest hurt. Instead, he imagined a rabbit jumping from each of his siblings' hats to the last and tallest—his half-brother Robert—home from school for the funeral.

A strong, cold gust of air struck John's face. He hated the sharp sting. The wind wouldn't leave him alone, whipping at his clothes like it wanted to tear them off. It nipped at his nose and made it run. On blustery days, even if his brothers and sisters wanted to stay outside and play, he'd go inside. But wind in Yorkshire was as common as grey clouds.

He went to wipe his nose on his sleeve.

Over the top of William's head, the nursemaid gave John the eye of admonition.

Remembering the stranger's handkerchief he'd stuffed in his pocket, he used that.

"Oh, holy and most merciful Savior, deliver us not into the bitter pains of eternal death . . ." The preacher obviously felt he hadn't said enough in the church and repeated his long sermon in prayer.

The wet lawn soaked through John's shoes and chilled his feet. He wished the old man's wig would blow off, but he kept a firm grip on it as he prayed.

Everything here appeared old—the vicar, the headstones, the church walls, the brittle trees. But his mother wasn't. She didn't belong here.

Last sennight, she'd cheered him on while he played with his whirly top. Eyes burning with tears, he tried to make the image leave his head by forcing himself to think of the hopping rabbit, but it did no good. Not even Thom grabbing his hand helped. Since Mother had left, everything felt dreary. He choked back a sob, but his throat was too tight to swallow it.

Father narrowed his eyes in warning.

William became restless too, having been so long in the nursemaid's arms. He pushed against her, hollering to be released.

John's sister, Anne, strangled a sob. And she wasn't a one-year old like William, but a big girl of eleven. Older half-sister, Isabell, took her in her arms, both crying loudly while Mary stepped toward John with a look on her face that told him she needed to be held too.

They all came together, the older ones trying to hold to Father's commands to keep quiet, but eventually crying too. The sound of their wails flew with the wind and swirled around the ancient cemetery stones.

Jaw clenched, Father stared at them with bloodshot eyes, and John stepped behind Mary to hide.

A long time later, the people from the church followed them home.

John found a spot alone in front of his favorite stone-arched window. Outside, the lawn stretched toward hedgerows with fields behind, waiting for crops to be planted. Dark clouds hung low, threatening rain. All around him, adults spoke in whispers and half-sentences.

His father stood not far away, speaking with Uncle Edmund.

Even though Uncle lived less than an hour's ride, John rarely saw him, which he was glad for. Uncle was often cross.

John wished he could escape to his room before he attracted either of their attention.

"Come here, John," Father commanded.

Too late. Father was never in good humor, even before Mother's death. Whenever John stood in the same room, he was expected to "remain silent and not display a childlike disposition." The few words Father had ever spoken to John were those to condemn, reprimand, or remind.

John moved toward him slowly.

Someone nearby prodded her companion. "Poor, motherless orphans. They do naught for their keep."

"And too many dependents," another whispered to someone else. "Some must go before he's penniless."

Father stretched his arm toward Uncle, who'd been peering at Thom and John all day as if he thought them distasteful to the eye yet couldn't stop looking. "Bow to your Uncle Edmund," Father said.

"Good day, Sir." John bowed deeply to his mother's brother. He didn't look like her at all. John wished he did.

As if done with him now that he'd performed his duty, his father turned to Uncle. "He has been a strong, healthy child since the day he was born."

Surprised and confused at the compliment, John stood taller.

Why did Father display such courtesy to Uncle? John looked for Thom, who he spotted holding the hand of Uncle's wife—their rich, sickly, childless Aunt Melly.

As if knowing someone spied upon him, Thom turned toward John and creased his brow in query.

John was anxious to be alone with Thom. He'd so many questions about the day's curiosities. And Thom knew so many things.

His father leaned closer to Uncle. "The eldest can be your heir and the next for the Church. Their grandfather was a charitable and distinguished vicar."

"Thank you for hearing me out," Uncle said quietly. "I'll need to consider all you've aforementioned." He bowed to Father and strode to his wife and whispered in her ear.

Her face beamed with pleasure, and she bent to kiss Thom.

John covered his mouth in a giggle, but then felt something cloud his heart. He'd never want anyone kissing him other than Mother. And that could no longer happen. Ever.

Thom had all but stopped himself from backing away from Aunt Melly. Biting his bottom lip, he looked to Father to see if he'd witnessed the act.

"Get Thom and go to the nursery," Father said without looking at John.

Borne off to bed early by the nursemaid, William lay on a small pallet nearby, already breathing in slumber, and Thom lay beside John. Rain beat on the roof, and the wind still howled.

The darkness and memories of the day swam before him. He missed his mother. Could her ghost visit? If she came, would he be happy or scared? Would he talk to her like he used to? Would she smell like the lavender she kept tucked in her bodice? Would she tickle his face with her long dark hair?

John rolled to face Thom. "What does it mean to do naught for our keep?"

"I think it means we don't earn money."

"I heard someone whisper it to another. I think they were talking about us."

"I cannot see how." Thom said. "Children don't earn their keep. If they were referring to us from Father's reckoning, I wouldn't worry over it. It's useless to try and win Father's favor."

John rolled onto his back. "Can Father not love twelve children?"

Thom made a noise of dislike. "Father does not love. Such

affection was for Mother only."

The words pinched John deep inside his chest. He squeezed his eyes against tears. He'd cried more this day than any other. He needed to stop acting like William—a baby.

John smiled out the carriage window, glad for the unexpected trip to Uncle's nearby mansion, even if the man was sometimes mean. And the day was extra special because John's brothers and sisters were with him.

Home wasn't the same since Mother had died eight months ago. He didn't like it. Sometimes he still forgot he couldn't run and find her when he wanted to share good news. His older siblings went about their days as they had before, but John had always been with William and Mother in the nursery. Now that he'd turned six, he had to spend time with the tutor. The tutor smelled of sour sweat and hair oils. His large crooked teeth protruded from his too small mouth and made him look like a rabbit.

When they arrived at Uncle's estate in Leconfield, Father dismounted his horse. He poked his head into the hot carriage, looking at them one at a time, as if counting all five—Anne with William on her lap, Mary, Thom, and John. "Stay here until I tell you otherwise." He strode away, his leather boots clacking across the cobbles of the courtyard.

John's brothers and sisters stared at one another as if they were as muddled as John about this strange, sudden outing.

Anne kept glancing out the window. "I suppose he's seeing if anyone is at home?"

"It's stifling in here." Mary wiped at her forehead. "I hope he's not long,"

John loosened his collar ruff. Nursemaid had bedecked him in his finest, as if he was going to church.

William settled into Anne's lap and fell asleep.

John dozed also and was awakened by Father's voice. "Come out of the carriage and bestow courtesy to your new father and mother."

What? What was Father talking about? John shook his head to clear it.

Anne jerked forward, startling William. "What do you mean, Father?" Her voice trembled.

John pushed back against the carriage seat. No one ever

questioned Father.

Father's face became red like cook's when she stirred stew over the fire. "Do as I say and get out of the carriage."

Uncle Edmund stepped up behind him. "Your father has spoken the truth, child. You *all*," he harrumphed, "have come to live with me and Aunt Melly." He didn't seem very happy about that.

Why would they come to live with Uncle if he didn't want them? John didn't like home anymore, but now he wanted to go back.

Anne stared wide-eyed, her face pale. Mary whimpered. Thom grunted.

John's stomach felt as if his midday meal would leave as they stumbled from the carriage.

"Why so many long faces?" Uncle squinted like the sun was too bright in his eyes. "Do you not want to live in this fine home?" He waved to the mansion beside him, windows glistening in the sunshine, stones as permanent as the Yorkshire Wolds.

None of them said a word.

John was sure Father preferred they not speak. That worked at home. If they stayed quiet, he ignored them. Maybe if they were quiet now, he'd let them come home.

"Come here, Thom." Uncle reached out. "You're the new heir of this grand estate."

Thom's eyes widened, and he stepped to Uncle as if he were sailing toward the whole Spanish Armada.

Aunt Melly took his hand like she had at the funeral.

Thom shuddered.

"And you, young John." Uncle turned toward him. "You are meant to be a preacher, if you've the tenacity."

A preacher? Never! Not like that old vicar. He was mean. And John hated sermons. They made him sleepy. He scowled even though Father would be angry.

Father shuffled his feet as if he wanted to leave. "I'll send this carriage back with their clothing." He waved the driver away.

Wanting to spit on his father, John clenched his fists behind his back. What had he done to make Father give him away?

"I pray they're not troublesome children, Thomas. You told me otherwise." Uncle frowned, examining all five faces.

Mary stood with her arms crossed, staring at the ground. Anne had tears on her cheeks. Still holding William, she tried to hide her face behind his head. Thom's face flushed so red John feared his brother would say something and make Father angry. And then he would never come back for them.

"They're as tame and obedient as lambs." Father stepped to Uncle Edmund, shook his hand, kissed Aunt Melly's free hand, and mounted his horse. Then he left without even saying "Fare thee well," or "I will miss you," or "I'll visit often."

John shook all over. He didn't want to run after Father, but he couldn't stop himself. "Don't leave us here!" He swept his arms forward, his heart pounded in his ears, tears ran down his face.

"You know naught of what's best for you," Father shouted over his shoulder.

Coughing from the dust, John stumbled and stopped. His heart slowed. His throat tightened. How could Father just leave them here?

With Mother in heaven and Father gone, who would take care of him?

Chapter Two

Twenty-one years later, August 1610
The county of Kent, England

The Lord forsook me to let me be born a woman.
    Hannah sighed and shifted in the stuffy carriage. The road, rutted from days of rain and then a dry spell, agitated her insides and matched her frustration.

"What ails you, daughter?" Sitting across from her, Father's jowls jiggled like the gelatus confiture Mother had served that morning.

If only she could share her thoughts with him. He'd been ignoring her as of late to spend time with her brothers. She'd lost his attention. Because she was a woman. "I don't know who to emulate, you or Mother."

If Hannah had been born a man, she'd preach every Sunday like Father, serve his Anglican parishioners, and study Church doctrine—letting God's word enlarge her soul. Years ago, in secret, Father had taught her Latin so she could better understand his books. Now it was as if she didn't exist when it came to her education. And because of her sex, the only *public* praising she could offer God was in song.

Father chuckled, oblivious to her strife. "Don't emulate me. I daresay you won't want my balding head or double chin." He winked at her.

Usually one to jest with him, today she was in no mood. "I

crave to preach the Gospel as you do."

Shaking his head, he let out a long breath. "All your wishing won't amend the fact that you'll one day marry and have your mother's duties."

Mother's life *would* one day be hers—sooner than later since Hannah was already sixteen. 'Twasn't that she didn't want to marry. It was more that she desired to spend time serving her Lord. Her mother and sisters spun yarn, embroidered aprons and sleeves, laundered clothes, brewed beer, made candles and soap, kept bees, cooked, cared for the young ones, and attended to Father's needs. But that wasn't for her. True, Father couldn't satisfy his important duties as vicar without their help but being male would have let Hannah fulfill her ambitions.

Father glanced away and tightened his jaw, his flabby profile hardening. "I'm to blame for your confusion. I shouldn't have let you study with me." He turned toward her and frowned. "You being the eldest and me not having sons for so long, I welcomed your interest. Your mother has scolded me. We're done with all that, and you'd best accept your fate."

Her fate. The fate of unfulfilled dreams. The fate of a woman. She clenched her fists.

Until now, she'd believed herself fortunate to be the eldest of seven. As a child she'd enjoyed much of Father's time, choosing his attention over Mother's, giving close analysis to his ecclesiastical duties. Her education had been looked to more fiercely than her younger three sisters. But now she had brothers who were old enough to start their own education.

He leaned toward her and clasped her hand. "I believe you misunderstand the importance of being a woman and the great gifts that come with motherhood."

Not that lecture again. She kept from rolling her eyes. "What's your sermon to be next Sabbath?" She deviated the subject to something Father would desire to discuss. He wasn't teaching her anymore, but she suspected he'd always be willing to have a good doctrinal analysis—as long as it was in private.

He let go of her hand. "I'm considering teaching about the gifts of the Holy Spirit," he said without hesitating, thankfully ignoring the fact that she was a woman.

She smiled to encourage the switch of discussion. "Where do you suggest I begin my study? Perchance with the book of Numbers, chapter eleven, verse twenty-five? 'And when the spirit rested upon them, they prophesied, and did not cease.'"

"Aye, a fine place to start."

The carriage stopped and Father peered out the window. "We're to Egerton vicarage."

The coachman opened the door.

Faint smells of late lavender and honeysuckle greeted her. She inhaled deeply. As much as she hated women's work, gardening she adored.

Father stepped out. "Come along, Hannah."

Taking his hand, she descended and peered about for a flower garden but saw only a tangle of what had probably once been glorious. Other than a few birds perched on the crest of the roof, the ancient two-story vicarage appeared abandoned. A squat edifice, with two dormers protruding from a slate-shingled roof, it had been built centuries before. An archaic stone Maltese cross stood at the roof's peak. Under deep eaves, arched windows of thick beveled-panes distorted what little sunlight reached them.

Hannah slid her hand into the crook of Father's arm and proceeded down a brick walkway to the portico, cool in shadow, framed by intricately hand-carved lattices of an outdated design.

Father's rap resounded off the aged wooden door. No one answered. He knocked again. "How now, anyone about?" he called.

But the new perpetual curate, John Lothropp, didn't answer.

"Let us roam the grounds to await his return," Father suggested.

"Aye, 'tis a splendid day for a walk. I do love Egerton."

"Shall we head toward the church?" He pointed up the hill at the square bell tower that rose taller than the trees and could be seen from nearby hamlets.

"'Twould be lovely." Hannah pushed back her lace-edged coif, releasing some of her curls, and raised her face toward the sun. The warmth helped release her foul mood. August had brought too much rain, and she wanted to bask in this clear and sunny day. She smiled. Alone with father, she'd bring out more theological discussion as they walked.

Strolling uphill along a well-worn path—probably used for centuries by preachers heading to the church in all kinds of weather—she admired the countryside. A flock of ewes on a distant hill, spots of white against lush green, grazed before a backdrop of dense woods. Small farms bordered by hedgerows stretched behind a farmstead clustered with meager thatched-roof homes.

"I enjoyed your sermon Sunday. Do you reckon the parishioners understood that evil speaking can also pertain to discourses about nonconformist views against the Church of England? Just yesterday I heard men at the mill yard talking of their disdain for clergy."

"I've heard the murmurings." Father pushed out a frustrated breath. "The danger with their philosophy is that congregations determine affairs without having to submit their decisions to the judgment of any higher human authority, and as such, they eliminate divinely appointed bishops."

They skirted the borders of the church's cemetery. Some headstones were at least two hundred years old, sinking crookedly into the earth. The recent ones had winged skulls carved onto their surfaces with solemn epitaphs prompting the passerby to contemplate the fleeting nature of life.

"Is it true the Puritans believe in predestination?" she questioned, hoping for more discussion. "It seems foolish to me."

"They imagine most people are depraved and undeserving of salvation," Father answered. "To them, salvation is a gift from God that will be bestowed upon the very few who were predestined. They say belief in Jesus Christ and participation in the sacraments doesn't affect one's salvation."

"I believe God is just and fair and will treat people in the afterlife according to how they lived their life on earth. I cannot fully comprehend these ideas of predestination."

"No offense, my dear." He chuckled. "But it's rather disappointing you *aren't* a man. You'd make a splendid preacher."

Aye, she would. His chuckle stung, and she chose to not laugh with him. "It's a shame it takes more than writing speeches to make a good preacher." In her heart she knew she'd be a great preacher. "Besides being *a woman*, I'm afraid I'd fail quite miserably at listening to everyone's opinions."

Father's chuckle deepened. "I won't disagree there."

She swatted his shoulder, her usual playful mood returning, despite the way the conversation had gone.

"But since when was listening to differing opinions the trait of a preacher?" Genuine mirth twinkled in his blue eyes.

Strolling to the entrance of Saint James with its tall windows of leaded diamond-shaped panes and walls of common ragstone, they stepped into the courtyard. Years of cool shadows cast from the great building permitted moss to grow between ancient ground stones.

The Pulse of His Soul

Continuing around the church and down a grassy slope, they came upon two men lounging on a blanket, a pewter pitcher and mugs between them. They faced away from Hannah and Father, oblivious to their approach. She couldn't see their features, only the backs of their heads. One man had auburn hair, the other brown, both held back with ribbons.

"I shall never marry and have children," the gentleman with the brown hair said.

"Funny coming from you, the man with nineteen siblings." The redhead's chuckle rang carefree and pleasant. "Your father would not fathom such an idea, John."

John? Aye, this man must be John Lothropp, the new perpetual curate. She hadn't expected to see him in recline, wearing a jerkin over a white linen shirt with no wig or collar ruff. Her imagination had decorated him in church robes of red with a white embroidered silk scarf trailing down the front.

Considering the private discourse, Father and she should head another way. She tugged on his sleeve.

He seemed oblivious to courtesy and strode toward the men.

"Mayhap that's exactly why I've sworn off the family life." Reverend Lothropp sighed. "I know well what it's like to have children underfoot who need money for food, clothing, and education. Nay, I cannot risk the distractions of a wife who demands attention and children who require care. I need time to carry out the duties of a parish priest and study for my sermons."

"Bishop King knew what he was doing when he brought you here to Egerton. More devotion to the Church a man cannot find. We all knew at Cambridge you were his favorite," his friend teased good-naturedly. "Do you have aspirations toward becoming a bishop?"

"I dare not allow such a lofty dream. I'll serve where God sees fit. I'd love naught more than to show others my convictions that the Lord is good."

Hannah listened in spite of herself, intrigued by this man who thought as she. Although as much as she loved the Church, she didn't reason her devotion would keep her from marrying. Did that somehow mean her faith wasn't as strong as she thought?

Moving closer, she glanced at Father who appeared highly interested in the conversation. She hoped he'd call out a salutation.

Suddenly he threw his arm out to stop her. His expression transformed to curiosity.

She held still, hardly breathing, embarrassment tingling up her neck. What if the men turned and saw them spying?

"Why can't you have a family *and* teach others of your convictions?" the redhead questioned.

"God before man!" Reverend Lothropp said, as if there were no truer words. "My profession would be placed second if I had a family. Which is why I won't marry."

His friend shook his head. "I've heard it said that if a man doesn't know how to manage his own family, he'll not know how to care for God's church."

"Same ol' Robert. Condemns with humor. You jest of things that shouldn't be made merry."

"Same ol' John. Doesn't know how to laugh." He nudged the reverend's ribs. "Come now, these are words amongst friends and will go no further."

Hannah swallowed, wanting to turn and run.

"All words are said before God," Lothropp argued.

"Truly John, your devotion should be admired," Robert said.

Father shifted slightly, and she tried to catch his eye. Why had he not called out to the men? Should they not make their presence known? Interrupt them somehow? The situation highly inappropriate, her face warmed. 'Twasn't her place to interrupt men. She pulled at Father's arm.

He frowned, then tipped his head, and loudly cleared his throat.

Reverend Lothropp leapt to his feet while Robert casually looked over his shoulder, then stood.

The reverend appeared young. In his late twenties mayhap? She'd expected him to be much older. She found herself drawn to his brown eyes, struck by the gentle slope at the corners. She discovered kindness where she expected agitation at their intrusion. Catching herself staring, she quickly looked down.

"How do you fare? I apologize to come upon you like this." Father pulled Hannah forward. "We went first to the vicarage but found no one home." They stepped to the blanket. "You're John Lothropp, the perpetual curate, I assume?"

"Aye." He nodded. "To whom do I have the pleasure?"

"I'm John Howse, the vicar of Eastwell, within this same county." He pivoted to her. "And this is my eldest daughter, Hannah."

"Reverend." Hannah curtsied, but didn't look up. She feared he'd read in her eyes that she'd witnessed his private discourse.

Reverend Lothropp cleared his throat. "Reverend, Miss

The Pulse of His Soul

Howse." He motioned to Robert. "May I present my colleague, Mister Robert Linnell."

Father stepped forward. "Mister Linnell, pleasure to meet you. Are you visiting our lovely Kent then?"

"Aye, reverend. John . . . er . . . Reverend Lothropp and I were companions at Cambridge."

"Well, I hope you enjoy your stay," Father said.

Hannah curtsied to Mister Linnell, keeping her eyes on the hem of her dress where the embroidery of the apron swirled into pink and green floral designs. She savored the well-bred manners of the men, wondering if they came from wealth.

"I couldn't help but overhear some of your conversation upon our approach," Father said.

Hannah winced, then glanced up.

Mister Linnell grinned, but Reverend Lothropp frowned.

Father chuckled amiably. "If I may say, a preacher must be devoted to his wife. First Timothy teaches, 'If a man desires the office of a bishop, he desireth a worthy work. A bishop therefore must be unreproveable, the husband of one wife, watching, temperate, modest, harberous, apt to teach . . .'"

A sermon now, Father? She clamped her jaw.

"'. . . One who rules his own house honestly, having children under obedience with all honesty. For if any cannot rule his own house, how shall he care for the Church of God?'"

Mister Linnell bit back a smile, clearing his throat and shuffling his feet.

Poor Reverend Lothropp looked at the grass, the sky, the church beyond.

They couldn't know Father was much like Mister Linnell and spoke partly in jest. How could they? But she knew Father's temperament and the merriment he withheld. She bit her cheek to keep herself from laughing.

"God created woman from Adam's rib. The rib is over the heart to protect." Father wasn't going to easily exonerate Reverend Lothropp. "Woman wasn't made from a foot bone to be stepped upon or from the head to be ruled over. The woman is to stand at her husband's side, his arm around her to protect her. Man shall cleave unto his wife."

Red crept up Reverend Lothropp's neck. "You need not preach scripture to me. I know it well. Forgive my ignorance toward whatever you may have heard me say."

Father finally chortled and stepped forward, clasping his

shoulder. "You're young and yet to learn the greatest joys in life." He motioned to Hannah. "You gaze upon one of mine." He beamed at her.

She curtsied to Father and braved another peek at Reverend Lothropp. That's when she noticed his prominent nose. But his reluctant smile was larger and directed at her for a brief moment. She got the impression he'd finally understood Father's wit.

Father stepped back. "We came to bid you welcome and introduce ourselves, but as you're with company, we shall return at a more appropriate time. Forgive our intrusion." He bowed. "Good morrow."

The men bade their farewells.

"You're right not to marry," Hannah said quietly to Reverend Lothropp as Father started away. She wanted the reverend to know she found rapport with his ideals. "A wife should be first preference to her husband. I see the Church would be yours." She spun to catch up with Father. But as she did so, she caught a curious look of uncertainty cross Reverend Lothropp's face.

Chapter Three

Could John live a life that God approved of? Was Reverend a title really meant for him?

Shoving aside his quill, he straightened his papers, finally done writing his sermon. With a heavy sigh he stared at a carving of Jesus's apostle Paul hanging above the desk, its deep-chiseled cuts hardly distinguishable in the dim room. That zealous apostle had also felt inadequate. Mayhap that could ease John's misgivings.

He stood and stretched tight muscles. Candles still burned in the late morning, and the low-beamed ceiling of the gloomy, old vicarage closed in on him until he thought he'd suffocate. He couldn't burn enough candles to brighten the large room to his liking. He wasn't sure what he expected after Cambridge, but 'twasn't this.

He picked a tight path between too many chairs and massive case furniture in designs of a century before, the dark antiquated pieces as heavily carved as Paul's plaque. At least the rain had stopped. He opened the diamond-paned window and pushed the sashes outward.

Cloud cover hung low and dark—as dark as his parlor and mood. The moist air smelled of mildewing vegetation, making him sigh again.

After a few minutes, a carriage rattled down the road. If only 'twould halt and bring visitors to alleviate his boredom. He leaned his forearms on the windowsill. Somewhat surprised when the conveyance did stop, he hurried toward the door to deliver a hearty welcome to whomever had dispelled his monotony.

The floorboards above creaked, and Robert rushed down the narrow staircase. "Do we have a visitor?"

"It appears so."

The two men stepped from the portico onto a wet brick walkway.

Reverend Howse came around the carriage, greeting them with a tip of his tall-brimmed black hat. "Good day, gentlemen." He opened the carriage door.

His daughter bent forward and placed a hand in his, a smile on her lovely face.

John's breath caught in his throat. A second visit from the vicar and the beautiful Hannah in as many days. It disappointed him to see her pretty blonde curls hidden under a coif and steeple-crowned hat.

Still smiling, she stepped toward him and Robert. "Reverend Lothropp, Mister Linnell." She curtsied.

She smiled a lot. Mayhap too much? When he saw her last, he'd the impression she'd had to withhold her mirth when her father chastised him.

John and Robert made their salutations to Reverend Howse and his daughter, then John invited them in and hung their hats on pegs. "May I offer refreshment? Ale and some bread and cheese? Widow Reynolds, our maidservant, hasn't yet come with the midday meal."

"Naught for me, thank you. Hannah?" Reverend Howse gently laid his hand on her shoulder, an endearing paternal gesture that appeared so natural.

And so foreign. John swallowed hard. He'd never had the same consideration from his father or uncle.

Hannah turned to address her host. "Nay, thank you." She gestured toward the expanse of the room. "It hasn't altered from when we visited last, Father."

Reverend Howse chuckled. "I fear it hasn't changed in the time a dozen vicars have lived here."

"Do you come here often?" John asked.

"I was Curate for Egerton from 1592 to '96. Hannah was born in this village." Reverend Howse's blue eyes gleamed kindly.

John could see where Hannah got her cheerfulness and her eyes. Reverend Howse's smile hadn't drooped since he'd entered John's home.

"Tell this old man," the vicar said. "has my friend, Richard Clayton steered Cambridge away from its Puritan sympathies?"

"He's still intolerant of Puritanism, to be sure," Robert said.

John nodded. "Clayton is now Master of Saint John's College, but I don't believe he could ever rid Cambridge of the strong Puritan sentiment."

Reverend Howse looked teasingly at his daughter. "Hannah wishes she could attend Cambridge."

Annoyance seemed to flash in Hannah's eyes for the briefest moment, and then she quickly shrugged. "You'd think he'd notice the skirts I'm always wearing." Fighting a tug on her lips as if she withheld yet another smile, she scrutinized her father. "Have you taken another dip into senility?" She spoke slowly, as if speaking to a child, then looked innocently at John.

He hadn't gotten past his shock at the disrespect she'd heaped upon her father when she and Reverend Howse broke into hearty laughter. John would never understand their easy relationship. He disremembered even once laughing with his father and certainly would never insult him, even in a jesting manner.

Not surprising to John, Robert hooted with them. He'd always been the opposite of John—carefree and jovial. He moved closer to Reverend Howse and delved into a discourse about the many aspects of Cambridge's politics.

"I bid you sit." John motioned Hannah toward the only cushioned chair in the room. The others were tall and hard-backed with rushed or solid-wood seats and not at all comfortable. He became suddenly aware of how the room smelled of fetid animal fat from all the many tallow candles he'd burned. He'd have burned beeswax if he'd known visitors were coming.

As Hannah passed John's desk, she glanced at his papers. "Stand for what you believe? Hmm. An unfortunate topic to preach."

A spear stabbed at his pride. It wasn't what he'd planned to preach, but a subject that weighed on his mind. "Do you not find it interesting?"

Hannah sat in the offered chair by the hearth, far enough from her father and Robert to have a more private conversation. "May I be candid with you?" She glanced briefly at him as he sat, her fists balled. "I daresay I'm not as those women you may know."

"Oblige me with your thoughts." Would he be sorry for it? He found himself immensely curious about what took place inside her head.

"There are many dissenting *against* the Church who are preaching the same sentiment. Methinks whatever you preach, your listeners need to hear the Lord speaking through you and into their hearts." She looked at him briefly, her face growing pink.

Fascinating. In all his life he'd never had a theological discussion with a woman. He settled further back into his chair. "I'd preach to both the dissenters and those true to the Church of England with the same words and passions. The Christian religion should be free to every man's conscience."

She cocked her head. "I'm not sure I understand your full meaning."

'Twas a topic they'd debated at Cambridge for weeks. "A man's religion is between God and himself." The statement stood at the core of John's true passion, but he'd surprised himself by sharing it with her. What did he expect her to say?

All the pink from her face gone, she looked fully at him. "Why, pray tell, have you taken orders and become a pastor?"

He caught and stopped a sigh in his chest. Then he coughed to relieve the awkwardness. She wouldn't understand. "It does the Church of England no good to be unyielding. If in this day the Catholic religion were enforced upon us and I as a man of God hungered to serve the Lord, I'd become a priest."

Her eyes widened in alarm, and her small gasp disturbed him more than he wanted to admit. Why did he tell this young girl his innermost beliefs? The daughter of a vicar no less.

"Isn't that sacrilege?" Amazing how her thoughts played out so evidently upon her features, her worry obvious and almost endearing. "Are you going to mention these ideas in your sermon?"

"Nay. Our kingdom is too full of fear and distrust to broach such a subject in public."

"The way you speak ill of the Church chills me."

It was he who felt chilled. "Then let us talk of something else." The conversation had gone too far. How would he take it back?

She fidgeted with her skirts, her lovely blue eyes no longer watching his. "Do you really have nineteen siblings as Mister Linnell has mentioned?"

"Nay. Twenty-one."

"Ha!" Her laughter rang bright in the dull room.

Robert and Reverend Howse looked her way, then resumed their discourse.

John stiffened. He found no humor in the fact. "Two are deceased."

Her face immediately grew serious. "I beg forgiveness for intruding where I did not belong. I offer sympathy for those siblings you've lost."

He didn't like sympathy. He gave a nod and cleared his throat. "How many siblings do you enjoy?"

"I'm the eldest of seven. We're a loud home of women at housework, boys being tutored, crawling about, and one still within the cradle."

She'd never known loneliness as he'd experienced in a house full of children. "My mother was my father's second wife, and I her fourth child. She died when I was five."

"I'm sorry to hear that." Her eyes held true sympathy.

"No need for condolence. I don't remember much of her."

Hannah sat mollified, as if she didn't know what to say.

Perchance he'd been too forthcoming? As much as he loved teaching the Gospel, he'd little practice in conversing with young women. He did appreciate her beauty and in the quiet moment took it in.

"What are you staring at?" she asked pointedly.

Caught in the act, he swallowed uncomfortably. "I'm looking for even one freckle." Not good at concealing his thoughts, he decided to be honest. "Your skin is so fair, I can't imagine how you don't have a smattering of them across your face."

"I hope that's a favorable thing. For you see, I don't attract men by being well spoken and intelligent. And I'm pleased that's not a subject on *your* mind. After all, you never plan to marry." Her face lit with mischief.

Did she remember everything? John floundered for a change of subject. "I know no university that permits women. Where have you acquired your education?"

She bit her lower lip. Charming. "I have comprehensive discussions with Father on all subjects, especially religion. And I use his large library extensively. Being a younger son of a minor noble family, Father didn't acquire much, but to us the books are treasured and a great inheritance."

Her eyes perplexed him. 'Twas as if she held humorous secrets about every subject.

"There'd been a time he simply didn't want to believe I

wasn't his son." She laughed.

He found himself staring again, this time at her bright smile. That she seemed unaware of her easy playfulness disturbed him. He admired her wit and intelligence but thought her too lighthearted. Although, when she'd mentioned the word "son," he'd sensed some sadness in her.

Yesterday he'd wanted to believe her naïve and dense so he could suppress thinking about her. Today he wanted to get to know her better.

Chapter Four

The chime of the tower bells from Saint James sounded across the small village of Egerton.

Hannah clasped her sister's hand as they ambled toward the church. "I'm pleased you're with me today. I'd not have courage without you." Penninah was Hannah's closest confidant, less than two years younger. Although she acted more like their mother in feminine interests, she complimented Hannah's temperament and the two often enjoyed a good banter.

"Do you expect the new reverend will eat you for supper?" Penninah thinned her lips to keep from smiling. The morning sun made the soft wisps of reddish-blond hair that escaped from her cap sparkle like gold.

The memory of Reverend Lothropp searching for freckles heated Hannah's face. "He did capture me in his snare . . . I mean, stare—as if he'd take a bite." But that wasn't what she feared. She feared appearing foolish. She feared his opinion of her. And, a sennight before, her fears had kept her from his sermon about standing for what one believed, which she deeply regretted. That's why she'd talked herself into coming today.

The bells continued to peal through the bright, chilly morning, calling both sinner and sinless to church. At least a hundred people walked toward the great edifice of Saint James—rich and poor, noble and servant, adult and child.

Hannah passed an elderly man wobbling along with a crooked cane made of a tree branch. A young woman in a threadbare dress clung to his elbow, patiently matching his slow gait. He pivoted to Hannah and acknowledged her presence with a grin and nod.

She returned the smile. "Good Sabbath Day, sir."

The old man's eyes instantly showed appreciation for the notice of his person. "To be sure, a good day."

She and Penninah walked on, nearing the crush of those entering through a wide, keel-arched doorway.

The bells stopped, the hammers stilled, and vibrations drew to an end. The bell tower stood like a castle fortress with a parapet at the top. A small circular turret rose along its side. It looked more a battlement for defense than an ecclesiastical edifice.

"I don't want to go in," a child whimpered to his mother.

The mother gave him a stern stare. "You've no choice," she whispered.

Her words found their mark in Hannah's heart. She recalled Reverend Lothropp stating with conviction that man's religion should be between God and himself. She'd pondered those words. The Anglican Church had no qualms in forcing people to worship as their king did, suffering fines and imprisonment if they disobeyed. She'd been comfortable with the idea, approving even, before meeting John Lothropp.

Arm in arm, Hannah and Penninah stepped into the stone building. Thick rock walls cooled the air inside and smelled of mildew. Father always said it was good for the church to be cold. It kept the people awake.

Footfalls of the growing crowd echoed as they moved with the congregation down the nave where tall-backed wooden pews stretched toward pointed gothic arches, towering up on both sides.

Hannah breathed deeply. A chapel—any chapel—was one of her favorite places to be. It helped her more fully imagine herself behind the pulpit.

Unlike her father's church, Saint Mary's in Eastwell, which displayed grey stone winged buttresses, the ceiling of Saint James stretched high with wooden beams, as if reaching to God in reverence.

In front of the congregants, the chancel's barrel-vaulted ceiling was painted a deep azure-blue with golden stars and fleur-de-lis, and the arched window with flowing stone tracery glowed in the eastern sunshine.

They found a seat amongst strangers and Penninah nudged Hannah's arm. "Look at that painted wooden beam in the chancel. It has words written on it."

The Lord is in his holy temple: let all the earth keep silence before Him. Yes, Hannah did feel a reverence in this church. "That's from Habakkuk," she whispered, wondering if the beam used to hold a rood screen.

Within minutes, Reverend Lothropp entered from the vestry and ascended the spiraled stairwell to the pulpit, his white wig a stark contrast to the red robe and embroidered scarf that draped almost to his feet. "Good Sabbath to you." His deep, kind voice resonated through the chapel as he searched the faces lifted to him as if he were looking for kindred souls.

An emotion moved within Hannah that she didn't recognize. Who was this man who had such an effect on her? Was this new feeling spiritual or . . . something else? Unexpected tears formed at the corners of her eyes. Mayhap God was trying to speak to her?

She closed her eyes and inhaled deeply, letting her breath out slowly.

God, what is it you want of me?

No answer came.

Again, she implored her Lord. *I'm but a woman.* As soon as the thought came, she knew God didn't view her as any less than a man.

You are My handmaiden.

Her tears fell. She'd heard that voice before with the same sentiment. But how was a handmaiden to serve the Lord?

Penninah gave her imploring scrutiny. "Do you fare well?" she whispered.

Hannah could only nod, the lump in her throat too large for words. She wiped her face. She must regain control.

Reverend Lothropp read from *The Book of Common Prayer*, then said, "Today I've been called to sermonize on the Sabbath Day." His compelling voice carried through the nave. "'Tis the fourth commandment and an eternal principle, existing since Adam walked the earth. Before I speak, we may praise God with song. I bid arise for the hymn, 'Sing to God.'"

They all stood and joined voice in the glorious hymn. Penninah and Hannah harmonizing so perfectly that people swiveled to stare. The acoustics of the church sheltered them in celestial chorus, the music seemingly reaching to the heavens. She never ceased being moved when heavenly melody intoned to esteem God.

After the hymn, all sat and Reverend Lothropp moved again

to the altar. He opened the large Bishops' Bible on the pulpit. ". . . God blessed the seventh day, and sanctified it, because that in it He had rested from all his work . . ." He read from Genesis.

She imagined sitting under a shade tree, eyes closed, listening to the timber of his discerning voice. Easy to listen to, even when sermonizing, he gave scripture a sound of eternity.

"Today is the *first* day of the week." He looked out to the congregation. "Yet we call it the Sabbath, the day we rest, as God rested on the *seventh* day. The Roman Catholic church amended our day of worship from the seventh to the first, a tradition we've followed."

What an odd way to start a sermon. To announce what the Papists had put in place and the Church of England still followed was bound to anger the nonconformists. Hannah searched the expressions of the people around her. Were Puritans and nonconformists amongst them? It seemed they always were.

"Make no mistake," the reverend continued, "Sunday we commemorate God's seventh day, and we should abstain from all manner of toil. 'Tis a holy day when we solemnly delight in His creation of our earth, a day in which we should assemble. The day, *not the principle,* has been changed."

Hannah had heard of people who were adamant about changing the Sabbath back to Saturday. Was that really what Reverend Lothropp alluded to? The man bewildered her.

"Christ obeyed the spirit of the Sabbath but did not follow the traditions of the Jews. Remember this and follow the *spirit* of the Sabbath, not placing worry on traditions."

His extraordinary eyes found hers.

A shock ran through her body. She blinked.

Pausing heavily, he looked elsewhere and cleared his throat. "After the ascension of Christ on a Sunday, His followers kept holy the first day of the week, giving the church in Rome some substance to their decision." Reverend Lothropp never smiled as Father did during his sermons, yet his eyes showed gentleness and he looked closely at many. "None of this history alters the importance of a sacred day to rest from labors and assemble in our Lord's church for worship. Doing so can satisfy man's need for spiritual sustenance. 'Tis the principle of a holy day that we would do well to never forget." He spoke with compassion, not piety as so many preachers did, thinking they knew all the answers.

"'Tis through God's grace that He has released us from our labors. Can we see it as a celebration for all He gave us? And

I'm not referring to dancing, archery games, festivals, or bear-baitings."

Chuckles, gasps, and harrumphs came from many.

Hannah had sometimes participated in those common Sunday activities, as she supposed most of the congregation had as well. After all, they labored every day of the week but Sunday. When *were* they to enjoy such activities? Yet, Hannah felt in her heart he spoke truth.

"Profanations of the Sabbath contributes to moral decadence and disturbances of peace. It displeases God. If we follow principles of caring for our poor and sick and spend the day in worship, we'll come to keep the Sabbath day holy out of love of God. 'Twill become your most favored day—a day of rest from all but charitable works and seeing to those in need. We're all sinners and we all need Christ. Let us all then live more holy."

After the sermon and communion, Reverend Lothropp uttered a prayer from the Common Prayer Book to conclude services.

Hannah stood and leaned close to Penninah. "I've never heard before the reverend's style of preaching, and he showed passion about his subject today."

"I believe you speak truth, sister." Penninah moved toward the aisle. It took several minutes to file behind others toward the door.

Hannah had told Reverend Lothropp that whatever he preached, his listeners needed to hear the Lord speak through him and into their hearts. In this, he'd satisfied her, and she hoped many others. He'd also not been as severe in his sermonizing as she'd expected, seeing as he rarely smiled and had unrealistic notions about having time for church work but not for family.

As people stepped outside, he greeted them. Hannah felt a flicker of astonishment that he already called his parishioners by name and that he responded attentively to the widows, asking after their needs.

A lovely young woman with brown hair adorned with a gold comb moved in front of him, her face animated as he spoke. She giggled, and he shared a longer moment of conversation than with the others.

Hannah pressed her lips and glanced away, a bitter taste in her mouth. Rubbing her hands down her skirt, she smoothed wrinkles that weren't there. "Penny," she said in her sister's ear. "What if he thinks I'm a ninny for coming all this way when he knows I should be at Father's sermon?"

Penninah rolled her eyes. "You're a Howse, of course you're a ninny."

Hannah giggled despite herself. "You jest when your sister is distraught?"

"'Twasn't a jest." Penninah wrapped her arm around Hannah's waist and squeezed.

They stepped to Reverend Lothropp. Hannah wanted to squirm under his dignified stare but held as still as possible. "Good day, reverend." She curtsied. She smelled something earthy like cedar. Was it the powder on his wig or the way he always smelled? Whichever, she liked it very much.

He inclined his head. "I'm honored to see you in my congregation. You and your friend are always welcome here."

"Thank you, reverend, but this is my sister, Penny . . . Penninah. May I introduce . . . she's my little . . . my younger sister." Good heavens! She was making a fool of herself, muttering like a halfwit.

Penninah pinched Hannah's waist, her eyes dancing, and Hannah knew she'd hear her sister's thoughts later, over and over, all day long.

The reverend bowed to Penninah. "I should have recognized the eyes." Then he shifted to Hannah. "How old are you, Miss Howse?" His expression felt far too penetrating.

What an unexpected question. "Sixteen?" She gulped. "Yes, sixteen." What was happening to her?

His eyes widened. "I thought you much older." When he moved to touch his brow, he accidently brushed her hand.

They both paused.

Skin tingling where he'd brushed it, she looked to the churchyard and forgot to breathe.

"I'm privileged to have met you." He bowed to Penninah again, then to Hannah. "Misses Howse."

That was their dismissal, but she wasn't yet done. "My father begs you and Mister Linnell dine with us tonight at six. Does that suit?"

Reverend Lothropp showed a moment of joy, and then he just as quickly masked that emotion. "We would be honored." He bowed.

She and Penninah curtsied and moved on. Hannah wiped at her forehead. So many comments she could have offered about his sermon. Instead, when he looked at her with those compassionate brown eyes that slanted just so at the corners, she found herself tongue-tied.

"Well, thankfully he didn't eat you, but somehow I feel you worried he might." Penninah's piercing stare agitated Hannah. "Where are your thoughts, dear sister?"

Obviously absent. She wanted to moan.

Of all the things they could've talked about, he'd questioned her age. She had a list of questions she desired to ask him. Like, why did he start his sermon on a contrary note? Did he believe the Lord approved of celebrating the Sabbath on a Sunday? Did he miss his mother? Was his childhood lonely? Because he swore to never marry, could they safely be friends? And what about that girl with the brown hair . . .?

But what had she done?

Floundered like the greatest of all Howse ninnies.

Chapter Five

John laid his hand upon Goodwife White's fevered brow. "I saw this ailment in others a sennight ago, and those parishioners are now returned to health. I'll pray for your full recovery."

The warmth from the hearth kept the autumn chill at bay. The one large room of their home was cramped but clean and filled mostly with cots. It smelled of rabbit stew, reminding him of the dinner invitation to the Howse's.

He offered a small smile to the five children huddled close to their mother's bed. "Now, who here can recite the Litany for Common Plague and Sickness?"

"I can, sir." Davey, who appeared to be about nine, looked toward the wall in concentration. "'Almighty God, which in thy wrath in the time of King David, didst slay with the plague of pestilence threescore and ten thousand, and yet remembering thy mercy didst save the rest: have pity upon us miserable sinners, that now are visited with great sickness and mortality, that like as thou didst then command thine angel to cease from punishing: so it may now please thee to withdraw from us this plague and grievous sickness, through Jesus Christ our Lord, Amen.'"

"Amen," chorused by all, including his sick mother.

"Very well done, indeed," John praised. 'Twas a shame Mister White fought in the war against Portugal and couldn't be here to feel pride in his son and care for his wife.

Hannah would probably have patted Davey on the head or wrapped an arm around him, something he'd never do. He cleared his throat. Why must he keep judging himself against that girl? He

The Pulse of His Soul

pulled a shilling from his pocket and handed it to Sarah, the eldest. "Goodwife Hodges is selling her apples. Hasten and buy enough to fill your apron."

Sarah's eyes lit, and he witnessed the first glimpse of a smile since he'd entered the White's cottage.

He turned to the other children, thin and in threadbare clothes, but each with lively anticipation on their faces. "Help with chores and do as Sarah says while your mother is recuperating. All of you remember that no one is useless who alleviates the afflictions of others."

"Aye, Reverend Lothropp," the older children said.

The youngest sucked on a rag, staring at him.

John gave his fare-thee-wells, sure Goodwife White would soon be able to care for her young. He felt relieved to leave the last of those who were ill this day. He'd been at his visits for hours and was anxious to join the beautiful Miss Howse for supper.

As he exited the cottage, an herbalist entered with a basket of plant remedies. She'd probably been waiting for his departure. He dared not tip his hat. Did Goodwife White hold to the mystical powers of herbs or was she a woman of faith? Who exactly were followers of the King's church in his congregation?

Untying his horse from the goat pen, he heard footfalls behind him. He pivoted to see a feeble man shabbily bedecked in homespun with no collar or cuffs.

"Reverend, m'Lord." The hair on the man's face was matted and dirty, his smell a sour odor of ale and unwashed clothes and body.

John reached out a hand, his first reaction one of sympathy, but then considered the man's plight may have been self-inflicted—a grog-swiller mayhap. "How may I be of service, good fellow?" He bowed slightly.

"I've not eaten in days." His gaunt face attested to that fact.

"Why be that?" John had never experienced hunger, but he'd seen its foul effects during his stays in London.

"Me cottage burned, and me wife died in it a fortnight back." His harrowed countenance spoke the truth of his words.

Mayhap that's why the man had taken to drink? John chided himself for the hasty judgment. "Are you of this parish?"

"Nay, I've been travelin' to dwell with me brother in Woodchurch."

Poor Fund Taxes were collected for those in his parish only. Yet how could John deny this man? He reached into his pocket but found it empty. He'd dispensed to Sarah his last coin. "The funds for the poor are at the vicarage." He'd give the man money from his own coffer. He needed to join Robert anyway. "Ride with me."

John gave the old man a leg up, grateful the beggar was strong enough to mount, and then he settled into the saddle in front of him. Given the man's stench, John would need to change into his fine-spun wool before supper. He hoped he wouldn't be overdressed.

Upon their arrival at the vicarage, John gave the old man money and some bread and cheese. "Remember to always dedicate yourself to God. If you do so, man cannot hurt you."

"Beggin' your pardon, man can always hurt and 'tis a risk we must take if we're to love." The beggar shook his head as if sorrowing over John's idiocy.

John contemplated the statement as he watched the feeble man amble down the road. The beggar was wrong. Once John had placed God before man, he'd no longer felt abandoned and the hurt his father had heaped on him diminished. He'd long ago dedicated his life to God, the father who would never leave.

Robert came out of the vicarage, scrunching his nose. "Perchance you should change clothing, for we best be on our way to delicious victuals and lovely maidens."

John quickly changed, and then he and Robert rode at high speed to Eastwell.

Light from the large candelabra overhead gleamed off the Howse's fine pewter and silver settings. It was the table of country gentry with white linens and handkins folded in elaborate shapes. Occasionally the maidservant, Molly, came in with necessary items.

John was reminded of his childhood in that *many* children sat around the table, but the similarities stopped there. In his home, they weren't allowed to speak during supper. Here, everyone spoke at once and the laughter sometimes felt pernicious.

As a child, he couldn't address an adult unless spoken to first, whether at the dining table or not. The Howse children not only spoke constantly amongst themselves but also to their parents. And he didn't know if he should be pleased or disturbed that Hannah kept looking at him and occasionally blushing. He did find his heart rate quicken when she did so, howbeit.

"Would you like some more stew of mutton, Reverend Lothropp?" Mistress Howse asked, her cap askew, showing reddish-blonde hair like Penninah's. She was a handsome woman. "Hannah made it herself."

John caught himself from wincing. This didn't fare well for Hannah's cooking. He very much wished he hadn't eaten the stew of mutton with its overuse of turnips and pepper. "Nay, I've had my fill. Thank you for your generosity."

"Well, I hope you've left room for warden pie. Hannah made that also."

Mistress Howse must not have had the stew if she thought that would persuade him to try the warden pie.

Hannah frowned at her mother. "The food is almost inedible." She turned to John. "My parents believe 'tis their failing that I'm not adept at women's work. But in truth, I've no interest in cooking."

Mistress Howse sputtered and gave Hannah a glare of warning and then turned to John, smiling as if she hadn't just scowled. "Hannah may not cook as well as some, but she has a merry disposition. She never argues with her siblings and ofttimes fills the house with singing and flowers from her garden. She's my husband's favorite to take on his Sunday visits. All the parishioners love her."

Sitting across from him, Robert winked at John, while Hannah stared into her plate.

"No need to try and pair the two, Mother." Reverend Howse's eyes gleamed as they often seemed to do when he was about to jest. "Reverend Lothropp doesn't plan to marry."

John cringed inside. He didn't like having his personal life discussed at the supper table.

One of the Howse children—Priscilla, who was mayhap five—swiveled toward John and stuck out her tongue. Her brother, younger than she, pinched her leg, and she stuck her tongue out at him. The adults seemed oblivious to the interchange.

"Do you not cook, Penninah?" Robert set down his pewter goblet, the candles overhead shining a warm light on its rim.

Penninah blushed. "I made the bread."

"Which was delicious!" Robert responded as if the bread had broken a several-day fast.

John had never seen his friend so animated toward a woman. Curious that.

"And what about you, Mister Linnell?" Mistress Howse turned

an interested gaze on Robert. "Are you without wife?"

"Mother!" Hannah and Penninah said at the same time.

Hannah's creamy skin flamed red. Penninah glanced away, pulling her handkin to her face.

A sharp sting of jealousy pierced John's chest. Would Hannah find interest in Robert? Could John watch his best friend marry a woman he . . . he what? Felt tenderness for? Couldn't thwart wondering about? He shifted in his seat.

Robert looked a bit dumbfounded, speechless—a rare occurrence. He looked to John.

John shrugged ever so slightly and took a sip of ale, hardly able to swallow it past the tightness of his throat.

"As lovely as your daughters are . . . your two eldest, that is . . . well, not to slight the others . . ." Robert gave an apologetic nod to the younger blonde, blue-eyed daughters who would one day be beauties themselves. "I cannot settle into family life here." His eyes kept wandering, more to Penninah than to the others. "I'm here but two more days, by the by return to London where I'm employed as a tutor."

Reverend Howse's face dropped in disappointment. "We'll be grieved to see you go and anticipate you'll come visit Reverend Lothropp again soon."

"I shall, to be sure," he said to Penninah more than to Reverend Howse.

After dinner, John found himself in the company of Hannah and Penninah as their mother took the children to the nursery. Robert and Reverend Howse sat several yards away speaking of politics.

John couldn't help but notice Hannah smelled of flowers and that her small hands, clasped together on her delicately embroidered underskirt, were so very different than his own.

"Tell me about your mother." Hannah gave him full attention.

This topic he stayed away from. "There's little to tell."

She arched a brow. "Do you remember anything?"

He never visited that deep place of pain. Ever. "I remember her bending over me when she came in to say goodnight." He cleared his throat, wishing he were talking politics with Robert instead. "And her giving me a hoop and stick to play with." And her standing close by when Father was home.

"What did she look like?" Penninah asked.

What had his mother looked like? He'd been so young when she'd passed. "I disremember." Admitting it hurt somehow. He'd never spoken of these things with anyone.

"I see we've made you unhappy. Forgive us." Hannah smiled sympathetically. "Your face is even more severe than usual."

"My face is usually severe?"

Hannah reddened and then shrugged. "You always look in need of comfort."

"And you never appear so," John countered before he could restrain himself. The woman was flippant.

"Sullen is a better description of your expression." Penninah added thoughtfully, her lips quivering with a repressed grin.

Hannah's eye filled with mischief. "'Tisn't from indigestion is it?"

Penninah giggled, and Robert glanced to her from across the room.

"You still look a bit hungry, Reverend Lothropp." Penninah elbowed her sister.

Baffled, John asked Hannah, "What does she mean?"

"She means mayhap you need to bite something." Hannah's warm smile didn't alleviate his confusion.

"May she offer you a leg"—Penninah winked at Hannah—"of mutton?"

Both girls laughed so senselessly John stood to leave.

"Nay, reverend. I beg forgiveness." Hannah grasped his hand. "Please sit. We're foolish sisters who share jests between ourselves. We've been rude. Pray pardon our frivolousness."

A bit unraveled that she was so casually touching him, he did sit.

"Avail us, how you're becoming acquainted with your parish responsibilities." She let go of his fingers.

John frowned. Would they have teasing barbs for all his comments? "Well." He rolled over in his mind what discourse would not be spun to folly. "Even with Mister Linnell visiting, I cannot get used to the extended times of silence. I'll not like living alone." It was a serious statement that shouldn't be made fun. But why was he telling them?

"Methink after all those siblings you grew up with and your mates at Cambridge, you'd be happy for the silence." Hannah's demeanor remained serious.

Perchance the jesting was over.

"I visit parishioners ofttimes to help with my boredom. Next to writing sermons, 'tis my favored activity. They're worthy people."

"As in our parish. I too enjoy the visits." Hannah mirrored his tone.

"Do you really not intend to marry?" Penninah had also quieted her laughing eyes.

How could he make them understand? "I fear to love any earthly thing above God." He briefly glanced at Hannah and her quickly narrowing eyes. If he ever were to take a wife, it could not be someone like her. Did she not realize she was too witty, too humorous to be the wife of clergy? Yet something about her invaded his thoughts almost daily, and he wished he could rid himself of the unwelcome introspections. But her intelligence fascinated him. Her lavender fragrance relaxed him. And her beauty captivated him.

Later that evening, John and Robert rode home slowly, the refreshing cool night probably one of the last before frost set in. The stars above overfilled the dark sky, a marvel to ponder, bringing heaven closer. Methodic clopping of horses' hooves and an occasional hoot of an owl lent a calming backdrop to John's reflections.

As unorthodox as the Howses were, he somehow enjoyed their hospitality. Mayhap it was the affection they had for one another. He was still trying to sort it out. His father and uncle had taught him laughter was light-mindedness and evil. The jests at Cambridge had fallen into those categories. Yet Reverend Howse, a man of God with unassuming grace, took his calling seriously. And somehow, he still jested with his children.

"Are your thoughts about a beautiful blonde who doesn't know how to cook?" Robert asked lazily.

"How do you know I'm not planning my next sermon?" Cheeks warm, he was glad for the darkness. He was probably blushing like Hannah.

"'Twas hard not to notice how ofttimes you two looked at one another tonight."

"She makes me uncomfortable, to be sure. She's a wretched cook. She smiles far too often. She's only sixteen."

"Aw, all reasons to love the girl."

"Love?" The word bounced back at John, echoing off a nearby outcropping of boulders.

Robert chuckled. "And there you have it."

Chapter Six

Hannah brushed a fly from her face.

"Hold still!" Penninah stood at her easel quite a distance away, pointing her paintbrush as if it were a sword. "I can't paint your profile if you're always moving about."

Sitting on the grass, Hannah placed her arm along her side in the same position she'd been trying to hold for over an hour—hair down around her shoulders, knees up, sapphire blue skirts flowing about, a basket of golden pears at her side. At least she was sitting this time. And their siblings playing on the grassy hill with autumn leaves gave her a pleasant prospect to stare at.

"Pretend you're watching for a certain reverend," Penninah called.

Hannah frowned. She suspected Reverend Lothropp avoided her. What would she do without Penninah to listen to her misgivings each night in bed, the hour when she fretted the most? Thankfully, by morning, her worries were forgotten and her hopes again high.

But it was getting harder to hope, even for his friendship. Hannah had seen him a sennight after Sunday supper at the harvest festival. He didn't dance. They barely shared a conversation, his gaze on everyone but her. Mayhap her mother scared him off with her talk of Hannah's qualities as a wife. Did he envision *she* was prodding him to wed?

Yesterday, she and Father had visited, and Reverend Lothropp spoke with Father the length of the stay. She'd wished Mister Linnell hadn't left, being the one who usually held Father's attention.

She imagined Reverend Lothropp bored in his quiet vicarage as he'd suggested to her once. But she hadn't come up with a plan on how to call on him without Father. 'Twould be unseemly to visit alone.

How could she make him think about her as she did of him?

Later that afternoon, Hannah settled into a chair in the library to read, her body weary and skin tight from the sun. She pulled her legs up and tucked them underneath her, sagged against the wing of the cushioned chair and dozed.

Robust knocking on the front door woke her.

A familiar masculine voice spoke with Molly. Reverend Lothropp!

Hannah stood so fast the book fell to the floor with a thud. Straightening skirts then hair, her hands froze. Her hair was still down and uncovered. She'd no time to remedy it. Her coifs were upstairs. She self-consciously hurried toward the front of the house.

"May I tell the master you called?" Molly asked Reverend Lothropp.

"Good morrow, reverend," Hannah said.

His gaze fell on her hair, and his expression softened. Removing his hat, he bowed slightly. "Miss Howse."

"Mayhap you've been advised my father is not at home. He's at the lake fishing with my brother, Jack. May I walk you there?"

Reverend Lothropp's dark eyes took on a look of uncertainty. And he glanced again at her hair. "I'm not troubling you?"

"Not at all. A walk would be invigorating." She grinned as she caught his eye, but her cheer didn't seem to fully register in his countenance.

Fingering his large ruff over a black cassock, he dropped his hands and fisted them.

Molly removed Hannah's cloak from a peg, draping it over her shoulders. The servant then pulled Hannah's hair loose from under the cloak and handed her a hat.

She tied on the steeple hat as she stepped out. Her automatic response was to loop her hand into the crook of the reverend's arm, as she always did with Father, but instead she crossed her arms over her chest. This wasn't a good way to spend time with the man she'd been wanting to see. How was she to get him to openly converse?

"Have you spent much time in Eastwell? 'Tis not as hilly as

Egerton," she began.

"Nay," he said almost in a grumble.

She ignored the tone. "I look forward to showing you our lake."

"As of yet, I've only seen what's accessible along the road between the two villages."

"Then perchance this stroll will delight you?" She pointed to a lane in the distance that led to the lake.

They hastened past her flower garden where birds chirped.

The reverend made no comment as to its beauty and only stared straight ahead.

She wished he'd glance over. Stop. Wander in. If he could have seen the garden turn from spring to summer with its early pink roses and tall foxgloves in differing shades of blue, maybe then he'd have been enchanted. Relaxed a little.

In silence they moved through a tranquil path of trees in autumn shades of golds, reds and greens. A breeze caused leaves to flutter down. She inhaled deeply the smell of the wet leaves—a boon to the autumn air.

The reverend strode in front of her at a faster pace than she'd have liked.

A dog barked from a cottage in the trees but didn't approach. She spied purple crocuses in bloom where the woods opened to a soft patch of earth. She wanted to pause and examine them further, but the reverend marched on unaware. She'd visit them later.

The crisp air invigorated her mood, emboldening her to step quickly to his side and speak on friendly terms as they once had. "I've thought often of you alone at the vicarage. Is boredom a distraction still?"

"Aye. The reason I chose to come beseech your father. You spoke of an extensive library. Perchance would it be appropriate to ask him if I may borrow some books?"

"I'm sure he'd be delighted to serve you in such a way."

They walked along, her mood reposed with a comfortable silence, his closeness making her heart beat faster. She was close enough to notice the fine tailoring of his black cassock and smell the hint of balsam soap. With her eyes at the height of his shoulder, she imagined she'd fit quite nicely under his arm.

They came into a clearing of short green grass with a slight slope toward the lake not far distant, partially behind a row of dark green conifers. Two ducks flew low over the lake, landing on the sunlit water.

She stopped to admire the tranquil view.

Reverend Lothropp marched on.

She hurried to catch up.

"Do you have a favorite book?" His voice displayed genuine interest. Mayhap he was enjoying their walk after all?

"It depends on my disposition. When I'm not studying doctrine or Foxe's *Acts and Monuments*, I might read a Shakespeare quarto."

He shook his head. "I've never met anyone like you."

"I'm not sure if that's a compliment or an affront."

He was silent yet again.

"You aren't sure either, are you?" Her laughter fluttered with nervousness. "Have you associated with many females?"

"Nay, I suppose not. My sisters are much older. They didn't spend time in my presence. But . . ." He sounded unsure of himself. "I don't understand when you laugh at a time when you should be sober. Is this common of your sex?"

She didn't have an answer to that. Was he insulting her? "Is happiness a sin?"

"Do you not think too much laughter is ungodly?" The timber of his voice sounded overly noble.

Her chest tightened. He was calling her to repentance. "My conscience tells me when I sin, and my laughter has never felt like an offense to God." She studied his hard profile. "You're very judgmental. I didn't realize you to be overtly self-righteous."

He stiffened. "I'm ordained to judge." Clasping his hands behind him, he didn't regard her, check her expression, or even pause for her reaction.

Her throat went dry, and she found herself speechless. Her feelings didn't matter to him.

He adjusted his stiff lace cuff. "As taught in holy scripture, the woman is regarded as the weaker vessel—a creature intellectually, physically, morally, and even spiritually inferior to man. I cannot say these things of you. I fear a man would feel he couldn't dominate you, as would be his right."

She stopped, fists clenched.

He took two more steps before pivoting, his brows drawn together in question.

"These are your thoughts of me?" Tears stung her eyes. "I've been berated by a man who has forgotten what it's like to have gentle and loving females in his home. Has it not occurred to you that a woman could alleviate the silence at your vicarage? A wife could do your rounds with you and discuss doctrinal concepts. She might even overlook that you've *only the capacity* to love your God." Hannah didn't realize she'd shouted until the shrillness of her voice echoed back to her.

The reverend turned pale and stricken.

She covered her mouth. 'Twas sacrilege to have said that. Tears wet her cheeks. She swiped at them then swept up her skirts and ran back toward the house.

John dropped his shoulders. He'd been raised a gentleman, but his manners had been atrocious to have made sweet Hannah cry. Right in her supposition of him being severe, he was a brute. His mood had been melancholy all day and he brought it to her. He turned toward the lake to try and find Reverend Howse on his own.

He came upon the vicar sitting on a large boulder along the lakeshore, directing his son—who stood thigh deep in the water in canvas breeches—on how to net a fish. "That's it, son, you're doing splendidly."

John had never seen Reverend Howse in common clothing before, and the scene was one of father communing with son. The sight made John even more melancholy. He'd never had a mutual interest with his father.

Reverend Howse shifted at the sound of John's approach and smiled broadly. "Have you come to fish? Don't tell anyone where you found us because this is our secret spot."

"I came to ask a favor. Do you mind?" John questioned.

"Of course, I don't mind. What ails you, son? It appears you've eaten rancid meat. Did Hannah cook for you again?" He chuckled.

John sighed and looked away. "I fear I've made your daughter cry."

"Which one? I've but four." His grey brows knit together.

"Your eldest."

"Hannah!" There was much surprise in his voice. "I've not seen Hannah cry since a wee child. Pray tell, how did this come about?"

"I'm not exactly sure. I fear I overstepped propriety and insulted her womanhood."

"Oh dear! Care to recount your words?" He bit back a smile.

What was humorous in this situation? Hannah's father was just as perplexing as she.

John's neck warmed. Would he get another sermon about Adam and Eve like at their first meeting? "I spoke of the woman being the weaker vessel."

The vicar threw back his head and bellowed heartily.

Astonished, John's mouth fell open.

"I feel your misery." The vicar stood and squeezed John's shoulder. "You've come up against a female Howse. They know naught about being *a weaker vessel*. I'm glad you made it here alive." The squeeze turned into a robust pat. "Come. At last I have a comrade." He motioned to where he'd sat moments before. "We need to commiserate together. This is a first for me." He lowered his generous body onto the rock. A creature hidden in the brush skittered away. "Are you sure you don't want to marry one of my girls and be my son? I'd welcome you into the family."

John sputtered and fell next to him with a plop. Pain tingled up his back. "Uh . . . you surely jest?"

Reverend Howse's kind blue eyes met John's. "I could not ask for a better son."

John's pulse pounded in his ears as the words pierced his soul. A lifetime he'd longed to hear that sentiment.

"Marrying Hannah will bring you closer to God than you comprehend." Reverend Howse shook his head. "Without realizing it, through my own selfish needs, I've trained her well to be a reverend's wife. Imagine that! She may not be a 'weak vessel,' but she'll be a strong helpmate. Withal, I'd advise you to keep Widow Reynolds as your cook." A smile touched his eyes.

"Father, look!" Jack held up his net, a fat fish within its twine, flipping wildly.

"We shall feast abundantly tonight," Reverend Howse said. "We'll have Penninah make us loaves." He grinned at John. "We've caught us another of God's good followers." He thumped John on the back.

Chapter Seven

Late that afternoon, John delved into his doctrinal studies at his desk. He found himself staring at the page but instead of seeing words, he saw Hannah's tear-stained face while she told him he couldn't love.

He dropped his head into his hands, torturing himself with the image of her standing at her door, hair the color of a golden wheat field flowing over her shoulders, skin barely touched pink from recent sun, blue eyes bright with affection. Was there more than friendship between them? Had he damaged that? Why did he care?

A man must get permission from his intended's father to marry. He'd gotten that without even asking. He'd also gotten the chance to become a cherished son to someone.

But that was no reason to marry. He tapped his fingers on the desk.

It wouldn't be fair to Hannah. She deserved full devotion and love from a husband. Although the Church of England didn't require celibacy from its ordained clergy, he long before required it of himself. 'Twas the only way to keep God first in his heart.

Besides, if he allowed her to know him, there'd be no doubt she'd find him unlovable. She'd be miserable married to him. He needed to stay distant. Other than serving the needy, he couldn't afford to develop an affectionate relationship. He'd been called to serve the Lord. And only the Lord.

John leaned back, remembering a rare time alone with his father, Thomas. He'd become sentimental and told John he was much like John's grandfather, who'd served as vicar in Yorkshire. Thomas had looked up to that man more than any other. Having lost his father as a young man, Thomas always felt a great preacher had been taken too early.

John had thought if he became like his grandfather, his father would admire him too. Mayhap even love him? But when his father died while John was at university, there was not even a mention of him in Father's will.

He threw the book aside and stood, pacing between the packed furniture, stubbing his slipper against a chair leg. "Jehoshaphat!" he exclaimed and dropped into another chair. He refused to let his dead father rule his emotions another minute. He kicked the hassock in front of him, causing it to tumble onto its side. *That was childish.* He got on his knees to right it.

Finding himself in a position of supplication, he felt called to prayer. He clasped his hands. "Dear God," he said aloud, considering which of the Common Prayers he should utter. Nay, this prayer needed to be more personal—a prayer to a loving Heavenly Father who knew him as a son. The Father who in time had replaced his earthly one and to whom he owed his life.

John looked to the heart of his soul. "Oh, gracious and loving Father," he started again, searching for the feel of his Holy Father's presence. "Find pity on your son and comfort me. Show me the direction to go and still follow Thee."

Hannah appeared in his mind again.

He tried to shake her image away but paused when his heart sang of a spiritual presence—a listening ear of Someone who loved more thoroughly and deeply than anyone on earth could. "Can I serve Thee, bringing changes to the lives of those in my congregation, bringing them to Thee, and still marry the woman who has taken my heart?" He stopped.

Taken my heart.

Having voiced the truth of his feelings, he knew then that he loved Hannah. His pulse raced at this emotion that was so very new to him.

"I cannot give myself if I'm less a man than she deserves." With his heart open to the love he felt for Hannah, a stronger, greater love came to him from a divine source.

Hannah is My handmaid, raised up to bring others unto Me. She is your ordained priestess. Your companion for life and the hereafter. Take her unto yourself and protect her from evil.

The message came with a light that filled his body. It spoke of truth he couldn't deny. On bended knee, John's eyes moistened in rare emotion as he thanked God for the startling new vision of how he could serve Him with a wife at his side.

Molly showed John into the Howse parlor and requested him to wait. Children romped upstairs. A squabble took place, and Mistress Howse's kind voice soothed the ills.

He sat but for a moment. Then stood. Then paced. He paused to inspect his pocket watch, dropping it in his nervousness. He picked it up. Almost two.

How was he going to convince Hannah to marry such an unlovable man as himself?

He paced some more, then looked at paintings of Howses on the wall. The blond hair had come from generations before. Would his children be blond? He scratched his head. *Getting ahead of yourself, you are.* He looked at his watch again. Half past. Was she so angry with him that she'd make him wait 'til dusk?

Many minutes later, a light footfall in the main hall alerted him to her presence.

She stepped into the parlor. Her beautiful face and floral scent made him grin. "Are you pleased with yourself about something?" Her features were closed to him. She was still angry.

His heart thudded so hard in his chest he feared he might lose his breath. "May we talk?"

"If there's no sanctimonious sentiment to your discourse, we may." She wouldn't meet his eyes.

"I promise I left my idiocy behind."

The corner of her mouth rose a fraction, but she still kept her gaze elsewhere.

Was he making headway? "Your father tells me there's no Howse female who is a 'weaker vessel.'"

"Father is a wise man—and *perchance* intimidated by many females." She finally smiled, showing lovely white teeth, but quickly regained her blank expression. "Shall we sit?" She perched on the wooden settle covered with brightly colored cushions.

He sat facing her, clearing his throat. Where to start? Wiping his palms on his breeches, he took another deep breath. "I consider my ordained calling with the Church of England to be lifelong."

"I wouldn't have thought otherwise. You're a good preacher. I enjoyed your sermon about the Sabbath. Mayhap someday we can discuss your reasoning on some issues relating to the subject."

She was sharp, this one. She'd have him delving into all of God's mysteries.

"My income is moderate, but comfortable."

"I'm pleased for you." She didn't appear pleased.

Not used to her being austere, he couldn't read her eyes. What was she feeling? How could he turn this conversation to matrimony? Could she not jest now? He needed a diversion—something to burst the pensive atmosphere. He stood and wandered to the window.

"Are you upset about something?" Her voice showed genuine concern.

His shoulders relaxed a wee bit. "Aye." He rubbed his face. "Nay." He shook his head. What was he saying? "I want to tell you something and can't find the words."

"Unusual for you." Her skirts crinkled as she stood and moved in behind him.

"I'm a man of faith and pray to God for answers I cannot know myself."

"I am a *woman* of faith and do likewise."

He swiveled.

She was closer than he'd realized.

Breath caught in his chest. He marveled at her clear skin. Still not a freckle. "Have you ever heard *His* voice?" The words sounded strangled. He needed to breathe. A burning developed behind his eyes. He blinked a few times. The memory of God's message was too recent. Too real.

"Aye," she answered reverently. Her eyes spoke of mystery and truth and eternity. She was pure, righteous.

He craved to envelope her in his arms. Hold her to him until his heart stopped thudding. "I prayed to ask my Lord . . . How do I say this?" He turned from her.

"Have you come to ask about a certain doctrine? I do enjoy discussing scripture. My father could join us if you wish?" *Now* she sounded passionate.

He stared at her and frowned. Did she not know what he was getting at?

Her countenance fell. "You're invariably annoyed. Again. Did you come to quote scripture at me about loud laughter?"

"With profound respect, I must say you've misunderstood me. Aye, I do often ponder on what lessons can be learned from the scriptures—"

"Stop there." She held up her hand. "I'll not have you preach to me."

"I'm not here to preach. I'm more interested in seeking after that which is eternal."

"You're arrogant to assume your goodness is meant to disparage me." Hannah glared at him and moved to leave.

John gently caught her arm and turned her toward him. He clasped her other arm and gazed into blue eyes full of distrust and anger. "You don't understand." He took in a deep breath and kissed her forehead.

She trembled.

The heat of her skin sent a small shudder through his body. He stepped back. "What I'm trying to say is that you're part of that eternal plan. We two can be one before the Lord."

Eyes wide, mouth hung open, he seemed to have stunned her senseless. She sank against his chest and he embraced her, bringing her closer. Nothing felt more right.

She wrapped her arms around his waist. "Is that a proposal of marriage?"

"It is." He inhaled the scent of her hair and closed his eyes.

"Your words have brought my soul comfort at last." She buried her face in his neck.

He'd never known such joy. He wanted to laugh—and did.

She pulled back. "A laugh from the severe preacher?" Her face was beautiful, eyes shining with love.

Love for him! He laughed again. "I cannot contain this joy. And you're right. 'Tis not evil to laugh. It's pure joy from God. He's blessed me with you." He hesitantly kissed her on the lips and received a warm and welcoming kiss in return.

He'd never been happier in his life. This was love.

The kiss grew deeper.

Guilt from carnal feelings of Hannah in his arms stunned him, and he backed away. Had he already let love fill his heart so completely with this girl that he'd stepped away from God?

Chapter Eight

To be married in the church meant it was approved of by God, Hannah hoped.

After their banns were read three Sundays in a row in both parish churches, Reverend Lothropp and Hannah were allowed to marry. They stood before Hannah's bewigged Father for the ceremony, Hannah's knees shaking, her heart pounding. Almost every Sunday of her life had been spent in Saint Mary's church. But today . . . today would be the day she'd always remember.

The church bells faded away, and Father's voice echoed into the vaulted chapel as he recited the beginning of the matrimonial service from *The Book of Common Prayer*. "Dearly beloved friends, we're gathered together here in the sight of God, and in the face of His congregation to join together this man and this woman in holy matrimony." He grinned at Hannah.

She returned his smile but felt her lips tremble.

Father took her right hand and placed it over his right hand.

Reverend Lothropp laid his on top of theirs.

She wished she wasn't wearing gloves. She couldn't feel the reverend's skin on hers. But the exquisite blue gloves had been a gift from him. Her first gift. Gloves were typically a gesture of the hand of friendship. Was that his message? He'd had the gloves sent to her that morning with a note that read: *I hope these fit your delicate hands.* After which Robert and John's brother, Thom—two bachelors, as was the custom—led her to church while carrying branches of rosemary that they waved to those lining the lane while voicing their fare-thee-wells.

"I require and charge you . . ." Father went on with the ceremony all priests recited.

Her hand was between the hands of the two men she loved. Did Reverend Lothropp love her too? He hadn't said as much. She slept little the night before, wondering if she was making a mistake. What did she know of this severe man of God who'd held her in his arms only once these past weeks?

Father turned to the reverend. "Wilt thou have this woman to thy wedded wife . . . love her, comfort her, honor, keep her in sickness and in health, and forsaking all other, keep thee only unto her so long as you both shall live?"

Would he do all those things for her? Was she standing before her father, this congregation, and most importantly, God making the biggest mistake of her life?

"I will," Reverend Lothropp said.

Knees still trembling, she looked him in the eyes for the first time that morning. And saw fear. Her lungs froze. Her mouth went dry.

Father turned to her. "Wilt thou have this man to thy wedded husband . . . obey him and serve him, love, honor," he went on.

He'd not requested Reverend Lothropp to obey and serve her. These stipulations were for women only. Stipulations she'd always worried over. *The Lord forsook me to let me be born a woman.*

". . . so long as you both shall live?"

Hannah swallowed, her throat dry. "I will," she croaked.

Reverend Lothropp's eyebrow raised.

She glanced away.

Father withdrew his hand, and they dropped theirs to their sides.

"Who giveth this woman to be married to this man?" Father gave an incredulous stare toward the congregation, widening his eyes as he looked from one person to the next, and then shrugged a shoulder when no one responded.

Many in the audience snickered. Someone loudly guffawed.

Father winked at her. "I do," he said happily.

Hannah's chest loosened a little. She should find comfort in that Father approved of the marriage. Many of her friends married without even knowing their intended but followed the counsel of their parents. Had Father really let the choice be hers?

"Reverend Lothropp, I bid thee to take Hannah by her right hand and recite your vows," Father said.

"I take thee, Hannah." The reverend stared at their hands, his skin ashen.

Why wouldn't he focus on her?

His mouth said the words, but she didn't hear anything he recited. Would she really be kissing that mouth tonight? Would he allow it? Would he hold her again? Sweat broke out on her upper lip and forehead.

"Hannah," Father said.

And somehow she recited her own vows. But 'twas as if she hovered outside her body, prodding it to perform as expected. Again, she had to say she'd obey him when he didn't say it to her. ". . . and thereto I give thee my troth." She swallowed hard.

John's brother, Thom, stepped forward and placed a small gold band on the Bible Father held.

Father picked up the ring between two pudgy fingers and gave it to Reverend Lothropp. "Place this on the fourth finger of Hannah's left hand."

Hannah removed her glove.

"With this ring, I thee wed . . ." Reverend Lothropp repeated the ceremonial words he regularly officiated. "With my body I thee worship . . ."

Heat moved throughout Hannah. She licked her parched lips.

"Let us pray," Father intoned, calling on God to bless the union, and then he pronounced them man and wife.

Man and Wife.

Hannah didn't believe she could stand much longer, but Father sang Psalms 128 and then requested her and Reverend Lothropp to kneel before the Lord's table. After the eucharist, they recited the matrimonial prayer and Father prayed they'd be fruitful in procreation.

Hannah frowned. She'd never noticed before how often the wedding ceremony spoke of breeding. She desired to feel exhilarated. Instead, she ducked her head in embarrassment and anxiousness while Father implored another lengthy prayer. After communion they arose and stood to Father's side still facing him.

And he preached a sermon.

Hannah swayed with lightheadedness. She feared the ceremony would never end.

Reverend Lothropp clasped her elbow, steadying her.

After at least twenty minutes, Father concluded his sermon by telling of Sarah "who *obeyed* Abraham, calling him Lord." He stared directly at Hannah in warning. "Amen," he said with finality and mayhap admonition.

The Pulse of His Soul

How grateful she was for the crisp October air that cooled her body as they left the church. Reverend Lothropp took her hand, and guests rained wheat kernels on their heads, a hope offering of fruitfulness.

Again, the denotation to breeding. She forced a smile.

For twenty yards they passed guests bedecked in ribbons of every color to symbolize the tying of the knot. Wheat fell into her hair. She'd dressed it with myrtle from her autumn garden, the dark green, leathery leaves a strong contrast to the white flowers. 'Tis said myrtle was the emblem of love. She could only hope. She also used it in her bouquet, paired with orange mums, lovely against her blue dress and ivory-colored lace underskirt.

The wedding feast took place on long tables near a line of trees God had adorned in leaves of glorious golds and reds. There was beauty to the autumn day, even if it was a little cool. The sky was blue and clear, free from the rain so common for the season, that she sent a prayer in thanks that the heavens hadn't wept on this day, as she wanted to do.

Guests from both parishes helped provide a feast for over two-hundred people. Father contributed the wine.

Hannah and Reverend Lothropp were so busy visiting with well-wishers that they didn't have an opportunity to say but a few words to each other. Gratefully, the reverend's color had returned, and he appeared to enjoy his conversations with his brother and friends.

Penninah stepped forward, her face open with delight, and tugged Hannah a few feet away. "He'll be feasting on you tonight."

Hannah gave her a cold stare.

Penninah's laughter fell short. "Are you not happy, sister? Your expression gives me a chill."

Hannah moved in close. "Have I made a mistake?" She struggled to hold back hot tears. "I love a man that I fear doesn't love me."

Penninah wrapped an arm around her shoulders. "I'm confident you're wrong. I've seen how his gaze falls to you whenever you're near. Although stern in manner, he's the best of men. He'd not have requested your hand if he didn't love you."

"Mayhap he wanted a companion to rid him of the boredom he spoke of?" She quickly swiped at an escaping tear, glancing around to confirm no one saw.

Two of Mother's friends headed their way, carrying between them a silver platter with a tiered cake of small buns built into a tall pile, all covered with a honey glaze.

"Come, Hannah." One of the women inclined her head and several chins folded onto each other. "It's time to try and kiss your bridegroom over this mound of cakes." Her joviality jiggled her large bosom.

The other woman said, "If your lips manage to reach each other, you'll be guaranteed plenty of children." She wagged her unruly eyebrows, the longest white-grey hairs spiking heavenward. "We built it to challenge even the most persistent, as we know you two are."

They placed it on the table. Someone called to Reverend Lothropp.

He stepped to the opposite side of the table. His face blanched, and he wouldn't meet her eyes.

She clenched her jaw. How was she to kiss a man who was colder than the October chill?

"Make sure you mash those lips real good, now." Guests gathered around, calling out impertinent slogans. "How many children depends on how many kisses." They laughed. "This is only preparation for something much better tonight."

Hannah's heart all but stopped as she leaned over the sticky mound of buns toward Reverend Lothropp.

With downcast eyes, he slowly moved toward her.

If she hadn't kept her eyes on his face, she wasn't sure his lips would have made it onto hers. She'd the impression he'd rather be kissing a dog.

Guests cheered.

Hannah blushed.

Reverend Lothropp wiped his mouth with a handkin.

As people moved away, Mother's two friends handed both Hannah and Reverend Lothropp a plate with some of the uppermost buns. "Sit and enjoy," one of them said as they returned to the banquet table.

Reverend Lothropp stepped around the table and sat next to Hannah, then waved his brother over. "Thom, come join us."

Penninah smiled sadly, shrugged and strolled toward Robert, who was laughing with some of the guests. Musicians arrived and set up their instruments for dancing and continued festivities.

Thom sat on the other side of Hannah. He wore the fine tailored clothes of a gentleman. His hair wasn't quite as dark as the reverend's, but he displayed the same prominent nose and his eyes likewise sloped in an affectionate manner—even though his were blue instead of a deep, warm brown.

Hannah smiled at him. "Your brother speaks little of his childhood. Mayhap you can avail me of Yorkshire and the great land holdings of the ancient Lothropps?"

Thom pivoted her way, as affable as the reverend was discordant. "For generations Lothropp ancestors have served as clergy in the county of Yorkshire, although our father served as squire with divers landholdings. As I'm sure you know, John falls in the middle of the great brood of twenty-two children."

Reverend Lothropp fisted a hand. "I'm grateful you're here, brother. I fear Hannah will not believe I have a large family when only one member comes to my wedding." He kept his eyes hooded, but Hannah sensed his torment.

"Did you expect otherwise?" Thom shook his head. "We're outcasts."

Outcasts? Hannah looked sharply at the reverend, waiting for an explanation.

He set down his spoon. "If you'll excuse me Hannah, Thom, I'll return shortly. I must welcome some members of my parish I see have arrived." He stood and strode away, his back stiff.

Confusion swam in her head. "It appears your brother hasn't found peace because of some aspect of his childhood."

"His feelings are understandable. He's never overcome Father giving away all five of us."

Hannah gasped. "What?"

"'Twas perchance not as it seems now. I've found peace, but I fear John has not."

"What do you mean 'giving away all five' of you?"

"It's not such an unusual situation with landed gentry to provide a younger son to a childless family member, insuring an heir."

"And are you this heir?"

"I am. Has John not spoken of this?"

Hannah shook her head, not knowing if she should be disconcerted or angry about her ignorance.

"Uncle Edmund, my mother's brother, had no children. Father was a widower with twelve children, willing to dispense of five. Mayhap 'twas a prudent decision to give away so many?" Thom lifted his mouth in a smile that never quite formed. "Father would not agree to Uncle taking just me and insisted he take all of his sister's children if he wanted me. Father drew up a legal document stating Uncle Edmund must supply sustenance and housing for us and also an education for John, William, and myself."

Hannah sipped her wine to sooth her dry throat. Why had Reverend Lothropp not spoken of this?

"My uncle wanted us—well, *me*. I'm selfishly pleased Uncle was stuck with all of us. After losing my mother, I'm not sure I could have borne losing my siblings too." Thom's eyes clouded. "I was eight when we went to live with Uncle Edmund in Leconfield. Even though we lived a little more than a league from Father, we rarely saw him. Mayhap once or twice a year, and even less often during the years he sired nine more children by his third wife."

Hannah's stomach flopped, and she clenched her spoon. John wasn't wanted by his father *or* uncle? What must that do to a man? "The reverend told me your father is now deceased."

Thom nodded.

She watched him carefully, wondering if his feelings could give her insight into Reverend Lothropp's, but she detected no sorrow.

"John and I were at Cambridge the day our father's solicitor told us Father gave no mention of us five in his will. We hadn't even yet heard he'd died—so unimportant and forgotten were we to the family. It struck John hardest. He's never had a carefree nature, but since father died, he's rarely been at ease. He refuses to discuss his injuries." Thom looked at her as if he felt sorry for her. "And it seems he hasn't discussed them with you either."

Reverend Lothropp has been hurting. She longed to hold him and talk of these things in the privacy of their home. Would he allow it? "'Twould be good for the reverend to have family close by. When Uncle Edmund dies, will you stay on his estate in the north?"

"John is living the life I desire." He smirked. "I'm sure John's told you about his misgivings behind becoming a minister."

He hadn't, but she nodded like he had, embarrassed she'd married a man she hardly knew.

"I regularly talked him out of his slump of feeling inadequate. He wrestled with the notion that man's conscience must choose the religion he was to follow and not be forced into the King's church."

Alarm shot through Hannah. She was reminded of the conversation she'd had with Reverend Lothropp about standing for what one believed. The discourse had frightened her. She wondered then if he'd Separatist leanings. He'd said people in the kingdom were too full of fear and distrust and he wouldn't discuss such things with his congregation. She'd shut him down from discussing it further with her. She regretted that now.

Thom smiled dolefully at her. "My heart has dallied with the idea of taking Orders, but my uncle has no such profession in mind. He expects me to be a landowner in Leconfield and manage his estate." He shrugged, as if resigned to his fate. "Kent is lovely country though. I wouldn't mind living close by—close to John. After Uncle dies, we'll see where William settles before I decide my fate."

"You're a kind older brother." Hannah's heart warmed knowing the reverend had someone who cared for him. So unlike him, Thom spoke freely and didn't keep secrets about his past.

"I've an inheritance that will afford me to live comfortably, but John will receive naught from Uncle Edmund. In fact, Uncle's contract has been fulfilled, and he expects John to support himself and whatever family may come to him." Thom blushed slightly.

Hannah tittered. "Well, don't expect us to have twenty-two children." The jest fell flat, her sadness not soothed. "I'm sorry you can't live the life you desire."

"No need for sadness." He gave Hannah a crooked smile. "My sister, Mary, is enjoying courtship with a gentleman in East Riding and William's happily studying at Cambridge. I stopped there on my way and hoped to bring him to the wedding, but he adamantly stated he couldn't miss classes."

"What of your other sister? Are there not two?"

"Did John not even tell you that?" He shook his head. "Anne died a year following Father, soon after John was made curate in Benington. Because of his new duties, he wasn't able to come home for the funeral."

Reverend Lothropp had shared none of this with Hannah. She felt disparaged and unimportant. These were aspects of his life that had affected him deeply, yet he must feel so distant from her that he'd chosen not to speak of his most intimate feelings.

"You must come to Yorkshire to meet Mary and her suitor. She'd want a new sister. And we also live near Catherine, our half-sister from my father's first wife. Her husband, William, is an excellent fellow." Thom's eyes gleamed with apparent love for his family.

She'd never seen such a look on the reverend's face.

"Avail me about Uncle Edmund." She prayed he wasn't a fiend and had treated Reverend Lothropp fairly.

"My uncle is stern but not violent. He's elderly and often in ill health. I don't expect he'll live much longer."

"And your aunt? How does she fare?"

"She died years ago, not long after we moved into her home."

Mayhap raising five young children scared the life out of the barren woman? Hannah chided herself for such an ungodly musing. "You had no mother's influence at Uncle Edmund's?"

"Nay. We had nannies and servants to tend to our needs."

And who gave a dark-eyed little boy affection? Hannah frowned.

"Forgive my talk of orphaned children," Thom said kindly. "It's a glorious day of celebration." He raised his pewter cup in a salute. "Happy shalt thou be, and it shall be well with thee."

Hannah recognized the matrimonial blessing from Psalms. It didn't buoy her. She couldn't bridle the aching in her chest.

"And may you both find a deep, abiding love." Thom took a sip.

Must he remind her that Reverend Lothropp never talked of love? They really didn't know each other. Thom convinced her of that. They'd been brought together by some kind of ancient longing—a sensual attraction—and the Holy Spirit. Could such a beginning produce love?

Reverend Lothropp approached, eyeing his brother.

Thom gave no indication of their discourse, smiling like she wished the reverend would smile.

Saints preserve us, 'twas his wedding day. Was he not happy?

Thom excused himself to find more drink.

"Are you upset about something?" John questioned Hannah as he sat.

"I was about to ask you the same. Are you unhappy to have married me?"

His face displayed such bewilderment that Hannah knew he couldn't have forced the emotion.

She regretted her words. "I apologize." She reached out and squeezed his hand, pleased for the physical contact.

His shoulders remained stiff. "Does this concur amidst your discourse with Thom?" He stared at the guests eating and chattering, but she guessed he was very mindful of her reaction.

She wished he'd look at her. "Mayhap." She sighed. "We've much to discuss." She squeezed his hand again.

This time he turned his palm up and clasped hers in a gentle embrace.

The musical strains of a lute and citterns produced a seductive appeal. The day's events took her mind to what was still to come. She would've liked to dance, to calm her anxiety, but the reverend never asked.

Going to bed that night wasn't going to be private or romantic. She and the reverend would be escorted to bed by Penninah, other single women, the bachelors at the party, then any guest who so desired would come into the bedchamber to wish them luck.

Luck? She'd need that and more. So much more.

Chapter Nine

The crispness of the air beneath the canopy of mature beech and oak trees amplified the laughter and conversations of the young adults, but John could hardly concentrate on what they were saying. The day's festivities weighed on him. So did whether or not his new wife was happy.

"Do you fare well?" Hannah's voice tremored.

Was she cold or nervous?

He studied her, trying to gauge her mood, then wrapped his arm around her shoulders. Pulling her close, he hoped to provide either heat or comfort, whichever she needed. When she came willingly, wrapping her arm around his waist, his chest filled with foreign contentment.

"It's a shame we're too late for blooms on all the orchids along this charming path." She sighed.

Peculiar the places her mind went. Would he ever come to fully know who she was?

With the lowering sun came temperatures cold enough to force the wedding guests to return home. As the bats started to fly, Thom, Robert, Penninah, and Hannah's childhood friends, Eleanor and Katie, led John and Hannah down a path. Ivy inched its way to shroud the seldom used lane. Their destination—the empty, old curate cottage not far from Saint Mary's—could be seen in the distance. Someone had lit a candle on the window ledge.

John hoped a fire had also been laid. Shame his vicarage was too far for the wedding party to escort them to bed there.

Bed. Strange this tradition of escorting the newlyweds to bed. What if he did something that made him appear foolish? Also strange was this fear that kept his heart thudding. *I'm a grown man and fear is not a part of who I am.* He drew in a deep breath. If only he could believe that sentiment.

Inside the cottage, someone had not only been kind enough to lay out the fire but left a loaf of bread upon the table with baskets of food covered with cloth.

Penninah grabbed Hannah's hand. "Come with us into the bedchamber." She stifled a giggle then turned to John. "We'll prepare your bride," she said in a serious tone, much out of character.

Hannah was quick to blush then laugh spuriously.

Penninah curtsied to the men and pulled Hannah into the bedchamber at the back of the cottage.

Eleanor and Katie curtsied and joined the giggling women, shutting the door.

Hannah's forced laughter worried at John's gut.

"Shall we sit, men?" Thom said, flopping onto a cushioned chair of fraying needlework.

John sat. Then immediately stood.

Robert chuckled. "It can't be that bad. I'm convinced God truly does love John Lothropp because He's blessed him with Hannah."

John paced to the kitchen and then to the window. Darkness had fully settled. Pinpoints of light from torches glowed along the distant path. His new family was on their way to wish him and Hannah luck. The plan was for both to be in bed before the family arrived. His heart pounded so hard in his chest he placed his hand there hoping to soothe it. He bowed his head. *God, you commanded me to marry her, and I was obedient. What now? I can't do this alone. Don't forsake me! I don't know how to love her.*

"Brother, come sit." Thom motioned him over.

John sat, uncomfortably. He stewed over the fact that he'd never spoken with Hannah about their argument and her accusation that he was unlovable. She was right. So why did she marry him, and what now did she expect?

"You look as nervous as a mouse in the cat's barn." Robert winked at John, his eyes bright with mirth.

"I know what I've gotten myself into. Marriage is as a parallel to Christ's bond with His church." That didn't come out quite as planned. 'Twas a sentiment John had tried to convince himself of these past weeks.

"Is that so? Next are you going to avail me that passionate love between husband and wife is regarded as undesirable?" Robert grinned, but worry crinkled the freckled skin around his eyes.

Thom waved a hand. "Leave him be, or the sardonic questions might come to haunt you on your wedding eve." He looked at John with what at first appeared like pity, but then it became affection.

If anyone should understand his misgivings, 'twas Thom.

"You're blessed above many to have married such a devout woman," Thom said. "She'll match you perfectly. I know you reflect about what lesson the Lord intended you to acquire from any experience. But right now, this night, try to concentrate on Hannah's needs."

Thom was right. He taught the simple and sometimes complex lesson of charitable love. That truth pulled John from his dark worries. He could do that. He could do that well as he'd proven with those in his parish.

The bedchamber door opened, and three overly joyous women entered.

The men rose.

Giggling, the women gestured John to come.

Penninah stepped forward. "Reverend Lothropp, your appetizing bride awaits." She swept her arm toward the open door.

John swallowed. Not quite sure how he made his limbs function, he moved toward the bedchamber. Could he give himself to Hannah? What if afterwards she couldn't love him?

"Call when you're ready," one of the women said.

The unfamiliar bedchamber smelled of sandalwood and cloves.

Hannah sat in bed, leaning against an absurd number of pillows. She wore a white bed-gown tied with a pale blue ribbon at her neck, lace spilling over. A gift of innocence and purity.

In fact, everything appeared to be tied with ribbons. There were silk ribbons of blue tied to the pillow covers, window sashes, bed curtains, posts, and canopy corners.

Hannah wore a cap of lace with another blue ribbon tied upon her head. He wasn't sure where the lace from the cap ended and the lace from the neck began—it surrounded her like a halo. As lovely as it was, he'd hoped to see her golden hair down around her shoulders.

"Welcome, husband." She smiled tentatively. "Your marriage nightshirt has been left behind the screen." She pointed to the corner of the room by another crackling fire.

John stepped behind the wooden screen and removed his clerical robes, folding them reverently upon a chair, and pulled the nightshirt on. As he did so, he heard the others entering the cottage in the room beyond.

Stepping up to the bed, he was at a loss for words. The fear of the unknown caused him to tremble. *You're a man, John, control yourself.*

Hannah hardly looked at him, her face flushed in shyness. Lovely.

"Recline beside me and call to the others." She pulled back the linen sheets and coverlet.

He removed the lavender stem that had been laid there to sweeten their bedsheets and stiffly positioned himself between the cool sheets. All this tradition felt paganistic and ridiculous. Where had it all begun? Probably schemed up by someone like Robert, who found humor in all things solemn. "Come in," he called, the words catching in his chest. He cleared his throat and called more clearly, "You may come in."

The wedding party—all of the Howses and a few esteemed friends—entered the room. There was hardly space for the crowd. They all spoke at once, none of which made sense to John.

Hannah's siblings climbed onto the bed, and he stiffened to where he could hardly turn his head without straining. What did they expect of him now? He should have quizzed someone with these private questions days ago. He was normally confident and moved toward what he wanted with no self-doubts. Yet all he could do was doubt this marriage, doubt his abilities, doubt that Hannah loved him. Matrimony went against what he thought he desired. Against the way he'd planned his life. Would it deter all he could attain? What had he done?

Thom stayed against the wall, subdued but smiling while the others in the room communed and chortled at childish jests, sounding as if they'd had too much wine. One by one, they approached the couple and blessed them with well-wishes.

Reverend Howse, of all people, told him, "Bless me with many grandchildren." And then howled a laugh loud enough to quiet the room.

All stared at him and then broke out in their own uncomfortable and overly loud laughter.

Mother Howse blushed and covered her mouth in a giggle, then hiked baby Samuel up higher on her hip. The natural nurturing of her young gave John hope that Hannah would be the same. Somehow, he thought not.

After a much longer length of time than John would have enjoyed, Reverend Howse finally called out, "Come to our home for warm ale."

Cheers went around, more congratulatory wishes to the couple, and then the door closed, and all was still.

John twisted toward Hannah. His neck sore, he rubbed at the tight muscles and forced a smile. Thom had told him to concentrate on her needs. He wasn't yet sure *exactly* what those were.

"Your rare smile is a wedding gift to me tonight. I do hope to see it more now that we're married." She laid her hand on top of his. "Are you happy, Reverend Lothropp?"

"I believe it's time you called me John."

Her face pinked. "'Tis time I acquire to know my husband." Her eyes held an emotion he couldn't name. "John." The name sounded foreign on her tongue. "Can you find happiness with me?" Before he could answer, she added, "And what does that happiness entail? Have you married me to alleviate your boredom? Help you with parish visits?"

He was stunned to silence, but her direct question needed an answer. Her sometimes teasing eyes were serious and completely focused on his.

He swallowed. "God's voice told me to marry you." It wasn't what she was asking him. It didn't mean he loved her. He hadn't yet told her so.

Some of the light went from her eyes. "Always obedient, you followed that voice."

"Thom told me I was blessed above many to have married such a devout woman and that we were perfectly suited." He couldn't bring himself to say what she desired to hear, even though he did love her.

"Your brother is protective of you."

"Thom had had his doubts about me finding happiness. He mentioned this morning that he liked you for bringing that to me."

"Have I brought you happiness?" The warm candlelight played across her skin. "What is it you expect of a wife? Thom told me about your upbringing by your uncle, that you rarely saw your father, and that your oldest sister died. Why have you not spoken to me of these things?"

John shrugged. He'd wanted to tell her, but he feared she'd

look on those events as unattractive weaknesses. She wouldn't understand an inaccessible family like his. If they couldn't love him, what made him conceive she could? "I'd written home asking for my uncle's permission to marry you. He gave it upon learning you were the descendant of a noble family, even though you came without a dowry. He supposed I could do no better." John glanced away. "I'm sorry for his insult, but 'twas directed at me. He also wrote that his health would keep him from attending the wedding and he would send Thom in his stead."

"Would Thom have not come without your uncle's permission?"

"I've no doubt he'd want to be here, but his livelihood is beholden to our uncle and he does whatever Uncle Edmund commands. Thom said he was glad for my contentment."

"So, you're happy? I've not yet learned the clues that tell me so." She grinned mischievously.

He feared a teasing barb was coming, yet he was filled with her, wanting to bring her to him against his heart, but her regard seemed far from that affection.

"You told Robert you would never marry." She turned, keeping her face hidden. "Now that you have, are you penitent?"

Had he not had those thoughts this very night? Did he even know? "I trust the Lord and know my career as a servant to Him is to be accompanied by a wife and mayhap children. The pull to place God before you hasn't diminished. I feel this may be your wifely sacrifice. Are there not sacrifices for all women regarding their husbands, whether clergy or not?"

She played with the ribbons at her neck. "I've yet to learn that answer. I suspect I'm not what you supposed either." She shrugged a shoulder ever so slightly. "If I must be second to God, I can accept it as so. I can support you." She still kept her face from his. "I didn't envision marrying so young. I watched my mother and sisters doing the chores of a woman and I remained uncertain *that life* was for me. I've had no interest in wifely duties. If I were a man, I'd be doing exactly as you—preaching the gospel." She turned to him and an unexpected tear slid down her cheek. "Perhaps we're two of a kind—asking to be accepted for what we are."

He wiped the tear with his thumb.

She clasped his hand against her cheek. "With all of our differences, I feel I was guided to you."

Her skin was amazingly soft. "Many have found that love

comes after a wedding."

Her eyes spoke of sadness, not happiness.

So why could he not tell her he loved her now? He kissed her forehead and he knew he couldn't bear it if she pulled away. She didn't. He lowered his lips to hers and found only warmth and acceptance.

Chapter Ten

"I suspect you need this blood tonic." Hannah handed to John a pewter goblet of powdered nettles mixed with warm ale. "Your illness is understandable, with your company seldom required by anyone this past winter and you cooped up in this dark house reading." She motioned toward the low ceilings and overstuffed room.

He grunted.

She opened the door leading to the backyard. The fresh air instantly revitalized her dour mood and she stepped onto the gritstone flags she'd unveiled days before. In the six months since they married, she'd been taming the weeds and creating a garden. It looked as if years before someone had cared for the large, tiered yard, and she planned to bring back its beauty.

"Mayhap you should let Widow Reynolds retrieve the local physician?" John called to her.

She stepped back to the open door. "He'll blood-let and weaken you further. I believe 'twould be more dangerous to employ the physician than for me to treat you with my herbs. Would you prefer bloodletting, an enema, and plasters applied to your feet?"

"I'd say not." John's skin paled further. "You're certainly gentler than a doctor would be."

That was as close to a compliment as Hannah had received from John in months.

Hair loosed from his ribbon, he brushed it away from his face. "Either the Church heals or herbs heal. Be careful the cure you follow. I don't want rumor spread that you're a superstitious herbalist." He motioned toward her basket of newly picked spring herbs. "You know how such talk alters lives and becomes a story about witchcraft."

His comment didn't surprise her. She'd found through the long winter with John that he was prone to sullenness and worry. "There's not a person in this parish that doesn't know I'm a devout Anglican." She stepped to the chair where he sat wrapped in a blanket and caressed his shoulder. "Come out into the sunshine. 'Twill do more for you than a physician can."

John finished his drink, set his cup aside, and stood.

Hannah carried his chair to the courtyard. Before he sat, she relieved him of his blanket and while doing so suspected he wanted to caress her. The moment passed as quickly as the realization entered her mind.

He sat.

She must have been wrong. "Do you mind if I bring some of the old chairs inside the house out here?"

"Please rid that room of the obstructions." He scowled.

"Mayhap we can donate the furniture to the poor? But then I suppose they'd want to use it as kindling as I do?" She attempted to tease a smile out of him.

All she got was silence.

Her days of laughter with a companion were gone. She missed Father and Penninah and promised herself to visit them as soon as John felt well.

After setting out a comfortable grouping of chairs and a small table, Hannah wandered toward a hedgerow of wild berries. A brace of chicken eggs lay in a nearby bush. She'd noticed the chickens wandering the land. With the eggs in her yard, she claimed them as hers and deposited each into her apron pocket. She'd talk to Widow Reynolds about giving the chickens a place to roost so they could have fresh eggs more often. The widow's cold repast of pork, goat cheese, and dry brown bread each morning kept Hannah bound up. But she did no better with the cooking. In fact, she only did worse. She giggled to herself.

When she turned, she found John watching her, and her heart spoke of the love she kept hidden. 'Twas enough to tighten her chest in discomfort.

For months she'd laid next to him in their bed each night. He'd hold her as if he expected her to leave at any moment. Innocent. Childlike. With a tentativeness that surprised her. Yet he couldn't seem to bestow her that last piece of himself. She'd fallen in love with John, but he had not fallen in love with her. She wondered if he'd come close at night in the dark. Yet by day, he turned distant.

She'd had no interest in marrying young, but it was the right choice, as if she'd been guided by a divine hand. She'd make the best of the situation by helping her husband with what was important—the church and his parishioners. Her daily routine had changed drastically, and she couldn't go back to her old way of life without returning with a broken heart.

And what was John's wound? He wouldn't talk of his past, and Hannah knew he carried scars she couldn't heal with her herbs. She sat beside him. "Can I bring you something for your comfort?"

"'Who so findeth an honest, faithful woman—she is much more worth than pearls.'" He looked at her with a longing she didn't understand. "'Yea she stretcheth forth her hands to such as have need.'" He took her hands and kissed each one.

Such a gentle and good man she'd married. "I love you," slipped from her heart into the world for the first time.

His mouth tightened. He gently released her hands and glanced away.

Her breath hitched as sadness settled into her soul. Would she ever be able to reach his heart? In the loud silence where he should've professed his love for her, she became uncomfortable and searched for a new subject. "I hear the king and his Hebraists and Greek scholars are done rewriting the new Bible. King James has said the Geneva Bible the worst translation. What's your opinion on this?" Theology they could talk about.

"The king doesn't like the marginal notes of the Geneva Bible, such as the one in Exodus which allows disobedience to kings. There's another note claiming the pope is an antichrist. But there have been more than fifty scholars to complete the new translation task. I studied with some of them at Cambridge. I can only hope they've rendered it to be more accurate than the Bible I've grown to love." He looked toward the open door, as if wishing he'd brought his Bishops' Bible with him. It was usually within arm's length at all times.

"Is it not interesting that the king's translators were instructed to make the Bishops' Bible the basis of their work and not the Geneva Bible?" she questioned.

"The Geneva Bible was created from the original Greek and Hebrew texts. I studied both languages in school. One word in

Hebrew can have many meanings. I've heard that the scholars are indeed drawing largely from the Geneva Bible but without the offending marginal notes."

Hannah enjoyed having canonical discussions with him. He reminded her much of her father with his considerable theological knowledge. And John hadn't yet belittled her womanhood with excuses of the fairer sex not needing to know such things. He'd implored her not to display her knowledge to other men. "Why do the Puritan's love the Geneva Bible so?" Hannah asked.

"Beyond the extensive marginal notes, the scriptural aids add to their examination of the texts. It's considered a Protestant Bible and another means in which the Puritans can show their departure from Catholicism."

"Many labored and died that we might have the word of God in our hands." 'Twasn't a small thing to have the Bible in English. Father had taught her about the selfless work Tyndale and Wycliffe had done decades before. "I want to understand the wisdom of the Bible as close to the translation as possible."

"I'm confident the king does likewise. We'll know soon enough what amendments there may be in the new translation."

"On the day I met you, you spoke of 'God before man'—which if I recall was your reasoning behind not marrying." She chuckled.

He didn't seem to find the comment humorous. "I believe there was never a moment when Christ wasn't loving God with all of His being. Methinks the only way to love God more than man is to be like God. Man hasn't the nature to not sin, but I'll put forth the effort to always have God at the helm."

"I'm blessed to have married such a devout man." She meant it, yet something inside her grieved.

He didn't acknowledge her compliment. "And thou shalt love the Lord thy God with all thine heart, and with all thy soul, and with all thy might."

She wished John would love *her* that way. Was that such a selfish thing? Aye, it was. Of course it was. She looked away in guilt.

Late in the day, John strolled toward the church for his Thursday sermon. The new year was welcome after the long winter of adjustments to his life. He felt better. Days were getting longer, allowing light to encourage growth. The transforming powers of spring gave him a feeling of wellbeing.

He considered all he'd learned about Hannah in the six months they'd been married. Surprisingly, he found her to be an untidy kind of person, her hands often muddy from gardening—on her knees, no less. He shook his head. No refined lady did such things.

And it wasn't just her amusements that weren't genteel. She studied the Bible with him as if she were a preacher herself, which he knew she wished she was. He hoped to keep these things hidden from his parishioners. Not that he was ashamed of her, but it was possible she could create trouble with the more pious. As much as she claimed to be Anglican, her actions were more of the Puritan bent—the women being allowed to study scripture alongside the men—though he'd never tell her that.

He very much enjoyed their doctrinal conversations. They complimented each other well in more than their intellect. Hannah naturally understood his needs and didn't hesitate to offer kindnesses. But did he do the same for her?

When he came home each day, he could tell everything she'd done. An apron draped across his desk chair, seeds left on a plate in the parlor, sewing in a tangled mess next to the hearth. Widow Reynolds huffed and puffed, muttering under her breath how she wasn't hired to be a housemaid. He'd soon need to hire a girl to clean the vicarage.

He respected Hannah's knowledge of plant virtues and how she took tiny seeds and planted them in such a way to create beauty. Already waves of color cloaked the stone-edged beds and tiered backyard, fragrance wafting inside. She snipped fresh flowers for the house. Scents of lavender, honeysuckle, and jasmine made the once dreary vicarage a Garden of Eden. Not to mention the floral smell of her skin when he held her at night.

He stopped halfway up the hill and shook his head to bar that line of thinking. He looked out to the weald. 'Twas a land unfamiliar to a Yorkshireman, a land of rich soil to grow much of England's bounty.

In the distance, rectangular barns with oast kilns—cone-shaped ventilation on the roofs to dry hop—dotted the darkening horizon. The first green shoots of hop were starting to emerge in the fields, their stringing and pegs standing bare above them.

John was trying to develop a taste for the common beer of the region so unlike the ale he'd grown to enjoy. Taxation on hop and other produce was a highly contentious subject among his neighbors. Tithes payable to the clergy gave John the right to ten percent of the crop for the church, which didn't endear him to the farmers when he'd arrived. He hoped they realized it was for their own good. It would help them serve their Master.

He continued his climb to the church, finding a gathering of parishioners waiting on him near the porch. He was pleased that so many had come.

"Reverend," several mumbled. They bowed and curtsied in respect.

He inclined his head and strode to the door, a following behind him.

The church was musty and cool. A clerk inside greeted him and then continued to light candles throughout the nave, warming the church in golden color, if not temperature.

"God be merciful unto us, and bless us: and show us the light…" He started the meeting with prayer as Hannah slipped in with other goodwives.

Later that evening, after all had left, John stayed at his pulpit with only one lit candle, searching the scriptures for doctrinal truths about where he set his heart—God before man.

In Paul's writing the Epistle to the Romans, John read about how God had been merciful through the death and resurrection of Jesus Christ. In chapter twelve he found: 'beseech you therefore brethren, by the mercifulness of God, that ye give up your bodies a sacrifice, holy, acceptable unto God, your reasonable service. And fashion not yourselves like unto this world, but be ye changed in your shape, by ye renewing of your mind, that ye may prove what is the will of God, good, and acceptable, and perfect.'

Before he gave himself away in mercy to man, he needed to give himself in worship to God. It satisfied his belief that he should build his life on service in God's name. He could let his concern be genuine and always give to his parishioners.

But Hannah? Could he bestow his full love to Hannah and not forsake his God?

The door by the narthex opened and a group of men and their young sons entered.

John knew them all well. They regularly came to his sermons, and they'd all been present tonight. Did one of the boys leave something behind?

"Good evening," he called down the dark nave. "Have you misplaced something?"

"Nay," said Ned Fenner, his jaw set, stiffly stepping forward with his fourteen-year-old son, Jonny. "We're here for answers."

"That's the very reason I'm called to serve." John felt unease but tried to remain calm.

The party of four men, two older boys, and a male child of mayhap six, gathered around the pulpit. John descended the spiral stairs to join the group.

Fenner, the oldest of the men—perhaps in his forties—with grey hair and a leathered face that attested to the amount of time he spent in the sun, asked, "If each man be responsible for his own salvation, then should he not have direct access to God?"

"And by 'direct access,' am I to assume you mean *prayer*?" John cross-examined.

"Our discussion outside centered round common prayer cited from the book written by clergy and monarchs."

Fenner teetered on treason to denounce common prayer, and John wasn't going to be led into such a discussion. These men balanced along a line of nonconformity to the Church and their sovereign.

"The book was influenced and enriched by our superiors. I often feel God's guiding hand while echoing the prayers." Even as John said it, he wondered if he believed it. Cambridge had taught him to question and he'd spent the last year trying *not* to do so. He'd also recently experienced a personal prayer about marrying Hannah, where he'd witnessed God speak directly to his mind. He could still remember the feeling of truth coursing through his body. He'd never had such an experience when he offered common prayer.

Samuel Hinckley, a young blond man of about twenty, stepped closer. "I know you're a Cambridge alum. May I ask what you studied at that institution?"

Odd question and one John didn't expect. Were these men trying to snare him in some way? "I matriculated at Oxford in 1602 when I was seventeen. My older brother convinced me to come to Cambridge where he studied. I entered Queen's College there and following four years of philosophy, rhetoric, logic, and Latin, I studied Greek, Hebrew, astronomy, and theology, graduating with a master's degree in 1609."

Hinckley's eyes grew large. "I enjoy your sermons and meant no offense as to questioning your education. What I hoped was to understand your ability to reason."

Nate Tilden guffawed. "Come now, Sam, whether you're meaning to or not, you're insulting the man." He turned to John.

"Our local reverend is not an educated man. We . . ." He motioned to the other men. ". . . want to *responsibly* follow our clergymen in all things."

About John's age—in his late twenties—Tilden had a closely groomed and pointed beard and mustache, was dressed finer than the others, but similar to his brother, Joseph, who stood at his side. They came from a family who held official roles in their community of Tenterden, and a family history of aristocrats who'd served monarchs.

Hinckley stood taller, his eyes earnest. "I do *not* mean to insult. I travel over three hours to hear your sermons. I wouldn't do so if I didn't feel your word to be powerful."

"I'm pleased, Sam." John laid his hand on Hinckley's forearm. He knew him to be an honest man who attended Thursday sermons regularly. Sermongatting was a habit of forsaking one's parish church to hear a better preacher elsewhere. John assumed he and the Tildens attended only their Sunday meeting closer to home. "I'm not offended. I'd like to understand better your earlier conversation and what led you to my counsel."

Ned Fenner stepped in front of Hinckley before he could reply. "There be some preachers who don't completely conform to the way of Anglican preachin'. They're more tolerant of an open discussion and teach the word of God as *they* find to be true," he bluntly stated.

John could be punished for that.

"Tell us, are ya open to teachin' doctrine in this manner?" Fenner's eyes looked weary, as if he'd come to service after plowing a field.

"As our king has said, a body—meaning the church—cannot stand if it isn't whole and undivided," John answered. "Our sovereign is the head of that body. Ministers are necessary to interpret God's word. I'll serve you and the others of this parish in the manner requested of me by my king and our new Archbishop George Abbot. If you like my sermons as Sam does, then I'd encourage you to attend and feel the Spirit of God. I'll not steer you wrong." John regarded each of them. "In Hebrews 11:6 we read: 'But without faith it is impossible to please him: For he that cometh to God, must believe that God is, and that he is a rewarder of them that seek him.'"

"I seek God." Fenner turned to the other men. "We all seek God."

They nodded.

Fenner looked John in the eyes and held his stare. "This be why we've come tonight. To tell ya that we want to follow ya in purpose and want to believe that you'll guide us down a road of truth unsoiled."

Fenner's intent was worthy. And John assumed that intent also held true for the others. He wanted them to keep attending—nonconformists or not. They were good men who looked to God as their ruler. He'd consider their needs as he prepared his sermons. "I'm here to serve my God and bring souls unto Him."

Fenner nodded and motioned to his son. "Come, Jonny, let's be gone."

All the men bowed to John and departed.

John felt in his gut that these men were going to be trouble with their Separatist leanings. He'd try to keep an eye on their movements *and* their after-sermon gatherings. He needed to keep them from talking to others. How he was going to do that, he wasn't sure.

Chapter Eleven

Entering Canterbury in Father's borrowed carriage, Hannah and John traveled past the wooden city port and crumbling Worthgate walls.

The smell of horse manure soured the air. People of all classes dressed in silks, satins, and common linens ambled along the storefronts of haberdashers, apothecaries, goldsmiths, and craftsmen.

A fishmonger calling his catch, "Perch, pike, chub," among cries from peddlers selling their harvested autumn produce and shouts of an argument between two men faded behind as the carriage headed northeast.

The noise was both exhilarating and frightening.

Hannah placed a hand on her belly. Married almost a year, at last a child grew within. Yesterday she'd felt flutters of movement and thrilled at the sensation.

"Are you well, wife?" John took Hannah's hand.

The carriage stopped, and the driver called to someone in the path to move aside. Carts trundled over cobblestones.

"I'm overmuch used to the quiet of the country." Hannah's heart beat a little faster.

John squeezed her trembling hand. "We've hours before the assembly. Is there a particular place you'd like to visit?"

"The few times we came here as a family, we picnicked near Saint Martin's Church. 'Twas peaceful over there."

John stuck his head out the window and called to the driver, "Good man, drive us to Saint Martin's."

The carriage lurched forward.

When they arrived at the church, Hannah took John to the incline next to the oldest part of the building and a view of the partially dismantled Saint Augustine's Abbey. Over seventy years past, it had become property of the Crown in King Henry the Eighth's time. The last abbot and monks fled when the country's religion reformed, leaving the building's ancient manuscripts to be plundered. A campaign to destroy Catholic icons swept over the country. But Puritans still complained that the Church of England venerated relics and effigies of saints.

"The light on Canterbury Cathedral is magnificent." Hannah said, breathless. The cathedral's creamy-yellow limestone and tall spires were set solidly against the clearest blue sky they'd had in a fortnight. Some of the trees were starting to turn russet. "This is a lovely day to come. Autumn will soon settle in. I don't look forward to being in that cramped house for winter."

"While here, I'll ask again for a new vicarage to be built," John said. "The commission's been ignoring my pleas for a year and a half."

They picnicked on cold mutton, pickled eggs, apples, and oatcakes with butter. Seagulls hobbled about, hoping for crumbs.

"Is it not prodigious that one woman can alter history and bring a nation to God?"

John cocked his head. "To what woman do you refer?"

"The Christian Queen Bertha, of course! You must have learned of her in school. She's a legend in Kent."

"I don't recall one woman bringing our country to God."

Hannah held in a sigh. "The oldest part of this church . . ." she pointed to Saint Martin's back wall where the stones appeared less uniform than the rest of the structure. ". . . was a private chapel of Queen Bertha's in the sixth century. She influenced her pagan husband, King Æthelberht, by making a condition to their marriage that she could continue to practice her Christian faith. She brought a bishop named Leodheard with her, and they used the church of Saint Martin. Christianity grew in this country from that time forward and—praise be to our Lord—hasn't stopped."

She smiled at John.

But he didn't see it because he was staring toward the cathedral.

"Thus, one *woman* who came to her husband's pagan country changed the history of England by bringing Christianity." She wondered if he was listening. "King Æthelberht was a wise man to listen to his queen, don't you see?" Her laugh sounded forced.

"I deduce Saint Augustine had more to do with the spread of Christianity in England."

She clenched her fists. "History is written by men about men. Don't you think there are good women alongside those men, and that women can also reshape history?" Even though she spoke of Queen Bertha, Hannah held her breath, feeling John's answer was important to their own relationship.

"I don't know." He said it with such a lack of emotion that Hannah wanted to shake him out of his dispassion.

Terribly disappointed, she exhaled.

"Hannah! Is that you?" a woman's voice called. "Hannah Howse!"

Hannah swiveled to see her childhood friend, Dorothy, with an older man.

John stood and helped Hannah up.

"Dorothy, what blessed chance to see you here." Hannah held her hands out.

"'Tis you!" Dorothy disregarded Hannah's hands and embraced her.

How marvelous it felt to be in her arms. Dorothy had been one of Hannah's dearest friends. Someone she used to tell all her secrets to, giggle with, and spend hours with in the countryside. She'd missed Dorothy when she'd moved to another county.

Dorothy pulled away. "Hannah, this is my husband, Sir Thomas Denne, Esquire."

Hannah curtsied, and John bowed. She was a bit surprised at how old the man appeared. In his mid-to-late-thirties, he already had receding hair, which curled over his shoulders. His clean-shaven face was long, his forehead high, and his eyes were as dark and impenetrable as John's. They also shared a similarly long nose.

"And this is my husband, Reverend John Lothropp."

After formalities the women giggled like young girls, and the men both inched away.

"When did you marry?" asked Dorothy.

"Eleven months back," Hannah said.

"We were married six months back."

Hannah wasn't surprised Dorothy had found a rich husband. Even the most beautiful women couldn't compare to Dorothy. The brown hair and green eyes were much as she remembered, but Dorothy's face had thinned, accentuating her high cheekbones.

Dorothy leaned in close to Hannah. "I'm with child." Her smile grew, and her deep-set eyes twinkled.

"As am I," Hannah said with delight.

"I'll come visit you for your lying-in and perchance you can come for mine?"

Hannah wasn't sure she'd have the convenience of a lying-in. John was a gentleman but certainly not rich. Besides, she'd miss the visits she made with him to the parishioners.

John shook Denne's hand. "Do you live in Canterbury?"

"Aye. As a solicitor, I'm employed to record and read for the court. I also assist in London." Denne's elegant lace collar draped over a stylish burgundy velvet doublet and fur-trimmed cloak. The cloak tied over one shoulder gave the impression of confidence. His golden pantaloons were complete with bucket-topped boots.

He had an intent stare about him, as if he studied all things, including people. "Do you hail from Canterbury or hereabouts?"

"We're here but a day and night for the ecclesiastical assembly. We'll be lodging at the inn near the River Stour. Our home is in Egerton—a four hours ride west."

"I know Egerton. I originally hail from Denne Hill, not eight miles south, near Kingston.

"Come to our home for tea." Dorothy gently grasped Hannah's arm in a familiar embrace as she used to when she wanted Hannah to come down to the lake or go for a walk to bird watch, one of Dorothy's amusements.

Hannah looked to John.

He bowed to Dorothy. "'Twould be our delight."

"Will you be attending Archbishop Abbot's reception tonight?" Denne questioned.

"We've been invited," replied John.

That was why he'd brought Hannah this day, to have her meet the new archbishop.

"I'll not compare to those women from London," Hannah said to John, worry in her eyes. She stood close to him in their small rented room, the muffled voices of other guests distinguishable on the opposite side of the thin wall.

"Vanity doesn't become you, wife." He thought her as lovely as ever. She wore her finest blue gown, the same she wore for their wedding, and the gloves he'd given her that day.

"Oh, John." She shook her head. "You don't understand. I'm a girl from the country, and I feel 'tis written plainly on my face and figure."

"Most of the guests are clergy from the far reaches of the Canterbury Diocese, and I'd assume are much like us. You'll not enjoy the reception of our new archbishop if you're fussing over yourself."

She looked at him with what he assumed was dismay—as she often did.

Mayhap a husband shouldn't be truthful to his wife?

Before it became completely dark, they strolled through the cathedral where a dozen brown-robed clergy lit tall candles in massive candelabras.

The musty odor of the ancient stone walls reminded John of his own parish church. But as exceptional as that church was, this one's vaulted ceilings lifted his soul to the heavens. The arches caught what amber light remained of the setting sun through the many windows—some stained-glass—creating shadows on the uppermost ceiling, which reinforced the depth and height of the buttresses. This was a glorious place of his Lord. It wasn't his first visit, but the feelings were much the same each time. No other building affected him in such a way. God was undoubtedly in this place. Surely the craftsmen had the Lord's help as they brought glory to Him.

The effect it had on Hannah altered every contour of her captivating face and lit her pale blue eyes with wonder. "Gloriosum," she said in awed reverence, using the Latin form of *glorious*.

"There are no words," he said, understanding her wanting a sacred language to express devotion.

John's testimony burned within him. He was following the plan God had chosen for him. His bosom was branded with the truth of it and the love he felt for a God who was aware of him. Without a doubt the gospel would be his lifelong focus, his rock.

After leaving the cathedral, they strolled through the vaulted passages around a magnificent cloister. Stone carvings of animals and archaic heads lined the walkway, with bosses of stone heraldry engraved into the ogive of the ribbed ceiling.

Evening had settled in, but light and music flowed from an open chamber ahead. With Hannah's arm tucked into his, they stepped into the Chapter House, a large stone-walled expansive room on the north side of the cathedral. Tracery-arched windows reached to a golden-oak wagon-vaulted roof.

Hannah gasped softly. "Lovely!"

The women were advantageously dressed in furs, velvets, and satins with embroidered skirts and sleeves. Now he understood why Hannah might feel like a country wife. He was pleased he need only wear his black double-breasted cassock, gown, a ruff, and a cap.

The room held a mix of Kent clergy and Canterbury's elite citizens, assembled to celebrate their new archbishop. A consort of lutes, a flute, and viols played at the far end of the crowded room. As they ambled toward it, attendants offered them drinks from a silver tray.

"Isn't the music captivating?" Hannah whispered, swirling her wine gently in a goblet.

"A disappointment we were not called here to dance," he said, not truly disappointed at all.

Her eyes smiled as she held in a laugh. "A sardonic jest? Such a rare joy." She saluted him with her goblet and took a sip.

He felt the corners of his mouth inch up a fraction.

Moving about the room, he introduced Hannah to some of the clergy he'd met earlier that day.

Sir Thomas Denne and his wife approached, one of the most handsome couples in the room. Dorothy grasped Hannah's arm and brought her close. They immediately began to whisper.

John stepped close to Denne. "We're unaccustomed to such refinement. Are there many of these receptions?"

Denne, wearing more formal clothing than earlier that day, surveyed the crowd. "Far too many." He scowled. "What are your thoughts regarding the assembly this afternoon?"

"We were interrogated about our education and tested concerning our intelligence."

"Trying to appease the uproar of the Church from being overrun with imbecile preachers, no doubt." Denne frowned.

John thought of how Hinckley and others were coming to his sermons because of inferior preachers. "There was an emphasis to confirm we are holding sermons every sennight and that they were sanctioned."

Denne nodded. "That's King James trying to create uniformity."

Uniformity. The word jarred John. He'd spoken to the group of men after his Thursday sermon of the church being one body— uniform. Uniformity was the opposite of diversity of ideas and values. *Uniformity.* The word buzzed in his head. Was it really the right choice?

Denne stared at him as if waiting for a comment.

John cleared his throat. "The majority of the conference was spent emphasizing that we now use the King James Bible and not the Bishops' Bible." In that there was uniformity too. The idea of not being able to use his Bishops' Bible sat in his stomach like souring milk.

"Has our king's massive new Bible been chained to the pulpit in your church at Egerton?"

Hannah pivoted toward the men.

He could tell by her grasp on his arm that she wanted to be part of the conversation. He hoped she wouldn't speak about religious matters. They could discuss it later at home where only he'd be privy to her theological views. Denne may be shocked at her effrontery.

John patted her hand to try and convey *be still* then addressed Denne. "Seeing as the Bible *is* chained to the pulpit, I've spent a lot of time at the church studying it." For a sennight now, he'd spent so much time doing so that he'd not gone home until late at night, his back aching. He *needed* to understand the differences between the texts.

Hannah drew closer. "Mayhap the new Bible is the final evidence that King James won't champion the cause of the Puritans."

Denne folded his arms across his chest. "I don't consider it politically wise to ignore the Puritans." He looked at John as if he'd made the initial comment.

John spoke before Hannah could answer. "Most Puritans are loyal to the crown and only want more distance from Papists."

Hannah shook her head. "They're a small minority and not strong enough to become a force that will stand against the Church of England."

John tried to catch her eye to let her know 'twas improper for a woman to voice these issues in public. He suspected she already knew that and was ignoring convention to get her ideas addressed.

Still looking at John, Denne stroked his beard. "But there's a significant Puritan representation in Parliament. They're intent on expanding their power."

John gave a slight tug on Hannah's arm. He refused to stand by while his wife spoke of church polity to a solicitor. "Shall we speak of things that might be more innocent for our womenfolk?"

Dorothy smiled at Hannah in a knowing way. "Do you still study with your father?" Understanding dawned in her eyes. "Well, of course! You've married a preacher. If he's as dedicated to God as you, you're a perfect match! I recall your father playing games to help you learn Latin. I still remember *et nolite audire loquentes*—stop talking and listen."

They all laughed.

Hannah wrapped an arm around Dorothy's waist. "Father probably said that more than anything else when we were together. No wonder you learned it."

Dorothy looked at John and then her husband. "Being an educated woman is unusual, to be sure." She turned to Hannah. "But my elderly neighbor has told me much about Margaret More Roper, Sir Thomas More's daughter. She too was taught by her father. She wrote Latin translation and lived and died here in Canterbury."

"I happen to know that any work Margaret Roper completed remained within the private sphere, as per her father's requirements." Denne lifted a brow at Hannah. He was putting her in her place.

A warm flush crept up John's neck onto his ears. Why couldn't he have chosen someone timid?

Hannah made a noise in her throat.

Because God had chosen her for him, that's why. He needed to keep his faith. By the by, there was the complication that he loved her.

The music stopped, and the archbishop's introduction was announced.

Everyone bowed as Archbishop George Abbot entered dressed in rochet and chimere, his sleeves as full as pillows, grey beard resting on his ruff. A big man, he moved amongst the guests slowly, visiting like any person of influence would do—succinctly and expeditiously.

Some faces held adoration for the diocesan. Others flushed as if embarrassed to be caught in a situation where they didn't know how to act.

John rendered his own feelings and found that he felt great honor for the man but saw him as only a man. God was John's monarch.

Denne leaned in, probably so Hannah wouldn't hear and comment. "He's being called 'the Puritan Archbishop.' He's promoted some Puritans to high ecclesiastical and academic appointments."

John whispered back. "I'm sure he won't be in opposition of

our sovereign. The king gave him a leading part in preparing the New Testament for the Bible translation."

Archbishop Abbot stepped to the consort and requested they play "Psalms Five," then turned to the guests. "Please sing with me."

Coming together in song gave John a sense of rapport with those in the room—teachers of the Lord's gospel, as he was.

Hannah's voice rang truer than the rest—clean and pure.

With John at the pulpit on Sundays, he was never able to stand beside her when she sang—although he could always pick out her voice. Sometimes he'd hear her singing outside as she gardened. He should find an excuse to have her sing after morning prayer and before their scripture study.

Hannah's voice in song warmed his heart. Somewhere in his memory was another voice. His mother must have sung to him as a child. He moved closer to Hannah. Her scent did something to his desire for her that terrified him. That's the place he ignored—where his fear warned he shouldn't deliver himself to someone who could possibly mean more to him than God.

Was he a fool to imagine she could love him enough to not leave him? And what if he gave her his soul and she didn't want it? She wouldn't leave him, would she? She could die though. She *was* carrying his child. Childbirth took many women, as it had his mother.

Chapter Twelve

Inside the coach traveling to John's childhood home, Hannah placed her hand on John's, pleased that the last travelers disembarked the coach in Rawcliffe and she and John were finally alone. "I see worry written plainly on your face." *Your family cannot torment you anymore*, she longed to say. *Because our coming child and I are your life now, and we'll safely hold your heart.* She couldn't say it aloud because if he rejected her 'twould hurt too much. If he loved her, why hadn't he said so?

"'Twas a mistake to come so far in your condition." He shifted on the seat and glanced at her belly then out the window. "If you see worry, 'tis for you only."

She squeezed his hand and kissed him on the cheek. "Your sister's marriage is a perfect opportunity to meet your family. Once our child arrives, it won't be so easy to travel across the country."

"So you've said." He huffed. "Take care to avail me if you're uncomfortable. These days of travel cannot be easy on you."

Did his attentions speak his feelings? Since her pregnancy, he'd been more attentive, something she held onto for comfort. If only he were more generous with his words.

She snuggled against his chest, forcing his arm over her shoulders, and nestled her ear over his heart. The steady rhythm spoke of vigor, stability, humanness.

An hour later, they neared John's second childhood home, that of his Uncle Edmund in Leconfield. The wind blew relentlessly against the coach, rocking them as they rode along a rutted lane.

The Pulse of His Soul

Hannah sat up. "I can see now what you've meant about Yorkshire. It's quite windy, but the terrain is lovely."

"This is East Riding. The low hills are known as the Yorkshire Wolds. In the summer they're painted in shades of purple heather."

She was charmed he realized she'd like to know that. "I'd adore the sight! We must come back sometime."

He shrugged. "Much like southern Kent, the hills are made of chalk. We're only a half-day's ride to the North Sea."

They passed a crossroad with a sign pointing left, *York, Scarborough*, and *Whitby* engraved deeply into the wood.

"Whitby is near your home? Surely you know the story of Saint Hild of Whitby?"

"I do."

She didn't like that he sounded bored. "Then why did you not tell me you knew of Queen Bertha since she's Hild's great-aunt?"

"I didn't say I did not know about Queen Bertha. I said 'twas Saint Augustine who spread Christianity in England." He rubbed his temple.

"You're discounting righteous women, as men have done for centuries." She clasped her hands in her lap. "Hild was abbess over several monasteries not only Whitby. Kings came to her for advice because of her great wisdom. Being a niece to the Northumbrian King Edwin, she was brought up in his court. When Edwin became widowed, he married Æthelburh of Kent, the daughter of Bertha and Æthelberht." Had he even heard her last sennight when she'd told him about Bertha?

John stayed quiet.

She went on, knowing full well he knew this story too. "And as part of the marriage contract—as was true of Queen Bertha's—Æthelburh was allowed to practice her Christian faith. She influenced King Edwin, as Bertha did King Æthelberht. King Edwin and his entire court were baptized Easter Day in 627. Hild was one of those baptized."

It didn't hurt to remind John how important women were to his country and religion. "Another person baptized that day was Hild's sister, Hereswith, who later married Æthelric, brother of King Anna of East Anglia. The couple and *their daughters* became esteemed for their Christian virtues."

Hannah raised an eyebrow to John. "Do you see the reach of good Christian women?"

He shook his head. "Women didn't have the capabilities to travel about the country for years as missionaries, and I still contend that Saint Augustine, although mistaken on some theological points, had a far greater reach with his writings and travel."

"Aye. More proof men have been holding women back for centuries. We've the ability to write. We can travel. And we can hold in our hearts a testimony of God as ardent as any man."

"Women are the weaker sex by nature. Methinks 'tis as God instituted." He looked away as if to say he was done speaking of it.

She clenched her fists. The way he dismissed her convictions exasperated her. She moved to the seat opposite and pressed against the far wall, crossing her arms over her chest, staring out the window at nothing. When he didn't accept the role of great women in the gospel, she felt he didn't clearly see her character either. The Lord had spoken to her, and she didn't doubt she was important to Him. Why could she not be as important to her husband? Would she become her mother and spend the day tending children, curing meat, and embroidering fabrics? Is this what God implored of her?

John sat subdued for a spell and then tapped his foot and shifted endlessly in his seat.

"Fare you well?" Hannah asked.

"It's getting late in the day. Let's halt and lodge here at Cherry Burton."

It dawned on her that he was nervous. He'd never admit as much. Her heart softened, dissolving her anger. "Thom may be insulted by that arrangement." She sat next to him. "I'm eager to meet your family."

"You've probably never met anyone like my uncle." He brushed his hand across his eyes. "He is . . ." John clenched his jaw, seemingly searching for the best description. "Minimizing."

"I'm a woman. I'm quite used to being minimized." She squeezed John's hand, hoping she'd get a reaction from her teasing.

He drew in a long breath. "It's not just that. He can be disrespectful in a way that's infuriating."

Interesting. Hannah wondered if Uncle Edmund had often infuriated John. She'd never seen him angry. When she thought he should have animosity, he'd act dismissive or aloof. A learned self-protection mayhap? "Well, this will be my only chance to visit Mary before she marries on the morrow and moves to her new husband's home. And I really wouldn't want to insult Thom." She leaned closer to John. "Would you?"

He sighed. "You're right. Let's pray Uncle doesn't bring up all my past failures. You may wish you'd never have married me."

"Never." Hannah turned John's face to hers and kissed him just as her babe fluttered within her womb.

They arrived as the stars decorated the sky. Wind whistled through cracks in the carriage and the wheels clicked across the cobblestones of a grand courtyard. The discoloration of the limestone on the mansion gave the house an ancient and unfriendly appearance.

Hannah shivered.

They disembarked near an expansive porch entry.

The coachman lowered their trunk to a servant who greeted them in the drive. The wind blew up their livery jackets like puffed-out bellflowers.

Thom stepped from the house. "At last! I've been watching for you all day."

"See," Hannah whispered.

Thom kissed her hand in welcome and embraced his brother.

A dark, small woman stepped out, smiled awkwardly, and looked to her skirts. She wasn't young, perchance in her thirties. Strands of coarse grey ran through her black hair, pulled into a matronly bun with no ringlets or hat.

Hannah supposed she'd do the same if the wind were always blowing. The woman was either a servant or John's sister, Mary, but no introduction was forthcoming.

Hannah curtsied and smiled.

The woman stepped forward tentatively.

Thom let go of John and he motioned her closer.

She smiled up at John, her eyes as dark as his.

John took her in a gentle hug. "Mary, how good you look," he said in a tender expression Hannah had never heard him use with her.

Her heart thudded with jealousy. *Silly*, she chided. *She's his sister.*

Thom finally introduced Mary to Hannah, and they touched hands lightly. Mary kept her eyes lowered and curtsied. She reminded Hannah of an Eastwell grey hare who lived in shallow ground depressions, peeking out tentatively. The animals were so shy, a sighting of one was rare indeed.

"It's well on dusk. Let's retire inside." Thom motioned them toward the door. "Uncle is anxious for supper and awaits us in the dining room."

John let out a breath of air Hannah guessed he'd been holding for some time, and she squeezed his hand.

She was a little addled by not being able to wash or change before their meal, but Thom gave no such courtesy as they hurried to the dining room. 'Twas a large room with splendid hanging tapestries of golds, greens, reds and blues—all with scenes of people and animals lounging outdoors under canopies. On the fourth wall, a massive breakfront cabinet was filled with silver tankards, plates, spoons, and candlesticks.

Hunched over an empty delicate china plate, a very elderly man sat at the head of a long table with exquisite inlaid marquetry. The wood surface as shiny as glass, it reflected firelight from the overhead candelabra that must have burned twenty tapers.

Thom stopped near him and looked to Hannah. "May I introduce Sir Edmund Howell." Thom bowed slightly, but Uncle Edmund didn't stand. "Sir, this is John's wife, Mistress Lothropp."

The old man looked as if he'd have a hard time lifting his head, so bent was his spine. His hands rested on the table, the knuckles large, fingers as crooked and thin as twigs on a curly oak tree. "My pleasure," he mumbled as if it took a stern mother's gaze to prod the sentiment out of him. He gave no welcome to John.

"I'm delighted to meet you, Sir Howell." Hannah curtsied.

"I'm hungry," he answered.

Thom pulled out a chair for Hannah one away from his uncle and then he sat in the chair at his uncle's left. John sat across from Thom, and Mary across from Hannah.

Servants immediately lifted covers off food waiting on the sideboard and judiciously served those at the table. No blessing was offered.

Uncle pivoted his head toward John without lifting it. "Eat."

After a few minutes of clinking utensils and awkward silence, Hannah said, "The ride here was uneventful. Yorkshire is quite lovely."

Uncle dropped his spoon onto his plate with a sharp clatter.

Everyone stopped eating.

John shook his head pointedly at Hannah, his eyes telling her something that she didn't understand.

What had she done wrong?

She glanced at Mary, who looked at her plate, hardly moving. Hannah considered what she'd said and couldn't conceive what had been wrong with the words. If anything, the host should have questioned how their travels had fared.

They continued to nibble in silence, the servants attending to them without words.

Strange, this household.

When Uncle was done with supper, male attendants stood to either side of him and helped him stand. They walked him slowly to the drawing room, his legs as bent as his fingers.

Hannah wondered if he were in pain and felt sorry for the man. Mayhap she'd act vile too if she lived in such a body.

Uncle was settled into a large, cushioned chair near a carved-stone hearth with a blanket draped across his legs. Thom and John sat in chairs flanking him, and Mary and Hannah sat on a settle. The fire popped, and a servant closed the door behind her with a click.

Would this hour be as censored as supper had been? No wonder John said so little. It appeared to be tradition in this household.

Hannah grasped Mary's hand in a gesture of sisterhood.

Mary flinched like she'd been stung.

But Hannah didn't let go, thinking 'twas Mary's peculiar shy way that made her startle so easily.

Even with a fire burning, the room felt cold in identity. Perchance it was the lack of anything personal. No partly read, overturned book had been left on a side table or portraits of family hung on the walls. The two paintings that were on the walls were old landscapes of the wolds, faded and uninteresting in color.

Uncle looked to John as well as his drooped head would allow. "I can't contend with all the deaths and births of you Lothropps. Your father's widow died, leaving eight more orphans. 'I can't take on anymore,' I told them." His claws grasped at his armchair.

"I was sorry to hear of my stepmother's passing. Where are the children?" John asked.

"They're still in the manor house. Their eldest, a newly-married sister, has moved back in."

"I see." John creased his brow.

Did he feel some kind of responsibility for the children? Hannah tried to catch his eye, but he didn't notice. Did he even take note of her being in the room? His thoughts appeared very distant, his lips pressed tight.

"William drains my coffers with his education but cannot return for holidays or his sister's wedding." Uncle made unsatisfactory noises in his throat.

Hannah counted exactly six grey hairs on the top of his dry, bald head. The hair remaining on the sides was long with no sheen.

"I'm sorry to hear that." John shook his head, probably realizing he'd done the same.

"And now for me to spend an exorbitant amount on Mary's dowry and a pretentious wedding for a spinster of three and thirty!" His voice went up in volume.

Mary's hand shook and Hannah embraced it gently.

"A silk gown will not make her more attractive." Drool dribbled on his chin, and Thom wiped it away with a handkerchief.

John's jaw ticked. "Mary deserves a lovely gown and lavish wedding. She has ever been a devoted nurse to you."

"Augh," Uncle grumbled. "You're a disrespectful man of God who doesn't honor his elders. Do you not live by the commandments now that you're not under my roof?"

Maybe this was more why John was a quiet man at home. Being reserved wasn't *tradition* in this household, but a means to avoid criticism.

Thom cleared his throat. "Being so far south, you probably haven't heard about what's happening here in Yorkshire—as close as West Riding even."

"What's that?" John asked, looking relieved Thom had changed the subject.

"Do you remember the Bradfords of Austerfield?"

"By name only."

"Well, recently an entire congregation of Separatists—led by John Robinson and an educated man, William Brewster of Scrooby—went to Holland to escape prosecution for their nonconformity. William Bradford was among them, leaving his inheritance behind."

"I'd assume his inheritance is safe under the Crown in the event Bradford returns," John said.

"But how does one return after separating from his church and country?" Hannah truly desired to know.

Uncle's head jerked up so suddenly that Hannah worried he'd afflicted damage. "Proper ladies don't talk politics," he thundered. His head dropped back down. "Go on, Thom."

John gave her a warning look much like his uncle's.

It took all of her energy to not respond then storm out of the room. She took deep breaths and decided it wasn't worth discussing further with either of them.

Mary's other hand was suddenly on hers.

Hannah slumped back, weary.

Thom said, "According to them, they're still defenders of the

Church of England and are asking for a choice in beliefs."

John nodded. "Typically, these Separatists are faithful to God. I can understand expelling the Catholics, but the Crown needs to contrive how not to push away some of our most devout."

"You've compassion for Separatists?" Uncle shrieked.

Uncle's bellow alarmed Hannah again, but her thoughts were along the same vein as his. She'd not heard these sentiments from John before.

John's hands clenched. "In Canterbury, I've become acquainted with Sir Thomas Denne, Esquire. He complains the courts are being tied up with Puritan and Separatist cases when they should only be handling civil transgressions."

Uncle wagged his head. "You're sounding like a nonconformist who shouts that man's religion should be between God and himself."

"I don't mean to present that impression. I'm, as always, a devout follower of King James and the Anglican Church."

"Bah!" Spittle flew onto the blanket. "Thom, take me to bed. I won't listen to this heresy in my own home."

Thom sprang up and helped Uncle to stand. A servant came forward, and together they walked Uncle Edmund out of the room.

Hannah leaned close to Mary. "The best thing about that man is he can't look me in the eye when he trivializes me."

Mary giggled a most charming laugh that gave her the appearance of a young woman.

The next morning, food was brought to her and John's bedchamber with apologies that the family had no time to dine together. They'd meet at the church in an hour. Hannah was glad for food at anytime and anywhere. Her appetite had almost doubled the last few weeks.

The church was too far from Uncle Edmund's estate to have a processional. But the wedding was well attended with more Lothropps than Hannah could count. She met at least twenty and knew she'd not remember all their names. Very aware that her accent was different and that she was the lightest blonde in the church, she felt a bit conspicuous. They were kind, but a bit distant, not just to her, but also to John. 'Twas obvious that he, Thom, and Mary were of a different mother and upbringing.

There were more stares than conversation.

"I don't see Uncle Edmund," she whispered to John once everyone was seated in the Lothropp pews.

"He's not here."

"What!" she said a little too loudly.

People peered her direction, disapproval written on their faces.

She smiled her apologies and asked no more. This family was as odd as she suspected—the man who raised Mary didn't come to her wedding. He'd not come to John's either now that she thought about it.

For Mary alone there was a short procession down the church nave with a bagpiper marching ahead. All rose to their feet and dipped a curtsy or bowed as she passed.

Hannah was filled with gratitude that so many honored the shy woman. She hoped Mary would take heart and always remember this moment.

Someone had styled her hair in a simple fashion but much prettier than the day before. Her veil flowed over a headpiece and onto a gown of light green silk brocade. A lace frontal piece matched the tightly corseted bodice. Her sleeves puffed twice, tied with cream-colored ribbon between. Ruffled lace cuffs draped over her small hands. Pinned at her gown's neckline was an emerald brooch with seed pearls that matched her earrings. Luxurious lace had been delicately tucked into the gown's low neckline.

"Lovely!" Hannah said under her breath, again delighted that Mary had this moment to be noticed, even though she wouldn't look up from the stone floor as she walked slowly behind the piper. As she neared, she did glance toward the Lothropps, smiling with only her lips until she met Hannah's gaze and showed her teeth before ducking her head.

Near the preacher, the musician stepped to the side and his pipes weaned out the last bits of air.

Mary moved to the groom, John Gallante, a widower of five and thirty whose seven young children sat in the front row.

After the ceremony, there were no festivities, wedding feast, dancing, or joyous traditions like John and Hannah had on their wedding night. Mayhap Uncle was too frugal and bitter to pay for such merriment?

Mary and Gallante ascended into a coach with their seven children and headed off into the distance to Mary's new home.

Hannah prayed in her heart that Mary's husband was gentle and that she'd be blessed to at last be away from the minimizing cruelty of her uncle.

When Uncle retired, John stretched his legs out in front of the fire in the drawing room, feeling discord in this house that had so many bad memories. He'd also nearly forgotten how exhausting the struggle was to make himself feel merited by his uncle.

Hannah had retired early, no doubt to avoid Uncle, but Thom took a seat beside John.

"You're a blessed man to have a wife so in love with you."

"What makes you think she loves me?" John asked.

"It's written all over her face. Do you not recognize her tenderness?"

John didn't want to hope. All the Howses were tender. 'Twas her nature to be affectionate with everyone. "Can her love remain after she's seen firsthand how Uncle feels about me? What must she think?"

"She sees the fool that he is."

John stared at the fire's flames that should warm him, but he was always chilled in this house. He'd be glad to leave soon. The sooner the better. "What say you of our orphaned half-siblings? What's to be done?"

"I visit often. Father may not have left us an inheritance, but he left *them* enough to live comfortably. The problem lies with the three oldest being girls. One is married, as Uncle said, but two are not and must be found husbands. Then there are three boys between twelve and sixteen that need schooling. A tutor is there daily but doing more may not be financially possible. Eleven-year-old Jane comes after those three boys and has two younger brothers besides. Being between those five boys with the closest sister seven years older leaves Jane somewhat forsaken."

"What kind of disposition has she?"

"A quiet child as far as I gather. They all still peer at me as a stranger, I fear, and don't often converse. Jane is but eleven, so mayhap her character is still to be discovered?"

"We need a house girl," John considered out loud. "She's younger than I'd envisioned for help in our home, but perchance her youth makes her amenable?"

"Robert, being the oldest, will make that final decision."

They sat for a while in their own thoughts.

"John," Thom's voice sounded forlorn.

John had a sudden rush of alarm. "What is it?"

"Why did you choose the life of a clergyman?"

He settled back in his chair glad it wasn't something serious. Thom deserved the truth. "I'd thought if I became like our grandfather, the vicar, then Father would admire me." Mayhap even love me. "Then when he died, I continued to follow the profession so my family could be proud of me." He swallowed, embarrassed at his shallowness, but Thom didn't appear shocked. "When I realized my loving Heavenly Father knew me as a son and that *He was the father* that nourished my soul, I hungered to serve my parishioners for Him. In this, I've truly found joy. I now endeavor to serve unselfishly. There are people who need God's word delivered to them with real intent of salvation."

Thom nodded as if he understood and didn't judge John's shortcomings. "When Uncle dies, I'll not live here." He closed his eyes and laid his head back against his chair. "Speak of this to no one."

"Your words are always safe with me." If there were anyone to understand, 'twas John. There were times, even now, he relived the day his father rode away—the fear in Anne's eyes, the coldness of the new house, Thom holding back tears. John had been provided a room to himself, and he'd laid awake all night trying to remember the comforting sound of Thom and baby William's breathing.

"I want to serve our Lord and become a preacher." Thom watched John for a reaction.

John sat up and stared into his brother's face, trying to judge the truth of it. Thom's earnest expression quickened John's heart.

"I want to live closer to you and Hannah. Do you think that reckless?"

"There's naught I could desire more."

The men stood and embraced.

Chapter Thirteen

Dorothy had come for Hannah's lying-in and was gracious enough to not complain about the small vicarage. The dark front room made it hard to sew by, but she and Dorothy were doing their best.

"Is your marriage one of love?" Dorothy asked Hannah, green eyes as intent as a hawk's circling its prey.

Hannah ducked her head as if she were engrossed on getting her stitches right. "I love my husband," she all but whispered.

"You sound as if your love is to be kept a secret." Dorothy set her sewing aside.

What would Dorothy think if she told her John said God's voice had told him to marry her? Always obedient, he followed that voice, but it didn't mean he loved her. He hadn't yet told her so. "The reverend is very attentive to my needs." As a doctor might be.

She'd sometimes caught him looking at her, fear in his eyes. He'd been different these last few months. He wouldn't touch her. Almost as if he were afraid. She told him the midwife said the marriage bed couldn't hurt the baby, that that was an old idea proved unsound, but he'd disagreed. She worried the religious teachings of married life as a parallel of Christ's bond with his church meant John regarded passionate love between husband and wife undesirable.

"He treats you cordially, does he? Well, that's fine if he's your clergyman, but I'm asking the state of your *marriage*."

"He's a man of goodness. His life is the church, I've come

to accept that." Hannah kept her eyes on the stitches she sewed onto a baby cap, held above her swollen belly. "Perhaps he's not very forthcoming with his affections. He's a bit reticent with his parishioners too—his feelings not always evident—but I see his affection in the way he tilts his head forward, eyes lowered, listening intently as they tell him their ailments or fears or questions. He goes out of his way to dispense to them what they ask." But it did plague her that he smiled as seldom for her as he did for them.

"I always thought you'd marry someone passionate. But now that I've spent some time with the reverend, I see that his intelligence is something to admire. You couldn't have lived with a man who wasn't highly educated."

She admired his intelligence too, but whenever she complimented him, he'd turn from her, sometimes leaving the room without a word. His moods had been hard to get used to. Now that she'd met his uncle and family, she understood better.

Dorothy stood, stretching her back, which brought her round belly forward. She massaged her lower hips. "As afraid as I am of childbirth, I suppose I'll welcome it in a few months." She sighed. "Whereby women have done this since the dawn of time, 'tis a great wonder why. Every part of me has grown. Even my feet."

"True, but I could swear my bladder has gotten smaller."

Dorothy laughed and stepped to glimpse Hannah's handiwork. "You never have had the talent for such invention, have you." She picked up the embroidery, examined it more closely, and tossed it next to hers. "Your lying-in is dreadfully dull in this dark vicarage. I know it's chilly outside, but there's no wind. Let's slip on our mantles and take a stroll in your lovely garden, seeing as your confinement won't allow a romp in the woods." She chuckled. "Those were convivial times when we were young, were they not?"

"They were. Once this child can walk, I'll use the excuse of giving *him* exercise in order to enjoy the countryside again. It's a shame there's no lake close by like at Eastwell."

Dorothy brought Hannah's pattens over and knelt to put them on, knowing full well that Hannah couldn't hunch to do it herself.

Grasping the wooden chair arms, Hannah jostled herself out of the chair. Her body ached from lack of movement and the size of the baby she carried. She took a step. "Ooh! My feet are so swollen it hurts to walk."

Dorothy took her by the arm. "Something I've yet to look forward to."

They crunched along frozen grass, Hannah more waddling

than strolling. Wood smoke suspended in the chill air. At the lower yard, they brushed off the bench seat and sat looking out at a large beech tree, lovely in spikey silhouette, even with its leaves gone. The barren field beyond lay covered with frost.

They snuggled close to keep warm while they talked about their childhood and their dreams of future family life.

Awhile later, footsteps approached. Hannah twisted to see her sister. "Penny! Oh, how I've missed you."

"I was here not three days past, you nonsensical girl. I've heard that pregnancy makes a woman's mind go thick like pea soup."

Hannah chuckled. "That's a good description."

Penninah handed Hannah a basket of soap. "Mother and I have sympathy for the attempts you've made at making soap with all that lavender you grew, so we've made some for you."

Hannah held the basket to her nose. Little flecks of lavender were scattered throughout the squares of ivory-colored soap. The sweet, subtle aroma reminded her of summer. "Lovely. Thank you and be sure to thank Mother. How is she feeling?"

"Probably like you and Dorothy. She expects her baby will come along in June. I fear my life will be spent holding other women's babies." An expression that was possibly disappointment crossed Penninah's face before she adjusted it to a look of teasing.

"Your time will come soon enough," Dorothy remarked.

Jane found them a few moments later. "The reverend and Reverend Howse have returned and ask that you accompany them for dinner." She smiled shyly and dipped a curtsy, her brown hair pulled back and covered by a coif.

Hannah loved having Jane there. She was a subdued girl, who'd appeared very homesick at first, but after a few months had become amiable. Hannah surmised her easy-going nature was something Jane wasn't used to. No Lothropp was used to it, but as they talked, and Hannah taught Jane how to garden and work on her letters, the girl showed her affable nature. She took well to Widow Reynolds' instruction as well.

"What has Widow Reynolds cooked up today?" Hannah asked.

"What do you say to a duck with berry sauce?" Jane answered as they stepped into the house.

"I don't know. I've never spoken to a duck before." Hannah smiled.

John's eyes tightened in disapproval.

Jane giggled.

At least Hannah was teaching one Lothropp to laugh.

Father stepped to her and kissed her on the cheek.

"I don't miss those bad jokes at home," Penninah commented as she passed.

Father patted her shoulder as she walked by. "Of course, you don't. My jokes are just as bad, and I offer them all the time."

Penninah rolled her eyes.

"Food has been my torment." Hannah said as they entered the dining room. She breathed in the aroma of roasted foul and steaming gourd with butter. "John brought me enough marchpane to last a month, but I ate it in a couple days. Now I'm shaving the sugar cone before and after meals." She motioned to her sister. "You need to place it where I can't reach it, Penny."

Penninah looked slyly and pointed to the floor. "I dare say I could put it down here and you wouldn't be able to stoop to retrieve it."

They all laughed. Even John.

There were many ills and hardships John could bear for other people but a scream from his wife wasn't one of them. He couldn't help her. What if she died with him wringing his hands, doing naught downstairs.

Another wail drifted down, this one lower-pitched and longer.

His mother, the one person who loved him more than any other had left him this way—in childbirth. He wiped his brow and continued his march around the furniture, hating how vulnerable he felt.

He'd told the midwife that if Hannah were anywhere close to death to be sure and let him know immediately so he could bestow on her the sacrament of Christ's blood and body.

Hannah had refused to lay by a burial sheet for the baby like most women did. She'd said, "I see in my mind's eye that I'm to birth a son. That son will grow strong in the Lord."

How could he argue those words? He wanted to believe. He prayed morning, noon, and night that she was right.

The next scream came so heart-wrenching he had to hold himself back from rushing up the stairs. He bent over, feeling like he was going to be sick. He quickly ran outside and vomited in the bushes then came into the kitchen to find a cup. He filled it with ale to clean his mouth.

The Pulse of His Soul

Dorothy, Penninah and Mistress Howse accompanied the midwife upstairs. Surely with all those women helping naught could go wrong. But he was fooling himself. Something could and often did go wrong. He'd presided over many funerals for both baby and mother. Sometimes for both in one day. *Save my wife, God.*

He went back to the main room and plopped onto a chair then looked up at the rafters, wishing he were in the room above.

Silence.

He strained to hear.

More silence.

Oh God, don't let her die. I love her so. I promise I'll tell her if You will only let her live. He swallowed back the frustration. This wasn't who he was. Fear in a soul could take a man to the devil.

The silence went on and on.

I'll tell her, I vow, I'll tell her. He silently recited every prayer he could recall from the prayer book.

"John?" Penninah stepped close.

He leapt to his feet, looking closely at her for any display of grief.

She laid her hand on his arm. "Would you like to come see your son?"

Tears stung in spite of Penninah's stare so close to his face. "The child is alive?" Could it really be so? "How is Hannah?"

Penninah squeezed his arm in reassurance. "She's resting. Come." She pulled him along and let him go up the narrow stairs before her.

Could this really be happening to him? His pace slowed. Well, he surmised, they both could still die. His legs felt heavy, harder to lift with each step. He squared his shoulders and entered the room.

Mistress Howse, Dorothy, and the midwife all watched him closely. How he wished he were alone with his wife and child. Why did such a private moment need to be shared with so many? It reminded him of his wedding night.

Hannah lay partially reclined on the bed, her pale features strained. She watched him as if she were afraid of his being in the room.

He stopped.

"Come see your son." Her voice scratched. She pulled back the blanket exposing his entire naked body. Two legs. Two arms. A collapsed tied-off cord, and his maleness was there for all to see.

Stepping to the side of the bed, John's words lodged in his

throat. The baby had his eyes open, looking at John as if in deep concentration. The room went still. He swallowed. "He's . . . magnificent."

A feeling came over his entire body—similar to when God spoke to him, private and sacred. He knelt beside the bed and let his tears descend, ducking his head so no one saw.

Hannah reached her arm around his shoulders. "My sentiments as well." She kissed the top of his head. "Is he not a miracle?"

John looked at Hannah, who gazed on him with all the love he desired but hadn't figured out how to accept. "How do you fare?"

"I am well." She wiped perspiration from her forehead, her coloring aflush, but healthy.

Relief washed over him like he'd been bathed in sweet tears of gratefulness. His love for Hannah caused a deep pain in his chest.

The midwife stepped forward. "There were no problems whatsoever. Your wife is strong and can bear you many more fine sons."

Hannah wrapped the baby, leaving his face showing.

The child stared from those celestial eyes at his mother as if he'd the soul of an adult in the temple of a wee babe.

John received the impression that it hadn't been long since his son had looked on God's face. He thought of the words of Jeremiah. 'The word of the Lord spake thus unto me. Before I fashioned thee in thy mother's womb, I did know thee: and before thou wast born I sanctified thee.'

Again, the feeling of a sacred reverence came over him. He stroked the boy's wet, dark hair.

A couple days later, John was anxious to talk to Hannah. To hold her again. To somehow say those things he'd told God he would. He tried to talk himself out of it a few times, but the dishonor of not following through on his promise was more than his integrity could bear. Before the baby was born, for months they'd slept in different rooms, but tonight John would approach Hannah while she was alone.

He stepped out of his room. All was quiet.

Jane and Penninah would be asleep, Mistress Howse had returned home to await her birthing, and Dorothy had left for her own lying-in. Hannah's lying-in would last forty more days, all of them attended during the day by her female friends and family.

He tiptoed across the landing. The floor squeaked, and he stopped. He drew in a deep breath and opened the door to Hannah's—no, to their—room. A candle burned on the bedside table, Hannah had her gown down, and the child suckled.

Desire drew him forward. Not of lust but of wanting to belong. He sat at the edge of the bed, and Hannah placed her hand on his. The baby continued his vigorous sucking.

"Is he healthy? Is there any worriment for him?" John questioned.

"Nay. He's a healthy boy, always ready for another meal." She smiled down at the baby with a look of adoration.

"What do you ask of me? I can't do a thing for him, and I'm at a loss."

"You can name him."

"I've been considering Thomas, after my brother. How does this sit with you?"

"'Tis your father's name as well. Does that present you indecision?"

He grieved the loss of what he never had with his father. Suddenly, he desired to tell Hannah everything and be done with it. "My father never shared aught about himself. He was never hostile, but he didn't express interest in me. He didn't tell me what problems he wrestled with, if it saddened him to lose my mother, or how he spent his time. I've had to imagine it all for myself, and I'm never sure I get it right."

Hannah stroked his cheek with her soft hand.

He'd missed her touch more than he realized.

She smiled sadly. "Even more striking than the wounds is the longing he has left in you. To finally share these feelings with me is to hopefully rid yourself of a great deal of rejection and sadness. Know that I love you fully and so will your son." Her blue eyes pierced his soul. "Do you fare well, my husband?"

How did she understand so completely? She never experienced such rejection with her own father.

"When I first learned of your pregnancy, there was a sudden resurfacing of my childhood. These were largely unpleasant recollections of neglect by my father. And an anger at my mother for leaving me. I didn't want to deal with the upsurge of memories. It caused intense resentment. I tried to push it away, but I can't seem to do it completely."

"I'll help you."

"What if I turn out like my father?"

"That isn't possible since you embraced a different path years ago. You chose to serve and gift your loving kindness to others. If I'm to believe what you say of your father, that path was something he would never have chosen. I suspect he had his own demons."

"I've considered that likelihood. I'm not sure what. He had a caring father."

"Perchance he developed bitterness from his trials? He lost two wives, after all."

"Aye, but he was bitter before my mother died."

"I don't believe we'll ever have the answers. You need to find peace without them. In your adolescence you weren't able to form a strong attachment to either parent."

He appreciated how she spoke without degradation. "You're right. Let's talk of kinder things." He brought her hand to his lips and lingered there. Could he tell her his feelings? He placed her hand over his heart. "I'm overdue in saying this. . ." He looked into her eyes. Her own love for him held him steady. "I love you, Hannah. I always have. You're dearer to me than anyone on this earth. I'm sorry for not having told you sooner."

She tried to embrace him, but the babe was between them. "Why have you kept these feelings from me?" Her eyes glistened in the candlelight.

"I suppose I thought 'twould make me weak and not bestow to God all His due."

"Vulnerable too, mayhap?" Hannah asked with understanding.

John nodded. "I've pushed you away because of the pain I felt by losing my mother—the only person who ever loved me. I never wanted to feel that again. Can you forgive me?" The senselessness of it was unfortunate. How had he gotten himself into this situation?

Hannah wedged her finger into the sleeping baby's mouth to get him to release her breast. She set him on the bed and closed her shift. "Come lay beside me." She gingerly slid to the center of the bed and pulled the coverlet back.

He slid in beside her.

"Oh! Your feet are freezing. Why didn't you say something sooner?" Hannah giggled.

"I hadn't even noticed." He pulled his feet away.

She grabbed them back with her feet and stroked them. "I'll take you any way I can get you." She wrapped her arms around him.

He pulled her closer. 'Twas a shame it was too soon to love her like he wanted. At any rate, being in her arms was much more than he'd had in months—and it felt exquisite. "You smell different."

She chuckled softly. "Is that favorable or distasteful?"

"Neither. Just an observation. Mayhap it's the smell of motherhood."

She sighed. "Thomas is a good name. I don't believe we need a third John in the family right now, but someday I want to name a son John. And I hope he'll be as kind as his father and my father."

"What can I do for the babe?"

"I'll supply him nourishment; you can teach him later. He'll need a father to teach him to walk in the way of our Lord."

There was naught that mattered to him outside that room. His world was with Hannah and little Thomas. He knew the perils of loving someone and was finally willing to risk it all.

Chapter Fourteen

On the first Sunday morning in April, Hannah stood in the narthex. A few steps higher than the congregation, she faced east. A white fringed veil masked her hair and face and kept her from seeing clearly. 'Twas the first time she'd been to church in months. She'd come for her churching ceremony to purify her and to end the forty-day confinement and to thank God for the safe delivery of her child.

In front of her, John stood in his white robes. He blessed her, making the sign of the cross, giving thanks for her wellbeing, and then read from *The Book of Common Prayer*. "For as much as it hath pleased Almighty God of his goodness to give you safe deliverance, and hath preserved you in the great danger of childbirth: ye shall therefore give hearty thanks unto God and pray. I have lifted up my eyes to the hills: from when cometh my help . . ."

As his prayer continued, Hannah considered how her perspective had changed since giving birth to Thomas. She'd amended her view of being female. To her astonishment, she'd found a love of motherhood and a new realm of power.

John allowed their home to be an exclusively female disciplined domain where she could nourish her baby and spend time studying medicinal herbs. She'd found that fennel mixed with a little sugar-water comforted Thomas's fussing in the afternoon and that comfrey relieved her nursing blisters. Providing healing with herbs gave her a new focus.

She admired the midwife who'd gently taught her how to bring a child into the world and used herbs like betony to lesson childbed pains and horehound to ease the delivery. Mayhap Hannah could study midwifery or become a domestic healer?

Her skills disquieted John and she understood his worry. The association between female influence, midwifery, and herbs for healing sometimes led to accusations of witchcraft. She'd need to find a balance somehow.

'Twas in this very church God spoke to her mind, reminding her that she was His handmaiden. She hadn't comprehended it completely then but now felt it had to do with motherhood. Perhaps her children and their children would serve God in such a way that *they* would bring many unto Him?

The timber of John's voice shifted, letting her know it was almost time for her prayer as he'd instructed her earlier that morning. "And lead us not into temptation," he said.

"But deliver us from evil," she countered.

Light from the high lancet window far behind John surrounded his silhouette. Through the veil, she saw his affection as he regarded her. "Oh Lord, save this woman thy servant." His words sounded more tender than when he'd done this ceremony for other women.

"Which putteth her truth in thee," Hannah said to John, the congregation, and to God.

"Be thou to her a strong tower," John quoted, his deep voice resonating through the nave. He was a man who believed what he was saying and wanted others to join in the grace of his personal testimony.

She liked this rapport between the two of them, and it was the first time she alone was able to voice scripture in church in front of a congregation. "From the face of her enemy," she said so all could hear.

John angled his head toward the wooden-domed ceiling. "Lord hear our prayer."

"And let our cry come unto thee," she said with emphasis. Hannah remembered all her parts by heart without reading the Prayer Book for guidance.

John swiveled toward the congregation. "Let us pray."

"Almighty God," everyone read together. "which has delivered this woman thy servant from the great pain and peril of childbirth: we beseech thee . . ."

This praiseworthy custom, churching a woman and giving her a blessing of purification, made Hannah feel loved by both her God and her husband. Could there be anything better?

John requested her to come forward into the chancel and kneel near the communion table.

As he prayed over the holy sacrament, she thought about teaching Thomas and her future children how to understand the Bible the way she did. Soon she could at long last teach the gospel—to her children.

After church, John changed from his robes and joined the party Penninah had organized—a celebration in honor of Hannah's churching. Parishioners and Hannah's family had arranged blankets on the grassy slope behind the church and shared their food with one another.

Reverend Howse brought beer and asked John to help serve it. John visited amongst the guests as he filled goblets.

The spring weather rejuvenated people. Much goodwill was amongst them.

John had long learned that any event with the Howse family brought joviality. Still deeply suspicious of too much enthusiasm, he cringed at the bursts of laughter coming from Hannah, Penninah, their mother, and the many Howse children—and on Sabbath, no less.

Jane sat subdued amongst the fair Howses, as dark-headed and different as him. She didn't laugh, but shyly looked about her at each of them. She'd need to find her way as he was doing.

"Good Sabbath Day, Reverend Lothropp." Nate Tilden held his goblet up to the jug John held.

This was the first time he'd seen Tilden at aught but a Thursday sermon. Many times, over the months, John had found Tilden and others outside whispering together after his sermons. Occasionally, they'd come privately to him with doctrinal questions.

"I'm pleased to see you here on a Sabbath with your family," John said.

"With the weather so fine, I decided to bring my wife. She's heard me speak about your thought-provoking sermonizing for a year now, and I thought it time the whole family experienced it for themselves. 'Twas an added surprise to attend Mistress Lothropp's churching." He stood and motioned to a woman seated on his blanket. "This is my wife, Mistress Lydia Tilden."

Lydia went to stand with a baby in her arms, but John held his hand to motion her to not do so.

She inclined her head. "Reverend." The child squirmed to be let free. Two older children played with stick poppets along the blanket's edge.

"My children are Thomas, Mary, and baby Joseph." Tilden smiled at them with endearment John understood now that he had his own son.

He glanced to Hannah bouncing his fussy Thomas in her arms. Her golden hair caught the sunlight. The baby's hair had lightened enough over the past month that John suspected he'd be a blond too.

These last forty days had shown him what an exceptionally conscientious mother she was. Not only that, their relationship had become stronger, more satisfying, since he'd professed his love. His happiness had become deeper than any time in his life.

"Sam Hinckley also came from Tenterden with us." Tilden pointed out Hinckley, a look of deep curiosity on his face as he visited with Jonny Fenner.

"I hope you'll come again soon." John bowed to the Tildens. "'Twas my pleasure to meet all of you. I'll go welcome Sam as well." He saluted with the jug of beer.

He also needed to visit Widow Fenner. Jonny's father, Ned, had died a few months back. John had officiated the funeral and afterwards visited the family almost sennightly. Ned had left a large parcel of land which Jonny Fenner, almost sixteen, was planting by himself.

When John approached Hinckley and the Fenners, all conversation stopped. He got the impression they'd been talking about something they had no interest in sharing with him. He felt a bit wounded, but it wasn't the first time others didn't want to have a casual conversation with their preacher.

After preliminaries and pouring of beverage, John welcomed Hinckley to their parish and turned to Widow Fenner. "How are you and the children getting by?"

Widow Fenner sat upon a pillow while her two daughters and two sons ate meat pies. They wore the clean, simple, sturdy clothing of yeoman, with an appearance of good health. The widow placed her pie on a handkin and brushed crumbs from her fingers. "Jonny has spent these last weeks putting in the hop pegs."

Upon hearing his name, Fenner pivoted. "Reverend Lothropp." He stepped closer. "Why do you use the sign of the cross as papists do?"

Widow Fenner's face flushed a bright red. "Jonny!"

His sisters gasped. His brother appeared too young to understand the crime. Hinckley shuffled his feet and looked away.

Fenner was obviously as headstrong as his father had been. Being young, he didn't know to bridle his passions and not openly question the practices of the Church of England.

John took in a deep breath. "I serve as my king has requested." He bent toward Widow Fenner and said quietly, "I've spoken with Jonny before, and we agreed that I'd be tolerant to an open discussion regarding gospel principles. I'd rather he discussed his questions with me than with a Separatist."

She nodded, but fear remained in her eyes.

Overly loud laughter came from the folks on the Howses' blanket. Many picnickers spun to regard the lighthearted group and smiled their approval.

Heat crept up the back of John's neck. He didn't approve. Additionally, he needed to concentrate and provide Fenner his full attention. He stepped closer to Fenner. "Can we speak privately? No need to further upset your mother."

Hinckley asked, "May I come too?"

"By all means." John motioned him forward.

They walked a distance down the hill. Fenner's ox-like body clomped in purposeful strides. In contrast, Hinckley was slow-moving and taller.

"How old are you now, Sam?" John questioned.

"One and twenty, sir, and still single," he answered lightheartedly.

John admired his easy-going nature.

They stopped next to a rock wall surrounding a newly planted field. Green shoots barely peeked from the soil. A hazelnut tree shaded them.

"How are you managing without your father, Jonny?" John asked.

Fenner's eyes dulled for a breath then brightened again. "As long as I get the dried hop sold in September, we'll survive. No need to reckon we be on the parish poor list." He smirked and shrugged his wide shoulders. A lock of wavy-brown hair fell across his face, and he jerked his head to move it back from where it had come.

"Your family is blessed to have your able labor," John said.

"I been in the fields with my father since I be a lad." He shrugged again as if 'twas no big compromise for a fifteen-year-

The Pulse of His Soul

old to carry the burden of supporting a family of five. "I didn't mean to offend earlier. The others didn't realize we've 'ad an open discussion 'bout such things. And I'm troubled by the sign of the cross and the many vestiges of the Roman Catholics in our meeting today."

John admired his honesty, integrity, and the hard laborer that he was. He saw in Fenner a leader. "You and I know that, but if you speak to the wrong people about your concerns there could be punishments—fines, stocks, imprisonment even. Your family needs you to be reliable and always there for them. Anyone who overhears your worries about the Church can report you to the church warden."

Fenner bent and picked up a small stick from the ground. He broke it in half, and then broke half of that in half and tossed the remnants away. "It's my right and duty to know God for myself."

"You can do that and remain in communion with the Church." Disobedience to church ordinances was treason, and John hoped he could keep Fenner from getting to that point.

"Obedience to conscience should be granted to every individual. If we don't speak up, how will this come about?"

Hinckley startled at sounds of footsteps coming toward them.

Tilden came into view as if he were on a stroll, but John knew curiosity had brought him.

"Your discourse seems serious." Tilden joined the group. "May I be allowed to confer?"

"Jonny is anxious to understanding why Catholic vestiges are still part of the Church of England's services," Hinckley explained.

"I admit I'm uncomfortable with the same." Tilden stroked his closely groomed beard.

"In school, I had studied a 1589 document written in response from the Church to the Puritan threat," John said. "It read, 'The Prayer Book contents are not repugnant to the Word of God; the vestments are not against the Word of God, and therefore should be used.'" The quote sounded erroneous. 'Twas no debate to their questions of papist evidence still within the Church of England.

Fenner cocked an eyebrow. "Those words ring false to my ears and heart. Your ordination is as a perpetual curate, and a curate is assigned to cure souls, is he not? My soul is ailing, yet I'm not sure you've the power to cure it—certainly not with that sentiment."

Hinckley shook his head in disagreement. "God is the physician. Clergy shouldn't meddle with matters of conscience or force religion on us."

Yet John did want to cure souls. Especially those of these young men. "When I was awarded my license to officiate, I agreed to advocate the idea of one land, one church, one absolute power on the throne. Loyalty to king and to church with its divinely appointed bishops and clergy encompasses this concept. Clergy isn't meddling with your choice. They're attempting to bring you closer to God." He looked each man in the eyes. "Uniformity takes discipline, and discipline will help you progress."

Tilden sputtered a sardonic jeer. "Uniformity doesn't lead to progress. I believe in the truths revealed by God in the Bible and in the virtue of personal faith. I freely accept Christ. 'Tis not a forced conversion. A forced, *uniform* conversion of *all* doesn't create testimonies of faith." He pointed at John. "Are you saying by disciplining people if they don't believe the same religion as you that you're doing something ordained by God?"

John had debated these same subjects with Thom and others at Cambridge. He too had wrestled with the notion of man's conscience choosing the religion he was to follow. And he certainly didn't agree with the king punishing those who didn't believe as he. But he couldn't tell these young men that. 'Twould cause them to stray, he was sure. "There's really no choice at present to learn of God and follow Him in peace and harmony without being a worthy member of the Church of England. The purity of one's religious principles is confirmed by collaboration."

Tilden turned his back to John.

John didn't want to lose this good man on the principles of conscience. He wanted to show him that he could find happiness within the Anglican Church. 'Twould take more time. "Look at me, Nate."

Tilden shifted back. With jaw set and eyes hard, he folded his arms across his chest, as if daring John to teach him something of truth.

With all the affectionate concern he could muster in his tone, John said, "I'd rather you were on the right side of the Church." He motioned to all of them. "And not separating yourselves from affiliation with the Church. Nonconformists attend church and, in my eyes, are those who are trying to come to an understanding of unity and gospel principles, even if they disagree with the use of the prayer book and the concept of an established church."

He looked more closely at each man. Did they realize his sympathies were with them? "If you leave the Church and become Separatists, then your problems will multiply and it's likely you'll end up in jail or find yourselves hiding from the authorities. That's not a course that is conducive to supporting a family and will only bring sorrow."

With their intent stares on John, seemingly listening well to his words, he suddenly felt as if he were standing at a crossroads, deciding if the pulse of his soul beat with God's. Could *he* make a choice that would afflict his family? He loved Hannah and Thomas more than he thought possible. Did God still come before man?

His heart quickened as if something was about to happen that would alter his life completely. He placed his hand to where his heartbeat flew. "I'd suggest we keep these conversations between ourselves. If you all continue to meet after my Thursday sermons, mayhap you can do so *in* the church and let me participate?"

PART II
Chapter Fifteen

October 1615
Charing, Kent, England

John adjusted his hold on a basket heavy with food for those unable to care for themselves—vagrants and the old—and then helped Hannah down from the wagon. They'd caught a ride to Charing and now stood at the crossroad.

"We're blessed, you and I," she said to John.

"A good thing to remember as we visit the poorhouse where so many are not as blessed as we." John stuck out his elbow to invite her hand into the crook of his arm.

Five years of marriage had brought Hannah to the point of feeling as if she and John were of the same heart and mind as disciples equally committed to their service to the Lord. She shared with him the concerns he had for his congregation and made visits to parishioners when able. She offered hospitality to all and often found herself serving as a conduit for those who wished to pass on complaints to her husband.

Finding time to study together in private was harder than it had been before children, but when they did, John still allowed her to voice her views, discussing Latin or Hebrew roots of the words and gleaning added truths from biblical passages. As long as it was in private, "Just between the two of us," he'd said.

Life had become comfortable and rewarding. The year before, they'd had another child and named her Jane, in honor of John's sister. They called their baby Janie, to distinguish between the two Janes in the household.

Now Hannah was pregnant with their third child.

She snuggled close as they strolled the road not far distant from Charing. 'Twas autumn again. The smell of a farmer burning leaves filled the crisp air. "What do you hear from Thom?"

"He's built a new manor in Dengie and wants us to visit again. I advised him that you're with child, and he said Elizabeth is expecting also. Amusing that soon after becoming a vicar he found his wife, as did I."

Amusing? It was a word she never thought she'd hear John use. He'd transformed over the years, even laughing quietly with her over some silly pun or expression. "I'm pleased for him and Elizabeth. I wish Dengie were close enough for us to enjoy each other's lying-in and for the cousins to play together."

"He offered to pay for the two-day's coach ride when you're able. I'm uncomfortable with him always offering money. Since Uncle's death, he often tries to convince me to accept the allowance Uncle never gave. It's tempting, and I wish we didn't need it. He says he no longer pays for William's schooling because William has gone into the military."

"You've provided me a comfortable living. Are we really so poor?"

"Well, if we had a conveyance, we wouldn't be begging rides on wagons, now would we? Our family soon grows to six, and my salary stays the same. I've written to the bishop countless times about the need for a new vicarage but hear naught in response." His arm stiffened under hers. "I'd like to acquire another benefice."

"How will you find the time?" She barely saw him now.

"That's yet to be determined. Perchance a clerk could be found to help with some of my responsibilities?"

Nearing the village, they passed small homes made of wattle and daub with thatched roofs and gardens turning golden-brown from the chilly air. Remains of old stone walls surrounded properties that stretched to fields beyond.

"Who are we visiting today?" Hannah asked.

"Because of the Poor Law, it's our government's responsibility to care for the impoverished. The Church no longer runs the poorhouses, but I feel we must be accountable for our own Egerton parishioners who reside there."

He blew out a long breath. "I'm afraid Mister Mills has found himself on hard times. I'd like to see if I can work out a contract with him and Sir Warren—to work his fields and bring Mills closer to home. Also, Old Tilley is being auctioned off as a pauper in a few days. I spoke with Sir Quitly, and he's agreed to let her do what little housework she's able in exchange for her meals and a bed in his tenement cottage. 'Twould be best if she can stay closer to home and not here in Charing, farther from family than she can walk. I need to advise her of the arrangement."

They neared the poorhouse on High Street. The building looked as if it had once been grand—probably donated by gentry who had since moved on to a more affluent life. The village square had little activity, and only a few carts moved down the lane.

When they entered, the smell of burning leaves faded and noxious odors of unwashed bodies and human waste stung Hannah's nostrils and eyes. She covered her nose. "Deplorable conditions," she said under her breath to John.

"I did warn you not to come."

"Aye, but my place is supporting my husband in matters of the Lord." She uncovered her nose and braved the smells.

They stood in a small entry hall filled with ravaged humans. People of all ages and sizes, most dressed in shabby clothes, some even shoeless, leaned against the walls and reclined upon the floor. How many were thieves and cheats, and how many had just fallen on hard times? A baby crawled across the filthy wooden-planked floor.

Hannah shivered.

A man in shirtsleeves and breeches with no jerkin, hat, or collar stepped forward. "Are you looking for someone, parson?"

"Aye," John glanced about. "Mister Mills of Egerton and an elderly woman known by Old Tilley."

"The beggar's in there with the other paupers who can do no hard labor." He pointed to an open door. "Mills is out breakin' stones and should be along shortly." The man eyed the basket of food.

"I've brought it for my parishioners," John said.

The man shrugged and ambled away.

The bigger room off the entry was as cold as outside but smelled not as fetid. They found Old Tilley sitting by a window amongst about thirty other women. She held up a square of fabric in her knobby hand, examining it in what little sunlight came through the begrimed glass.

As they grew closer, Hannah saw that it was a monogrammed handkerchief, stained and ragged.

Coming to her side, John said loudly, "Good day, Old Tilley."

She startled at the use of her name, but then saw John and revived. Her cheeks pinked as if he'd come to court her. Her smile held no teeth, but her eyes beamed with genuine pleasure. "Reverend Lothropp!" she said loudly, her hearing having gone.

Hannah suspected Old Tilley's dreams were fanciful, but what did she have but dreams?

John sat in a chair beside her, and Hannah stepped to his side.

"Good day, Mistress Lothropp," Old Tilley said with no cheer then immediately turned her attentions to John again.

Hannah almost chuckled but bit her tongue. "Good day to you as well."

John handed Old Tilley the basket of food.

Her face lit almost as charmingly as when she first saw John. "What a pleasure you make my life."

As John and Old Tilley spoke of the arrangements made with Sir Quitly, Hannah strolled about the room, speaking with the women and trying to understand what brought them to such a place.

Most were widows without property of any kind and no family. They spent every day in this room darning odd pieces of clothing. They were women who for one reason or another, couldn't work hard labor. Most were old, some lame, and one was deaf.

Hannah stepped back to John's side and listened to him dispense comfort to Old Tilley with promises of rejoining her with her children and grandchildren.

A middle-aged man entered, set his hands on his hips and surveyed the room as if it were his domain alone.

John stood and leaned toward Hannah. "I've only seen him a time or two, but I gather that's Mills."

Mills stood tall in sweat-stained clothes that hung as if they belonged on a much fuller man. His acrid stench reached Hannah from across the room. "Can nae one keep the fire a-burnin'?" He stomped to the hearth and energetically poked at a green log. Little wisps of smoke escaped up the chimney, but the wood barely burned. Mills mumbled something under his breath.

John stepped closer to him. "Mister Mills?"

Mills leaned the poker against the wall. "Wha' can I do ye?" He came to John, a look of suspicion in his brown, hollow eyes. His thinning grey hair hung scraggly and in need of a ribbon.

"They tol' me you was 'ere. You's the minister in Egerton."

"Aye. I've come to discuss a matter with you."

Mills wouldn't remain still, teetering from one foot to the other. "I'm a church-goer and know the Thirty-Nine Articles. My testimony is stronger than yours, I 'spect."

"I don't grasp your meaning." John tilted his head.

"You forget, I sleep in doorways and under eaves—the church's cemetery even. There's much to learn about people in the dark. I've seen you meetin' with those nonconformists after Thursday sermon."

Hannah rushed forward. "That's a lie! My husband is an obedient follower of God."

The women spun at the pitch of her voice. The room stilled.

Mills's hands on his hips became fists. His sunken eye sockets and sharp cheekbones showed his skeletal features. "I may be a swill-belly, but I'm honest." His knuckles went white. "I know what I saw. And I see'd it more than one season." His breath smelled of whiskey.

Hannah backed away.

Old Tilley stood, her chair scraping across the floor. She positioned herself before Mills. "A banbury story if I ever 'eard one." She took his stance, hands on her hips. "The liquor's gone to your head."

Hannah pivoted to John. Why was he not defending himself? "Say something."

"I'm devoted to God as my wife says." The statement fell flat with no passion.

Mills shoved Old Tilley and came within inches of John's face. "What God is yourn? The one that our divinely empowered king esteems or the one Puritans say only takes the foreordained?" Mills swayed like waves on the beach.

Hannah had been holding her breath. She tried to let it out slowly without gaining more attention from those scrutinizing the scene. It'd all happened so quickly she didn't know what to do or say. It wasn't a gentlewoman's place to bicker with a man, but she desired to defend John as Old Tilley had done, knowing his heart was true to the Lord. The strangest memory came to mind of when John told her that as a child he was to keep his mouth shut unless bidden by an adult to speak. Did he need someone to come to his rescue? *Speak, John. Speak.*

"I see yourn wifie don't know about those meetin's." Mills continued his swaying. He brushed his hair from his eyes.

"Leave her out of this." John appeared frightened and would not meet her eyes.

Dread settled in her stomach. Usually his presence filled the room. Today she saw the boy inside.

John turned from Mills and took Hannah's hand. "You've no quarrel with me, Mills. I serve the Lord now as I always will." He pulled her toward the door.

"The bishop might reckon different on that." Mills's snicker sounded forced.

Hannah couldn't suppress a tremble as they stepped from the building.

While they'd been in the poorhouse, it had begun to drizzle. The soft wetness cleared Hannah's nostrils of the putrid smell within but didn't settle her mind.

More people filled the streets and shops with the afternoon rush of men returning home from their labors.

"I apologize for bringing you into such a den of liars." John brushed off his black cassock as if trying to wipe away Mills's words.

Was the verse not thieves? "If there was a time for anger, 'twas in that room. I've never seen you angry. Even Christ had anger when He cleaned his house of thieves." She was afraid to ask him what she really needed to. Did he meet with nonconformists? Was he separating himself from the Church? But no, she must trust him. He'd never . . .

Commotion in front of a tavern caught her attention.

John wrapped his arm around her. "What now?"

They neared slowly.

Two men were bickering, one muscular and much bigger than the other. The smaller one said, "For your disobedience in matters of religion, you'll be fined."

"Devil rot thee, I won't!" The muscular one raised to his full height.

Hannah knew them both. One was a churchwarden, the other a man her age who lived in her father's parish. "I know the younger man. His name is William Granger. His father owns a mill in Eastwell," Hannah explained quickly. "He's big because he carries large bags and barrels of grain for the mill. He has three older brothers almost as big as he. They're all a bit hot-tempered and lean toward trouble."

The concern in John's eyes deepened. "I need to help him."

Hannah shook her head in confusion. "Oh! You mean the

churchwarden."

"Nay. I mean Mister Granger."

What? "But John!" she called after him, but it was too late.

John jostled through the crowd and approached Warden Smith and Mister Granger. "May I be of some help?"

Smith's eyes looked heavenward in an expression of relief. Rain misted his face. "Reverend Lothropp." He smiled and inclined his head.

Granger jutted his chin.

Smith said, "This man, William Granger, hasn't been to church in two months' time. He refuses to pay the fine. I'll need some help getting him into the stocks."

Granger's eyes narrowed at John. "Have you come to give spiritual enlightenment? There's a thing or two I'd like to tell *you*."

The curious crowd grew around them.

"Filthy Separatist!" Someone hollered.

The taunt became a chain of insults: "Antichrist," "Traitor," "You would betray your God and king?"

John wanted to reassure Granger that he was there to mitigate. He laid his hand on Granger's arm to extend friendship. "I would like—"

Granger shook John off, punched him in the stomach, then bolted.

Hannah screamed.

Women and children cried out.

Pain seared through John's gut. With the breath knocked out of him, he doubled over.

"Stand fast in the name of the king," Smith yelled.

The world erupted into chaos. The mob surged to entrap Granger.

Three men tried to bring him down, but he twisted and turned, throwing them off. He struck out, but one of the men threw his body over Granger's outstretched arm, pulling him down with the help of the others. Granger stopped struggling and wrapped his arms around his head to deflect the blows.

The drizzle became a downpour. A man who struggled to control Granger slipped in the mud, his pants and hands covered in slime. One pulled Granger's arms behind his back.

Warden Smith bent over to speak to Granger. Water ran off the brim of his hat. When Granger shook his head, Smith straightened and called, "Take him to the stocks."

The three men took him away and most of the crowd followed. Others moved toward whatever the rest of their day entailed.

Hannah ran to John. "How do you fare?" Her gaze flew from his stomach to his face and then over her shoulder where Granger disappeared.

He straightened as tall as he could and rubbed where his stomach ached. "I suppose I'll be agreeable soon enough." He'd never been punched before and didn't know what to expect. "You're with child, calm yourself."

"Oh, John!" Hannah embraced him in the middle of the lane.

He pulled her away, embarrassed at such affection. "Not in public, wife." He looked around at who was still about.

A woman smiled and ducked her head, but no others paid them mind.

He gently pulled Hannah under an eave and out of the rain. "Men are heading home for the day, and we need to find a ride to Egerton."

Hannah looked incredulous. "Why are you calm? You've been assaulted and still you aren't angry?"

Shocked, John looked closely at her. "I don't know a wife who would want an angry husband. What are you saying?"

She sighed. "You're right. I'm blessed to be married to a man who professes peace." Her words agreed, but her eyes spoke of mistrust.

"Let us not be weary in well doing: for in due season we shall reap if we faint not." He quoted scripture because sometimes that's all he knew to do to comfort his wife.

Hannah cocked a brow. "Why did you want to help Mister Granger and not the warden?"

John looked away. "I weary of doctrinal arguments causing the breaking of charity with one another." He gazed again at Hannah, trying to make his point by looking her in the eye. "Love and respect bind individuals, and I wanted to explain my sympathies to Granger."

"Do you not worry people will believe you a traitor as well?"

Aye, he did. Mills had the ability to entangle John in a snare. He also brooded about the conflicting feelings he had regarding his relationship with the Church. But those concerns would worry Hannah. So he didn't share them. "I'll serve our parishioners and hopefully that will build the household of God. I pray it's not too much for you to be by my side in this endeavor." He needed her more than she could realize.

She grasped his hand. "I'll always be at your side."

Chapter Sixteen

With a loud *whoop*, Thomas grabbed the poppet from Janie, making her scream as if he'd punched her—an overreaction and so common for the girl.

"Will I never have peace?" John grumbled under his breath, dropping his quill to his desk. The vicarage grew smaller and smaller every day.

Jane ran in from the kitchen, drying her hands on a cloth. "Come, Thomas, let Janie be." She threw the towel over her shoulder and handed the toy back to Janie.

Teeth clenched, John rubbed at his face. He didn't understand his daughter's drama. And he didn't understand the bishop. Why wouldn't the man respond to his desperate letters? 'Twas nigh impossible to concentrate on writing sermons in the close quarters of this ancient house. He needed a chamber where he could shut the door. He needed a larger vicarage. He'd been asking since he'd first arrived.

The stairs squeaked as Hannah made her way down, singing a charming lullaby to baby Anne in her arms.

Her enchanting voice mollified him. He could listen to anything she sang. Would Janie's voice ever carry such a melody?

Hannah glanced at John and then at the children. "Jane, would you kindly take the children outside to play? We shouldn't waste such a glorious summer day."

After six years of marriage, he was amazed at how well she knew his needs.

Jane opened the door and the children ran out, Thomas

shouting, "Let's hide amongst the foxgloves, Janie."

The strong fragrance of honeysuckle wafted in. Hannah placed Anne in a cradle and rocked her until she fell asleep and then came to stand by John, looking over his shoulder. "We seldom have time to discuss the Bible, and I miss it."

"Aye. Children have changed both our lives, to be sure. I'd get more written hunched over that old lectern at the church than trying to do it here. Can you not teach them to be quiet? They're constantly shouting or arguing about something."

Hannah raised one eyebrow and chuckled. "Parenting is a cumulation of everything I've never learned."

He couldn't understand why she jested about something so serious, although he did appreciate her sharp wit. "You know I've a great fondness for them, but mayhap there was some good in the way I was raised where children only spoke when requested by an adult."

She shook her head and sighed. They'd had the conversation too many times and 'twas obvious her patience was thinning. "Mayhap you'll be pleased to hear I received a letter from Dorothy today."

John swiveled in his chair to focus on her.

Hannah brought her hands together. "She and Denne are back from London and in their home at Canterbury. She's begged that I bring Thomas and Janie to play with her two little ones."

That was a relief, but he didn't imagine he'd like *that* much quiet. "As long as it doesn't cost too much," John mumbled, feeling petulant about the plan.

"We'll visit at her expense, as usual."

"I wish it weren't always so."

"I think Denne is very pleased to have visitors that occupy his wife's time. Dorothy gets so lonesome for countryfolk."

A knock sounded at the door.

John answered to a stranger—a gentleman about sixty years or more in finely tailored clothes. Standing confidently, straighter than expected for a man his age, he smiled warmly, his long dark hair and beard clean and trim.

"Will you invite a wanderer and missionary into your home?" Eyes clear and perceptive, he watched John with alertness.

"What's your name, stranger?" Something told him this was no ordinary man.

"I'm the nonconformist, Robert Browne." His chest puffed at his own title.

Hannah gasped so loudly John's face heated at her rudeness.

He turned to her. "I desire you leave the room, Hannah."

Her fingers clenched and unclenched, her face went red, and her lips thinned.

He'd never seen her anger grow so quickly. "Obey, wife," he said louder and more harshly than he meant, and his chest had tightened over what she'd do next.

She didn't leave.

He wasn't surprised. "Excuse us, Mister Browne. I pray, step in, and I'll be with you in a moment."

Leading Hannah by the arm, shaking her a bit to snap her out of her shock and antagonism, he took her to the kitchen.

She yanked out of his grasp and expelled air like she'd been holding her breath for a sennight. "Why don't you make him leave? He's a radical Separatist!"

John clasped both her arms and hovered closer to keep his conversation from Browne's ears. "Keep your voice down. He separated from the church years ago and has come back. He calls himself a Nonconformist now. You heard him."

"When men like him came to my father's house, he *always* implored them to leave."

"You're overreacting." He loosened his grip and rubbed her upper arms, hoping to soothe her with compassion. "Besides, I love a good debate—it reminds me of the best times at university." He tried to smile, but the tightness of his face made it feel more like a grimace.

Hannah appeared so flustered she couldn't speak.

"Why do you worry? Do you not know me well enough to know I'm for the Church of England?"

Her shoulders dropped, and she nodded once.

"'He that fear men shall have a fall: but whoso puts his trust in the Lord, is without danger.'"

She nodded again and looked out at the children playing with Jane.

He embraced her quickly and left, knowing full well she'd listen in as well she could.

Browne waited at the open door. "Am I welcomed into this clergyman's house, or will the vanity of a licensed preacher's wife keep me out?"

He was here for a reason. He obviously knew who John was. Why such an infamous dissident would choose to come to the vicarage, John couldn't fathom. "Excuse my wife. She's unused to notorious nonconformists coming into our home."

Browne chuckled, and John gestured for him to come in, taking the hat he held. "Have a seat." He hung the hat on a peg. "What brings you here?"

"Your name came to me by some in London who meet in Henry Jacob's new Independent Church." Browne sat.

John all but fell into his chair. Who was talking about him, and what were they saying? "I know no one there."

"Methinks they originated from your own county of Kent." Browne's piercing stare seemed both to study and pass judgment.

Could this man see inside his soul? It felt that way. John calmed a shiver. He couldn't imagine who might be sharing his name with a nonconformist. "Who is Henry Jacob, and what's the Independent Church?"

"Reverend Jacob has lived the last six years in Holland with John Robinson's Separatists. He plans to model his church after theirs. His heart still seems to be with the Church of England and the communion, but he rejects the bishops and deacons."

John nodded although it still wasn't clear how his name had become entangled with Separatists.

"Where were you educated?" Browne interrogated.

John cleared his throat. "I received my masters from Cambridge."

"A university education is not necessary for understanding the scriptures." Browne studied the dark vicarage the way he studied John. "Are you a man who can debate the finer points of teaching a congregation?"

Was he trying to trap John with words? "I don't need to debate such a topic. My congregation is content with my teaching methods."

"All true Christians can understand a simple sermon style. Do you preach plainly so the simplest man may understand your teachings?" he asked as if he were questioning a pupil.

"My style is as the Church of England demands." John tugged at his collar. "I'm well learned and believe canonical words should be used throughout the church so there can be no misunderstanding or corrupt use of scripture."

"Aye, the church denunciates rhetorical elements of style. Have you read Tyndale's *The Obedience of a Christian Man*?"

"I have."

"Then you'll know the literal meaning of scripture is primary to developing a testimony of our Lord."

"I've said naught to you that would say otherwise. I agree with your statement."

Browne grinned as if they were chatting about what to eat for supper. "I've a disgust for intellectual rhetoric. 'Tis the vain shows of learning."

"I don't exaggerate during my sermons or while teaching the individual." The insult stung. "I do believe the Thirty-Nine Articles as defining statements of doctrines and practices, and in which it states that the ministry is both the leadership and agency of Christian service. The offices of ordained clergy must be upheld and respected. My means of sermonizing are respected by my parishioners."

Browne shrugged. "That may be. It doesn't alter the fact that the Church of England is unreformed and has too many Catholic ideologies. Their means of preaching can fall into that dogma. As Plato wrote, 'rhetoric is an art of flattery like cookery which only bad men use to defend falsehood and their unjust deeds.' Those who are wise to that which is simple concerning evil have no need of exaggerated speech."

John wanted to participate in a debate, not sit here and be belittled by this man who kept telling him he was preaching wrong. How would Browne know anyway? Who was talking about John behind his back? "I don't embellish my sermons, and I seldom read from other men's texts." Although the Church had encouraged John to read approved sermons, he didn't have the stomach for it.

Browne nodded. "'Tis good."

Was John supposed to be relieved that this rectified apostate approved of his sermons?

Browne relaxed into the chair as if he'd be spending the afternoon there. "I'm also a Cambridge man, well trained in the rhetorical arts, but have since come to testimony that plain English reaches the innermost regions of one's heart—where our Lord resides. Is the Gospel not to teach the unlearned? Do you sprinkle your sermons with Greek and Hebrew?"

John tapped his fingers on the chair arm. What gave this man merit to question him so? "It depends to whom I'm speaking. If my motives are to show academic honors, I see the listeners as having respect for such an education." He didn't want to say that it was to his own wife he spoke the ancient languages.

"Then you're an elitist and serving out the doctrines with vain logic," Browne said. "You're shutting out your congregation from talking and having a mutual edification toward their testimony."

John let him misunderstand. He didn't need to prove himself to Browne. The more they talked, the less Browne's cocky banter annoyed John. He didn't need someone to tell him how best to preach to his flock. But this conversation did help him see where he stood with the Lord. And with himself. "Matthew chapter twenty-three—only one is my Christ."

Browne acted as though he hadn't heard.

He probably wasn't there to debate whether or not John had a testimony of faith. He supposed Browne was there in concern for the common man—the ones who weren't educated and needed the Gospel as much as anyone. John had the same testimony in his heart.

Browne said, "Is not every Christian to rule with Christ? Let all seek out the works of God. Logic is filthy stuff which like vomit can obscure the scriptures." He leaned forward. "When you preach, do you bang upon the pulpit or raise your voice to the non-listener?"

"Nay, I do not." In this John found favor with Browne, who finally gave him a small, kind smile.

"Nae pulpit-barking? Ha! That is good. I too don't go in for the dramatic."

Somehow John doubted that.

"Meaning of scripture should be our primary concern." Browne banged on the chair arm. "Matter must predominate over style."

John nodded. "My sermons are in agreement with all scripture."

Browne flicked his hand at John. "The king has enslaved you, and the Church of England cannot admit how papist they are. They've walked a crooked path and are part of the Anti-Christ."

Anti-Christ seemed harsh. "I welcome debate but must ask you to refrain from accusation and slander toward my church."

"Then, may I ask, do you gather your tithing more often than you gather your flock?"

Browne's way of speech was dangerous—he was an enemy of civil order—an extremist.

"You cannot discredit the Church of England with me. We debated your treatise at university, and I know your tactics well."

"You've conformed." Browne's features lit as if he'd come here to prove John wrong and finally succeeded.

"I've taken orders to serve my Lord. I'm a preacher for a flock of believers who need a shepherd."

"If I may leave any heartfelt sentiment with you, 'tis that the common people should pray directly to God and no monarchy or bishop have the right to intervene."

John agreed with the sentiment, and it disturbed him—had been disturbing him for some time now. But he must not let his guard slip with Browne, who wanted to make his points heard and didn't care what John had to say. Browne had a talent to manipulate conversation. "What drives you to preach to clergy? If you love the common people as you profess, why are you not with them this day?"

"To reach the preacher is to reach the flock. I come to you at my peril. I've been thrown in gaol for such acts more times than I can count. My beliefs are stronger than any iron of man's making. I'm a blessed man. My departed wife, Alice, suffered by my side and never let me down."

John could only hope he'd married a woman as devoted. So far, he wasn't sure Hannah would follow him to another city let alone to gaol.

Browne frowned. "My sorrow is that my literature has caused the hanging of many of my followers." Sadness reached his eyes. "That sin is on the king's head." He stood and placed a hand on John's shoulder. "Simply speak the word of God." His eyes now held tenderness, not radicalism or anger, insanity or evil. The man was as eclectic as his beliefs—judgmental but also kind.

The Spirit of God testified the words to John. He couldn't understand it, but the nonconformist's words 'simply speak the word of God,' sank into his soul as if Browne commended a calling upon John—that which his clerical orders had never done.

After Browne left, Hannah stepped to John's side, obviously having hovered closer than he'd realized. "He's a theological rebel who attacks my cherished beliefs. A destroyer of religious veneration."

John had accepted the calling awarded to him by the Church of England, but had he accepted it in his heart and soul with the same passion as Browne? "He's a man with a purpose. I should have such devotion."

Chapter Seventeen

Hannah gently rocked her baby's cradle, although he slept peacefully. They'd named this fourth child after John.

Little Anne toddled about, raising her short legs high enough to not trip on the courtyard stones as Penninah and Hannah conversed. Soft brown curls fell about Anne's face, and she kept brushing them back with a pudgy hand.

Penninah raised an eyebrow and pulled her mouth down. "Baby Johnny is two months old. I expect you're already carrying another?"

Hannah looked toward the house to make sure no one was near. "Penny, you shouldn't say such things. What if Jane or the children heard you?"

"Nay, they won't hear. I saw them when I stabled my horse. Jane's showing Thomas and Janie the new cow."

Surrounded by spring flowers—snowdrops, daffodils, and tulips—it was a sign that winter had finally released its hold. Hannah breathed in the lovely scents.

"The children are less than a year apart. How do you manage?" Penninah asked.

"I don't know what I'd do without Jane's help. Some days I can't pick up yet another toy or put two sentences together. Last night, Janie started to bawl about not finding her favorite blanket, which made Anne cry, which made Johnny wail." It had been late, but John walked out and went to the church in the dark.

"Well, in my eyes, if you can have four children in five years, you can do anything." Penninah's smile was genuine, and it cheered

Hannah.

Sunshine caught on Penninah's golden-red hair along her lace-edged coif. She was unaware of her beauty, but men were not. Hannah often wondered why her sister hadn't yet married. At one time, Hannah had presumed Penninah waited for John's friend, Robert Linnell, but it had been years since they'd seen him, and she'd stopped bringing up his name.

Anne tripped on a stone then righted herself and toddled toward a clump of bluebells, not yet open. She coughed. She'd been doing that for a few days.

"You're keeping your midwife busy, to be sure, but I'm surprised Reverend Lothropp is agreeable to more children. He seems troubled with raising the ones he has."

Although true, Penninah's comment stung. Hannah's and John's ideas about caring for the children were as different as a coddling mama cat and a bird who leaves her young unattended while foraging for food.

"Did you hear what happened to the Indian princess—Rebecca Rolfe . . . or Pocahontas . . . whatever they're calling her—from the Virginia Colony?" Penninah gratefully changed the subject.

"John told me Bishop King in London entertained her with great pomp. Imagine, a savage being converted to the Gospel and then celebrated like royalty." Hannah shook her head.

"Not only that, she attended a masque hosted by the king himself. But that's not what I was referring to. It seems she left to sail for the Virginia Colonies a fortnight back, but took ill, forcing the ship to dock at Gravesend here in Kent. She died and is buried there. She was no older than you, God rest her soul." Penninah clasped her hands.

"How very sad. I pray her husband and son will be comforted."

"Aye. But speaking of righteous women, you know how we used to find women in the Bible who did great deeds?"

"I've shared some with John but he's little impressed."

"You'd have to be Mother Mary to impress him." Penninah grunted. "Surprisingly, I've found two women we've never discussed. In fact, they were so righteous they saved a nation."

Hannah was greatly curious. "How could we have missed such noble women?"

"These women reshaped the course of events that have affected all of us."

Hannah swatted at her sister. "Come now, do tell!"

"In Exodus, we read of the midwives Shiphrah and Puah,

who were called before the king of Egypt and told to kill the male children when they were born."

Hannah looked at little Johnny in his cradle and shuddered. "Ah, aye. How could we have not discussed them? Such brave women to go against the Pharaoh."

"Because they feared God more than the king, they were blessed with their own families. The king became angry and told his people to cast all the Hebrew newborn sons into the river and drown them. Consequently, when Moses's mother delivered him in secret, she hid him for three months and then made an ark of bulrushes and floated him down the river."

In the distance, Hannah heard something that stole her attention.

"Have I lost you, sister?" Penninah smirked. "Am I boring you?"

Hannah strained to listen but heard naught more. An unmilked cow bellowing mayhap? "Nay, my apologies. Uh, aye, Pharaoh's daughter drew the ark from the river."

"And so later, Moses leading the Israelites out of Egypt hinged on Shiphrah's and Puah's righteousness and courage." Penninah sat back with satisfaction.

Shouting in the lower yard brought them to their feet.

A young, stocky man ran by with the churchwarden following. Penninah gaped. "Who's that?"

"It's Jonny Fenner. He's in our parish." Hannah placed her hand to her quickening heart.

The churchwarden, young himself, gained on Fenner. "Stop in the name of the king!"

Fenner stumbled, and the warden was on him instantly. They wrestled, dust flying in the air. "Get off me," Fenner yelled.

John ran up to the men. "Release him!" he shouted. "It wasn't as it seemed."

Hannah gasped. "Is John involved?"

"How could he be involved in a crime?" Penninah's voice hitched.

Hannah ought not to have said that aloud. She'd never told anyone of the accusations Mills made against John at the poorhouse, nor how John had defended Granger, or that Robert Browne had come to visit.

John tried to hoist the warden off Fenner and got pulled into the brawl. He fell on both men and then rolled off onto his back and quickly stood, again shouting, "Stop!" He tried to pull the warden away.

Penninah grabbed Hannah around the waist. "What shall we do?"

Anne was suddenly at Hannah's skirts, pulling on them. "Up," she said, then coughed.

Penninah released Hannah, who bent to pick up her child. She brought her close and rubbed her back until the hacking subsided, all the while watching the savage scene in front of her.

Another man neared the group—Bishop Buckeridge who served over John. He was dressed in his surplice and stood a distance off. "Reverend Lothropp," he called in a stern voice.

The warden had a now motionless Fenner pinned under him.

John rose to his feet, brushed off his clothes, and jogged over to the bishop.

Buckeridge spoke to John, but Hannah only caught the words, "charges of," "nonconformists," and "commission."

Oh! This couldn't be happening. Was John being reprimanded in some way?

Penninah must have heard some of what he said for she gasped.

"Nay!" Tears burned Hannah's eyes. Was Browne's visit more than she'd supposed? After he'd come, John had sworn to her that he knew no one in London that would accuse him of nonconformity.

John glanced toward the house, and she knew the minute he realized she'd witnessed everything. Shoulders slumped, he shook his head as if to convey the accusations weren't true.

But were they? If John had fallen from the Church, would he confide in her? The thought of him keeping secrets caused her heart to ache.

The warden forced Fenner to stand and grabbed his hands behind his back.

Bishop Buckeridge called, "Take him to the stocks. I've been instructed to bring Reverend Lothropp to Canterbury to stand before the commission." He took John by the arm and pulled him away.

John acquiesced but glanced over his shoulder at Hannah with a look of guilt.

Hannah stumbled forward. She needed to talk to him.

Catching her arm, Penninah pulled her back. "Best to stay here. The bishop will not appreciate a meddling wife."

Neither would John. She clenched her jaw.

That night, Hannah didn't receive word from John. What if the Church no longer considered him capable of leading their congregation? What if he were released from his work? They'd lose their home and occupation with one fatal decision. Where would they go? What would John do to take care of the seven of them? They'd have to send Jane back to East Riding. She'd become like a sister to Hannah. 'Twould shatter her heart to lose the quiet and kind young woman who always desired to please.

Since Robert Browne's visit, Hannah had often tried to understand how to navigate the doubt and uncertainty she felt about John's activities. The last thing she wanted to do was tell her father about John's waywardness.

Through the night, Anne's coughing grew worse.

Hannah walked the floor with her. She tried all her herbal concoctions but not a one helped.

Anne burned with fever, and Johnny cried incessantly because Hannah wasn't producing enough milk, mayhap because of her anxiety.

By sunrise, she sat with the children in the kitchen, spooning warm cow's milk into Johnny's eager mouth. "Jane, ride to my mother and bring her and Penninah." Hannah took a risk sending for them. She'd make them promise not to tell Father of John's disgrace.

Jane curtsied. "I'll stop at Widow Reynold's and ask that she come help thee." She placed Anne on a blanket on the floor.

Normally up and roaming as soon as she was set free, Anne flopped her arms out at her sides and closed her eyes. Her head fell to the side. Curls wet with perspiration stuck to her face.

Hannah sighed in relief that she was finally sleeping. Poor thing.

Once Jane was gone and Johnny settled in his cradle, Hannah went to Anne and gently stroked her cheek. She was still hot but no longer perspiring.

"For catechism Thomas, quote the Litany for Sickness and the Articles of the Faith, then Janie recite the Lord's Prayer and the ten commandments."

She listened to her children for a time but couldn't focus on their recitations. Where was John? She picked up Anne.

Her daughter's head flopped back.

Hannah looked more closely.

Anne's blue lips parted slightly.

Hannah's heart stilled. She shook the baby.

Anne's brown curls bounced, but her eyes remained closed. "Wake up, Anne!" This couldn't be happening.

"Mama, what is it?" Thomas asked, fear evident in his words. Janie stood upon her chair to see better.

Hannah's mind screamed to God for help as she shook Anne harder. "Wake up!"

When John was released from the provincial court, he sent a missive to Denne, needing a place to sleep and a ride home.

Denne obliged, and the next day they rode toward Egerton. Dark, low-lying clouds created gloom in the otherwise fine carriage. Moist air trapped in the small space made it hard to breathe. It smelled like rain, but none fell.

As they rode, John chastised himself for not putting God before man. Hadn't he learned long ago that if he dedicated himself to God, man wouldn't be able to hurt him?

He'd stood before the ecclesiastical court the day before, accused of meeting with nonconformists, and realized he'd been focused on Fenner's, Tilden's, and Hinckley's concerns more than on the rest of his congregation who believed his teachings. He mourned his choices. Worry gnawed at his stomach for Fenner. His family depended on him for support. 'Twas time to plant hop.

After some discussion about the proceedings, Denne asked, "Why were your charges dismissed?"

"They saw that I was only trying to help the men *not* leave the Church. I was reprimanded but not fined." Gratefully they knew naught of Browne's visit. John had to make some quick decisions because he couldn't lie to defend himself. "I told them as little as possible about the men, yet I fear I've caused consequences to come to them. Who knows how the court will deal out those punishments?" He rubbed at his temples.

"Did you supply evidence that could cause severe penalties?" Denne questioned. Being a solicitor, he had an understanding of the law and what could and had happened to those who fought the Church—fines, prison, tortures, hanging.

"I pray I didn't cause them harm. I met with Fenner and the others because I didn't want the breaking of a community." But maybe *he'd* created the break? What was his part in it? "I tried to downplay that the men only asked questions, and I confirmed many times that they all attended church regularly."

The Pulse of His Soul

The bell on Saint James tolled through the woodland dell that led to Egerton, cutting off anything Denne would've said.

Is it already time to recite the Lord's Prayer? John pulled out his pocket watch, thinking it later than he supposed and that the canonical hours were upon them, vespers needing to be said.

But then the bell rang again.

Stiffening next to Denne, John held his breath, waiting for another toll. Had one of his parishioners died? No one had been ill.

A third chime peeled through the air.

And then a fourth.

Silence settled, the heavy finality dropped in his stomach like lead. Four strikes and no more. The death knell of a man 'twould have rung three times three strokes. For a woman, two times three. But this, one times three, meant a child. But whose?

He listened for the strokes of how many years the child lived.

The single chime shot through his heart and shoved him back against his seat. One year. His own Anne was one. How horrible for this child's parents.

His court proceedings and now this. If ever he needed Hannah's cheerful countenance, 'twas now. She always found the light in the dark. He missed his children and even the chaos of their household. Even though the small vicarage with so many in it frustrated him at times, it had become home.

A home he craved to go back to was new to him. He'd fight to stay there. He hadn't appreciated what he had. But being taken away with the threat of not returning for a long while changed that. He needed to be more involved with the children. They needed a firmer hand than Hannah displayed. But what if he couldn't do it? What if he was like his father?

"I best go to the church instead of home," John told Denne.

"I'm sorry to hear the death knell. Who could ever get used to such a chime? And a baby, no less. I don't envy you your calling."

"'Tis at times like these I'd rather be a yeoman."

"I could never see you as a farmer. You've chosen your profession well." They stopped at the path that led to Saint James. "God be with you." Denne tipped his hat.

John descended from the carriage. "Go on to the vicarage and have Hannah serve you supper."

"Thank you, but nay, I best be getting back to Canterbury before it gets dark. The coming rain could make the whole affair that much worse."

"I understand. And thank you again for the ride. I'm much obliged and hope I can repay the favor in the not too distant future."

"No worries, my friend. I enjoyed the distraction from the many seditious cases I've been laboring over."

John waved and pivoted, hiking up to the church.

As he entered through the back door into the narthex, the clerk, Albert Bonney, was opening the door leading from the bell tower. When the Scot saw John, he stopped in his tracks. Shock, then worry, then sorrow played over his features. "Reverend—"

"Mister Bonney, I've just arrived from Canterbury and heard the death knell. Pray tell, who has died?"

"Why . . . um . . . Reverend." His eyes watered.

John stepped forward to comfort him by placing a hand on his arm. "Your kinsman?"

"Nay, reverend . . . yours." He lowered his eyes.

John swayed. His?

One stroke of the bell.

In his mind, he heard it again, and again it pierced his heart. "Nay!" The word caught in his throat.

Bonney's chin trembled. "I did'na know ya was away. I thought ya was home mournin'. My deepest sympathies." Now the one comforting, he set a hand on John's arm and led him to a pew.

John's legs gave under him, and he fell onto the hard bench. "But how? Why? She wasn't sick."

"Who understands God's reasons for calling home the wee bairns?" The Scot was sympathetic—the way John had planned to be with the baby's parents.

Only he and Hannah were the baby's parents. "Anne," he softly said his daughter's name. There was such a final sound to it. "Anne." He dropped his face into his hands and wept.

Allowing him time for his sorrows, Bonney eventually asked, "Can I help ya ta home? I 'spect Mistress Lothropp needs your care."

Dear God, Hannah! She was probably sorrowing worse than he, knowing Anne so intimately. The girl was such a sweet little thing—never sick, always curious. Now he'd never again be able to rest his cheek against hers. Smell her hair and touch those curls. A sob escaped from deep within his chest.

Bonney shuffled his feet. "Let's get ya home."

Suddenly embarrassed to be a burden, he swallowed hard and forced his voice steady. "Nay. Return to your own. I'll go now to mine. Much obliged for your service to this church and to my family."

The path home had been traveled so many times that John need not have his wits about him as he stumbled along. It was a good thing because he knew not how he was stepping one heavy foot in front of the other.

Misty rain sprinkled his coat as he stood before the black wreath on his door. He held the latch for a long moment, dreading to see Anne's stiff body, dreading to see Hannah grieving, dreading for this to become real.

Nothing like this had ever happened to them. How would his lighthearted Hannah react? Would she need comforting, or would he? Would she be angry that he hadn't been there? Could he have saved Anne if he had? Near the end, had she received the sacrament of Christ's blood and body and have a last blessing?

He swayed.

Had his sin caused his daughter's eternal soul to hang in abeyance?

God was punishing him for questioning the Church's stand on common prayer, consciousness of faith, considering the ideas of others. With his thoughtlessness, he'd put himself in a place to be reprimanded by God's anointed. And he hadn't been here to help Hannah in such a time of great need.

He pushed the door open. The black wreath swayed.

No one greeted him. The windows were shuttered, the room empty, the hearth cold. Being a priest entering the home of a recently deceased, he somehow pushed out the words he said on other such occasions. "Peace be in the house and to all that dwell in it." He made the sign of the cross.

He hung his hat and mantle on pegs then slowly lumbered upstairs. At his bedchamber door, he stopped.

Hannah's back was to him. She stood near Anne. Dressed for burial and laid out on a table, her form was astonishingly small.

John's chest grew so tight he feared he'd never take another breath.

Johnny lay asleep in his cradle. A lamp on a table threw Hannah's shadow on the far wall. Anne's body and profile played out against the wall too. Hannah swayed slightly. Anne was still as stone.

Shadows were only created by standing in the light. Hannah had never liked darkness. He loved her for that and so much more. At least he could say the words now, but he hadn't told her often enough.

'But he that doeth truth, cometh to the light, that his deeds may be known, how that they are wrought in God.' He desired to quote the scripture to her now, but something held him back.

As the light illuminated her, he found no flaws. She'd tell him otherwise. She examined herself in the light often enough—always striving to be better, exposing herself to John without reserve. Everyone should be like Hannah. He should be like Hannah.

He was suddenly aware of the darkness in the hall. He didn't love darkness and would never again risk his soul to step away from the light and speak to others of the Church's failings. He stepped into the room, his shadow falling over Hannah's.

She turned, her face a mask of almost inhuman pain.

He strode to her in three bounds and took her into his arms. "My love." He kissed the top of her head. "Forgive me for not being here."

She grasped him back and they kept each other erect.

"What happened?" His words caught, and he swallowed a sob. But not before it made his chest heave.

"'Twas my fault." Hannah wept. "She'd had a fever less than a day. I didn't pay close attention to her cough. I didn't know she was so ill."

John rubbed her back. "These things are no one's fault."

She shook against his chest. "There must have been a sign I missed."

"Nay. I know you. You would not have allowed her illness to overtake if you'd known its seriousness."

Her shoulders slowly went rigid, and she stepped away from his embrace. "You. I'd been up all night worrying about *you*." Her jaw clenched. "So, it's true. You've been meeting with heretics. No wonder you invited Browne into our home. Do you love us so little as to threaten your livelihood?" Her lips turned pale. "Threaten your *salvation*."

John pulled in a deep breath. "Forgive me for my foolishness. Although, I did *not* meet with heretics. I *did* meet with men who questioned many of the Church's teachings and needed guidance. I'll not meet with them again." It didn't matter that he would miss the peaceful harmony he felt with them. "Avail me, could I have saved Anne if I'd been here?"

Her face and body softening, Hannah collapsed into his arms again. "I think not."

They cried together for some time before John released

Hannah and knelt in front of Anne's still body. "In thee, Oh Lord, have I put my trust. I am the resurrection and the life . . ."

He stopped.

Did he need a king to tell him what prayer his daughter deserved? For what Hannah needed at this time? What *he* needed? There—that rebel spirit spoke again, but it spoke to his heart. How could he deny it? He sent his soul heavenward, needing communion and comfort from his Lord.

He sat back on his heels, hands clasped, eyes closed. "Oh God, hear our words, know our pain, and send us the comfort only You can bestow." He sobbed.

Hannah knelt beside him and placed a hand on his back.

He took a deep breath. "Bathe my wife in Your goodness and help her find the cheerfulness that seems to come so naturally to her. Help us endure this great loss and be stronger for it. Bless my family, Dear Lord, and give us health to rally and serve Thee."

Chapter Eighteen

Hannah stood next to John outside the church of Saint Laurence at the south end of Hawkhurst village. The church's tracery east window, one of the largest and finest in the county, was as beautiful outside as it had been inside. She always felt more at home in churches and churchyards than anywhere else, even more than her garden. As a child, she'd played games amongst the pews and headstones of Saint Mary's while her father performed his ministerial duties.

Samuel Hinckley and his new bride, Sarah, came into the sunshine from the church, and well-wishers surged forward.

Hannah and John stepped farther into the crowd as guests threw wheat kernels, a hope offering of fruitfulness. Although Hannah didn't know the couple, she smiled, remembering her own wedding and how the day had felt like a discourse in fertility. Well, it had certainly come true. She hugged Johnny closer in her arms.

As if on cue, he brought up milk on her black sleeve.

"I'm naught but a rag for baby vomit," she mumbled, softly chuckling, and wiped at it with a small blanket.

Wearing mourning-black himself, John looked at her with a question in his eyes. "I'm glad to hear your gaiety, but what produced the chuckling?" He smiled, still a rare occurrence and even more so since Anne's death.

"Because laughing is better than weeping." She always thought 'twas her love of the gospel and Christ that would get her in heaven. Now she wondered if it was the endurance of raising children.

The bride and groom made their way down the lane to a wide open area of grass.

Tables surrounded the perimeter. Sprays of autumn wildflowers tied with ribbon lay as table adornments. Pleasant music played from a lute, harpsichord, and viols. The guests found places to sit.

John pulled out a chair for Hannah. "It's unusual for us to be alone—with but one babe."

She wished he hadn't said that. It made her think of Anne. Not yet seven months since her death, she'd still be a baby too. She shook off her thoughts. "If you can call this alone with at least a hundred people about us."

"What I meant was, we usually have the children at our feet." John took her hand.

"I know what you meant." She squeezed his hand. "I'm glad for the time with you." She couldn't leave Johnny at home because he was still at the breast. She hadn't come to celebrate Hinckley's wedding, for she didn't know him. She'd come because she wearied of the disquieting feelings about John's secretive doings. She wanted no more secrets.

A couple surrounded by numerous children passed, the husband handsome and well-dressed with a thin, grim face. He acknowledged John with a stiff dip of the head. His wife glared at John and pulled her husband away.

"Who was that?" Hannah questioned, stunned that anyone would be so rude toward John.

"That's Nate Tilden and his wife, Lydia." John frowned. "He's one of the three who was imprisoned for his nonconformity."

John had told her after Anne's funeral, when her deepest grief was no longer keeping her from facing life, that Tilden, Hinckley, and Fenner had all gone to prison for six months for discussing heretical ideas. When released, the three were no longer allowed to sermongat and had to attend sermons in their own parish. They were also not allowed to meet with John to discuss gospel principles.

But John wasn't told he couldn't go to them. When he and Hannah received the Hinckley wedding invitation, John's face had lit with expectation. Hannah guessed he felt as a father-figure to Samuel Hinckley.

They feasted for hours and conversed with strangers. John, as usual, would not dance. The celebration reminded Hannah there were joys to be had in her life, even after losing a child. She was glad she'd come.

Later in the afternoon, when she met Sam Hinckley, she was surprised at his easy-going nature and soft-spoken but sincere accolades of John.

She excused herself to feed the baby. When she returned, Fenner sat in her chair. Coldness hit her core. She looked about, but it seemed all were involved in feasting and celebrating the bride and groom. She hoped no one truly knew them here.

John saw her approach and ended his discussion.

Fenner immediately sprang from the chair and offered it to her. "I didn't mean to impose." He was much thinner than when she last saw him. Still a young man, he now had dark circles under his eyes and a gash on his forehead that appeared to be healing.

Hannah handed sleeping Johnny to John, telling him with her gaze she didn't like Fenner being there. But John only looked to the child.

The guests next to them bid their farewell and left their seats. Fenner brought one of the chairs closer to John, then sat.

Hannah clenched her teeth. Why would he risk being in John's presence? Why would John risk himself talking to Fenner?

"Fenner was telling me about his experiences in prison," John said to her, sounding abashed.

"They must not have been so dreadful if he's taking no precautions and sitting with you." Anxiety pinched Hannah's chest, and she didn't care that she was being rude.

John gave her a glower of displeasure.

She didn't care about that either. She was here to make sure they didn't talk about dissident ideologies.

Fenner didn't acknowledge her rebuke. He leaned forward with his forearms on his legs. "Prisoners were pilloried daily because they spoke their minds about their beliefs. When 'twas my turn, I came back with no feeling in my hands and my neck achin' from the thick wooden frame." He shook his head. "Some have come to calling it Christ's yoke."

"I pray you'll take the authentic yoke upon you and come back to Christ's true church," Hannah said. "For He's 'meek and lowly in heart: and ye shall find rest unto your soul.'"

Fenner looked at her with intense blue eyes for a brief moment, and she got the feeling that he was keeping himself from saying what he wanted.

John cleared his throat. "Were you in the same cell as Hinckley and Tilden?"

"Nay. They had their own ratholes. And I wasn't just with Separatists but with Presbyterians, Catholics, and other enemies of the king." He gazed to something distant. "Is it not ironic that our call for toleration creates harsher intolerance? We've been branded sowers of sedition."

"I warned you it could come to this," John said, true sympathy shining in his eyes. "Is the mark on your head a contribution from your gaolers?"

"Aye. That and scars unseen." Agony darkened his expression. "Their favored weapon was a whip of knotted leather."

Hannah winced involuntarily, picturing the lashes ripping across bare skin and blood ripening the wound.

John took notice of her reaction. "Best to not speak of this before women's sensitivities." He laid a hand upon Hannah's clenched fists.

Fenner looked at her with true contrition. "Beg pardon, my lady." His eyes held warmth and gentleness. "No harm meant."

Maybe she was wrong about him? She nodded. "The cruel acts do seem extreme, but I suspect what put you there was a crime against God and His anointed."

John shifted in his seat.

Fenner looked at his hands, jaw clenching, then held her stare. "I meant no disrespect, but I must follow my conscience as I'm sure you must do likewise."

Tilden stood across the table from them, the other guests having left. "May I join the conversation? My wife has retired with the children. It's possible this will be the only time I may ask your advice, Reverend Lothropp."

"By all means," John said freely.

He'd promised her he was done meeting with these men. Did his promise mean so little to him?

Sitting, Tilden looked closely at Hannah, as if judging how careful he needed to be with his words in her presence. He seemed to display the same deep agony in his eyes as Fenner, but as with Hinckley, she saw no scars on his face. "My kinsman's stepson is named Robert Cushman, of about my age," he said to John. "Robert hails from across the weald in Rovenden but has been in Holland as of late, meeting with the Separatists belonging to the Reverend John Robinson's congregation." Tilden looked at Hannah again.

She assumed he wanted to scrutinize her reaction, if she'd supply one. Were they edging too close to sedition by talking of other Separatists? She wasn't sure but didn't think so. Even she and Father spoke of the goings-on of those who'd left the Church.

"And what's your question?" John asked.

Tilden cleared his throat. "Cushman is in Kent to gather supplies for a journey to America. It seems the congregation in Leiden will be sailing to the Colony of Virginia. He said they're on a pilgrimage, looking for the promised land."

Fenner sat straighter, beaming. "I know of what Tilden speaks. He sent Cushman to me last sennight. Cushman bought my entire upcoming yield of hop. The Separatists will be taking over a hundred casks of beer onboard the ship. They expect the journey to take at least six weeks."

"I'm pleased the arrangement worked for you." Tilden smiled at Fenner then turned to John. "You've met my brother Joseph?"

John nodded.

"He's one of the investors funding the voyage, hoping to make a profit from the fur trade in the Colonies. Robinson's group plans to send beaver skins back to London in exchange for passage. Joseph is at present fitting out a ship in London, the *Mayflower*, that the Robinson congregation will travel aboard."

"And the king has agreed to their voyage?" John's voice held disbelief.

"Aye. It's a venture that should bring wealth back to him and our kingdom."

Hannah worried over this news. The Separatists were leaving under the guise of fur traders, but that's not why they were truly leaving. The Church wouldn't be able to stop these agitators.

"Cushman has invited me to go with them," Tilden continued. "He said it may be best to leave my family and send for them once we've established a colony there."

"You're leaving then?" John asked.

"I would prefer to not leave the land of my birth. My family has served king and country for hundreds of years. We're loyal Englishmen." He huffed and shrouded his eyes. "A voyage with small children is dangerous, even if they sail after me. Which leads to my question." He made a nervous noise in his throat. "Do you see Britain as a kingdom that can amend its ways? Will the Church of England ever reform? Do I risk my life and the lives of my family for an improved and safer way to worship? I know your feelings on the breaking of charity with one another and that a congregation's strength is in its members, but . . ." Tilden trailed off.

The relationship between these men and John suddenly became clear to Hannah. They obviously looked to John as an honest leader who cared about them. Hannah wanted to lament. Why had he become so involved? What in his failing avowal of faith pushed him to associate with Separatists? If a cleric heard their discussion now, they'd probably all be arrested.

John placed his hand on Tilden's. "You honor me by seeking my advice, but these are questions I cannot answer. Reform has been discussed for over fifty years and may take another fifty. Or may never happen. I wish I had the answers for you." John removed his hand. "The difficult course of faith and finding unification is a personal journey. Clergy can *help* with religious direction and mayhap show the most effective means to regulate behavior. If I, or you two"—He looked between Fenner and Tilden—"elevate the moral standard of our parishes, we can live more fulfilled lives. Love and respect bind individuals and is what Christ expects of us all. I've told you this before." He smiled sadly. "I'll play my part in the survival of our country's salvation by curing the souls of my parishioners and by building the household of God. But Nate, you must find the part you're to play in bringing your children and others to God."

Tilden dropped his head.

Fenner groaned. "How many good men will England lose before the Church relaxes its hold on the most faithful—the ones who care about following God's commands?"

Interesting that Fenner would think himself one of the most faithful. She'd have saved that title for those who weren't speaking against the Church and attended their meetings every sennight and followed their sovereign. John had told her what a hard worker Fenner was, and that he was a true leader. Who would he lead if not a faithful congregation?

This was a perilous decline for they were now speaking treason, planning to leave the Church and find sanctuary in the Colonies. She looked about, but no one seemed to pay them mind. She and John had to leave. In far deeper than she'd realized, she needed to get him out of the muck.

She leaned forward to take Johnny from him. "Shall we be going?"

Surprise flashed in his eyes. "As you wish."

"Before you leave," Tilden quickly said. "I wanted to share something I heard rumor of while in prison. Are you aware Archbishop Abbot has been suspended from his duties?"

"Nay." John's forehead creased.

Tilden nodded. "It's said that he's refusing to order his clergy to read the new Declaration of Sports from the pulpit."

"Declaration of Sports?" John quizzed.

"The king made a declaration to resolve a conflict over the subject of Sunday recreations in Lancashire, and now he has devised that all of England follow it. With his permission, we're allowed Sunday amusements of dancing and sports and the like. Women shall have leave to decorate the church with rushes."

John blanched.

He held to rigid Sabbath Day observance in their house.

Hannah had heard him preach about it on several occasions. Their home had become reverent and peaceful on Sundays. She very much enjoyed the quiet reflection and dedicating the day to her Lord. In this one instance, she wasn't sure she agreed with the king's declaration. And if what Tilden said was true, the Archbishop of Canterbury didn't either. "I suppose King James is trying to counteract the Puritan ideas of strict abstinence on the Sabbath."

No one made comment, and her observation fell flat.

About an hour before dawn, John sat on a bench in the garden, wrapped in a wool blanket. He'd made a habit of coming here each morning. 'Twas the only quiet time he could find during the day. The morning air chilled him, and he pulled the blanket up over his ears.

"What do you expect of me Lord?" He spoke to God from his heart. Something felt out of kilter. The balance of his life tilted too far from peace—if peace were found in one's thoughts and productions. He needed to know he was in the place God wanted him to be because he felt he was not. "Am I serving Thee to the best of my abilities?" He tried so hard to do just that.

Hearing no answer, he opened his eyes and sighed, leaning back onto the bench. He stared at the morning stars still in the darkness of night, the moon not in sight. From the southeast an object like a massive red-burning coal blazed across the sky, its tail a brilliance of greens and blues.

He sprang up, hardly believing such a thing. He'd seen a comet before, but this one was exceptionally bright. Its body was massive and its tail sharp with luminous rays. As quick as it had come, it disappeared into the northern sky.

He sat again, breathing as if he'd climbed a mountain. Did it mean something? An ensign for him? What a ridiculous thought! But was it a symbol of change? He'd witnessed God's power sweeping across the world to any who would look up, as if God was saying, "I've not left you. I'm still here."

That Sunday, dark clouds hung so low that extra candles had to be lit in the nave. Cold wind howled outside in spite of it not yet being winter.

From high above the congregation, John looked out from the pulpit. His family sat on the front pew.

Blond-headed Thomas, almost seven now, had become a serious child, despite Hannah's best efforts to bring him to her side of gaiety. Hands folded in his lap, he sat looking up to John, who wasn't sure how he'd been so blessed to have been given such a worthy son or any of his children for that matter. His little Janie was full of innocent happiness. She sang around the house like her mother. He found his heart tied to his children as tightly as it was to Hannah.

She smiled at him anxiously while trying to control a squirming Johnny on her lap. This was the day he was to read the Declaration of Sports. He could put it off no longer without getting censure. Hannah knew well his aversion, and for the first time, she didn't agree with King James's declaration either. Yet it did not seem to defeat her soul as it did his.

At home, they continued as they always had on Sunday, allowing scripture reading and catechisms with the children. Hannah was raising their children to know and love God and agreed that on Sunday they didn't play outside and found only subdued activities to do inside. She read to them from *Foxes Book of Martyrs* and played games to teach them Latin as her father had done for her. Often, John used Sundays as a day of fasting and self-examination.

Many of his parishioners knew what was to be read on this day as well, and the church was full, with some standing along the walls. He'd leave the reading of the Declaration of Sports until after his sermon to make sure they heard God's word first. The congregants of more Puritan opinion sat in the pews with their hats still on as a sign of disrespect. More and more of them had been wearing hats in church over the past few weeks.

King James hadn't held back his loathing toward the Puritans, calling them, "A pest, a fanatic, and a hypocrite, worse than a cattle thief." In some ways, John agreed. But he did hold closely to their convictions about keeping the Sabbath Day holy. And he certainly didn't loathe them as the king did. He did, however, find them to be hardhearted and unteachable in many instances.

After John quoted a prayer, all stood and repeated the Apostles Creed and then sang *A Mighty Fortress is Our God.*

He hoped his favorite hymn might comfort his anxiety. Hannah's clear and sweet soprano rose above the others and filled the stone church up to the wooden rafters. He closed his eyes and begged the Lord to quiet his heart.

After he sermonized for over three-quarters of an hour, the audience became restless. 'Twas nigh unto dinner time. He pulled from underneath his Bible the small book provided to him by his bishop. "I'll now read to you from the Declaration of Sports, an official proclamation given to all of us by our revered king and sovereign, James the First."

The wind rattled at the door, and many children swiveled their heads. The church stood atop a hill with no windbreak and took the brunt of the tempest.

John cleared his throat and read an explanatory introduction by the king. "'We did justly in our progress through Lancashire rebuke some Puritans and precise people, and took order that the like unlawful carriage shouldn't be used by any of them hereafter, in the prohibiting and unlawful punishing of our good people for using their lawful recreations and honest exercises upon Sundays, and other Holy-days.'"

Some Puritans got up and left.

John didn't acknowledge their departure. The majority of those in the congregation were the folks who labored hard all week. The king chose to appeal to them and insult the Puritans. He continued reading, "'. . . our pleasure likewise is, that after the end of divine service our good people be not disturbed or discouraged from any lawful recreation, such as dancing, either men or women; archery for men, leaping, vaulting, or any other such harmless recreation, nor from having May-games, Whitsun-ales, and Morris-dances; and the setting up of May-poles and other sports therewith used.'"

He'd never hated being at the pulpit until this day. He wondered if the king, who did naught to appease the unrest regarding the crisis in the economy caused by their endless wars with Spain, was now trying to make amends and control the populace, providing a release for discontent.

For another half hour, John read from the Declaration of Sports, refusing to look at his congregation. He ended with the written words, "God save the King," and a few offered an "Amen," but he didn't repeat it.

Wiping the perspiration from his forehead, he left the raised pulpit and descended the spiral stairway.

Thomas came and took his hand. "Father, can we now play May-games and dance on Sundays?" Confusion marred his earnest expression.

His children had listened to him repeat the words of the king and probably thought *he* believed those words. How was he to explain that Father taught things from the pulpit that he didn't believe? His stomach jerked and he felt ill.

Today, had he put God before man? Nay, he had not. He'd put king before God. But James was king by divine right, and to disagree with him was treason.

Chapter Nineteen

John accessed the River Thames by the Watermen's Stairs then rented a wherry to row him to Saint Paul's Cathedral. Cries of bargemen letting customers know their comings and goings rang out across the river. Seagulls flocked fishing boats.

"A lovely spring day to be visitin' the city. Come 'ere often?" The cheerful waterman smiled, showing few upper teeth and even fewer lower. His muscled arms pulled the oars of the skiff against the river's current.

"I'm here for Bishop John King's funeral at Saint Paul's Cathedral." John gazed across the water at the west bank where windmills slowly turned.

"'Tain't first I rowed for those solemnities. I see you're in clerical garments. Did ye know 'im personal like?"

"I first met him at Oxford when he sponsored me as sizar," John said.

Bishop King had shown interest in John when he was sixteen, becoming his mentor and a man he admired. King had come into John's path to bequest a great favor, and then they separated forever more. Yet John's life would not have been as blessed without King's kindness at a time when John didn't know which direction to follow. It was King who gave him his Bishops' Bible and convinced him to take his orders.

"A long time then. Have ye ever been to London?" The waterman waved at a large barge with a tall mast, heading the opposite direction, probably sailing to the North Sea.

"I was here ten years past when King James bestowed John

King the bishopric of London." It was when John was newly married to Hannah and his first trip away from her.

"Ye might not recognize London if it be ten years since ye last visited. I'm Jenken, by the by." He tipped his head. With his shirt sleeves rolled up, his arms were as brown as strong tea. He made pulling the oars appear as easy as stroking a paint brush. "I'm sure ye musta 'eard all 'bout the beheadin' of Sir Walter Raleigh for conspirin' against the king. And now folks upset over the prospect of a marriage proposal brewin' between Prince Charles and a Catholic wench. I fear for our country if that 'appens."

So did John.

Jenken spat into the brown river. "They say Francis Bacon is sure to be convicted of corruption. And then there's always the Puritan's puttin' their bills before Parliament to be defeated again and again."

John was surprised at Jenken's knowledge, assuming one in his profession to be uneducated. "How do you know so much of London's politics?"

"A waterman learns a bit if 'e's willin' to listen. I daily carry men to Parliament. They talk. I listen."

He did a lot of talking too—if this ride was to be an example.

Jenken went on about secret assemblies gathering to discover what they could do to reshape the Church.

John half listened until they neared the London Bridge where Jenken moored in the middle of the river in queue behind other boats. "It be some risky oar work to shoot the rapids through one of 'em small arches of ol' London Bridge. I'll need to charge ye extra if ye want me ta try. Elseways, I can bring ye to steps o' the bridge and ye can walk the distance to Saint Paul's. 'Tain't far."

"I'll walk, if you'd be so kind."

Jenken waited in line while other watermen deposited their customers at the London Bridge stairway.

When it was John's turn at the landing stage, he paid Jenken and made his climb into the city.

Smells of sulphurous coal fires, horse manure, and human sewage caused his eyes to water. He pulled a handkerchief from his pocket and held it over his nose as he worked his way toward the cathedral in the distance.

Even though its spire had been hit by lightning years before, it was still one of the tallest buildings in the city. The lightning strike had been proclaimed by Roman Catholics as a sign of God's judgement on England's Protestant rulers. All nonsense.

Cries of hawkers selling produce and peddlers their wares, rose above the clatter of horse and carriage.

John came to Saint Paul's on the northeast side where a public pulpit stood in the open space of the Cross Yard. Empty benches faced the unoccupied pulpit. There would be no preaching on this somber day of London's bishop's funeral.

A throng surged toward the cathedral entrance.

Other than unwashed bodies, the smells of the city were not as harsh here on higher ground. John tucked his handkerchief back into his pocket and strode toward the cathedral's nave.

After the funeral, the crowd moved as a wave toward the south aisle where King's body was to be laid to rest. For a crowd so large, it was a quiet, solemn affair, and John spent much time reminiscing about his youth and the kindness of Bishop King. 'Twas said in his funeral that he always preached on Sundays at some pulpit in or near London with excellent eloquence of speech. John didn't doubt it. The bishop was a great man of piety who John would always consider a person should emulate.

When the services concluded and the crowd thinned, John turned and saw an old friend in the distance.

"Robert!" John called out.

Robert Linnell raised a hand in greeting, his smile genuine even though he'd stopped corresponding with John years before, a loss John didn't understand.

He strode to Robert. "'Tis good to see you." He embraced his old friend. "I was hoping to bump into you here but feared it a chance encounter." John hadn't seen him since his wedding.

Robert's red hair had darkened and his freckles had lightened, but he still had the same silly grin. "God has always been with you John Lothropp, and with Him there are no chance encounters." He slapped John on the shoulder. "You appear well, old man."

John brushed at his greying temples. "We're the same age. Is seven and thirty really so old?"

"My mother thinks it's ancient, seeing as I haven't wed and provided her grandbabies. She doesn't understand that all those I tutor are children enough for me."

John wanted to suggest Penninah as wife but thought better of it. He couldn't fathom two jesters being able to maintain a household or raise Robert's mother's grandbabies in a safe, able-bodied manner. John would relish having him as a brother though—if only. "Shall we find a quiet place to talk?"

They left the great cathedral and found a bench to lounge on at Saint Paul's Cross, where the open-air pulpit still stood empty. Many had the same idea and sat on the benches conversing or eating a meal.

"How many children have you and the quick-witted Mistress Hannah produced?"

That question still found pain in John's heart. How could he not include little Anne in the number? "We have . . . had five. Our youngest is Barbara, almost two years old."

Robert smiled, but John could see loneliness in his eyes. "Every child comes with the forewarning that God is not *yet* discouraged of man." He patted John on the back. "How is the curating coming along? I bet your parish has only the most obedient conformers coming to church. You'd have it no other way, would you?"

John knew he was jesting, but something in him craved to tell Robert of his misgivings. That's what Robert always did to him—made him want to share his concerns. Even Hannah didn't have as strong a pull on him as Robert in that regard. He not only listened well, but he wasn't judgmental, other than some sarcasm.

"Come now, I sense there's worry. How many in your congregation have gone astray? Has it been harder than you assumed to keep everyone on the ladder to God?"

"There have been . . . contentions. Nay . . . questions with no answers, more to the point."

"Questions about what?" He leaned in, his expression earnest.

John sighed in relief that Robert hadn't changed. He draped an arm on his shoulders. "Do you have a more private place to talk?"

"Aye, I know the place to take you. 'Tis across the bridge, howbeit. Are you up for it?"

"I'd enjoy the walk."

The sun sank lower on the horizon and fewer people traversed the thoroughfares. Street sweepers cleaned manure and other unpleasant debris. Smells of alehouses and suppers cooking also helped deaden the more undesirable odors.

They paid the fare to cross London Bridge, a city in itself, with hundreds of shops and houses. Wagons, carts, carriages, and pedestrians shared a single file lane that was a man's height wide, going each direction. Near the end of the bridge, water wheels powering mill stones below drowned out John's and Robert's conversation.

At the southern gatehouse, they passed a display of tar-covered and boiled human heads impaled on iron pikes—executed traitors, criminals, and those tortured for their religious beliefs.

They stopped talking for a time, then strolled down quieter streets. As they walked, John told Robert about Fenner, Tilden, and Hinckley. John tried to put into words how he questioned certain church practices without sounding like he wasn't happy in his ordained calling. He shared his thoughts on the Declaration of Sports and common prayer.

Robert listened and only occasionally interrupted to clarify or ask a question.

The soot in the air floated onto John's black garments. He brushed at his sleeve but knew 'twould only be moments before more would take its place. They were in Southwark now, a place of distasteful establishments for prostitutes, gambling, and bear and bull baiting arenas. Refuse littered the narrow streets and beggars held out hands for coin. John had naught to give and had to sadly turn a blind eye.

Robert gave liberally to the destitute children.

"Will we be there before dark?" John asked, the shadows of the half-timbered houses already growing long. John worried Robert's fine clothing would attract a thief's attention.

"Just," Robert said distractedly, worrying his lip.

John had talked so much he hadn't realized Robert said little of himself in return. Now John wondered why. He interrogated Robert with questions but only received one-word answers.

After another quarter of an hour, the sun set and they came to terraced houses that looked alike, timber-framed with many mullioned windows, curtains drawn.

Robert stopped and looked about, then lifted his hand to knock at a door, but did not. He lowered his arm and shifted toward John. His face held enough sorrow to make John suppose he was about to weep. But there was also fear in his eyes. "I . . . I apologize, old friend," he said quietly. "For discontinuing my correspondence years back. I didn't want to experience the disappointment you'd have in me for separating from the Church."

John caught his breath. He couldn't have said anything more unexpected. "But Robert—"

He held up his hand. "I'm a coward, and I needed my friends to help me get through this." He turned and rapped on the door.

A petite woman answered. She narrowed her eyes at John, but when she saw Robert, her countenance transformed completely.

John could have been mistaken, but it seemed her love for Robert replaced her suspicion for himself.

Robert stepped in and pulled John with him. "May I introduce Clara."

Clara curtsied John's way but didn't take her eyes from Robert. When she finally did, she looked John up and down, her lip curling at his attire. "M'lord?"

Robert motioned toward John. "This is my lifelong friend. We're here to speak with Henry. Is he in residence?"

"Aye, 'e's in the back parlor with others. Be it wise to bring a stranger and preacher 'ere?"

"He's no stranger to me and I trust him as a brother."

Then why hadn't Robert trusted John? Why must he find out Robert's innermost secrets through strangers? Hadn't John just told of his own troubles with church doctrine?

"Let me speak with 'im." Clara left through a door at the back of the room.

John glanced about. The dimly lit room appeared to be a storehouse. Shelves lined the walls, holding bags of grain.

"This is the home of a young grocer, newly establishing his business," Robert said.

Clara entered with a short man who looked to be in his fifties. He carried himself with authority but had an openly welcome expression.

"Henry," Robert said. "may I introduce my friend, the Reverend John Lothropp."

The lack of a last name was discourteous, but John didn't say anything.

Henry stepped forward to shake John's hand. The lace cuff around his wrist was of fine cloth. His jerkin also that of a man of means. "Greeting, Reverend Lothropp. Many of us have believed you one of England's most promising ministers."

"I'm not acquainted with you, so how is it you know me?"

"Mister Linnell has shared his stories as have others. Robert Browne and I discussed your skill with sermonizing."

Who was this man who had watched John's career? "I'm at a disadvantage by not knowing your last name, sir."

"I'm Henry Jacob, the minister of the Independent Church here in Southwark."

An unfamiliar burning of anger tightened John's chest. How many years had he been trying to control that emotion? "How dare you call your following a church when only the Church of England is recognized here."

Robert placed a hand on his shoulder. "That's why I brought

you here, John." He tried to sound lighthearted, but failed. "To learn of my church. We're *semi*-separatists, if you will."

John snorted. "Either you're in the Church or you're out. There's no semi-anything when it comes to worship." How could Robert have placed him in this situation?

"Gentleman, please, come into the back parlor and let's start from the beginning," Jacob said with a smile.

Clara stayed in the front room, and Jacob led the men through the back door and down a short hall into a large room with many chairs and tables. Candles burned from the center of each round table.

Of five men in discussion, one of them sitting closest stood up so quickly his chair toppled.

Recognition hit John. This was the man the warden was trying to fine that day in Charing—who the crowd took to the stocks.

The man charged, his bulk towered over John.

Both Jacob and Robert grabbed the man's waist, pulling him back. "I thrashed him once and didn't do the job properly. Let me at him again."

"William Granger, act like a gentleman in this home or leave." Jacob, half his size, shoved him back when Robert released him. "We can discuss this like admirable men who follow the Lord's command to love our neighbor."

Granger sneered at John. "I'd been wanting to cuff you even before that day at Charing."

John had tried to help him then, but everything had all gone awry. "Why?" he implored incredulously, knowing his innocence in the whole affair.

"Because you took the woman I wanted as my own." He growled like a spoiled man-child.

Unable to form words, John combed his fingers through his hair. "Just how well do you know my wife?" he finally managed to say.

Granger stepped forward, looking down his nose at John. "Well enough to know her favorite flower is honeysuckle, and she speaks Latin, and she desired to be a preacher from the time she could talk. I suppose you don't allow her any of these things."

Jacob stepped between the two. "Mister Linnell has brought Reverend Lothropp here so we can explain our beliefs. Mayhap you can have this conversation another time?"

Granger swiveled abruptly and sat in the chair farthest away from the men.

A man who'd been with Granger stood. He was almost as tall as Granger, but half his size in girth. "May I introduce myself as it seems others have lost their manners." He glared at Granger then pivoted back to John. "This is my home and my name is Joseph." With his thin hand, he grasped John's in a firm embrace.

"Greeting, Mister Joseph." He assumed the man didn't supply his surname intentionally. "I didn't intend to bring disharmony into your home." He bowed.

"Oh, I saw the whole thing. 'Twasn't your fault. Granger is as easy to rile as a hungry child without a bowl and spoon. Please"—he extended his hand—"won't you have a seat?"

John set Granger's chair upright and sat. Robert, Jacob, and two other gentlemen joined them.

Joseph motioned toward the other two. "These are my cousins," he said, but didn't supply their names.

"Gentlemen." John stood again, shook the newcomers' hands, then sat. If anyone had questioned this morning what he'd be doing tonight, he'd never have guessed that he'd be surrounded by Separatists.

"May we trust you to keep our conversations here tonight hidden from others?" Henry Jacob grilled.

John hated keeping secrets from Hannah. This would have to remain one. Although, he was tempted to tell her Granger had gone astray. Had she had feelings for him as a young woman? Why had she not explained their relationship years ago when Granger punched John in the stomach? The fact that she kept her own secrets made him imagine there must have been more to their relationship. Keeping secrets—as he planned to now do to her.

Secrets.

"Reverend Lothropp?" Jacob prodded.

John came around. "I'm here to learn of Robert's new beliefs and have no plans to expose your clandestine meetings or those members who belong to your congregation." Something suddenly dawned on John and he turned to Robert. "Did you send Mister Browne to my home years back?"

Robert gave him a puzzled expression, but Granger sniggered in guilt. And that question was finally answered.

He shifted back to Jacob. "How many in your organization?"

Jacob looked at the others as if considering whether or not to answer. "Is that important to know?"

"I suppose not." John shrugged.

"Let me tell you some of my history." Jacob leaned forward.

"I too am from Kent, near Canterbury. This, more than any other reason, is why I've come across some of the same people who know you. I earned a master's from Oxford in 1586 and was precentor at Corpus Christi College. After reading Robert Browne's writings while there, I soon joined the Brownists and went to Holland with them in 1593. I formed a non-separatist independent congregation of former Church of England members. Later, in 1610, I went to Leiden to confer with John Robinson and his followers. I adopted his views on church government." Jacob rested his arm on the table. His eyes held sincerity.

Clearly the man had had issues with the Church most of his life. 'Twas no wonder he'd formed a church to satisfy his disagreements.

Jacob studied John intently. "Some of the congregation here in London traveled to America with Robinson's congregants. I await to hear word from them any day. They consider themselves Separatists from the Church. But I still believe that the Church of England is a true church in need of reformation. That's why I came back to London in 1616 with the express purpose of forming a congregation similar to Robinson's in Leiden, but not completely. I'm not a Separatist in all ways. Browne visited me here as he told me he did with you in Egerton."

Jacob did know a lot. Was he as interested in other preachers as he was in John?

"I'm now making plans to travel to the Virginia Colonies to teach my beliefs there. But I don't intend to leave the church I've loved since my youth. I even now attend Saint Andrew Hubbard Parish meetings on Sunday."

This surprised John. Jacob hadn't left the Church of England in his own eyes. But where was his heart? "On what accounts do you separate yourself from the Church?"

"I don't believe that ministers have the power to forgive sins." Jacob's tone went flat.

John assumed Jacob wanted him to refute the claim. He couldn't. He questioned it himself. He'd never admitted it to anyone and he wasn't about to start here with this group.

"I also don't agree that the Church forbids ministers to offer prayers from the heart before congregations, and only allows utterance from *The Book of Common Prayer*."

Granger cocked his head. "These are scripted performances in which you recite, sing, and have symbolic gestures." He pointed at John. "You wear a costume even. How is that worship to our

The Pulse of His Soul

Lord?" he shouted. "I don't go to church for theatre."

The man obviously had an issue with authority.

"The Lord also used symbols in His teaching. 'Tis so throughout the scriptures," John said to Granger as much as the others.

Jacob questioned, "How important is it to you, Reverend Lothropp, that as a minister you must confess that the Church of England is the only true church?" Articulate, Jacob seemed deeply committed to his reasoning.

John understood how Jacob had become the chief herald of the Separatist movement in London. *Semi-separatist* if he was to believe Robert. "When I teach that the Church of England is the only true church, I feel I'm bringing others to God in unity. 'Tis in church where they'll learn to follow in His ways and become happier people. There's strength in the wholeness and harmony of the church."

Jacob shook his head. "Methinks you're mistaking unity with unanimity—a forced, undivided opinion. Can your parishioners not learn God's teachings outside the Church? Is it right to deny men the right to assemble freely to meet and discuss the Bible? Those kinds of meetings would be no different than what you're wanting—for men to learn of the Bible's teachings so that they may become happier people. Right now, the bishops forbid men from speaking freely." Jacob ran his hand over his grey hair. "I'm not here to argue these beliefs. You asked me how I separated myself from the Church. These are some of the points where I find issue."

Jacob was right. 'Twasn't worth debating all his points. None of them were new to John. All were issues he'd discussed with Fenner, Tilden, and Hinckley. He wondered over them himself through the years, yet he wasn't ready to question all his beliefs. How could he leave a church that his wife and her family loved so much? That he'd been consecrated to serve? How could he leave his profession? He'd a family to support. He had no other skills to earn a living. "I see," was all he was willing to say. "Robert, I must go and find my inn. Will you come with me?"

Robert and John strode through the darkness in silence, John trying to keep his wits about him and watch for thieves and pickpockets.

Robert kept close to him, also glancing about them. "Are you angry with me?"

"Not in the least. I shared with you my own concerns earlier this day. I'm uneasy, howbeit, that you may be found out and imprisoned. Are you careful when you meet with those people?"

"I try to be. We have conventicles in different homes each time. I take my mother to her parish church on Sundays, and I don't believe others have reason to question my . . ." He stopped as if searching for the right word. "Incorruptibility," he finally said, chuckling. "I feel my newfound beliefs are the opposite of being corrupted."

"Robert, I hope you can honor me by allowing me to stay with the Church of England. Our beliefs shouldn't change our friendship."

"I suspect our beliefs are really not so different."

"That may well be, but I cannot renounce my orders with the Church. I've a family to support."

Earlier that day, John had considered emulating Bishop King and now his friend believed John had the views of a Separatist. The goodness on both sides pulled him in different ways.

"I do have one regret," Robert said.

"And what's that?" John stopped and turned.

"That I wasn't there to see Granger punch you." His eyes sparkled with mirth.

John had missed Robert. He'd make sure they kept in touch this time. He needed to know that Robert remained safe.

Chapter Twenty

"It's a lonely shoreline," Hannah said to John. From the guest bedchamber window at Thom's new manor house, she could see the North Sea and very little in between, other than flat salt marshes and a narrow pebble beach. "I don't believe I can even call it a beach."

John stepped to her side and gazed out the window. "It's a new day, and I'm glad for it. I plan to enjoy my time here even if there won't be strolls along the shoreline."

"Thom must like it well enough since he owns much of it." She couldn't tell if it was windy outside because there were no trees to sway in the breeze.

"He benefits greatly from the whelk, cockle, and oyster trade. But methinks his grain fields and dairy pastures to the west are of greater value."

Hannah sighed and turned toward the room with its high-poster bed draped in dark-blue silk curtains that puddled on the floor. "I'm already enjoying having ceilings over my head that I cannot touch." She chuckled. "But I suppose that's a vain thing to say." She glanced back at John. "I appreciate that roof over our heads in Egerton."

He shrugged. "I prefer not to reflect on it while here. Let's be about the day. Thom's promised a ride to one of the oldest chapels in England." John left the room.

Hannah hoped their time with Thom and his family would benefit John's mood. He'd been pensive for months—unhappy even. She didn't believe it was her fault but more to do with his church duties. He used to thrive on writing sermons and teaching God's word. Now he appeared to dread Sundays. She wished more than ever she could deliver sermons for him—a preposterous wish that still too often flitted through her head.

She placed her hand on her belly where another baby grew. Barbara would be four before this one was born. The years without a baby had rushed by, all her time spent with the charge of older children who needed to be taught to read and understand the joys of education. Father shared his extensive library and often came to spend time with his grandchildren. They adored him.

"Mama." Janie shuffled in carrying Barbara on her little hip, the toddler half her size, but she didn't seem to mind. The two could always be found together, Janie acting the part of a little mama. "Since my aunt is Jane and Uncle Thom's daughter is named Jane, how will we tell each other apart?"

"I think we should call you Poppet," Hannah caressed her shoulder. "Now go get your sunhat. We're going for a ride today."

They took two carts and a carriage to the old Saint Peter's Chapel at Bradwell-on-Sea. The servants followed behind in another cart with the picnic necessities. The scenery was more severe than at Thom's manor. Their only reprieve from the wind was inside the ancient church, its stone walls deadening the gusts. Sunlight from high, narrow windows exposed portions of crumbling walls infused by tens of thousands of prayers.

"If it's stood the tempest for a thousand years, it's likely to stand another thousand," she whispered to Thomas, whose head now reached as high as her shoulder.

He whispered back, "There's a true reverence in this little one-room chapel."

She watched her serious eleven-year-old son roam on, looking about with a faint crease to his brow. Blond and blue eyed like her, but very much his father in disposition, he was leaving childhood behind at an alarming rate.

To allow the holy atmosphere to soak into their souls, they sat on simple wooden pews, Hannah next to John and the children lined up on her other side with Jane at the end. 'Twas unusual to sit next to John in church. She reached over and took his hand, wanting to comment, but Thom stepped to the pulpit.

Had he brought them here for a personal sermon, or was he acting on impulse? He'd changed since she'd first met him. His untroubled attitude had become critical. And she sensed fear in his soul when he looked at John.

On a pew across the aisle, Thom's two daughters, Anne and Jane, sat subdued, hands clasped on their laps, their nursemaid paying them more mind than their mother, Elizabeth. She was a pensive woman wearing her dark hair in the most recent fashion under a delicate lace veil, her pale profile austere. Years past, she'd buried a daughter, Ellen, but recently delivered a fourth daughter, Maria, who stayed home with the wet nurse this day.

"'The Lord sent them two and two before Him into every city and place, whether He Himself would come.'" Thom quoted from *The Book of Common Prayer*. "Therefore, He said unto them, the harvest is great but the laborers are few."

'Twas an unusual situation—church with just her family—and she rather liked it.

John released her hand, face red, jaw clenching.

Surprised, Hannah stared at him. Is this not what he and Thom did? They were in affect two servants laboring for their Lord. Hannah had heard John repeat the same words numerous times both in and out of church. She must have misunderstood his displeasure.

"I send ye forth as lambs amongst wolves." Thom put the emphasis on *wolves*.

She reached for John's hand again, but he pulled away.

He seemed to be struggling to stay seated.

Bewildered, she checked on her children. They were sitting reverently, unaware of their father's reaction. Janie held Barbara's hand, and Johnny leaned on Thomas's shoulder. Jane's profile was unreadable. With both her brothers having taken orders, she was like-minded to them, attentive to Thom's words.

"For the labor is worthy of the reward." Thom ended the prayer and began a sermon about keeping faith.

John stared at his lap the entire time.

When Thom had finished, he motioned for John to come to the pulpit. "Come, brother. Let us hear from you."

John shook his head, gave Thom a glare of annoyance, stood, and strode toward the door.

They all proceeded to follow him as if it was a natural thing for John to disobey his older brother or not want to sermonize. He must not feel well.

They walked into the sunshine. The wind blew at a steady rate, flapping at their clothes. Hannah kept a hand on her hat. She knew how John hated the wind, but guessed his foul expression related more to Thom and his sermon on faith. John obviously wasn't getting the relaxation he'd hoped for this day.

Single file, they followed Thom along a dried brook-bed, stiff and brown marsh grasses hardly moving in the whirling wind. Johnny, Janie, and Barbara ran ahead chasing one another and squealing if one of them tagged the other. Anne and Jane solemnly followed their nursemaid.

They all came to an open area where the servants had arranged the horses, carts, and carriage in a semi-circle, acting as a windbreak. Blankets had been laid on the sandy earth. The sea sparkled close by. Hannah assumed if the wind weren't muffling her ears, she'd be able to hear the waves.

Sister Jane didn't recline with them but stood looking at the servants carrying food, drinks, and cushions for the comfort of all the Lothropps. Hannah sensed Jane's insecurity at not knowing if she should be helping the servitors or relaxing with her family. This was Hannah's fault. Jane had been trained to serve them, but Hannah needed to let her know that foremost she was family.

"Come, Jane, lounge with us." She patted the space next to her.

John and Thom had discussed Jane's situation the night before, deciding they needed to find her a husband, wondering if their older half-brother, Robert, would accept the responsibility. But his familial interests and correspondence had been minimal. Hannah selfishly wanted Jane to stay with them, but she'd no right to hinder the men's planning. She loved Jane as a sister.

Thom kept glancing at John but didn't address him. He and Elizabeth sat on a blanket with their children, the servants paying special attention to their needs. This would be how John would act if he'd married someone as resolute as Elizabeth.

Thomas crouched in the marsh grass, studying some insect or plant. Johnny, Janie, and Barbara ran and giggled, pouncing on one another while Thom's daughters sat quietly and watched, disappointment in their eyes. Anne's sober young face jumped with a nervous tick, her mouth jerking upward every so often.

John said under his breath to Hannah, "My children can laugh together and still serve God."

Hannah caught her breath. What brought that sentiment on? She remembered when she first met him how he'd discouraged laughter. They'd argued about it even. Was this what was irritating him? Thom had continued with his childhood disciplines, but John had not. Was Thom reprimanding John's parenting somehow?

The Pulse of His Soul

"The soul is rejuvenated by watching children at play," Hannah replied.

They picnicked until the fishing boats came in, their white sails drooped from lesser wind than when they'd left.

That evening, the children settled into the nursery with servants—something Hannah could get used to—and the adults ate a quiet supper with servants attending to their needs also. Hannah wasn't once interrupted by a plea for help with something-or-other from one of the children or called to clean up someone's mess. Yet, the supper was as quiet as when she visited Uncle Edmund's years before.

The deliciously tender seal meat, red smoked herring, and fresh oysters couldn't compare to any seafood she'd had before. She was also offered goose, lamb, and beef cooked to savory perfection.

With their stomachs full, they gathered in the parlor with its dark-paneled walls and elaborate fire hearth and drank hippocras from Venetian glasses.

Elizabeth soon excused herself, tired from the day's activities so soon after giving birth.

Jane too said she'd visit the children before retiring. Hannah surmised she felt uncomfortable in Thom's opulent parlor. She squeezed Jane's hand before she departed.

Hannah glanced about at the extravagant furnishings and draperies. She found it odd that, as in a church, Thom had a lectern in his parlor. A Bible sat upon it. Did that mean he lectured to visitors or he studied standing in front of it? The parlor would be a quiet place to study, she decided, considering no children were allowed past its door. John had been raised with these same demanding rules and luxuries, but never complained that he didn't now have them. Although, he did often lament that their vicarage was much too small for all of them and he didn't have a quiet place to study. He was right.

Sitting on a settle, John and Hannah sat across from Thom, who crossed one leg over the other and took a sip of wine, his lace-edged cuff a French export. "I assume your bishop gave you the dispatch *Directions Concerning Preachers*? How do you feel about the limits the king has placed on preaching?"

John's features tightened. He hadn't told Hannah about this new document, which probably meant he desired to stay clear of an argument with her.

"I've never limited my sermons to the two Books of Homilies

and the Thirty-Nine Articles of Religion. Nor do I *read* my sermons as the document has requested us to do."

Thom observed his brother a little too closely.

Both men held back their passions and their speech sounded casual. But there was something going on here of which Hannah was unaware. She'd sensed it earlier in the day also.

"The king is seeking to limit the range of subject matter we can teach to our congregations," Thom said. "I don't deduce this would have come about if there weren't preachers teaching false doctrine."

John stroked the stem of his wine glass. "Many believe the timing of the document has more to do with the king seeking marriage for his son to a Spanish Catholic princess. The people of England fear their country will become Catholic again, and it didn't help that he lately released from prison Jesuits and Catholics. I speculate the king is now making a *show* that he holds to Anglican beliefs and they need not fear."

Hannah sat straighter. She'd never heard John disparage King James. She opened her mouth to speak, but Thom spoke first.

"I don't infer it's all show, John. I think you better follow your king and cease your sermon practices of applying scriptural passages to our present time. And if it were about the king trying to show the people his convictions to the Church, why did he add the command in the document to stop invectives and indecent railing of speeches against Papists and Puritans? Wouldn't that further the anxieties about the country's conversion to Catholicism?"

"The king said that?" Hannah put in. "Where is this document? Thom do you have a copy I can read?"

Thom pointed out the door. "It's in my library on the desk."

She'd read it later. She didn't want to miss this conversation.

Thom glowered. "We study from the same scriptures and worship the same God. Why must you create this division in your heart?"

Hannah drew a sharp intake of breath. She wanted to ask *what division*, but she already knew. John was still exploring Separatist ideologies.

"Why can't the Church of England allow differing opinions?" John grumbled. "They don't want to lose control of the people, that's why. They don't want us to act on our own conscience."

Thom set down his glass and sat forward. "The Church should matter most to you but still you place your conscience as the priority. Is that selfish? A sin? Can't you be grateful that you live in a Christian kingdom?"

Hannah laid her hand on John's. "God doesn't want the Church divided against itself. I've heard you say that many times." She squeezed his hand, feeling guilty for aligning with Thom and opposing John.

Thom's lower lip protruded in a deep frown. "There's naught wrong with seeking unity in the church. All these dissenters you told me about in your letters can't even agree on what Christ's church should look like." His voice grew louder. "Henry Jacob's Independents don't agree on basic principles amongst themselves if I'm to believe what you wrote. There must be order. The Church of England achieves that. There's only one God." He held up one finger. "Who is a God of order. He has only *one* church." He shook his finger.

So, John had been writing letters to Thom, telling him all the things in his heart he wasn't sharing with her. Why? Why could they not discuss these things? These subjects that mattered greatly to them both. He placed his brother before her.

John set his glass on the side table. "'For where two or three are gathered together in my name, there am I in the midst of them,'" he quoted from the Bishops' Bible. Why he still used that edition, Hannah didn't understand.

"'But be you doers of the word, and not hearers only, deceiving your own selves,'" Thom quoted from the King James Bible.

John clutched the settle's arm. "You want me to obey and not question? Questioning brings wisdom and a fuller understanding of God."

"Don't you think Christ's apostles would've considered it strange if a congregation decided to imagine itself as following Jesus in their own way and gathered to fortify each other in this idea?" Thom cross-examined.

Hannah said to John, "I've often heard you speak of one land, one church, and one absolute power on the throne. You're a divinely appointed servant of the *one* true church."

John turned to her with a sadness in his eyes she'd never seen before. 'Twas obvious he felt she was against him in this. Although she was, she'd try to say no more. Her heart broke for him.

He shifted back to Thom. "I suspect that's exactly what happened at the beginning of the Church of England. Or any church other than the one Christ organized with his apostles. With Henry Jacob's gathering, I envision a church that's built on the Bible and populated by those who seek out other Christians and together determine their own affairs without having to submit to the judgment of any higher human authority. If such a church can stand, the power of the Holy Spirit will abide there. With the Holy Spirit's presence, people can be taught all that's needful."

"It's been tried time and again," Thom grabbed tightly to his chair arms as if he were holding himself back from springing toward John. "There will need to be governance and order, which is what we have with the Church of England. The Apostle Paul told the Corinthians 'Let all things be done decently and in order.' Order and structure are what the Holy Spirit uses."

At one time in her life, Hannah would have reported to the warden anyone who spoke against the Church of England. Could she do it now? If she reported her husband, would it in the end save him? Perchance having him punished would be better than him losing his soul to the Separatist organization? He could pay a fine and be reprimanded. She wanted to ask her father, but she couldn't bear him knowing John had these ideologies.

John shook his head. "How many people have acted out of fear of King James's power and have no relationship with God at all? The people separating from the church aren't doing so to live a life of sin or disbelief. On the contrary, they're searching for more of God's words and goodness. The ones who are not searching are those drowsily sitting each Sunday in the Church of England's pews, forced to listen to prayers by rote and sermons that were written decades ago."

"You don't—" Thom started to speak.

"Nay." John raised his voice over him. "I've been going against my sense of what's right, and my integrity suffered by reading the Book of Sports in church. My own children no longer know who to follow or what to believe. I need to be true to the whisperings of the Spirit and deny these Separatist ideas no longer. I respect you as my older brother and have always bowed to your commands, but when it comes to matters of my relationship with my God"— John stood—"you don't have the right to tell me what to do or how to think."

Fear and sadness pushed at Hannah's chest. She'd waited years to see John get angry. She didn't expect it to be at his brother or over the Anglican Church.

Thom stood too, his face inches from John's. "I'll turn my back on you if you renounce your orders."

"No Thom," Hannah shrilled, also standing. "Don't say such a thing." Thom was the only family John was devoted to other than

Jane. If John felt abandoned again, she feared he'd revert back to the days when he feared loving her or anyone.

John squinted. "Fine, if that's all our relationship means. Is this Uncle Edmund speaking through you? Have you become as closed minded as he? I never would have thought I'd see the day."

Thom marched away but stopped and pivoted before stepping from the room. "Contemplate well on what you're considering. If you renounce your orders, along with losing your home and salary, you'll squander your education and forfeit the only profession you know. If you believe you've tight living quarters now, how will a hovel suit? You and your wife and children will no longer be considered gentlepeople or respected in society."

"Aye." John barely whispered and looked to Hannah. "'Twill be harder on her than I."

As soon as the bedchamber door shut, Hannah turned on John. "How could you—"

He grabbed her upper arms. "Hannah, go easy. I've rebuffed the person who's loved me most next to you—*if* you do still love me."

"Don't start the conversation by bringing me to my knees. Of course, I love you. I can love *and* be outraged, can't I? If I didn't love you, I wouldn't be so upset."

"Come, let's sit." He felt so defeated he didn't think he could stand another minute. He fell onto the chair. "You can ask any question you want, and I'll hold naught back. I'm sorry you've discovered my feelings as you have." If he'd lost her trust, he'd much to ask forgiveness for.

She sat in the chair beside him. "My first question is, why would you keep these plans of renouncing your orders from me? I should be asking *you* if you love *me*. Do you not respect my feelings or care about the lives of your children?"

"I didn't have *plans* before this night. Thom forced me to face my beliefs and make a decision. I hadn't told you because I hoped all would be well in the end, that I'd find answers in the Church to appease my misgivings, as I usually did. Or maybe that the Church would become more lenient." He rubbed his eyes. "But instead, the king sent a farce of a letter dictating all preachers *read*—not sermonize, have you—from the two books of homilies and the common prayer book. I've been able to serve the parishioners all these years because I could teach what I felt God wanted for *their* benefit. Now that's taken away, Hannah. Do you understand?"

She shook her head, eyes moist from unshed tears. "Nay, I fear not completely. If I were a preacher, I'd teach as the king tells me. The homilies and prayer book are still scripture from the Bible."

"I don't believe we fully have the gospel the Bible teaches." He looked into her beautiful face and felt in his heart a great love for her and the goodness she pursued. She desired to do right, and he couldn't fault her that. "Questioning one's faith is not a weakness. One must question to find answers. For faith to grow, one needs to spend time with the Lord on more than just Sundays to search and pray for answers."

"Do you question my faith, John?"

"Nay." He laid his hand on her tightly clasped hands. "You're a good woman. I'm not trying to tell you you're wrong. I can accept that you'll attend the Church of England services when I cannot." Yet, he'd pray she'd understand him. He considered Reverend Howse and how he'd be disappointing the only man who'd acted as father to him. Could he really go through with this?

The Holy Spirit whispered to him *Aye* and his heart stilled.

Wanting to wrap her in his arms, he knelt before her. "Once the light of new knowledge had entered my body, I couldn't replace it with aught but more light. I couldn't help but listen to others who taught of God's fairness. This is more important than myself. I swear to you I'm doing this for God and for others. I pray God will let me know who those others are. If I can lead people to a higher cause, 'twill brighten further the light that burns in my heart."

"This light is invisible to my eyes." She looked away.

"I couldn't do this without God's permission." John turned her face back, letting his hand linger on her smooth cheek. He couldn't lose Hannah.

"I see that you feel so, but how will we live? What will you do with yourself?" A tear slipped from her eye.

He wiped it and she pulled away.

How could he put his family in this situation? "When I was young and had the guidance of Bishop King, I felt so sure about being a preacher. The Spirit whispered to me to cure souls in His church. But now, this night, I believe it's still whispering to me that I'll always be teaching God's word." He let out a long breath and sunk onto his heels. "Maybe the first ordination I received was to get me to this point. It gave me the experience needed for what's ahead. I'll serve God no matter where I am."

"I believe you told me something similar when we first met. But how is that going to keep food on our table—if we even have a table."

"Believe in me again." He reached for her hand, but she kept it clasped with the other on her lap. "My natural desire to serve will keep us secure, no matter the road we take."

"The road *you* take. I'll not follow on that road of separating from the Church. It's simply not right for you to make up your own religion. The Church of England dispenses all things to find inner peace. Why must you search elsewhere?" Her eyes held such despair. She needed to let him comfort her, but she wouldn't. "We were raised with catechizing to enlighten us, and I'm sure of our salvation through baptism and the sacraments. Why must you feel you need to assemble with heretics and place your life at risk? Do you not care for your family's safety?"

His temples pounded. The guilt of failing his family gnawed at his soul. He loved them more than any other people on earth. If he truly believed this step away from the Church could harm them, he'd not be able to do it. But the Spirit of God was urging him to follow the Independents. How could he deny his God? "We'll sell the horse and cow. They're our only true property. The money should be enough to live where we don't need either animal. London, I'm thinking."

"London!" Hannah exclaimed, her face reddening. She hugged her belly. "I don't believe I truly know who you are."

Oh, God, he sent up a prayer. *Soften her heart. Keep the child within safe through what's coming for our family.* "Please, Hannah. Have faith. Please stand by me in this."

"You're saying you're not only going to leave the Church of England, but you're going to lead people away as well? I'm sorry, John, I cannot stand by you." She spun from him and wept into her hands.

"Do you suppose I could do this if I thought I'd lose God's favor?"

"God's favor is more important than mine." She mumbled into her hands and then sniffled. "As it should be," she added softly, her voice full of dejection.

He wasn't sure she believed the last sentiment. "I pray I don't hurt you or the children in any way, but I must answer to God first."

Chapter Twenty-One

Insides churning, Hannah sat on the front pew of Saint James with her children and Jane. This would be John's last sermon. He was going to renounce his orders this day, and she could say naught to dissuade him.

He climbed to the pulpit and started the meeting with prayer—not from the common book but from his heart. He prayed for peace and understanding. He prayed for the Holy Spirit to rest upon them all. Hannah's heart ached for him, for them, for herself. He was saying farewell to the congregation without them knowing it.

When he finished, murmurings of astonishment ran throughout the chapel.

Head bowed, Hannah could not glance at the others lest they see the fear in her eyes. Breathe Hannah. Just breathe.

"Why are the people with the black hats leaving, Mama?" Barbara pulled on her sleeve.

"Shhh. I'll tell you later," Hannah whispered.

After a psalm was sung, John began speaking, his voice remarkably calm. "Today I've prepared a sermon from Second Corinthians chapters one through seven. These chapters pertain to the Apostle Paul when he was building the Church of God in Corinth, Greece."

Pausing for a moment, he gazed sadly upon his congregation.

Hannah imagined he was thinking about what he was giving up. She'd miss her life too, but she stopped her thoughts there. She couldn't think about what was ahead without crying, and she didn't want to weep here so openly.

"I'd like to start by asking you to close your eyes." John's smile genuine and encouraging, hit Hannah hard. "I know this is an unusual request, but you'll understand soon enough."

Like the others, she bowed her head and closed her eyes, but anxiety brewed deep. How had they found themselves a step from leaving all she'd ever known? Heart closed to him, she'd lost her faith in his judgement and didn't want to listen to him sermonize.

"Imagine being in total darkness," John said. "It's so dark you can't see your hand in front of you. Keeping your eyes closed, pretend you're lighting a candle you're already holding." He stopped speaking for just a moment.

People shuffled and coughed. A baby fussed.

"Watch the light shine on you and away from you, out into the darkness. Watch it blaze a path in front of you. It might not cast a glow all the way to your destination. It might still be dark far ahead. But the light is enough for you to follow. Now start walking." John let another moment of silence go by. "This is *your* path. Now open your eyes."

Hannah opened her eyes but kept the visual she'd seen in her mind, her path bright and precise.

"Remember what you saw as I give the sermon. In fact, remember it through your whole life. Sometimes spiritual light is hard to comprehend, and I'm hoping by teaching it metaphorically, 'twill help you understand light spiritually and physically because 'tis always both."

Hannah was almost afraid to listen. Afraid John would teach her something wrong.

"'Prepareth an exceeding and an eternal weight of glory unto us.' Second Corinthians 4:15-17 speaks of the losing, or the dimming, of our light by affliction and trials that pull us down. But in the end, knowing trials will make your light stronger. Make *you* stronger." John's voice fell over the congregation as if he were speaking to each person companionably.

"If your candle burns to a stump and dims, get a new candle."

A few people chuckled. Hannah did not.

"It's hard to stay on your path if your light is getting low. Where do you symbolically get new candles to keep your light strong? By reading and studying scriptures, praying, following the commandments. If you do these things, you'll always have a supply of candles to burn brightly through your life."

Hannah glanced at Jane, who appeared to be listening intently.

How was she going to take John's fall from grace?

"If you cannot find your candles and you're left in total darkness, call to God for help. You can also reach out to those who have candles burning brightly and ask them for help. Don't let yourself embark on despair. On the other hand, if you're persecuted for your strong light, ask those persecuting to walk alongside you. These people who believe not, won't believe unless they're given the light. Shine your light on others until they can get a light of their own." Not only did John display his God-given ability to share the gospel in every word, he displayed how much he wanted to help his congregation.

These were the things Hannah had fallen in love with about John. She sent a prayer, the same prayer she'd sent for days, asking that John see his errors in falling from the Church and for God to somehow keep them safe from poverty and strife.

"When your eyes were closed"—John looked out over the congregation—"I had you light a candle that was already in your hand. What does the candle represent? The answer may be different for each of you. You may have thought of the Holy Spirit, your avowal of faith, obedience to God, the Light of Christ."

Hannah had thought of the bedrock of the church.

"In Second Corinthians 4:6, we read: 'For it is God that commandeth the light to shine out of darkness, which hath shined in our hearts, for to give the light of the knowledge of the glory of God, in the face of Jesus Christ.'" John looked up from the Bible.

And he looked right at Hannah, with something in his eyes she could not read.

"The word *glory* is used to describe the manifestation of God's presence. He's usually described as being so bright we cannot behold Him. Our eyes have to go through a transfiguration to be able to see Him. Glory is also used to describe His greatness—something that's hard for us to truly fathom. The scripture is saying that Jesus represents this greatness and knowledge of what God is about and what He can do for us."

The congregation seemed to listen as intently as Hannah. Teaching God's word was what John was born to do. Why would he leave all this?

"If we could behold Christ in all His glory—which is greatness and knowledge and light—as is written in Second Corinthians 3:18, we would need to go through a transformation to be as glorious as He. We've access to the glory of God at all times. We keep ourselves from Him. 'Tis not a coincidence that the sun in the sky is called sun, sounding like son, as in the Son of God. We would die without the sun to supply warmth or grow our crops to nourish us. If we're in the dark too long, our eyes hurt when we come into the light. 'Tis painful to get back on our path once we get off. But 'tis possible to get our sight back and step back on our sun-lit path."

As John continued to read and explain more scriptures that referred to light in Second Corinthians, God's light shone through him.

Hannah was so touched by her husband's words that she knew it was the best sermon he'd ever delivered. Yet she didn't want to admit it.

"Our candlelight can only shine so far. According to Second Corinthians 5:7, we walk by faith. We cannot see the future, only guess at it. We need to have faith that we're walking in the right direction and believe that as long as we're following the light, the darkness will not destroy us. We must know what's in the darkness. On the outskirts of our light, we might catch glimpses of something that looks interesting or enjoyable. Sin is often enticing. It's the light of the gospel that saves us from Satan. Mortal trials are naught as contrasted to eternal glory. Gospel light will shine on all saints. Let me end this sermon by reminding you, light can overtake darkness, but darkness cannot overtake light." He paused as if to let the idea plant itself and grow roots.

And in Hannah's heart, it did. Her fear for John and what he was about to do this day thawed ever so slightly.

"You'd have to blow out your candlelight in order for the darkness to consume you. You can also get so far from the light that you disremember what the light once meant to you. Or how it felt to have light in your life. If you need to get your light back, repent, look for the truth again, search out all things that glow with light. Humble yourselves and realize your light depends on Christ's light. He is the light. Christ is the light of the world."

And her salvation. Hannah rubbed at the warmth in her chest.

"He *is* the candlelight guiding your path. He knows what your path should be—the path that will bring you back to God. Don't judge someone else's path, but pay close attention to your own and make sure you're always following your light, for your light is a representation of Christ's light. In John 8:12 we read: 'I am the light of ye world: He that followeth me, doth not walk in darkness, but shall have the light of life.'

"Consider the light your candle provides and believe that eventually your light will be joined with one so bright that all darkness will be dispelled. When that happens, you'll be safe in God's home. Amen."

Amen was repeated, with heavy conviction, from many.

Hannah stared at the unopened prayer book on her lap.

"There's naught I've regretted about serving you all in this parish." John grasped the pulpit's edge, his knuckles white. "Other than choosing my wife"—he looked at Hannah in a way that made her feel he was begging her to understand what he was about to say—"the choice to take orders with the Church of England and be amongst all of you has been the wisest of my decisions. I've been given the light."

He cleared his throat.

Hannah guessed he was trying not to choke up.

"It brings me sadness to leave you now."

"Nay," someone shouted. Others gasped, and voices rose.

John held up his hand to silence them. "Follow your paths of light as I'll be following mine. I'm as of this day renouncing my orders of perpetual curate with the Church of England."

He came down the stairs from the pulpit and took off his robes.

The meeting quickly turned to chaos.

A chorus of surprised, angry, and sad voices—so unlike the calming reverence displayed during the sermon—filled the chapel.

Tears ran from John's eyes, and he furiously swiped at them, turning his back to everyone.

Some left with a scowl of disgust. Others had their own tears.

The wide-shouldered Fenner stepped close and brought John around, embracing him as did others, one by one.

Hannah stood, and Thomas put his arm around her waist. "I don't understand what's happening." His voice quivered. "Why has Father taken off his robes?"

Hannah wrapped her arm around his shoulders and brought him closer. "Your father will be practicing his faith in another way. Our lives will alter greatly, Thomas. We've raised you to be capable and wise. Can you be strong?"

"I believe so, Mother. When my eyes were closed and I imagined my lighted path, Father stepped to my side and a warm feeling came over me. With his light combined with mine, our path was very bright."

PART III
Chapter Twenty-Two

1622
Southwark, England

The breaking of a holy servant. The fracture of an individual. The rupture of a marriage. The sever from family.

To Hannah, John seemed more flawed and human now—a boy abandoned by his father, still trying to find his way. Since renouncing his clerical orders two months before, Hannah only spoke to her husband when needful. The hurt and anger ran so deep she didn't know how she'd ever forgive him.

Almost touching knees, Hannah sat across from Dorothy in the Lothropp's new house—a small terraced home in Southwark.

Jane was close by in the kitchen preparing a meal. Hannah still had no interest in cooking and her family was ever grateful Jane had learned culinary skills from Widow Reynolds.

Dorothy's two children played with Janie and Barbara within inches of Hannah's feet. Dorothy's baby, Tommy, sat on her lap, and Thomas, Johnny, and Jack were upstairs in one of the two bedchambers. Floorboards creaked as they scampered about. There was no back garden to send them to, and she refused to let them play in the street where hundreds of filthy and hungry urchins roamed.

When Dorothy discovered John had moved his family to

Southwark, she'd "come to see her dear friend." When not in Canterbury, she lived across the Thames in "an attractive area of London."

Her words cut Hannah, deeply embarrassing her.

"If there were a place for me, you know I'd be here for your lying-in." Dorothy smiled, her eyes still the color of a country sky, only etched with small wrinkles now. She wore on her lapel a small nosegay of rosemary and lavender to ward off Southwark's stench. "After your churching, I'll send my carriage to bring you to my house for a visit."

Hannah once disliked the overcrowding of ornate furniture at the vicarage, but this place held only enough plain chairs for them to all sit. No settle, chests or desk.

Shame made Hannah want to hide. She placed a hand on her large belly where the child within stretched. "You've always been a kind friend." If she were to stay John's wife, she needed to learn humility. She hadn't realized she was vain until they'd moved to this hovel. "Did you fret over riding in your carriage down our street? Did anyone harass you?"

"You exaggerate." Dorothy huffed a false chuckle. "But if it eases your mind, my coachman carries a pistol."

Light seeped through the gaping crack at the bottom of the front door, one reason Hannah was forever sweeping soot out of the house. She heard noises from the road at all times of the day and night. Men peddling their wares and horses clomping down the lane. No birds chirped. No plants grew.

The walls were so thin, smells from the neighbor's dinner often wafted in—along with their arguments. The husband was a brute who didn't allow his wife to speak unless spoken to first. He'd hollered the previous evening, "A woman is to obey her husband. 'Tis God's own will that it be so."

John more or less had said the same thing to Hannah in Egerton but without the yelling. When her father spoke about obedience at her wedding, she never fathomed that meant following her husband to hell on earth.

"He's not the man I thought I married," Hannah blurted out, wanting to take the sentiment back as soon as she'd said it. Her face warmed.

Dorothy agreed with a nod. "What wife hasn't said those words? Denne prefers London. I love the countryside. He judges people on what kind of education they've gained. I want to know if they're likeable. I sleep 'til noon. He's up before the sun."

"Those differences I could manage." If only that were it. "John fell from the Church of England, for heaven's sake." Hannah's eyes burned. She'd cried every day since they'd left Egerton. "Forgive my impertinence, but my situation is not as simple as him waking at an ungodly hour. He has no consideration for my or the children's needs. He's lowered the children's position and prospects for a good marriage. He follows his desires only."

"Hannah, surely those aren't his objectives."

"The day we arrived in London, we descended the coach in front of an inn next to a brothel." Hannah's voice shook. "Carrying all we owned, we passed drunks, beggars, and thieves." And that didn't count the simple folk loitering along the squalid street in thread-bare clothing looking as though they'd lived in poverty their whole lives.

That day, John had pulled a small handcart with Barbara sitting upon his books. They'd come to the murky dregs of London because they'd no choice. The choice for how she desired to live her life was taken from her. "I'm bound to you with a vow of obedience," she'd told John when he made the plans to move to London. "But know that I go in sorrow. You tear me from my family to a place of whoredoms where my children may live next to brothels." John said he'd not subject them to brothels or taverns or distasteful establishments of any kind. He was wrong. She could no longer trust him. She shuddered at the thought of their future.

Dorothy bit her lip. "What of your family? Can they not help?"

It hurt to breathe, and Hannah closed her eyes. "I wrote to them before we left, explaining only that John had renounced his orders. I didn't provide an explanation." The guilt and regret still held on. "I told them that I'd send notice of where to write to us when I knew myself. I am a coward. I know. But if I confessed to Father in person, I couldn't bear his disappointment. 'Twas also possible I might've begged him to let me and the children live with him."

Dorothy frowned. "Maybe it's not as bad as it seems?"

Hannah had said too much and Dorothy couldn't understand. Maybe if she knew her daily routine. "I try to remain in the house, but once a sennight I go to the drying green and lay out our washed clothing to dry in the daylight." She tucked her hands into the folds of her skirt, hiding the raw skin she'd gotten from scrubbing. "I've never before witnessed so many bare-legged women in one place. Some with nursing babies clinging to them.

That will be my situation, soon enough."

Dorothy leaned in close and whispered, "Denne says the number of bastards rises with the number of ale-houses in Southwark." She moved back. "Since John has notions of separating from the Church, does he desire to go to America or Holland where the others have gone?"

"He's talked of it." 'Twould be the breaking of them for sure because she wouldn't allow the children on those death-traps sailing across the ocean. "But he's decided he's to serve the people of England."

"What will you do if he's caught in a secret conventicle?" Dorothy kept her voice low and tucked her child closer, as if trying to keep him safe from the evil, schismatic meetings.

"I don't know," Hannah whispered back. "I don't know when he goes to the Separatist meetings. I hardly see him anymore—he works many hours in London." Hannah's fists balled. "He's clerking for a beaver hat tradesman who is also Robert Linnell's employer. To make extra money, he's also teaching Latin to his employer's young boys. He works sunrise to sunset then there's the long walk home." She felt abandoned—a single mother. He should have been choosing her and their family. She couldn't imagine ever again finding unification with him.

Dorothy leaned forward and took her hand. "I'll not withdraw my friendship under any circumstance."

Hannah savored the genuine warmth flowing from Dorothy. She missed Penninah and her other siblings. She missed her father's lightheartedness and her mother's nurturing. She missed the visits to those in her parish.

Barbara leaned in, her long dark hair catching Hannah's attention. "Elizabeth said she has two poppets at home and that I may play with one when we come visit. May I, Mama? When will we go?" She danced on her toes in anticipation.

Elizabeth was Dorothy's four-year-old. Whenever the families met together, the two girls were inseparable. They were inordinately genteel, liking all things feminine.

Dorothy gave a weak simper. "May Barbara come stay with us for a time? Elizabeth is often lonesome for a friend."

The two girls jumped up and down, Elizabeth's copper ringlets bouncing, her eyes as green as her mother's.

"May I, Mama? May I?" Barbara begged.

"Aye, you may if you promise to be affable for your hosts."

Jane came in. "I've prepared soup if you'd like to come into the kitchen."

"Thank you, Jane. I don't know how we'd manage without you." Hannah kissed the girl's cheek as she passed into the kitchen and sat at the small wooden table that John had bought from the previous tenants.

Hannah doubted Dorothy had ever eaten at such a rickety piece of furniture. The humiliation of it all was enough to make Hannah long to run and hide in her bedchamber like a child.

After dinner, they returned to the front room and discussed what was happening with Dorothy's family.

The front door rattled with a knock, and Janie startled at the suddenness of it.

Jane opened the door. "May I . . . Robert!"

Hannah stood to get a better peek. She inhaled sharply. Robert Lothropp!

"Will you come in?" Jane half-curtsied to her half-brother and stepped aside, shooting a look of panic to Hannah.

"I prefer not. I've come to take you home," he said in a hard voice.

Hannah stumbled.

Dorothy jumped up to steady her. She set her baby on the floor.

It'd been almost twelve years since Hannah had seen Robert at Mary's wedding. He'd greyed, his face thicker and hard. Hannah imagined he probably looked much like John's father had.

She grasped her skirts with trembling hands, all sound diminishing around her. 'Twas as if time slowed. "Robert, how good it is to see you," she lied in an unsteady voice. "If you don't wish to come in, will you come back when John's at home? I'm sure he'd enjoy a visit," she said as pleasantly as she could. Her mind scrambled for a place to hide Jane while he was gone. There was no way she was going to let him pluck Jane away. She'd already lost Penninah. She'd not lose Jane too.

"I've no desire to see the apostate, and I no longer call him brother." He took Jane by the arm. "Come with me. No need to bring your clothes. I'll buy you more."

Jane looked back, her eyes wide in fear.

"Don't take Jane!" Janie screeched. Wrapping her arms around Jane's waist, she pulled. "She belongs to us."

"Can you not control your child?" Robert roared. "Why does she speak so loudly out of turn?"

Robert's insult and the panic in Janie's young voice spurred in Hannah a protectiveness that overwhelmed her with strength. "Robert, you cannot snatch Jane from us." She stepped closer to him, standing taller. "As Janie said, she's one of us now. She belongs here."

Not slackening his grasp, Robert dragged a crying Jane outside. "Let me go!" she wailed.

Hannah and the children jostled their way out, Dorothy and her young ones following. Hannah wished Thomas would come down. He was only eleven but maybe somehow, he could help?

"Please, Robert. She's our family." Hannah clasped her hands as if praying to him.

Barbara began to wail too. Dorothy's little Elizabeth clung to her mother.

"I'll not allow Jane to live in a home of heretics. Thom is with me in this. We want what's best for her, which is *not* John."

"Not" vibrated loudly in Hannah's ears.

"Heretics, are they?" A woman said from behind. "I coulda guessed. Keepin' to they'selves in their fancy clothes. Too good to be mixin' with the likes of us." With hands on her hips, Hannah's neighbor glared, her stringy hair framing her thin face.

Others on the road stopped to watch the spectacle of shame.

"If you don't want Jane here, let her live with me." Dorothy spoke above the bawling girls. "We're loyal Anglicans who can take her with us to our London church each Sunday."

Dorothy's coachman bounded down from his carriage seat and with hand in jerkin, headed toward Robert. Would he pull his pistol?

Hannah's heart raced. Just as she was about to scream, "nay," Dorothy held up her palm to halt him. He planted himself close to Robert, not removing his hand.

Robert scowled at him. "No need for you to get involved in a family matter."

"Robert, please." Hannah was ready to beg on her knees. "Don't take Jane from us. We love her so and—"

"I'll not change my mind in this matter," he boomed. "I'm the patriarch of this family and know what's best." He pulled Jane toward a waiting carriage.

"Nay!" Jane wailed, pulling and jerking wildly, dust flying up around her.

Dorothy drew back Janie from running after them, and wrapped her other arm around Barbara, who sobbed uncontrollably.

"Shall I stop him, Mistress?" the coachman implored Dorothy.

"Nay," said Dorothy, her shoulders sagging in a defeat Hannah felt all the way through her body.

Following Robert, Hannah kept trying to convince him of the mistake he was making. "This isn't right. How could you snatch her from us?"

Robert wrenched Jane so hard, Hannah feared he'd snap her arm.

Jane whimpered.

"Sister Jane!" Hannah called out as Robert shoved Jane into his carriage. "Know that we'll not recover from this tear in our hearts." Her heart literally felt as if it were ripping.

The horses lurched with a crack of the whip, and Hannah jumped back.

The carriage quickly rode away, and Hannah rushed back to Dorothy and fell against her, weeping.

"That's what you get when you're a friend with Satan, witch," a woman called from an above window.

Their upstairs window flew open with a bang. "My mother is Godfearing," Thomas thundered.

Dorothy coaxed them all back into the house.

Two days later, the landlord came to their door and told Hannah they needed to move out immediately. "I'll not 'ave an antichrist in any of my 'omes," he'd said with a cynical sneer.

And the division between John and Hannah grew wider.

Chapter Twenty-Three

Standing at his upstairs window, John could barely make out the tallest buildings in London to the north. After his family was evicted from their home, he'd had no choice but to move them quickly. This house, owned by a fellow Independent Separatist, would at least be more secure than the last. It certainly wasn't quieter. Drunken shouts came from the stadium constantly, even on the Sabbath. The crowds roared as loud as the bears, and dogs barked ceaselessly, all displeasures of living near a bull and bear-baiting arena. But at least it was more convenient to London Bridge and closer to his work in London. Disappointingly, it was still within Southwark's cheap but corrupt bounds.

He turned to Hannah, who'd given birth to a baby boy the day before. They'd named him Samuel after Hannah's venturesome and strong-willed brother. She said it might help her feel closer to her brother, and their son would certainly need those traits to get by in the life they now led.

"If the baby had been a girl, I'd have named her Penninah," Hannah told him in tears yesterday, missing her family. Would they have any more children? He couldn't imagine her agreeing to his affections. She hadn't embraced him in months and tried to not be close enough to touch.

Jane's absence had also darkened the cloud hovering in their home. He missed his sister. The hurt of his family's rejection was enormous. He and Hannah were alone in their new life. He glanced at her again. Or mayhap *he* was alone.

"Who will baptize him?" Reclining in bed, his wife could

barely keep her eyes open, weaker than after her other births.

John feared she was going to cry again. When had she last smiled? Her lightheartedness had disappeared completely. He missed her singing as she went about her chores. It couldn't be good for the new child to have such a melancholy mother. "I'll speak to the vicar of Saint Saviour's and arrange for his baptism."

John wasn't sure how he now felt about baptizing infants. He'd been studying the Bible, trying to come to a conclusion. Could it be that people should be old enough to personally confess faith? He'd not contradict Hannah, howbeit. He didn't need to give another reason for her to despise him.

"I wish we had the money to travel to Eastwell to have my father baptize him as he did Thomas." She scooted deeper into the feather mattress John had spent a week's wages on, hoping the gift would soften her toward him. It hadn't. She rolled away. "I'm tired and will rest now."

Staring at his newborn son sleeping peacefully beside her, John looked forward to finding out what this one would be like and marveled again at how he could love someone he'd just met.

He checked Hannah's bedwarmer and stirred the coals in the grate, adding a chunk, then pulled the thin curtains over the oily window and left the room. The only other place to go was the one other bedchamber the children shared or downstairs in a room that served as parlor, dining room, and kitchen. At least this house had a backyard patch of dirt with a back-house where one could have privacy. The yard had no space for a garden, howbeit, or for children to play.

What had he done to his family? He spent equal parts hating himself and being eager for what the future might bring. The future for him, that was. Hannah insisted the children attend church with her. He'd gone occasionally, not wishing to draw attention from authorities to his illegal religious activities. But unlike Henry Jacob, he didn't think he wanted to be a Semi-separatist and attend both churches graciously. He was done with the Church of England. At the Independent meetings, they covenanted together to tend to one another's needs. They tendered protection and trust.

In the front room, the children gathered around Johnny as he showed them drawings in one of John's books, outlining the laws of planetary motion. Almost six, his son had picked up on his letters with fervor and was highly intelligent, always searching for something new to learn. Unlike Thomas, he'd no interest in religious matters and often complained about going to church or performing his catechisms. John hoped that would amend with age.

"Father, how is Mother?" Janie came to where he sat and leaned against him. "Would she like me to bring her soup?"

"She's sleeping. Thank you for your concern. We're all blessed for your efforts at cooking." He patted her arm. "Will you care for her while I'm at work tomorrow?"

She nodded and joined her siblings lounging on the floor. She'd shown notable weight loss since Jane was taken. Now that he looked at his children more closely, he realized they were all thinner. He didn't think it was only because of the lack of Jane's cooking. They each took their turn at being sick with some new illness never experienced in Egerton. Did it have to do with the soot-filled skies or the rats that scurried in the attic?

Johnny looked up. "Remember your sermon when you talked about the light of the sun? Where does the light of the stars come from?"

Is that all the boy had gotten out of the sermon—an astronomy lesson? John valued education and worried how his boys were going to get it in Southwark. Thomas was almost old enough for an apprenticeship—a skill instead of studies. The thought gnawed at John's belly. He needed to find time to tutor them. Hannah tried, but without Jane, she had so many other responsibilities.

Starlight. How could he teach Johnny a lesson? The memory of the comet that streaked across the sky in the early morning hours in Egerton came to John. He'd wondered then if it was a sign of change. He'd felt awe at God's capabilities. "The stars are God's manifestation of His power. The lesser lights rule the night. They're the same thing as the sun, only farther away. If one doesn't have faith, they need just observe the sky to see God's influence sweeping across the world. He hasn't left us nor will He ever."

Someone rapped at the door.

All the children's heads turned toward the sound.

John opened the door to a cold wind and Henry Jacob with two unknown men. Relieved Hannah was asleep upstairs, he shook Jacob's hand and invited them in.

"Excuse us for visiting on the Sabbath," Jacob said. "May I introduce John Bellamy and Henry Dod."

John took their hats and coats then introduced his children who stood and bowed or curtsied. "Take your book and go upstairs," he told them. He'd *rather* they listen to Henry Jacob for he greatly admired his goodness. Likeminded, he and Jacob had become close friends. But 'twould be a mistake for the children to know their father was breaking the law.

After the children left, the men sat around the table, the abject chairs squeaking under their weight.

Jacob motioned toward the young man with black hair and easy smile. "Mister Bellamy is a publisher and bookseller." He motioned to the dispassionate young man with sandy hair and pockmarked face. "And Mister Dod has recently come from university. He's found fellowship with our congregation. His leadership abilities are heartening."

Dod observed John coolly.

John recognized Bellamy from various meetings. Dod he did not.

"Bellamy has connections with our Leiden congregation and Mayflower passengers. 'Twas he that Robert Cushman came to when he arrived back from Plymouth. He brought with him a document that detailed the written journal of Edward Winslow and William Bradford. It described the exploration of the new colony." Jacob motioned to him with a wide grin. "He printed and quickly disseminated the booklet, *Mourt's Relation,* as widely as possible."

"I'm familiar with the document." The numerous deaths of the colonists were alarming, and John had been fascinated by the accounts of the relations with the Indians.

"We believe it's this document that caused King James to reissue the strict printing injunctions of Queen Elizabeth." Jacob's mouth hardened. "Publishers are now threatened with severe punishments and imprisonment if they don't conform. Sadly, Bellamy's presses were confiscated. We're not sure who informed against him but be wary of strangers asking questions."

"As always." John agreed. He doubted this was why Jacob had come. This was something he could have told him at their next meeting. John stood. "May I offer some warm ale?"

John stepped away, his spine tingling with the intense feeling in the room.

Bellamy and Dod were curiously quiet.

He gave them drinks and sat again.

Jacob cleared his throat. "John." He met his gaze. "As you know, I've started a community in Virginia. What you may not know is that I've had a few narrow escapes with the King's men here in England almost discovering conventicles I led. I often suspect I'm being followed."

Could someone have followed him to John's home? Would Jacob place him in such danger?

"After much prayer and begging from my wife," Jacob chuckled, "I've decided to return to the Colonies with my family."

John wanted to cry out nay but forced himself to hear the rest. He'd miss his friend greatly. He was more an example of peace than any clergy John had known.

"Since its birth eight years ago, there's never been another leader of our London group but me. Yet, 'tis time for change." He placed his hand on John's shoulder. "As you know, the authority resides in our congregation to choose by common consent a new pastor. It's you, dear friend, who we've elected to lead us."

The past years of spiritual struggle suddenly made sense to John. They'd brought him here. God hadn't let him down. He was to be a leader to guide others with what he knew to be truth—what was in his heart—as the spiritual promptings had told him he'd do. But this was something larger than himself. Overwhelmed with responsibility, he said, "I've not been here long. How could others know me well enough to trust my guidance?"

"As we've bound ourselves together with an agreement with God, others have noticed your integrity and passion for such a covenant. Those from your old parish have spread the word about your sermonizing. Is it that you don't recognize your own testimony strengthening others? You need not be a perpetual curate to share the Lord's goodness and teachings."

Other than the Book of Sports, John had never taught anything he didn't feel was God's truth. Was this what Jacob referred to? "I speak from the heart because of my love of God." Could it be that a congregation was *asking* for him, and he not for them? John's face warmed. In the past his congregation had no choice in the matter of who would be their clergy.

His mind suddenly fell to Hannah. How could he do this without her support? "Brothers, let me speak with my wife. She attends the Church of England, and I've hurt her concerning past events. I cannot place a larger wedge between us. She sleeps above, having just delivered a child."

Dod glowered. "Marriage is a male hierarchy constituted by God. Women are the weaker sex, and you must tell her you plan to lead us."

John would have bellowed if he weren't worried about waking Hannah. He suddenly missed his father-in-law. He needed to do what he could to heal that wound. If only he'd enough money to take Hannah to see her father—to have her father bless the baby, as she wished.

"You've much to learn, son," Jacob said to Dod without as much mirth as John. "My own wife is guiding me to America." He turned back to John. "Mister Dod is here because I feel he's a passionate leader who can stand by your side or fill in where you cannot. Someday, I hope he'll lead his own congregation."

John worried he'd have no support from Dod. When someone tried to appear holy, it sometimes became a question of faith.

But then Dod's face softened for the first time.

"I wanted you to meet Mister Bellamy because he's the channel to our congregation in America," Jacob said. "The letters from them are first delivered to him. He hears of deaths before the deceaseds' families are told. He tells me, and I gently break the news to them. Robert Cushman has brought the missives to him in the past but it may be someone different each time."

"I see," John glanced toward Bellamy.

"Your responsibilities will be quite different than with the Anglican church. You will guide and teach as before, but you'll be no kind of judge of the people. There will be no tithes collected and no payment made for your services."

John nodded. "As I said, I'll speak with my wife. I'd rather wait until she's recovered from childbirth. Mayhap after her churching?"

"There's plenty of time. I'm planning to leave in the summer if we can make arrangements by then. I wanted to give you forewarning. Take the time you need to work things out with your dear Hannah."

Although Jacob had never met Hannah, he was always kind about her rejection of his church.

By the time the baby was two months old, Hannah hadn't shaken her loneliness and anguish. John was no longer her companion, and Jane was gone. She'd decided to visit Saint Saviour's this morning to search for answers. She needed reverent time to pray and ruminate.

But the day didn't go as planned. Sam fussed, wanting to be held, and refused to suckle at his usual times, causing him to sleep later. By late afternoon, Hannah was exhausted but determined to pray alone in the church.

She approached Thomas playing chess with Janie, Johnny watching on. "Thomas, I'm going out. Keep an ear for Sam. I don't expect him to wake, but he's acting unusual today."

"Aye, Mother." Thomas didn't glance up from his game.

"Where you going, Mama?" Barbara asked from a chair where she practiced her stitches.

"To the church. I won't be long but I best be on my way so I can return before dark."

Outside, the sooty February sky appeared greyer than usual. Chilly air woke her from her lethargy. It had been a mild winter with little snow.

As she walked, she kept a sharp eye to her surroundings. Many people were on the streets, going about their business, but just as many seemed to be looking for a pocket to pinch. They'd get naught from her—she had no coin. Yet she feared others would misconstrue her clothing with the finely embroidered apron. How many years would her gowns last before they were threadbare?

The smell of baking pies reminded her of Jane, the loss almost as great as when Hannah had lost Anne. She tried to imagine Jane happy—mayhap married to someone who would cherish her as they had.

She pulled her shawl tighter and hurried along, coming to a street of haberdashers, apothecaries, artisans, and merchants—with less vagrants and more men in wigs. As she neared the river, she could hear the gulls calling and customers hailing watermen.

She'd no friends in Southwark. Her pride kept her from visiting Dorothy often. Hannah refused to associate with John's new friends. Sometimes she wanted to see Robert Linnell again but she'd not allow a Separatist into her home.

She lived in fear that her husband would be caught at a conventicle and thrown into prison. What would they do? They'd go home to her family. Isn't that what she wanted? She'd finally written to tell them where she lived and share the news of Samuel's birth. Father's return letter cautioned patience and Penninah's was of great cheer to her, but made her all the more homesick. She longed for Penninah's laughter and Father's comforting arms.

Inside Saint Saviour's, the strong scent of candle wax gave her a sense of coming home. Its massive stonewalls kept the inside as cold as outside. As she strolled the long, vaulted nave, her footfalls echoed.

She felt but a tiny thing coming to God in this grand building in her insignificant form. The church building in all its glory was the only thing she liked about Southwark. She sat in a pew and marveled at the high-alter screen statues, depicting various saints and bishops. 'Twas the most papist-looking relic she'd seen in an Anglican church, but she was glad no one had destroyed its beauty.

A few others huddled in pews, quiet in thoughts and prayers.

Pulling her prayer book from her pocket, she read at the beginning about the uniformity of common prayer and that no one was to alter the prayers. John did that, adding things as he saw fit depending on the situation.

She closed her eyes, to lament to God about her miserable situation. Loneliness and confusion and anger had kept her from her husband's tender embraces.

They'd argued the night before, and John told her she'd a problem admitting when she was wrong. It had infuriated her because she wasn't wrong and wouldn't admit to such. Life was unanswerable for men. They could do what they wanted when they wanted. Women had to answer to them and seldom won an argument. 'Twas the lot of a female. Hannah smacked her fist on her leg.

The woman closest turned and gave her a sharp glare.

Chastised, she looked down. She'd chosen to obey John when they married. On their wedding day, Father's admonition to obey was almost like a threat. He told the story of Abraham and Sarah. Abraham was commanded by God to move to Canaan. Had Sarah gone willingly? Had she believed Abraham had the Spirit of God with him? Had she longed to stay behind where her family lived? The scriptures didn't say.

Hannah had no role other than to be obedient to her husband and care for their house and children. In her heart, she desired to lighten John's load by taking some of it on like she had in Egerton. But she could not now. She would not.

Part of her wanted him to suffer with all the hours he had to spend clerking, tutoring, and worshiping with heretics. "Hannah" she chided herself softly. "You don't really mean that." But maybe she did. She didn't like the power he used over her. She tried to respect the fact that John had to follow his conscience, but he was surely misguided. Satan was doing his work on John.

"I grant that I may be inferior physically to a man, but I'm not inferior intellectually or spiritually," she whispered to God. "Am I?"

During their argument John had tried to convince her that he wasn't forsaking their marriage. To her this meant he wasn't seeing things as they were—bringing them to a place no one desired to be. The ache of the memory and the feeling of loss sent so much pain, she hugged her waist and slumped over.

As she prayed and poured out her heart to God, she realized how ungrateful she was being.

"May I comfort your soul this day?" a voice said.

Hannah sat up and opened her eyes to Reverend Osbourne's white-grey hair and gentle hazel eyes. He'd been kind to her, but his sermons lacked passion. 'Twas hard to compare any preacher against John. Reverend Osbourne had baptized Samuel and then performed her churching. That too was so different than John's. Same words. Different affections.

"Reverend." She stood and curtsied.

"Please be seated." He sat in the pew in front of her and turned. "You were in prayer so long I wondered if you'd fallen to sleep." His eyes twinkled much like her father's. "How's the babe?"

'Twas kind of him to have remembered her for he had hundreds in his congregation. "He's fussy today." She answered truthfully.

"Were you praying for him?"

"Nay, I expect it's naught serious." She wished she could tell him her real problems. She needed someone to talk to. "I was praying for my pitiful self, I'm embarrassed to say." Her face warmed.

"Are you unhappy in marriage? I've noticed your husband is seldom here." His brow crinkled in an understanding, fatherly way.

Hannah needed to be careful with her words. No one knew them here. She couldn't let anyone know John had fallen from the Church and was a Separatist. And if the vicar was noticing his lack of attendance, then she needed to direct him away from talk of John. "He's seldom home. He works long hours in London." She searched for what to say without saying too much. Yet she wanted counsel from the vicar.

"He's an affectionate husband then?"

"Aye," Hannah said, grateful to tell the truth and a little surprised that the tides had turned since they'd first married. 'Twas she who held back affections now.

"Is there something you'd like to talk about?"

She started her dialogue slowly, trying not to slip-up about her unhappiness with John. "I've forgotten who I am," she said simply. "God talked to me twice when I was a young woman." Before she married but naught since. Had she fallen out of favor? Had she married the wrong man?

"You're a daughter of God and always will be. Do you remember what He said to you, or do you need to be reminded?"

"I remember." How could she forget. He told her she was His handmaiden—such strong words. She was awarded spiritual confirmation years later that her motherhood was important to Him. Why had she forgotten this?

"If you want to find yourself, do the Lord's work. Help the hungry, lame, and blind as He did. Lift up those who have also forgotten who they are."

"But is not the growth of poverty around us associated with moral decadence? I cannot let my children outside for fear the urchins will teach them falsehoods or tear the clothes from their bodies." She'd seen that happen on her street.

"Those urchins are my flock."

The blood drained from her head. The shame of her words made her cower. She'd considered herself too good for her neighbors. They criticized her for it, and now she realized they were right.

"We need to concern ourselves with caring for those who cannot care for themselves," he said tenderly.

Those were Hannah's most important principles of Christian faith. She truly had forgotten who she was. She'd visited the poor and needy her whole life, first with Father and then with John. Why had she looked at those in her new neighborhood differently? Her opinion changed of Reverend Osbourne. He'd the heart of a saint, a wise man. She couldn't explain her past to him however. "I have no money or extra food to give. How can I help?"

"There are times during my visits when a woman would rather talk to another woman. May I call on you when that occurs?"

Her broken heart needed opportunities to love. "Please do, I'd like that very much."

"I often need help distributing food when it's donated."

"I'd be pleased to help with that also."

He hesitated. "May I offer some advice?"

She nodded.

"Every one of us are lacking in some way. Find in your heart the spirit of contentment by being grateful for what you do have." He smiled genially. "Grateful people are sociable people."

As she left the church, her mind swam with all Reverend

Osbourne had said. She wished she'd money or food to dispense now when she saw the poor huddling in alleyways or holding a hand out for coin. Why had it taken her so long to come back to who she used to be? Her own vain pride had blinded her to others.

Whether John didn't or couldn't carry the Spirit of God, the Lord expected the same of her. Her lack of being able to forgive John was harming her more than him. He seemed the man he'd always been. Quieter, maybe, but that was probably her fault. 'Twas her perception of him that had altered.

The qualities she loved about him hadn't changed. He was a visionary, which had gotten them into this mess. But he was also dedicated, compassionate, and a leader. All the traits she loved were also the one's that got him into trouble.

Deep into her thoughts, she wasn't watching where she stepped and tripped over something. "Oh!"

A hollow-faced man looked up at her, his eyes combing her face and body.

She shivered, as if she were suddenly undressed. "Pardon me." She marched on at a quicker pace, watching carefully where she was going. 'Twas later than she realized, the sun ready to set. She pulled her shawl tight and walked faster.

Footsteps seemed to follow.

She glanced back but saw no one in pursuit, only a few men entering their homes after a long day's work, and an empty street.

A minute later, something snapped, and she spun again. 'Twas dark now and the shadows were where evil hid. A tight knot in her stomach wouldn't release. Her heart raced. She all but ran toward home, scarcely daring to peer back again.

Suddenly the man she'd tripped over stood before her. His eyes deranged in his sun-browned face. He brandished a dagger and a sneer that tightened a band of fear around her chest.

Hannah tried to command her legs to move. To run. But that band cinched so hard, when she opened her mouth to scream, no sound came out. How could this be happening? She'd children to care for. *Dear Lord, don't let me die.*

The man wrapped his arm around her, holding the cold blade to her throat with the other hand. Crushing her against his chest, he pressed his hardness against her.

His sour odor made her stomach convulse. She felt faint, her head swimming in disbelief. "Nay," she choked.

Moving his stinking face to her neck, he slobbered a wet, cold kiss.

Suddenly, the hand holding the knife jerked away, the dagger clattering against a house. He went down, and Hannah fell with him. Her head thumped against the road, her teeth snapping together. The world went black.

When she came to, two men were on the ground throwing fists. One of them was John.

"Hannah run!" he yelled.

She'd not leave him. She ran for the dagger and then back to the men, holding it in front of her. "I found the dagger."

Her assailant scrambled out from under John and limped quickly down the road.

John rushed to Hannah and took her in his arms, his breathing rapid. "Are you unharmed?"

She dropped the dagger, sagging against him. "My head." She rubbed the spot that was sore. She'd forgotten how secure she felt in John's embrace. Aching head forgotten, she pulled him closer, kissing his face and mouth.

He stiffened but then met her kisses with passion.

'Twas as if she'd been in a desert and suddenly found water. Life-giving sustenance. She broke the kiss. "Could you not have left a few moments earlier from work?" The absurdity of her comment caused a giggle to bubble forth, and she pushed her face into John's body to restrain another. She felt his chest trying to control his own quiet laughter. How good it felt to be in his arms.

"If you're where you need to be, the Lord will create miracles in your life," John said.

She didn't want to imagine herself as a woman of little faith, but she also wasn't sure John still carried the Spirit of God with him to teach her about miracles.

Chapter Twenty-Four

Since King James's son Charles had come of age, beaver hats were his passion and those with means wanted the prestige of the same stylish attire.

Each pelt went through thirty steps to make it usable before it was sold to hatters. Although not part of John's responsibilities, he felt those thirty steps in each of his long, tedious workdays. Because of the hat's newfound popularity, John spent hours going over the numbers of pelts imported from the Colonies, making sure those numbers balanced to the final product.

He worked late and hurried through the London streets, trying to make it to the Independent meeting before it started. Meeting in various locations with different groups helped escape detection. As he turned onto Edgeware Road, he was surprised to see a large crowd.

A hanging was about to ensue—unusual for this time of day. Calls of "Sorceress," and "Agent of the Devil," alerted John to the fact that a witch was being executed. Many Puritans dressed in dark clothing and dire expressions stood about, probably the accusers of the woman, for they went often on witch hunts.

Fewer witches had been executed as of late however, the fervor waning from convicting the Catholics and witches and moving toward Separatists and those who were meeting in secret to practice their own religious beliefs.

Like John.

Who the Church feared and hunted often changed. The truth, howbeit, did not. The absolute truth of a loving God, His son

The Pulse of His Soul

who died for all, and the adversary, Satan, who tied people in knots of fear and pride, forever stayed the same. But God could not be mocked.

John shouldered through the periphery of the throng, only to notice a red-coated king's guard on the outskirts watching him closely, hand tight on his poleax. Then another turned John's way and twisted to discuss something with the first.

The hairs on John's neck raised. Moving away from them, he weaved through the crowd.

Under law, if he appeared upset or angry over the hanging of a witch and tried to leave, he could be branded with the same crime. Or if he showed fear about her being accused of witchcraft, then they could assume him to be guilty too. None of it made logical sense. But when it came to witchcraft, fear generated more fear and endless accusations. John wanted no part of it. He stopped before he got too close to the gallows.

The woman who stood accused was brought forward, hardly able to walk. Her skin was bright red, mayhap burned, and her hands swollen, probably from tortures such as thumb screws and the rack. She looked to the crowd as if truly not seeing them, her head wobbling about.

John twisted away, his chest constricting.

The women next to him were in deep conversation about the crimes of the convicted. "She wouldn't let her husband do his duty upon her," said a stout woman in a crooked hat.

"She has no need for a husband when she flies through the air to copulate with the Devil," said her neighbor.

Witchcraft was high treason against the king and confessions were usually extracted by torture conducted by the authority of the Church. The whole affair disgusted John, and he looked at people's hats instead of at the gallows. He'd have no part of celebrating such evil deceit. He glanced back at the guards, and still the one watched him closely. Had someone provided his description as an enemy to the king? Mayhap he shouldn't go to the meeting tonight.

A hush, then a gasp from the crowd alerted John to the hanging of the accused witch.

Shouts of delight chorused across the onlookers. The woman next to him called, "She rides with the Devil no more." The crowd bellowed uproariously, if not falsely, and then began to disperse. 'Twas time to be getting home for supper.

John removed his hat and ducked into the largest group of

people moving toward his destination. He looked for the sharp-eyed guard and saw him no more. Acting casually, he stayed near as many people as possible as the throng thinned. Soon he was alone, striding toward the meeting. He put on his hat and glanced casually about but saw no one. As much as he enjoyed meeting with the Independents, he hated this game of deceit.

He hadn't been to a meeting in a sennight and needed to find out Henry Jacob's state of health. Jacob hadn't yet sailed to America. He'd contracted an illness that lingered. His travel had been suspended until the next summer when it was warm again. Because of the change in plans, John never told Hannah that he'd been elected to serve as pastor.

Just as Jacob had brought Bellamy and Dod to him, Jacob also introduced John to the most influential people of the Independent faith. They were likely the ones to keep the organization from the king's attention.

From a distance, a fellow Independent, Marke Luker, strode his way, his manner stiff and covert. He walked past the house where the meeting was to be held and past John without stopping, but whispered, "Don't go."

The meeting place had been detected by the authorities. He kept walking indifferently and took the first street toward the bridge. Darkness fell. He passed an inn. The door opened to the aroma of roasting meat and loud laughter. A drunk and noisy patron tumbled into the street and the door closed.

When he arrived home, the warmth of the room greeted him. He removed his coat and hat.

Hannah glanced his way with a look of relief and a slow smile, which was the same every evening. "Janie and I have made your favorite tonight, stew of mutton."

'Twas a jest between them because the first stew she'd made for him had been almost inedible. It had improved only marginally.

The children greeted him warmly. The boys stood and bowed, and Janie and Barbara hugged him tenderly. Sam sat on the floor, gumming an apple, drool on his hands and on the fruit.

When John took Hannah in his arms, the children looked away with silly grins on their faces. She was with child again, and her belly nudged into his.

'Twas safer to not ever tell her where he'd been. And she never quizzed. He hated keeping secrets, but she was protected by not knowing the truth.

She kissed his neck. As shabby as the home was, 'twas the best place on earth because this is where his family resided. The peace that abided within was as holy as any cathedral.

To John's joy, Hannah gave birth to a son, Joseph, on a spring day in 1624.

The babe was healthy and she not as weary as the last childbirth. "I'm determined to have Father baptize him," she told John a sennight later. "Can we find the funds to travel home?" With her eyes, she begged him to oblige.

Home. He feared she'd never consider their humble dwelling as home.

"I'd set money aside in hopes of finding an apprenticeship for Thomas. I suppose we can use that since he still fights me on the idea."

"Oh, John! Thank you." The grin he received was worth whatever money he'd spend getting to and from Eastwell.

John didn't know how to tell Hannah that Thomas had confided his desire to be a minister. She'd encourage him to serve the Church of England, and 'twould fracture John's heart to see him do so. He and Hannah had come to a compromise, agreeing that the children would attend only the Church of England now. At sixteen, they'd be allowed to choose which church they wanted to attend. John didn't know how he could win Thomas over without taking him to the Independent meetings. But on the other hand, he didn't want to place his son in danger by attending those secret meetings. He needed to talk to Hannah about it soon, and he dreaded the conversation.

A sennight later, on an April day where they could actually see the blue sky, they loaded a rented wagon for the two-and-a-half-day trip.

Dod jogged up to John's side.

He heaved in the last trunk and then took in Dod's saddened face. "What is it?"

It took Dod a moment to catch his breath. "Where are you going? You can't leave now! Henry Jacob has died."

John's heart stilled. A lump in the back of his throat made it difficult to swallow. He turned from Dod, trying to regain his composure.

Hannah stepped out with a basket of food. When John didn't introduce her, she looked at Dod skeptically. Placing her hand on

John's shoulder, she asked, "What is it? Has this man brought bad news?"

John straightened and tried to find his voice. "The pastor of the Independents has died." He still hadn't told her about the congregation wanting John to be their next leader.

Hannah frowned and looked from him to Dod and back again. "God be with his family," she said tenderly.

He loved her more for it, for she'd once told him she didn't want to know about those men who took John from the Church. She'd softened since helping Reverend Osbourne with the parish needs. Her heart went out to those who suffered.

Dod stepped closer. "The brothers are asking for you to come and show the congregation that the organization will remain strong without Brother Jacob, and that you'll be their new pastor as planned."

Hannah gasped. "He's what?" She turned on John with fury in her eyes.

He tried to embrace her. "I'll explain."

"Let me be." She smashed the basket into his stomach, then stomped into the house.

John turned on Dod. In a fierce whisper, he said, "Can you not mind your youthful tongue? Not only could neighbors hear, if they'd a mind, but Mistress Lothropp need not know of the organization's polity either." He wished only to go to his chamber and mourn the loss of a dear friend. "Our organization will survive without me coming forward immediately. Its strength depends upon God's word, which is to love thy neighbor. Go and tell them I'll mourn with them in a fortnight but to remember their covenant of succoring one another."

Dod clamped his gaping mouth and nodded once, then trotted down the road from which he'd come.

After he left, John wished he'd warned Dod about attending Jacob's funeral. There'd be henchmen watching those who came to mourn. If he sent Dod a missive, it could implicate them both if intercepted.

He sighed and placed the basket in the wagon and went inside.

Hannah sat in their bedchamber weeping.

He knelt in front of her and pulled her hands from her face. "I've sent him away. We'll all be going to Eastwell."

She wouldn't look at him. "Why have you not told me about being their pastor? How can we trust each other with these secrets between us?" She looked in his eyes, hers still flowing with tears.

"I don't keep secrets from you."

"It's for your safety that I don't tell you what goes on with the Independents. If you were ever questioned, I'd want you innocent of knowledge so you couldn't be held accountable for my actions." He wiped her cheeks. "But 'twas wrong of me to not discuss the leadership position for it will require more of my time."

She blew out a noisy breath. "We seldom see you now. Are you saying you'll be gone more often?"

"I believe so, aye. If we could discuss my testimony of this God-blessed organization, things would be different. You'd know for yourself that I'm only in the service of my God." He kissed her wet cheek. "I'll try and be mindful of your needs."

"Again, the choice is not mine, but yours. I'm forever the obedient wife." Her tone held much regret.

Would they never find a truce? "I pray every day you'll be blessed for your service to me and our children. No man has ever had a better wife."

She snorted. "How can you say that when we're at such odds over what lies deepest in our hearts?"

"Because I sincerely believe every man should be able to choose his own path to follow God."

She leaned forward and cried on John's shoulder. "But I want our paths to be the same."

So did he.

"I'd not be able to endure this if I didn't love you, John Lothropp."

"I'm forever grateful for that love. I'm not worthy of it." He hoped she never realized how much more endangered his life had just become. Attending the meetings was one thing, but leading them—that was quite another.

Chapter Twenty-Five

Spending time in Eastwell dissipated Hannah's melancholy. Upon her return from visiting her family, in high spirits, she'd agreed to accompany John to Robert Linnell's wedding. She never would have done so if it were not in an Anglican Church.

The drive to London in a hired hackney was intriguing, as usual. She'd come to the city only a few times before by Dorothy's invitation and always enjoyed watching the people from the carriage windows. Riding purebred horses and dressed in extravagant fashions, the residents lived a life she never expected.

Nearing Bloomsbury, John said, "I suspect you'll have something in common with Robert's new wife, Enid. She's also an Anglican." He gave her a pleased glance that she assumed meant to encourage a positive response.

"I'll hold her hand and calm her fears when her husband is gone at night for hours—who knows if he be dead or in prison. Aye, I know the life well."

John took her hand. "God has kept me safe, has He not?"

"'Tis proof He listens to my fervent prayers."

John kissed her head.

After the ceremony, the wedding guests dined at a nearby inn. Robert had married a young Welsh woman who'd come to London as a baby with parents who were both now deceased.

Hannah suspected the parents left Wales to escape the Catholic persecutions, as many had. Mayhap Enid's sympathies stayed with them still. 'Twas hard to know, with her generation removed from all that, and she a composed girl. Had her parents secretly taught her Catholic ways, or did they shun the dangers? Hannah couldn't help but wonder if it hadn't always been God's plan to make following one's faith a risk.

John sat next to Robert, and Hannah sat at Enid's side. Robert's mother moved about the guests, chatting as she loved to do. Hair red and bosom large, she bounded about the room in animated happiness. Her son had finally married. She already spoke of grandchildren filling her home.

"Do you enjoy living in London?" Hannah spoke with the restrained and charming Enid, only to discover Robert had chosen a wife very unlike his mother.

"I know no other city." Enid shrugged delicate shoulders, her cascade of blonde hair shifting. "My parents would regale me with the beauties of Wales, but I've never been myself."

Robert and John appeared to be discussing something more serious, but occasionally Robert turned to stare at Enid, eminently aware of her presence and obviously smitten with her.

Enid never failed to timidly grin back at him.

Hannah found their exchanges endearing. Her own marriage hadn't started with so much adulation.

Leaning closer, Enid asked, "Do you not find a division in religious adoration a conflict in your marriage?"

There were so many warnings and answers to share. Too many. "Your knees will grow callouses from the hours you'll spend in fretful prayer." She'd tried to say it in a jesting manner, but her voice hitched. Not wanting to frighten the girl, she quickly added, "I love my husband enough to allow his misjudgments." That sounded wrong.

Enid's confused expression further solidified that Hannah shouldn't have shared her criticism of John.

Hannah sat at her table punching a pestle into dogwood, grinding it into powder for a poultice for her sick neighbor. The summer stench of the city made Hannah feel ill too, but she guessed her neighbor's illness was more than that.

John stepped in waving a paper. "A letter arrived from Jane. I can't imagine how she paid for and sent it without Robert's detection. Listen to this." He all but fell into a chair next to Hannah.

A letter from Jane would bring cheer. How Hannah missed

the girl's genuine goodness.

"Jane says they've had word from William. He's joined the Navy and is in Spain."

After the death of King James that spring, Charles declared war on Spain. Hannah feared her brothers would enlist for the high naval pay. As citizens, they paid King Charles's new higher taxes to equip that Navy.

John shook his head. "I haven't seen William since I left home for Oxford. He was but a lad of fourteen, not much older than Thomas. I doubt I'd recognize William if we met on the street." Sadness pulled at John's mouth.

He was likely to never see William again, unless, of course, John came back to the church. But she'd given up on that happening. They'd been in Southwark for three years now, and John had only become more enthusiastic about the Independents. He thrived as their leader.

"We didn't have much in common as children." John looked off as if his mind was elsewhere.

How grateful Hannah was for her loving family.

"Let's pray the war will be over soon." She set aside her pestle and smelled the dogwood, its odor weak. She longed for her fresh herb garden in Egerton. Who knew how old the herbs were that she bought at market. "If it's not enough that our nation's citizens are unnerved over having a Roman Catholic queen, we also have to send our husbands, sons, and brothers to war. The king's wife may be but a child, but her papist family have much royal power." Hannah sighed, worry pulling at her.

Thomas looked up from a book. "We can only hope the king will remember the past and not again reform our nation's religion."

"Who knows how many more thousands could die for the sake of their faith." Hannah wiped the perspiration from her forehead. The summer had been hot and muggy. "If the war and taxes aren't bad enough, we must also live with that threat."

John went back to reading the letter. "Jane tells me Robert has found her many beaus, but none interest her. She wants to be with us again." He went on reading the letter.

The next day, Enid Linnell sent a carriage for Hannah asking to visit. She'd done the same almost weekly since their marriage. She appeared unaware of Hannah's workload with six children, but Hannah didn't complain. She enjoyed Enid's company and the chance to get away from Southwark. At age eleven, Janie did well caring for the babies.

The Pulse of His Soul

When Hannah arrived at the Linnell's, she was welcomed by the housekeeper and shown to the parlor.

Enid came in looking rather sallow. "I apologize, Hannah, it's been another morning of illness." She gingerly sat and leaned against the sofa. "I felt perfectly fine when I sent you the carriage. I never know when it will come on."

"It usually passes by the fourth month." Hannah went to Enid, placing a hand on her forehead to be sure 'twasn't anything worse. She was cool to the touch.

"My mother-in-law didn't come down for her meal this morning. Her maid told me she's ill with fever. We're not going to be good company today. I do apologize for having you come all this way."

Hannah sat. "How could you've known? I was—"

A shout came from outside, and they rushed to the window.

Enid sagged against Hannah, a hand to her forehead. "I shouldn't have moved so quickly."

"Plague!" a young man shouted. "Plague in Saint Giles. Stay in your homes. Plague!" he kept up the refrain as he trotted down the street.

Hannah's stomach churned. Had she come into a house of plague? Was this what her neighbor had been sick with yesterday?

"Being so close in Bloomsbury, do you believe us safe?" Enid looked at Hannah with pleading eyes.

She didn't want to scare Enid. Surely her illness was from the babe growing within. But Mistress Linnell? She didn't know. "What are your mother-in-law's symptoms?"

"I didn't ask. She's often infirmed from old age." She walked to the parlor door. "Betsy, please come here."

A maid came down the stairs, worry on her face. She'd heard the warning from the streets, no doubt. She curtsied. "M'lady?"

"You've tended to Mistress Linnell this day?" Enid asked.

"Aye." Her eyes gathered moisture. "Do ya reckon . . .?" She clenched at her apron.

"What are her symptoms?" Hannah asked.

"She chills and complains of pain in 'ead and neck. She 'ad complaints yesterdee as well." Betsy wrung her hands. "I can'na die! Me children need me." She started to sob.

Dread filled Hannah's chest. As much as she wanted to rush home, she'd not bring the disease there. "Has anyone else been with Mistress Linnell this day?"

"Nay, only me." She wiped at her face.

In the hall, the other servants huddled close, listening to the conversation.

She shifted toward Enid. "It's possible Mistress Linnell is ill with some other sickness, but best to not take chances. I feel I cannot go home without knowing."

Enid covered her eyes. "I pray we've not brought you into a home of pestilence."

One of the servants gasped. "May I go 'ome, m'lady?"

The announcer ran by again. "Plague in Saint Giles. Stay in your homes. Plague!"

Enid looked to Hannah. She was so young, less than twenty. Hannah shook her head.

Enid stood taller. "Nay, Mary, 'tis too much of a risk."

"May I make suggestions?" Hannah requested of Enid.

"I'd appreciate your wisdom." Enid's posture slumped.

Hannah took in a deep breath, hoping to sound calm. "Separate the servants from those who have been with you and Mistress Linnell since yesterday. I'm sorry, Enid, but we don't know yet if your sickness is from breeding or . . ."

Enid bit her lip.

Motioning to Betsy, Hannah said, "Leave us and attend to your mistress only. Don't come from the room again. A servant will place medicine and meals outside the door, but don't open the door until she's well away."

Betsy sniffled and nodded.

Hannah looked to the two other servants close by. "Are you all well?"

"Aye, m'lady," they said in unison.

"You, like me, shouldn't leave this house until we know more of the illness that's within. Who is Mistress Enid's maid?"

A young girl stepped forward and curtsied.

Hannah addressed Enid, "May I ask that you also stay in your bedchamber with your maid?"

Enid simpered at her maid. "Will you stay with me Elin?"

She curtsied. "Aye, m'lady."

"The same rules should apply to Mistress Enid as Mistress Linnell."

Everyone nodded.

"For the cook, I'll advise her of the herbs for hot poultices that may help."

"Go tell the rest of the house staff," Enid said. "Lock the doors, and let no one in. When I see the watchman, I'll tell him from my window what has occurred."

"God save us," one of the maids said as everyone dispersed.

Enid stepped to Hannah. "What will you do?"

"May I use a guest room?"

"Of course." Enid's lower lip quivered. "I'll never forgive myself if you become ill."

"Don't blame yourself, dear one, you didn't know."

Before night fell, a red cross was painted on the Linnell doors to warn others to not enter.

Through her open window that evening, Hannah heard Robert calling Enid from the street. Hannah stepped to her window.

The summer's day had cooled little. Robert's red hair shone in the light of the full moon.

Enid called down in a faltering voice, "Do not fear, my love, I'm well. Betsy is with your mother."

"It's mother who is ill?" His voice cracked.

"She is." Enid's sobs echoed to the street below.

"If you're not ill, let me in. I need to be with you."

Robert's love for Enid touched Hannah's heart, but they couldn't let him in if they wanted to. All the doors had been hammered shut and a street watchman passed by often.

"Nay," was all Enid said between sobs.

"Robert," Hannah called.

He came to stand below her window. "What are you doing here?" he called up.

"When paying a visit, we heard of the plague and feared I'd bring it home if it truly is what's wrong with your mother." She didn't want to suggest Enid may have also fallen victim. "Please, Robert, can you go to my family? Let them know where I am. They must be frantic with worry."

"I will. I just left John walking home. I may come upon him with my carriage if I hie."

They must have had a meeting tonight for John to be heading home so late. "Bless you, Robert."

He cleared his throat, seeming unwilling to ask something.

"I've no symptoms and will stay in my room, Robert."

He nodded. "May God be with you all. I'll be back in the morning."

Hannah left the window and lay on her bed, still in her gown, listening to Robert encourage Enid that all would be well.

Hannah stayed awake, fearing she'd made the wrong decision. How would her family get by without her?

She slept a short while before the sound of a bellman awakened her. He called out loudly, "Bring out your dead. Bring out your dead."

He stopped and talked to the watchmen below, but Hannah couldn't make out their words. Did people really die of plague so quickly? One day it was discovered, the next they were dead?

"There's no need for your services." Enid called down.

Hannah got up and stretched but refused to peer out the window at the bellman's cart in case there were dead upon it. She spied a note near the bottom crack of her door. The writing was childlike, with words misspelled.

I beg thee and the Lord's forgivnes. I canna staye heer. Betsy

So she'd left. She had to have gone out a window for there was no way to leave by door. Mistress Linnell must be alone. How could Hannah let her suffer abandoned? What if there was something that could be done to save her or at least make the passing a little easier?

Hannah went to her bed and knelt beside it. If it were the plague, she'd be quarantined in this house for forty days. She didn't know what to do. "Dear God, bestow to me the strength to do what's needed. Care for my children if I never see them again." Her heart pumped slow. She then prayed the Litany for Sickness from the prayer book. After saying amen, she stood and knew she couldn't stay in this room while others needed her.

She opened the door to a tray of ham, eggs, and bread. She ate in silence. Very few conveyances traveled the road. When done, she steeled herself and went to Mistress Linnell's bedchamber.

A tray of cold food lay before the door, the makings for poultices with it. She picked it up and held it to her hip. Her hand trembled on the doorlatch. Was she sending herself to the grave?

She stepped into a stuffy room, decorated in expensive, but old-fashioned furniture and fabrics. The hearth lay cold and the window closed.

Mistress Linnell was an unmoving lump under the coverlet.

Hannah's stomach flopped. Was she already dead? Should Enid not have sent the cart away?

Setting down the tray, Hannah opened the window. Some feared humours from illness could fly out, but Hannah hoped not. The room was simply too hot. And she needed strength to help.

She approached the still form.

Mistress Linnell opened her glassy eyes. "Ms . . . Lothropp?" her hoarse voice questioned.

"'Tis I."

"How sick? Where is Betsy? Enid?"

"Enid is in her own bedchamber. She's well." Hannah hoped she told the truth. "Do you hurt?"

Mistress Linnell licked her cracked lips. "My head . . . neck. Under my arm." She tried to raise her arm but appeared to be too weak.

"Can you drink?"

"Perchance."

Hannah picked up a cup of cold tea from the tray. She tried to help Mistress Linnell sit, but wasn't strong enough and Mistress Linnell fainted with the effort.

With her unaware of the ministrations, Hannah examined her neck and under her arm. When she lifted the second arm, she found a buboe, black and tight, as if 'twould burst.

Cold fingers of fear ran down her back. "God help us!" she murmured. "*'Tis* the plague."

She'd need to build a fire and boil water to administer warm poultices. She lit a fire and then removed her clothing to her chemise. With Mistress Linnell barely conscious, Hannah pulled back the blankets and took off the woman's unnecessary clothing. Hannah needed to bring Mistress Linnell's fever down but had no cold water to do so.

For hours Hannah applied poultices, taking them off as soon as they cooled and replacing them with warm ones. Mistress Linnell's skin burned so hot, Hannah feared she couldn't live through such an inferno. She struggled to breathe.

Hannah prayed the litany of sickness again and again. Occasionally Mistress Linnell mumbled a few of the words.

Late in the afternoon, Hannah awoke in the chair with a start.

Mistress Linnell moaned deeply. And then went silent.

Hannah sprung to her feet.

Face so white, body so still, Hannah knew the woman must have died.

Uncontrolled tears fell. Robert would be devasted. She sniffled and smelled something awful. Never had she smelled such a stench. She lifted Mistress Linnell's lifeless arm and removed the black and oozing poultice cloth. The smell came from the burst buboe.

Hannah ran to the window and vomited. Had the humour pustules gotten into her body and now she had the pestilence? She vomited again until there was naught left. *Oh God, Why?* She placed a hand to her forehead but didn't believe she fevered.

Mistress Linnell moaned again. She wasn't dead!

Hannah staggered to her side, the stench in the room unbearable. She covered her nose.

Barely conscious, Mistress Linnell rasped shallowly.

Eyes watering and stomach turning, Hannah removed the poultice from the bed and threw it in the fire. She wiped Mistress Linnell's forehead with a cloth and could think of naught to do but talk.

She told Robert's mother about her childhood, her father, her deepest desires to preach. She spoke of her love for the gospel and Reverend Osbourne and her family and all her children's interests. On and on she talked, as if a lunatic. When she almost told her of her disappointment in John, she realized she'd gone too far. Robert may not have shared his Separatist activities with his mother. Too many secrets lived within families.

Hannah had moved into singing hymns by nightfall when she heard Enid calling down to John and him asking questions that were hard to make out. When all was quiet, she stumbled to her chair and slept.

Again awakened by the bell ringing in the morning, she listened more closely as Mistress Linnell's bedchamber was in the back of the house.

"Bring out your dead." The call came over and over. Sometimes all went silent.

Hannah assumed 'twas when the dead were being brought to his cart. When she heard Enid call down to him, Hannah heaved a sigh of relief that Enid was still well enough to do so.

Not sweating, Hannah presumed she didn't fever. She went to Mistress Linnell to discover she still breathed and slumbered with less of a fever. Hannah opened the door to find ham and eggs again with tea and more bandages. She had an appetite but couldn't get her patient to awaken enough to nibble.

The day passed much as the one before. Hannah couldn't cease worrying about her family in filthy Southwark. Why had John not come back? Or had he, and Hannah missed his discussion with Enid?

By the third evening, Mistress Linnell felt well enough to be spoon-fed tea. Each morning Hannah heard Enid call to the bellman and knew she was still well, as were all the servants. At week's end, Mistress Linnell sat up in bed and ate a small piece of bread.

Hannah left a note under the door to let the servant who brought the meals know that she presumed Mistress Linnell had made it past the worst of the pestilence and to please pass the message to Enid.

Forty days Hannah stayed with the Linnells. Neither Robert, nor anyone else, could enter the home during the quarantine. He brought food and sent it up through a window in a basket tied with a rope on its handle.

By some miracle the plague hadn't become an epidemic in Southwark but killed tens of thousands on the north side of the Thames. By God's grace, Hannah's family had survived.

Chapter Twenty-Six

John only intended to stay at the Independent meeting at Praise-God Barebone's home a short time. Baby Benjamin had fallen ill, and Hannah had asked him to bring home sow thistle. He'd picked it up at the apothecary and felt an urgency to get it to her.

Thomas stood at his side as John greeted people arriving for the conventicle. Thomas had been so adamant about his desire to worship with the Independents, that he'd been coming with John for over a year now. John felt unease leaving him there without him, though. "Best you come home with me tonight," he said to Thomas.

"I understand," Thomas immediately responded.

The easy acquiescence wasn't a surprise to John. Thomas was a gentle soul, obedient with inborn integrity.

Henry Dod approached and bowed. "Good evening to you, pastor." He'd been caught attending a past conventicle, and being imprisoned for a year had altered him. Jacob had been right about him being a leader. His heart had been softened and his faith enlarged during his time in gaol. He was no longer the young man who thought he knew all the answers.

Sam Eaton, a new member, was to speak tonight, having recently graduated from Cambridge. Praise-God himself was a worthy preacher, and he'd taken Eaton under his wing to teach him the admirable, if not dramatic, methods he'd so frequently used.

William Granger swaggered in and half shook John's hand, refusing to look him in the eye.

John still thought of him as *the angry ox* but tried to be amiable. They'd never spoken again about Granger's heartache over losing Hannah, and John felt it best to keep it that way.

A few minutes after Eaton stood by the hearth and began his sermon, John motioned to Thomas. They slipped out the backdoor and down a passageway.

Down the street, in the distance, a half-dozen men approached. In black clothing and carrying weapons, they were no doubt the Bishop of London's henchmen.

"Thomas." He spoke in an urgent whisper. "Walk casually home. I must warn the others." He tipped his head toward the men who were only now a block away.

"But, Father!" Thomas shook his head repeatedly, so unlike him.

By all that was holy, he couldn't let Thomas be captured. "Obey, son!" He ran back to the house and stepped through the front door.

"Laud's Henchmen! Go in haste!"

Men, woman, and children sprang to their feet as soundlessly as possible.

John helped them gather coats, hats, and anything that would give away their attendance.

Dod held the backdoor open as they slipped into the shadows of the oncoming night. "I'll not spend another year in that godforsaken prison," he mumbled.

When the house was empty save Praise-God and Sarah Barebone, John left out the front door, tipping his hat to them. "Good evening."

"God's blessings," Sarah chimed, a small warble of stress in her voice.

This time as John entered the street, the henchmen were upon him.

"Halt!" A tall, thin man with sharp cheekbones and nose blocked John's way. The man's thin lips pursed as he stared hard. "What are you doing this evening?" His breath reeked of mead and garlic.

The words were simple enough—it was the tone that carried the threat.

Tomlinson. John knew the man, although they'd never met. Bellamy had printed a drawing and distributed it amongst all the Independents. An over enthusiastic subordinate of the Bishop of London William Laud and his number one deputy. Tomlinson was an evil man who took pleasure in torturing Separatists.

"I was visiting friends." John caught a movement across the street. He prayed it wasn't Thomas.

Tomlinson placed a hand on his sword. "And to what reason were you visiting when you should be supping at home?" He narrowed spiteful eyes.

John knew the planned fabrication he was to use and sent a plea to God for forgiveness. "Mister Barebone bought some new tobacco he wanted me to try."

Tomlinson shoved John, sending him thudding against the Barebones' house. Sniffing, Tomlinson curled his lip. "The smell is too faint." He threw John aside and banged on the door.

Mister Barebone opened it, wafts of smoke coming from a pipe in his mouth.

John all but buckled at the knees, grateful Praise-God had remembered the alibi.

"What's this disturbance," Praise-God shouted.

John feared his acting too dramatic.

"Do you know this man?" Tomlinson pointed at John.

"Aye." Praise-God looked Tomlinson directly in the eyes, no fear evident. "He came here for a smoke."

John had been holding his breath, and slowly drew in air.

"In the name of the Bishop of London, I request to enter your home." Tomlinson stepped forward without waiting for a reply.

Praise-God stepped aside. "I bought the tobacco legally."

"It's not that, imbecile." Tomlinson turned on John. "You stay there."

Tomlinson and his henchmen filed into the Barebone home, their rapiers clanking as they marched. They all wore the black uniform with gold trim of William Laud. On their chests was the bishop's emblem of arms—two swords crossing over a red shield with the image of a bishop's mitre and sash above it. The crest evoked violence not peace.

Across the street, Thomas stepped out of the shadows of a narrow passageway between two houses. Heart racing, John waved his son away, and Thomas melted back into the passageway.

Tomlinson had left Praise-God's door ajar, and John lingered closer to listen.

"Why do you own so many chairs?" Tomlinson demanded.

"We have a lot of friends," Praise-God answered simply.

"I bet you do." Tomlinson growled.

Furniture thudded, and John guessed every room was being searched.

Not long after, Tomlinson and his men came back outside. He pushed his face within inches of John's. "What's your name? Where do you live?"

The hate in his eyes unnerved John more than the threat of discovery.

"John Lothropp of Southwark, my lord." He gagged on the smell of putrid breath as well as on the honorary title of *lord*.

Tomlinson motioned to one of his men. "Write that down." He spun back to John. "We'll be keeping an eye on you, Lothropp." He thrust John away and marched down the street, his minions following.

John tipped his hat to Praise-God and walked the opposite way. He motioned his head slightly to Thomas, who followed behind on the other side of the road.

John turned to glance behind him many times but Tomlinson had gone.

At the bridge, John moved amongst a crowd watching a jester entertain.

Thomas approached him. "They have your name, Father." He appeared worried, not afraid.

John was grateful for his son's bravery. The boy would need it if he truly continued with his desire to be an Independent. "That's regrettable. But they've no proof of me breaking any laws."

"What happened will frighten Mother."

John stopped and pulled Thomas by the sleeve. "Do not mention anything that happened tonight to your mother."

For the next few weeks, John came home directly after work, not only to throw off Tomlinson and his henchmen, but because Hannah had delivered a baby girl early. The child lived but two days. A shroud of sorrow hung over the family, and Hannah couldn't seem to rise from her bed.

He went upstairs to her. "May I bring you some soup Enid delivered?"

Eyes closed, Hannah shook her head.

"Dorothy brought fruit. Does that sound appealing? Or bread from the neighbor?"

Wrapped in blankets to her chin, Hannah opened her eyes. "Will you help me rise?"

This was hopeful. He helped her sit upright until her bare feet touched the floor, then rushed to get her stockings and slid them on. He brought her to standing and used a blanket as a shawl. "Shall we visit the children downstairs?"

"I'd like that." Her smile inched up a fraction.

The stairs were only wide enough for one, so John moved Hannah behind him where she could set her hands on his shoulders for support as they walked down.

"Mother!" Janie pulled out a chair. Only fifteen, she was already taller than Hannah. Janie led with her heart rather than her head. Thomas tended to be her guardian for that reason.

Johnny and Barbara looked up from chess and the three little boys from a game of marbl

Thomas wasn't yet home from working as a stockman for the grocer and fellow Independent, Joseph Grafton.

A knock sounded at the door, and John answered to a stranger in fine clothing. "Have I found John Lothropp?"

John's heart skidded to a halt. Was this one of Tomlinson's tricks? Was he checking on John's whereabouts? He wasn't usually home so early. Mayhap this man had come to question Hannah and the children?

After pulling in a deep breath, John silently prayed, *Thank you, Lord for this small blessing of being home early. As always, I am in your debt.* Out loud he answered, "Aye, I'm John Lothropp."

"My name is Charles Brock, solicitor. I've come on a matter regarding your brother's estate."

"My brother? Which one? Has someone died?" John's stomach tightened.

Brock's face stiffened. "May I come in, sir?"

John invited Brock in and hung his hat on a peg.

The children and Hannah quieted and focused on Brock.

In a powdered wig smelling of talcum, he looked about, not quite disguising a glower of disgust.

John motioned for Johnny to vacate his chair and pulled it away from the table, setting it by the window. "Please, have a seat." John brought a chair over for himself. "May I offer you some ale?"

"Nay, thank you." Brock pursed his lips. "You've been a hard man to find. It seems the rector . . . Lothropp's widow didn't know your whereabouts. I had to travel clear to Yorkshire to discover where you lived."

"Is it Thom who has died?" John didn't want to hear the truth of it, but he had to know what had happened.

"That is correct. Your brother, Thomas Lothropp, has died," Brock confirmed with not an ounce of empathy.

Hannah gasped, and John glanced behind him to be sure she stayed upright on her chair. Barbara and Janie both went to her side and draped their arms about Hannah's shoulders.

John covered his eyes. "When?"

"January. He'd been ill for a few months, writing his will October last."

If John had known Thom was ill, he would've gone to him. "And I was in his will?" He didn't believe it. Thom had said he'd disowned John.

"He's left the bulk of his estate and all his lands to his four daughters and widow and his northern lands to your half-sister's husband."

"But to me?"

"To you and each of your siblings, William Lothropp and Mary Gallante, he's left five-hundred pounds."

Not such a huge sum, considering Thom's wealth, but still surprising he had left John aught.

Thom gone. John hung his head, anxious for the solicitor to leave so he could mourn privately. Maybe his brother hadn't stopped loving him after all? John certainly hadn't stopped loving Thom. "God rest, Thom."

A hand caressed his shoulder. He turned to see Hannah there. She leaned against him, tears flowing down her face.

Brock cleared his throat. "Mister Lothropp, I'm afraid there's more news."

"More?"

"I've spent the last months looking for you three siblings, and I just missed the two others."

"What do you mean?"

"Your sister, Mary, died in the spring. William recently was lost in the war. And . . ." he went on.

But all John heard was a humming drone. Numb all over, he barely registered Hannah's fingers on his neck as she bent her head to his and whispered, "I'm so sorry."

"Since neither have offspring, you'll also be receiving their share of the inheritance," Brock proclaimed with finality.

"Dead . . . all?" A moan escaped from deep within John's chest. "All?" He was alone. Every one of his mother's sons and daughters were gone from this earth, in heaven with her. In one year, three deaths. How could this be? *Why God? Why choose me to be alone?*

Chapter Twenty-Seven

In the parlor, Hannah reached up again with both hands. Nay, still couldn't touch. She grinned.

"What are you doing?" Barbara questioned, eyeing her as if she belonged in Bedlam.

Elizabeth's green eyes shone with knowledge. "She's in disbelief that she has a home where she cannot reach the ceiling."

The two girls giggled.

"You're a wise girl, Elizabeth Denne." Hannah was indeed grateful for her new home in Lambeth Marsh, where the ceilings were tall and the rooms large.

Although they were still on the south bank of London, close enough for John to pastor the Independents, they no longer lived in the soot-filled air of Southwark. John's inheritance had bought them a home, carriage and horse, and sent Johnny to Eton. And having spent most of the money, John still needed to work as a clerk to put food on the table and clothes on their backs.

Hannah stepped outside to a garden in motion with birds and insects. She didn't want to disturb the symphony of it all—a curiosity of nature so near the city. This was their first summer in Lambeth and already her herbs and flowers grew lush and thick. The once marshland soil grew delicious vegetables too, the land so fertile her neighbors at a distance maintained a market garden. She picked one of the last tomatoes under a brittle leaf, the late August weather dry and hot.

Her youngest two coppery-blonds, Joseph and Benjamin, played ball by the chicken coop.

"Mother." Janie came outside dressed in a new green velvet gown. "You'll never believe who arrived." She smiled, showing her dimples. Although sixteen, Hannah's age at marriage, John refused to let beaus court his daughter. He said Thomas should marry first, knowing that Thomas wasn't yet interested in courting young women. It really wasn't the way things were done—waiting for a brother to marry—but Hannah agreed with John. Janie could wait a couple more years.

Returning inside, Hannah found her brother in the parlor, his face brown from being at sea, moving commerce for the king. "Samuel! When did you dock?" He visited occasionally when he was onshore.

"I've come from Eastwell, not the ship." He embraced her.

"Why?"

"It's Father." He dodged her stare and took her hands. "He's sick and asking for you."

"Is it serious?" Could he be dying? She didn't believe it. Father was always so full of life.

"I reckon it could be."

Samuel tried not to show concern.

But she knew him better than that. It must be serious to bring him here.

Her eyes teared. "Samuel—"

"Where's my namesake?" He spun away, probably trying to avoid fragile emotions. "Sam," he called.

The boy came clomping down the stairs, a book of short morals and comic tales in his hand. "Uncle!" He shook Samuel's hand like he probably presumed a big boy should, but Samuel enveloped him. "Can you tell me of your recent adventures?" Sam begged.

Samuel questioned Hannah with a stare.

She shook her head in dismay. He brought her news of father's illness yet avoided the inevitable tale. "You two spend time together, but soon your uncle and I need to make plans."

Later, Samuel found her where she went to work out her worries, clearing weeds from her physic garden where she grew herbs for medicine—feverfew, lavender, fennel, mint, and more. She brushed off her hands. "Are you ready to make plans for travel to Eastwell?"

"Aye." He smiled lopsidedly, looking like the young child Hannah left at Egerton eight years before. "We should leave in the morning."

Hannah's heart sank in disappointment. "Must we hasten, Samuel?"

He ran his hands through his long, blond hair.

She wanted to brush it and make him appear like a gentleman instead of an adventurous sailor.

"He believes he's in his last days, and I cannot say otherwise."

She pressed her palm into her chest to try and suppress the unsettling feeling. "You and I will leave in the morning then. John and Thomas must work. Janie and Barbara can care for the three boys."

"Where's Johnny?"

"He's at Eton. And I doubt he misses us. Thomas wouldn't go. He said he'd not take the Oath of Supremacy and acknowledge the Thirty-Nine Articles of Religion. Basically, by signing the admission papers into Cambridge or Oxford, he'd be denouncing Separatism."

Samuel nodded. "I don't blame the lad."

"What do you mean?" Alarm shot to Hannah's chest. "Not you!"

Samuel shrugged.

"Does Father know you sympathize with Separatists?"

"Nay. I couldn't break his heart as John had."

She gave him a bitter smile. Father had never told her that John's leaving the Church had wounded him. He'd only offered her encouragement to stay strong in the faith and obey her husband. He'd accepted John into his home but requested that they never discuss religion. And they hadn't. 'Twas one more person John afflicted with his choices. She sighed. "I see. We'll talk of it on our ride home."

Three days later, they arrived in Eastwell.

Hannah found her father very weak and her mother in a dither, trying to accommodate everyone who'd come to visit. Sending her to read to him, Hannah gathered Penninah and their sister-in-law, May, into the kitchen to help old Molly prepare food.

"Don't let Hannah do any of the cooking," Penninah loudly whispered to May. "We want to be able to eat it."

Hannah swatted at her with a towel. "I'm better at it, out of necessity, but you're right, Penny. I'll chop the onions."

Late that evening, when Jack and May had taken their children home and the others had settled into bed, Samuel, Penninah and Hannah sat by a dying fire and talked of their fondest memories of Father. Hannah had much gratitude for him and prayed he'd recover.

"Mother will need to relinquish the vicarage when Father dies," Penninah said. She wasn't her usual self, and though the mood had been rather somber for such frivolity, Hannah missed her sister's jests and laughter.

"I thought as much." Hannah glanced around the house she'd grown up in. "Are there plans to where she and the youngest will go?"

"If she sells the animals, much of the furniture, Father's books, china, and pewter, she expects she can buy a small cottage here in Eastwell."

Samuel leaned forward, staring at the embers in the hearth. "Can she not live closer to Jack?"

"I've suggested the same. She's considering it. Her friends are here though." Penninah frowned.

"She need not worry about my tenancy, for I'm loving the sea and will stay in Deal when ashore," Samuel said.

Penninah looked strangely at Hannah, as if she were uncertain of something.

"What is it Penny?" Hannah asked.

She glanced toward the dark window, seemingly considering her words. "'Twould be easier on Mother if she didn't have an old maid who needed a bed to lay her head on."

Hannah grabbed to the arms of her chair. "Penny! Are you wanting to come live with me?" Hannah's heart raced with the prospect. "How I'd love to have you."

Penninah grinned. "You wouldn't mind my dirty boots on your rug when I come in from my long, feeling-sorry-for-myself strolls?"

"Oh, Penny. I'll even put up with your laughter that cracks the windows."

Samuel chortled, but then quieted quickly at his sisters' stern looks.

"No need to wake Mother and Father." Penninah chided him.

The mention of Father sobered them, and they sat subdued for a while.

Hannah needed to know if Penninah had truly considered the consequences of living with her. "Would you be afraid to live with a Separatist? He's often gone, sleeping at a friend's instead of traveling the many miles home. Since the king made Laud bishop and a supporter of his tyranny, the streets are patrolled by his guardsmen, especially late at night."

"I'm braver than I appear, dear sister." She lifted her mouth into a delicate smile that opposed her comment.

"Tis no jesting matter. I can never be sure of John's safety, and now Thomas attends the meetings with him."

"He does?" Penninah eyed her in surprise.

"When they become sixteen, we've agreed to give all the children the choice to attend the Independent meetings. 'Twas a deal I made with John when they were all young. I regret it now."

"And does Janie go to Separatist meetings?" Samuel wanted to know.

"She's afeared but has much interest. I take them all to the parish church, for their safety and salvation, but it has been a burden to stand against John's convictions." If they only knew her sorrow over losing Thomas to the heretical organization. Would Janie hold back to not add another burden to her mother's worries?

Penninah leaned forward and squeezed Hannah's hand. "You've stood strong and upheld the faith. I'm proud of you."

Samuel leaned closer to them. "I've a Separatist friend on the ship, and he's truly persuading with his argument against following a king who shouldn't have authority to interfere in matters pertaining to God. And now that the king puts in effect policies that emphasize sacraments and ceremonies seen as a return to popery, I can see his point."

"Samuel!" Penninah whispered hoarsely. "Your words are treasonous. And have a care. Your sister hears this rubbish at home. You presume she wants to hear it from you?"

"It's all right, Penny. We talked of similar topics on the ride here." Hannah must be getting calloused to such talk for she didn't have as strong a reaction as she used to.

Samuel said, "It's been rumored amongst the crew that four ships carried Puritan gentry to America this last spring. They were not Separatists, like the first settlers of Plymouth. They're faithful to the Church of England. A Mister Winthrop is supposed to have said that he wants to extend our country's reach into the New World. It sounds to me like the religious battle that ferments here has been brought there."

On the third day of Hannah's visit, Father could no longer eat. He called each of his children to him and privately expressed his concerns and wishes.

When Hannah's turn came, she entered his bedchamber trying not to shatter with grief.

Father's once round face appeared disturbingly pale and saggy. His long white hair splayed across a pillow, and his hands were very swollen. "Come, sit by me."

She sat on the bed.

He took her hand in a weak grasp. "Where has my joyful daughter gone?"

"Must we talk about my sadness? 'Tis a hundred-fold to see you like this." Hannah knew he referred to the sadness that had befallen her since John had left the Church. She couldn't avoid the inevitable, and finally spoke about her situation. "I'm settling for a husband who hasn't lived up to promises made to the Church. I want to be close to him and share our love of the gospel again." She should have stopped. But if anyone was going to understand, 'twas Father. "I miss the man I married. I feel there's a hole in my heart that can no longer be filled." A tear escaped, and she swiped it away.

"The heart must break for truth and love to be poured in. You can have compassion . . . empathy . . ." He cleared his raspy throat.

"Can you sip tea?" she asked.

He shook his head. "Compassion and empathy can come without agreeing with your husband's beliefs. Even love." It sounded as if he had to thrust each word out, breathing hard between sentences. "If there's one thing I've learned in my years as vicar, husband, and father, 'tis that it's a sacred thing to be able to *feel* with someone."

Hannah laid her head on his chest like she did as a young girl.

"Your husband is a good man. Who are we to say how the Lord expects us to worship Him?"

Hannah pushed away. "Father?"

"'Tis possible that the church our Lord organized for us while here—a foundation of twelve apostles, the power of God, the priests and prophets—is supposed to be what the true church should look like. And that church is no longer on this earth." He wheezed. "How far away from it have we gone? Christ should be the head of the church and God the ultimate ruler."

"I suppose so." It made sense.

"Then 'twould also be true that those of us with testimonies of our Lord are trying to find ways to serve Him and create that church He organized."

"Aye."

"John is serving the best way he knows how. Do you believe that?"

"He's a man of faith," she admitted. Regret for turning from him seeped into her.

"You'll never be happy as long as you feel you're better than John."

Hannah sat up straighter. "I don't feel that!" But did she? "Oh, Father." She laid her head on his chest again and sobbed.

He patted her back. "Take upon yourself the name of Jesus Christ and do as He did—love and forgive."

Two days later, Father died.

Chapter Twenty-Eight

Hannah took a hat off the peg in her front hall. "Penny, having you as my companion once again has been a great blessing." Although she had no power to keep John safe, she found some relief in her sister's support of their mutual Anglican faith.

"I should have come sooner." Penninah pulled on her mantle. "And it's been years since I've seen Dorothy." Enthusiasm showed in her eyes. "I look forward to the visit."

Even though the November day blew cold, Thomas had today off work, which meant he could drive them in the carriage since she didn't know how to drive it herself. And that made today a good day for visits.

"I suppose I must meet Enid someday, but I fear I'll like her, and then what do I do with that?"

Hannah chuckled. "Robert chose a lovely woman, only second best to you. To the exuberance of his mother, they have two dear children."

"Men go for the beauties and leave nonsensical women like me alone." Unruffled, Penninah walked out the door with Hannah.

"Robert is nonsensical himself. Find heart that you're both not living a life of confusion."

When they arrived at Dorothy's grand mansion, they were shown into the parlor where they feasted on delicacies of tarts, fruits, and preserves on biscuits.

For the first time, Thomas came in to talk with them. Hannah considered it a good opportunity to practice manners and companionship with women. He appeared rather uncomfortable as they talked of trivial matters such as the price of fabrics and styles of hats.

"Denne tells me there will be a flogging at Westminster this day, to show all those who defame the Church what their punishment will be," Dorothy said.

Thomas suddenly became interested in the conversation. "Who is it?"

Penninah didn't miss his interest and flashed a look at Hannah.

"Alexander Leighton. He's no man from the street, but a physician—a learned man and Puritan sympathizer," Dorothy said. "He once was a minister of the Church of Scotland. I see no sense in him attacking the Church of England the way he has, and I wonder if he might be insane. John meets secretly with others. He's shrewd to not speak out publicly."

Thomas cleared his throat. "You should know, Mistress Denne, that I'm a Separatist as well."

Hannah cringed inside and set her fine china teacup on her lap. She didn't know he'd made a final decision, for he still actively attended the Anglican Church with her. Did he talk so openly about his feelings with others? Would she one day be watching him flogged? How grateful she was that she could trust Dorothy to keep her family's secrets.

"What more do you know of this criminal?" Penninah gave Hannah a look that said, *Listen up. This is important.*

Dorothy thought a moment. "He's a Scottish Presbyterian who opposes the bishops' abuses of power. He planned to appeal to Parliament with a manuscript he'd written in Holland that criticized the Church. Why he thought he needed to also brand Queen Henrietta Maria a daughter of Heth, I don't understand. Is his quarrel with the queen? We may not like her, but we don't need to go to Parliament with those feelings."

"She *is* Catholic," Hannah said.

"Because of her Catholicism, she's never been crowned our true queen." Thomas's relief showed in his words.

Hannah didn't quite understand Dorothy's explanation. "But the king has dissolved Parliament, so how did Leighton's manuscript become known?"

"He had it printed in Holland and left it there once he received word of the king's singular tyranny." The way Dorothy so easily threw out the word "tyranny" surprised Hannah.

'Twas the common sentiment of most Brits, but to say so risked punishment. She was grateful Dorothy was as comfortable expressing her feelings with them as they were with her.

"A few manuscripts were smuggled into the country and came to the attention of Bishop Laud," Dorothy continued. "And you know him, he's determined to strike terror into the hearts of any person who criticizes the Church. They say he was a key instigator into getting the king to dissolve Parliament."

"Has Leighton been in prison long?" Thomas asked.

"Over a year. No one thought the flogging would be carried out. But then Leighton escaped from the Fleet, and Laud thought to make a spectacle of him. Denne suggested I go and watch the flogging. *Why*, I implored. He said 'twas every citizen's duty to support the king when he assails his enemies."

Penninah squinted at Thomas.

Hannah knew that look. Penninah had an idea. How long would it take for her to come out with it?

Dorothy kept up her conversation of what Denne had told her about recent politics and then said, "I guess there will be no more disgruntled heretics sending pamphlets to Parliament. King Charles rules by himself as supreme leader. He's selling titles and church positions to the highest bidder."

"Dorothy." Penninah fidgeted with her skirts. "Will you be attending the punishment of Mister Leighton?"

"I try my best to be an obedient wife, but I've considered claiming illness." She smiled weakly at her admission.

Penninah again gave Hannah that look of there being an opportunity here. "Thomas, if your mother agrees, I surmise 'twould be a good opportunity for you to see such a flogging. Then you can decide if being a Separatist is really worth the risk."

Hannah could only wish watching the violence would turn Thomas from his father's ways, but she didn't believe she wanted to see such brutality herself. Would it be worth it to save her son? Aye, 'twould. "I agree with Aunt Penny, Thomas. You should understand the retribution that may be in your future if you continue to have sympathies with heretics."

Thomas flinched at the word "heretic." "If you feel I must." He looked unconvinced.

Hannah prayed this was a good idea. Penninah had gotten her into trouble many times in their youth.

Dorothy agreed to go, and they used her larger carriage to travel together.

At Westminster, a crowd of thousands congregated—people of all ages and stations, from the rich to the poor, threadbare clothing and fine tailored apparel, children and babes in arms.

Dorothy's driver parked on the periphery, to the side of the platform with other conveyances, and they stayed in the carriage to watch.

Mouthwatering scents of meat pies and sugared nuts gave the feel of a lighthearted social gathering. Bells on a jester's hat and shoes tinkled as he summersaulted in front of their carriage. Vendors brought carts of food. Families gathered for picnics. The festive atmosphere felt like a celebration—except for the men-at-arms standing about holding pikes and halberds.

Something in the pit of Hannah's stomach told her she'd regret coming.

Penninah took in the throng with wonder. "I'd no idea," she murmured.

"Different than the country, I must say, and one of the reasons I miss my childhood home." One side of Dorothy's mouth quirked up. "Denne said that after they arrested Leighton and threw him into a rat pit, agents burst into his home and held his five-year-old son at gunpoint, threatening to shoot him in the chest if he didn't confess to where his father kept his papers."

Hannah's head swam. "That's horrible," she whispered. Would men of Christ's church treat a child so? Men of her church *had* done so. She wished she could talk to Father, to understand the workings of men. This didn't feel right.

A man held a small pamphlet up to their carriage window. "Care to buy a copy?" The front page read: *Life, Character and Behavior of Alexander Leighton*. "Only a half-penny."

Thomas took it and gave the man a coin. He opened the booklet.

Dorothy leaned over to read the page. "Just rhetoric, Thomas." She shook her head.

The crowd cheered when a cart pulled up with the prisoner—a short man in filthy rags, his head bald in spots with strands of blond hair, and peeling skin. Who knew what vermin crawled in his beard?

Dorothy shuddered. "His physician friends reported he'd been poisoned in gaol."

Thomas said naught in return, jaw held tight, eyes furious.

Would he blame his anger on Hannah since she'd agreed they should come?

Leighton was brought to a high wooden platform with his hands in manacles in front of him.

The Pulse of His Soul

A tall man with sharp features, in the black livery of Bishop Laud, stepped onto the stage.

The crowd stilled.

"We bring before you Alexander Leighton, an enemy of King Charles and to all that's good. Guilty of sedition, libel, and treason, he is here today to suffer just punishment as set forth from the Star Chamber. Such sentence states he is to be degraded from his orders in the ministry and have his ear cut off, his nose split, and his cheek branded with the sign of a Sower of Sedition. He will then be whipped. In a sennight, he shall be carried to Cheapside on market day and have the other ear cut off, opposite nostril slit, and second cheek branded."

The crowd roared their approval.

Hannah clutched her stomach, fearing she'd be sick.

Also looking a little sick, Penninah placed her hand on Hannah's. "This is my fault. I'm sorry. Shall we leave?"

"I'd like to but how will I explain leaving to Denne?" Dorothy crossed her arms. "I hold to your first idea that this is what Thomas needs to see."

"There's no lesson here for me," Thomas fired back. "My thoughts are only of Christ and His suffering. This is not the first man to unjustly be punished in God's name."

"I apologize, son." Hannah offered, but he turned from her.

Two men tied Leighton to a stake. Keeping his head low, he didn't struggle. Many in the crowd elbowed their way forward, seemingly wanting a better view.

The hangman stepped up with a dagger in hand and grabbed Leighton's ear, swiftly slicing it off with the knife.

Leighton cried out with an inhuman wail.

Hannah gasped and twisted from the scene.

The crowd applauded, whistled, cheered, and yelled— "Heretic," "Son of Satan," "Anti-Christ."

"Must *I* watch and not *you*, Mother?" Thomas growled.

She'd never known Thomas to display such disrespect and fury. She prayed the trauma would not scar him for life. This had been a mistake.

By the time she glanced back, Leighton's nose had already been split, and the hangman was reaching for a hot poker. When he seared *SS* into Leighton's cheek, the man let out a high-pitched, soul-crushing scream. He quivered with spasms.

"Sower of sedition, sower of sedition," hundreds chanted until Hannah had to plug her ears.

The hangman dragged Leighton to the pillory, removed his tattered shirt, and locked his head and hands in the stocks. All the while, the onlookers mocked him for his beliefs.

Snow began to fall as fleecy as lamb's wool. Big flakes, floating softly. They landed on Leighton's blood-smeared, mutilated profile, and patchy-bald head.

The hangman threw his arm back with a leather strap in hand and whipped it forward to tear into Leighton's skin. He cried out, and after countless more lashings, he fainted.

"This public mocking and flogging will continue for two more hours," Dorothy said weakly. "Denne cannot expect me to suffer it all."

Suddenly a freezing wind whisked at hats and shawls. It whistled through their carriage.

"I've seen enough." Thomas rubbed tears from his face. "This brutal display hasn't frightened, but empowered me. Leighton has overpaid with his blood. His sufferings will one day be his glory."

Hannah had taken part in the celebration of a man suffering torture and her heart was stricken with shame. Never again would she do such a thing. *Please God, keep my son and husband from such brutality. No one deserves to be punished so. Hold Mister Leighton in Your hands.*

They went back to Dorothy's in silence for their own carriage, then traveled home.

That night, Hannah and Penninah sat in the parlor, together on the settle, grieving for poor Leighton. Neither of them could eat supper and Thomas had disappeared. "Do you think Leighton's wife and children were in the crowd?"

Penninah just shook her head, at a loss for words, and turned toward the fire hearth.

Hannah prayed once again for the comfort and safety of them all.

"Tell me more about this Bishop of London who executes the men who speak out against the Church." Penninah touched Hannah's hand.

"William Laud. John's worst enemy. He enforces a uniform system of worship through bishops. After today, I'm beginning to think he's not a worthy man."

"Laud cares naught for humans," John boomed, stepping into the parlor. "Only his great ability to control and inflame his enemies,"

Hannah leapt to her feet. She'd never heard him yell before

this day, and only once witnessed his anger at Thom when he denounced the Church.

Janie and Barbara peeked into the room, their faces full of worry.

John pointed at Penninah. "The persecuting zeal of Laud will destroy our God-given agency. I heard of Leighton's sentence from Thomas. 'Twas designed for terror, to control all of us to worship as only the king does." He spun on Hannah. "How could you have taken our son to such a spectacle?"

She winced. "I didn't realize—"

"'Twas my idea." Penninah stood and faced John. "The hope was to show Thomas what fate may someday be his if he didn't stay with the Church of England."

"The teaching of my son's religion is mine only." Again, anger boosted John's words.

"And not mine?" Hannah's own anger burst from her mouth. "Upon the handmaids the Lord will pour out His spirit. Women are meant to receive the Spirit too. I'm not a fool. I too have taught my children how to love God."

He tucked in his chin. "'Twas a *foolish* thing you did today," he said a little quieter, but still with force.

"Well, you renouncing your orders was the most *foolish* of all! When you left the Church, I settled for less and tried to ignore the hole you created by bringing me to Southwark and not caring to meet my needs. I finally found my self-worth by remembering my love for the Gospel and serving others. I may do foolish things, but I'm not a foolish person—as you are."

"How is what you're doing any different than what I'm doing? The king is not my Lord, and I'll not follow him as you have. Talk about foolish!" he said with a sting.

His words hit the mark. She observed today what the king was doing to God's followers. She wiped a tear. "You're right."

The shock on his face looked almost painful.

"I've followed a safer path. Not just for me, but for the sake and safety of my children. I'm not brave like you."

The question in John's brown eyes was more than she could decipher before he spun and stomped out of the room.

Janie and Barbara jumped out of his way.

Hannah plopped back onto her chair.

Penninah settled slowly into hers.

As John's footfalls neared the stairs, Benjamin asked, "Are you mad at Mama?"

John's footsteps halted and then became louder once again. He came into the parlor and knelt on one knee beside her. "I can't help but fight wrong, but I'll never again fight you. You've more agency than you realize. I cannot provide you courage, but if you choose to walk alongside me, I'll hold you up and I *will* protect you." He kissed her hand and left.

Weary from expended emotion, Hannah fell forward, face in her hands.

Penninah cleared her throat. "Now that you two are done wreaking havoc on one another, I need to say something," Penninah said gently.

"If you must." Hannah's words fell into her hands.

Out of the corner of her eye, Janie's skirts appeared and she rubbed Hannah's back.

All this time she'd tried to keep the truth from the younger children, now they knew of their father's secret activities. How could she make sure they didn't tell anyone?

"I'm surprised you aren't interested in the fact that women's voices are as welcome as men's voices at the Independent meetings." Penninah chided her.

Hannah sat up to gauge if her sister spoke truth.

Penninah's face was that of innocence. "Samuel told me. You didn't know?"

"Nay, I've requested John to not speak of what goes on at the meetings. And he keeps me from knowing where they meet or who he meets with for my own safety."

Penninah shook her head as if Hannah were a dunce child. "How could you be so adamantly against it if you've not gone to their meetings to discover their views and whether the Spirit resides there? I shall go to find out what it's about."

Chapter Twenty-Nine

At the kitchen worktable, Hannah punched the dough, taking out her frustrations with Penninah on the bread. She was probably ruining their Easter meal. "If I'd known when you moved in two years ago that you'd become a Separatist, I don't suppose I'd have taken you in." Hannah's chest burned "What would Father say?"

On the opposite side of the table, Penninah crimped dough along the edge of a tart and looked up and grinned, ignoring Hannah's fury. "Well, I do make the best tarts with custard and baked apples. Think of what you would've been missing. I know the children are happy I'm here."

"Truly, Penny, life has taken swings at me that I'm not sure I can avoid anymore."

"So cease ducking and come to the next meeting. You behave out of fear of damnation, as John said."

"John said that?" Hannah stopped what she was about to say when Johnny roamed into the kitchen, looking for whatever food he could find.

At Eton he'd grown into a young man with a deep voice and had done naught but eat since home on break. "Don't stop the conversation on my account. I'm very aware of Father's Separatist activities. It *is* news that you've joined them, Aunt Penny. I've been taught at school, as I'm sure Grandpapa taught you, that the best loyalty to a way of worship is set out in Common Prayer."

"Only fifteen and you envision you understand the most pertinent answers to life." Penninah arched a brow.

"What I don't understand is why Father has moved us to Lambeth, blocks from the palace where the archbishop lives. There are safer places to live."

"To hide in plain sight, is what he told me." Penninah filled her tart with berries.

Hannah knew that to be partially true.

"Good thing Bishop Laud has his own palace. But since I've been home, did you know I've seen him travel this street almost every day?" Johnny said.

Penninah rolled her eyes. "And a fine carriage he has with gold-spoked wheels and intricate gold fretwork along the top."

Hannah assumed Penninah was trying to open Johnny's eyes to the opulence flaunted by the Church clergy. And if Hannah were being honest, the opulence bothered her too. On her way to Dorothy's, she'd seen the stately grounds of Laud's Fulham Palace. He lived like royalty. "Moving here was also my idea since your father insisted on being close enough to access the Thames for his London meetings. I'd have much preferred the country, but this was the next best thing with clean air and a garden. And I very much like the parish church of Saint Mary."

"You're not alone in your beliefs, Mother. I plan to remain a member of the Church of England."

Hannah left her dough and hugged Johnny, leaving flour on his shirt. She tried to brush it off, only making it worse.

He laughed and brushed at it himself. "There's no fear of damnation, Aunt Penny. But there are expectations others have of us. I feel I must carry myself above reproach." He grabbed some radishes and left the kitchen.

"Well, he's gotten cocky." Penninah shook her head.

"He's a little full of himself, 'tis the age, but he's my son, and methinks he understands me more than all of you. Although Janie is a sweet thing, always considerate. It's a shame you've gotten her to go to the meetings too. How could you? Now Barbara's asking to go, and she's not much past thirteen. The rule is sixteen."

"Maybe their behavior is something you should consider. Your husband is a reformed man from when I knew him in Egerton. He used to be stern and unhappy."

"Unhappy?"

"In his soul." Penninah placed her hand over her heart. "He's found something that gives him purpose."

"Did he not have a purpose as a perpetual curate?"

Giving her a smirk, Penninah wiped her hands on a cloth and

left the room.

A sharp pain grabbed Hannah's womb. She'd lost her little girl at seven months, and then the last child only four months along, and this one had been threatening to do the same. She rubbed where it hurt. Feeling nauseous, she sat down.

A sennight later, Johnny went back to Eton, but Samuel stayed on and attended Independent meetings with the other adults. That afternoon, they all left for a meeting in London at different times, heading in different directions, to throw off anyone who may be watching their house.

At home with the youngest, Hannah sat and brooded. Not only did she have John and Thomas to fret over but now Penninah, Janie, and Samuel too. So far, she was able to keep Barbara from attending, but not without confrontation. Barbara had much curiosity about the meetings. Hannah supposed it was because she wanted to feel as adult as possible and do what the adults were doing. John had been quiet on the matter. She assumed he wanted Barbara to make the decision on her own, like he'd always told Hannah to do.

Joseph entered the parlor. "There's a man at the door asking for you."

"Did you get his name?" Being home without an adult male present made it unacceptable to invite a stranger in.

"Nay. He said he was from the Church."

Hannah found a tall, lean man standing at the door. He looked vaguely familiar, but she couldn't place where she'd seen him. At church, perchance.

"Good evening." He bowed.

"My husband is from home." Her womb ached again, and she'd started to bleed that morning. She hoped this visit wouldn't take long.

"I apologize to inconvenience you, but I'm the parson's clerk, helping Vicar Featley with church records."

"I see." Something didn't feel quite right. Hannah studied the man closer.

He wore finely tailored clothes for a man with the modest title of clerk. Mayhap they were paid more than she realized?

"How long have you lived in Lambeth Saint Mary Parish?" He looked from her face to something behind her, to the ground, and then to the book he held, where it appeared he wrote pertinent information.

"We've been here over two years." A memory of his face

played at the edge of her mind, but she couldn't recall seeing him at church.

He wrote in his book.

"And where did you come from?" His voice was high-pitched, like a youth not yet turned man. But his face showed a life of grievance.

"Southwark." Telling of her past made her uncomfortable.

"Does your husband work within the parish?"

Oh nay! Was this why he was here? Wherever they went, she had to dodge questions about John. "He works in London as a clerk for Henry Walters, beaver pelt tradesman."

The man nodded. "We've noticed that you haven't had any baptisms or other ordinances performed at Saint Mary's." This time when he glanced up, Hannah witnessed anger in his eyes, but he quickly looked again to his book.

"That's correct. I've not had any babes as late."

"Your husband and son don't attend services regularly. Can you tell me why?"

She panicked and tried to calculate quickly. Why was she not prepared for this question? She hid her shaking hands in her skirts. "Their work is . . . busy."

"They work on Sundays? I'm sure you're aware 'tis a crime to do so." His gaze now held hers, his eyes as intense as a snake wrapping around its prey.

Her stomach roiled. She placed a hand on the door frame to steady herself. "Oh, well, of course not. They're tired from the day's work before." She sounded like an idiot. Her womb ached, and she needed to lie down. How could she get him to cease asking questions?

"Where does your son work?" He held his quill ready.

The church kept such records of its parishioners? A tingling climbed up her back. Something wasn't right. "He stocks goods for a grocer in London."

"And do you know this grocer's name?"

"Joseph . . . um, nay, I suppose I don't know his surname."

The clerk leaned closer. "And where in London does he work?"

"I'm sorry, I don't know." Her voice squeaked, and she swayed.

He looked at her as if she were an imbecile and a liar.

"I'm feeling ill. Can you come back another time when my husband is home? I'm sure he'll have the answers you need."

"Are you sure?" He glared at her, not leaving.

She wanted to slap his face, shove him, scream at him. Anything to get him to thwart questions and go away.

"You do realize how important it is to attend services every Sunday? Our Lord has much to teach us through his servants, and how will you learn if not at church?" His eyes didn't match his statement of truth.

"Of course, we'll be there Sunday."

He spun and marched the direction of Lambeth Palace and Saint Mary's.

Chapter Thirty

John gently helped Hannah onto the settle in the parlor where she could be surrounded by the whole family so as not to miss any of the conversation when they were all together. Samuel had come earlier for Easter and would be here only one more day.

She moaned as she reclined against the pillows. The afternoon light coming from the window added little color to her pale face.

He'd stayed home from work, feeling the need to be here after she'd miscarried a third child. The fear of being caught by Tomlinson, even as the man heightened his efforts to round up every last Separatist, didn't come close to the fear John harbored over Hannah when she was unwell.

Each time she miscarried a babe, she became weaker. She was only six and thirty, but mayhap it was time to cease breeding. She loved her babies—and no doubt would argue with him—but watching her in this condition showed him it was time. If he lost her, he'd lose his world.

"May I get you anything, Mother," Janie asked.

"Nay, thank you," Hannah said feebly.

Hannah wasn't just ill physically. She'd withdrawn from all the adults. When he'd become an Independent, he never would have guessed how many in her family would also find peace in the organization. He'd stopped hoping years before that she'd join him. Yet when Penninah and Samuel covenanted fellowship, that old hope sprung to life—only to find sorrow. Not only did Hannah refuse to attend with them, she'd been deeply hurt by their decisions. When she lost this third child, her spirits were as low as when he'd taken her to Southwark.

Penninah glanced at him as if she understood both his and her sister's sorrow. She smiled at the children lounging on chairs and the floor. "Did you know that I met a Mister Praise-God Barebone in London?"

Joseph giggled. "That's a silly name."

"He told me it's his nickname." Penninah nodded. "His parents named him Unless-Jesus-Christ-Had-Died-For-Thee-Thou-Hadst-Been-Damned Barebone."

The children laughed joyously, and even Hannah softly chuckled.

John burst out in laughter.

Everyone in the room quieted and stared at him.

"What?" He lowered himself carefully next to his wife.

"Your laugh has a magical tone, Father. We didn't know." Janie blushed.

Hannah laid her head back and grinned.

"You should come meet Mister Barebone, Mother," Thomas said.

John's son had the same desires as he to bring Hannah into the fold.

Not surprisingly, she shook her head.

John needed to remind Penninah and Thomas that the congregation members' names were never to be mentioned outside of the meetings. Too much had changed since Penninah had moved in, and the rules had become lenient. He also regretted that she witnessed the first and only time he'd raised his voice at Hannah. He'd made a promise before he married her that he'd never act like his father. And he'd failed.

Hannah glanced at him, then to her sister and Thomas. "We don't mention the names of other Independents in this home."

How did she always know what bothered him? "Penny and Samuel, you two can leave now and go by wherry to Blackfriars. I'll wait for Dorothy to come this afternoon before leaving."

"Humphrey Barnett's?" Penninah questioned.

Hannah threw her a stern, disapproving look.

Penninah covered her mouth. "Oh, sorry." She shrugged and left with Samuel.

John turned to his children. "Your aunt has become negligent about mentioning names. Please, let's comply to the old rules for everyone's safety."

"Aye, Father," Thomas agreed.

John said to him, "You leave and go by bridge. I'll come soon with Janie by carriage."

He nodded and left to get ready. Soon the door clicked shut.

Barbara clasped her hands in front of her. "May I come tonight? I've only been once and very much liked it."

John glanced at Hannah. As much as he wanted Barbara to come, he didn't want to compound Hannah's pain. She was so frail. Should he stay home? He'd promised to sermonize this night, but maybe someone else could do it. "Nay, Barbara. 'Tis not Elizabeth coming with Mistress Denne? 'Twould be rude to not keep your appointment."

"We can wait until they come. Elizabeth wants to see what a meeting is like."

John threw back his head in alarm. "Boys, leave the room. Barbara and I need to talk."

They wandered out, heads down.

John knelt beside Barbara's chair. Her dark hair and timid brown eyes reminded him so much of his sister Mary. "You've been speaking to your friend about our meetings?"

Barbara nodded and looked to her lap. "My apologies."

Hannah offered no comment, which was unusual. She must be very ill indeed.

"Keeping the meetings and those who attend them secret could be a matter of someone's life. Do you understand?"

Barbara's eyes watered. "Aye."

He wanted to make sure she understood the seriousness. "There's an evil man who uses bloodhounds to sniff out people at the meetings. If he discovers them, they're all arrested and taken to prison."

Hannah's expression betrayed more worry than Barbara's.

He went to her and sat, taking her hand. "Should I stay home? I'm not feeling right about leaving you."

She stared at him, her blue eyes sad and forlorn. Her lightheartedness seemed forever gone. "Dorothy is on her way." She coughed. "She'll be spending the night in case you don't make it home." She caressed his cheek. "Be ever watchful, John." Her eyes begged him be so. "Something does feel amiss, but my siblings and Thomas have already left. I need you to keep them safe."

He kissed her tenderly on the brow. "As always. I'll take all precautions."

The Pulse of His Soul

The pain of walking up the stairs, even held between John and Dorothy, exhausted Hannah. She fell asleep instantly and awoke to Dorothy bringing her tea, the room faintly lit by one candle.

Setting the cup on a table, Dorothy placed a hand on Hannah's forehead. "I've never seen you this ill. Should I call the physician?"

"Nay, I'll recover." Hannah coughed and felt it deep in her chest.

Dorothy's forehead wrinkled. "That cough sounds like there's more to this illness than losing a child."

"Has John left?" Hannah glanced toward the bedchamber door.

"Aye, and he's taken the girls with him."

"What!" Hannah tried to sit up, but a sharp pain pulled at her womb. "*All* the girls?"

"Elizabeth has been hounding me for weeks to go to one of those Separatist meetings. I decided 'twould do her some good to finally get a glimpse of what they talk about. I'm guessing she'll be so bored she'll never want to go back."

"And Barbara went too?" Unease sent hairs raising on her arms and neck.

Someone knocked on the front door below.

Dorothy started to rise.

Hannah pulled her back down. "One of the boys will answer. Avail me Dorothy, was John in favor of taking the three girls?"

"He hesitated, and I told him 'twould make the home more peaceful for you. I promised to spend the night." She cocked her head. "Did I do wrong?"

Hannah felt she needed to get to the meeting. But how could she? Again, she tried to sit, and the pain shot through her womb.

"Hannah, what's wrong?" Dorothy's voice rose.

Joseph came to the door of her bedchamber. "Mama?"

"Son, please go be with your brothers."

He nodded, a little unsure. "That man from church . . . he came to the door again."

Man from the church? "Did you get his name?"

Joseph shook his head. "He asked for some clothing to donate to the poor. Said there was someone who was about Father's size that needed a hat. I gave him one off the peg."

"That was very kind of you," Dorothy said.

Man from the church? Who? The man who'd interrogated her

with all those questions last week?

Dogs barked in the distance. Many dogs.

"Oh, dear God," Hannah exclaimed. "Keep them safe until I can get there."

"What are you talking about? You can't go anywhere in your condition," Dorothy all but shrieked.

"Mama?" Joseph sniffled.

"Joseph," Dorothy said. "go tell Sam he's to care for you and Benjamin while I talk with your mother. All will be well."

He left, watching Hannah over his shoulder, tears on his face.

Could a ten-year-old care for his brothers late into the night? She considered the mischief they could get in, but it didn't matter. The rest of her family was in more danger. She knew it in her heart.

"We can't go anywhere, Hannah." Dorothy placed a hand on Hannah's cheek. "You're a bit warm. It must be the fever making you delirious."

Hannah grabbed her hand. "Dorothy, listen. Hear the hounds?"

"Faintly."

"That's because they're running away from us . . . toward Elizabeth and John and Barbara and Janie. Oh, Dorothy! They're bloodhounds on the scent of John's hat."

Dorothy paled, reeling back. "Elizabeth!" she gasped.

"We must take your carriage and try to reach them first, thwart them from making it to the meeting where all the others will be in danger as well." Hannah could hardly breathe. She coughed again and pushed through the pain of sitting up. "Help me dress."

John entered Humphrey Barnett's home to find everyone there waiting for him.

Penninah made room for Elizabeth and Barbara to squeeze in beside her, and Thomas stood to offer Janie his seat. The small room in the brewer clerk's home was packed with at least sixty people. Many of the men stood along the walls. The April night was warm, but they dared not open any windows for air. Curtains had been drawn and doors locked.

After a brother prayed and they sang a psalm as quietly as possible to not arouse the neighbors or someone passing, John stepped forward with a greeting. "I almost didn't come tonight, for my wife is ill. It's a dangerous life we lead to meet in Christ's name and commune in faith. Our testimonies that bring us here at our peril, are a personal thing. You must have your own and cannot live off of anyone else's. We shouldn't be here to please another, but because our souls cry to worship God. Allow your conscience to dictate." He cleared his throat to settle his sudden emotions. "I had respect for my holy orders to act as perpetual curate in Kent. But I found I don't need holy orders to serve God."

Many smiled in agreement.

"As with us, the Apostle Paul also met in secret with those who believed, and tried to teach those who did not." John stopped and smiled. "I just realized my thoughts were so torn with staying home with my beloved, that I forgot my Bible."

A few chuckled, and Eaton, sitting on the front row, handed him his.

"Thank you, Brother Eaton." He flipped to the chapters he'd read so many times before. "In Corinthians we learn of Paul's challenging ministry. He said: 'Of the Jews five times received I forty stripes save one. Thrice was I beaten with rods, once was I stoned, thrice I suffered shipwreck, a night and a day I have been in deep; In journeyings often, in perils of waters, in perils of robbers, in perils by mine own countrymen.'" John looked up after he emphasized the words "perils of mine own countrymen."

Many nodded.

He continued. "'. . . in perils by the heathen, in perils in the city, in perils in the wilderness, in perils in the sea, in perils among false brethren; In weariness and painfulness, in watchings often, in hunger and thirst, in fastings often, in cold and nakedness.'"

John handed the Bible back to Eaton.

In the distance dogs bayed.

John's heart skipped a beat. "Bloodhounds! We need to leave now." Panic flew through his veins.

The congregants leapt from their seats, faces masked in sudden terror.

"Hurry!" John shouted. He helped William Attwood hobble forward on a crutch. "Thomas, get the girls out of here." In a frenzy, John lifted the elderly man off his feet and hefted him toward the backdoor.

Penninah grabbed Elizabeth, and Thomas took a sister under each arm. Samuel helped Widow White, who cried and fussed and clung to his doublet.

Husbands went to wives, families congregated together, and

everyone jostled toward the backdoor, their bodies slamming together. The crowd so large it slowed their exit.

Someone banged on the door. "Open in the name of the king."

The smell in the room grew sharp, as if fear had an odor.

The banging grew louder.

Women screamed. Men called orders. Children cried out.

John feared the door would fracture before they could get everyone out.

Suddenly, those who were heading toward the back pivoted and ran into the room again, expressions of dismay and horror on their faces, their hands grasping air.

Behind them, men in black uniforms with the crest of Bishop Laud stomped into the room, grabbing at people, telling them to, "Stop in the name of the king!"

There were more Independents than henchmen, and they clambered as well they could around the guards, heading once again toward the backdoor.

John lost sight of his family. Dod appeared in front of him and took Attwood from his arms. John scrambled to see who else needed help.

The front door flew open with a loud crack and splintering of wood. Dogs rushed in snapping and snarling. The screaming and chaos heightened. Eaton smashed a dog's snout with his Bible.

Mothers and fathers threw arms around their young, pressing them to a safer place between them.

One dog leapt over the back of someone, flying right at John.

He ducked, the dog smashed into the wall and yelped, but then righted himself, snapping at John and baring his teeth.

John kicked at him.

The dog buried its teeth into John's leg.

Pain seared through his calf.

"Good boy, Beelzy." Tomlinson stepped forward, a pronged mace in his hand. "Lothropp. I knew I'd catch you and your evil apostates." His upper lip raised at the corner.

"These people have done nothing wrong in God's eyes. Let them go." John's heart thudded in his ears.

Beelzy took hold of John's pantaloons, pulling him toward the door. Fabric tore, and the dog took a firmer hold on John's ankle, sharp teeth burrowing into his flesh.

He went to smack the dog, but Tomlinson caught his fist. "Do you mock your king? They've done much wrong in the eyes of our sovereign, God's own divine." Tomlinson released John and grabbed Beelzy's collar. "Release."

The hound immediately sat on its haunches, panting, with its tongue hanging out.

"Move toward the front door, Lothropp, I'll be right behind you." Tomlinson's sharp features were honed like the edge of a sharp knife.

John didn't move. He'd not put his back to a man wielding a spiked club.

"Help me here," Tomlinson called to the guard nearest him.

Grabbing John on each arm, they dragged him toward the door.

In front of them, two men-at-arms hauled out Sara Barebone, who had apparently swooned.

Outside, the henchmen held torches high. They had at least thirty Independents lying face-down in the street, many of them women, with pikes or guns pointed at their heads.

Granger, on his hands and knees, vomited, grabbing at his gut, a glowering henchman standing over him with the butt of his musket toward Granger's stomach. Blood covered his face.

Penninah and Elizabeth lay beside one another, holding hands. Elizabeth shuddered with sobs. Samuel and Dod lay prone. Too still. Where were his children? *Please God, help them get far from here.*

Tomlinson kicked John in the back of the legs. "Kneel, heretic."

John fell to his knees.

Tomlinson punched him between his shoulder blades with the hard-metal handle of his mace.

An ache shot through John's spine all the way to his fingertips. He fell forward onto his hands, landing in the muck of the roadside, trying to catch his breath. The sharp odor of urine made him gag.

"Lay in the gutter where you belong." Tomlinson growled.

John turned his head to avoid as much of the stench as possible.

Far down the dark street stood a carriage with lanterns lit and horses dancing and throwing their heads, a coachman trying to calm them. Thomas helped Janie and Barbara into the conveyance. Denne's carriage? Lantern light fell on Hannah's pale, stricken face in the carriage window.

With a thud, pain projected like a missile into John's head and turned everything black.

Chapter Thirty-One

Hannah didn't know how someone could be angry, relieved, and terrified all at once, but that's exactly how she felt. Angry at John for placing her children in such danger, relieved they now sat safely with her in the carriage, and terrified for John, Penninah, Samuel, and Elizabeth.

As the carriage took them home, Janie and Barbara clung to one another, sobbing and blithering over their frightful escape and who'd been caught.

Thomas sat at Janie's side, rubbing her back but saying naught, staring at Hannah as if he expected her to make everything better.

She'd tried to make it better. For years, she'd prayed they wouldn't go to those illegal meetings.

Dorothy pulled at her skirts, wiping her eyes with a handkerchief. "Denne will get Elizabeth out of the hands of those filthy Laud subordinates. He must!" She leaned toward Thomas and grabbed his arm. "He can, can't he?"

Anger reddened Thomas's face. "I pray it be so, Mistress Denne. We must get them *all* out." He silently pleaded with Hannah again to make things right—the same look he'd given her at Leighton's flogging. "What shall we do, Mother?"

After his poor choices he expected her to make everything better. She wished she could.

Her eyes were suddenly blinded to what was going on in the carriage. She only saw what was in her mind—guns pointed at her sons. "The boys! Oh, dear God. The boys are home alone." She replayed the story Dorothy had told of how the henchmen went immediately to Leighton's home after the arrest and held a gun to his son's chest. "Thomas, we must get home and burn your father's papers. All his sermons, correspondence . . . everything."

Thomas shot up straighter. "They'll be heading to our house now. They'll need evidence of his crime."

"Can the horses go any faster?" Janie wailed.

Dorothy knocked on the ceiling.

That gripping pain that barely let Hannah climb from bed pinched her womb. Why now? Could God not heal her so she could deal with what needed to be done to help John and the others? "Do you have incriminating papers, too, Thomas? Or Samuel or Penninah?"

"I do. My journal." He confirmed.

They *had* to get home before the henchmen. She'd not let them capture Thomas too. "It all must be burned. They don't have you now, but they can arrest you if they find anything heretical in your writing."

"We'll stoke all the fires when we arrive." Barbara looked at Dorothy weeping in her hands. "I love Elizabeth, too. We'll get her out."

"Denne will blame this on me. I allowed her to go. How could I have been so foolish?"

Barbara moved across the carriage and squeezed between Hannah and Dorothy. She took Dorothy in her arms. Such a loving gesture for a girl of thirteen. Hannah's kind children were not all her doing. They'd learned compassion for others from John. His deeds were always for the troubled.

At last they arrived home. No horses or men appeared to be near. They disembarked, Thomas helped Hannah, and Dorothy sped off for her own house.

All was quiet inside.

She prayed the boys were in bed. To Janie and Barbara, she said, "Check on your brothers and then search through the parlor for any papers your father may have written. Build the fire in there." She spun to Thomas. "Your father keeps his papers in the desk in our bedchamber. Let's start there."

Somber, the girls left to perform her bidding.

Thomas helped her up the stairs and into the bedchamber then blew into the embers of the dying fire and added more wood.

Hannah had her ears trained to the street. "Go get your journal."

Thomas ran off.

Would they have enough time? She gathered all the papers she could find in drawers and leather satchels. John's life's thoughts and sermons—words of praise to God scrolled across the sheets. She piled them on the floor. What if he didn't live? She was destroying all she'd have left of him.

Thomas rushed in and threw his loose journal paper on the fire then picked up what she'd found. He added pages by handfuls to the fire. It smothered out the flames, and Hannah's heart stilled.

Thomas made a sound of despair in his throat then blew on the embers again. The papers finally caught, curling in the red and orange flames. John's beliefs were going up in smoke, years and years of his longing to please God turning into ash.

Exhaling, she turned back to the desk, double checking that she'd found everything.

Thomas came back. "I'll need to burn them slower in order to keep the flames alive."

"Aye. I wish we had a hiding place, and they didn't need to be burned."

Thomas stopped and looked at her. "Do you see goodness in Father's work?"

"Your father's heart has always been pure. 'Tis his judgement I've worried over. And now look what he's done—been caught and beaten and thrown in jail somewhere." John's foolishness tightened her chest. "He cannot live as he thinks God demands or care for his family when he's rotting in gaol."

Thomas thinned his lips and threw more pages on the fire.

The sound of a horse galloping down the street and stopping near their house caused Hannah to feel lightheaded. They still had so much to burn. She'd go down and try and stall. "Hurry Thomas," she said as she went out.

An impatient knock banged on the door.

Janie stepped from her and Penninah's room. "I found some papers in here. Barbara's checking Samuel's belongings."

"No time to get back to the parlor with them. Carry them to Thomas. Do what you can to destroy everything." Hannah held tightly to the railing as she made her way downstairs. Her chest and womb ached with pain.

The knocking grew more incessant.

Her heart thudded just as incessantly. What was she to say to the shrewd Laudian? Taking a deep breath, she opened the door. "Robert!" Her knees buckled.

He grabbed her before she hit the floor. "I came as soon as

I'd heard." He kicked the door shut and helped her onto a bench. "Do you know . . . ?" His eyes searched hers.

"I know. Not only did they arrest John but Penninah and Samuel too."

His face went ashen.

"Were you not at the meeting?" she asked.

"Nay. Enid still doesn't fair well with her pregnancy. I stayed home."

"Robert, what am I to do? I'm so ill." She brushed hair out of her face. "The children need protecting. A friend's daughter—only thirteen—taken too. She's the daughter of a solicitor for the Church." A tear slipped down Hannah's cheek. She swiped it away, wishing she were brave.

"From what I was told tonight, there were some distinguished people arrested. Ralph Grafton, a rich man, and Abigail Delamer, whose husband is a servant to the Queen."

"Will they have enough influence to get the others free?" She clutched her middle.

"I don't know. Some will be able to pay bond, perchance."

"And John?" Almost afraid to ask, her words were too quiet.

"If history serves, they'll consider him a heretical leader who persuades others to follow Satan. They'll use him as an example of what they can do to those who leave the Church. Prepare yourself for the worst."

"The worst?" Her breath caught in her throat.

A bang on the door brought on a shard of terror that sliced into Hannah's gut. *Keep calm*, she told herself and hid her trembling hands in her skirts. "Thomas is upstairs burning John's papers," she urgently whispered.

Robert nodded and opened the door. "May I help you?" he asked smoothly, without a tremble in his voice.

"Address me as Lord Tomlinson," the man growled.

Hannah knew that high-pitched voice. 'Twas the parson's clerk, and no doubt the man who took John's hat.

"I'm here on Bishop Laud's orders. In the name of the king we must be granted entry to search the home," he demanded.

"Search for what, may I ask?" Robert barred the door.

"Who are you?" Tomlinson snarled.

"I'm Robert Linnell."

"Mister Linnell, you're obstructing Bishop William Laud's guardsmen by not letting us pass. If you don't step aside, I'll arrest you."

Robert stepped aside. "There are only women and children here. Good Anglican church attenders."

"How do you know my business has aught to do with the Church?"

"You said you were Laud's man, did you not? What else could you want but to be about the Bishop's business?"

Tomlinson stepped in and stared down his sharp nose at Hannah on the bench.

She didn't stand for she feared she'd faint. "Are you not the parson's clerk?" She hoped to throw him off with his own deceit. "What right does a parson's clerk have to search my home?"

"I'm the deputy of Bishop Laud's guards."

"You mean to say, you lied to me when you visited last?" She wished to knock him down a few rungs on the holy ladder he stood upon.

He puffed up his chest as seven more men filed into the entry hall. "Why do you not rise and bow to me?"

"I'm ill," she said simply.

He glared at her with snake-like eyes. "Show me where your husband keeps his papers."

Hannah needed another tactic to stall him. He loved himself overmuch for belittling. Praying Thomas was getting everything burned, she told her own lie while asking God for forgiveness. "I don't believe he has any papers. If so, I'm unaware of where he keeps them."

"Now who's lying?" The man's nostrils flared.

"I rarely see him writing." Which was true. He wrote late into the night when she slept, exhausted from the day's chores. "Why not wait for him to come home and ask him yourself?"

"He'll not be home tonight, for I've arrested him."

Hannah gasped as if this was news to her. She didn't have to try that hard, his words felt like a punch in her already aching gut.

He turned to his guards huddled outside the parlor, dressed in the same black livery as he. "Search the whole house. Every desk, chest, cabinet. I want all of it examined closely." His nasally voice lacked authority, but the men left to do his bidding.

"Wait!" Robert held up his hand. "There are young children here. May I gather them in the parlor to ease their fears?"

"Gather them if you must, but I'll be talking to every one of them."

Hannah sucked in her breath.

Tomlinson had attached to his uniform a pronged mace, a

dagger, a long-barreled handgun, and a sword in jeweled scabbard strapped to his waist. Would he use his gun like someone had with Leighton's son? Hold it to their chests to get the truth from them? Grateful John was wise enough to keep his business from the boys, she hoped they knew naught incriminating about their father. Then she remembered Penninah had mentioned names. Would they remember? Would Thomas and the girls withstand Tomlinson's inquiries?

"Mistress Lothropp is not well. May I take her to her bed?" Robert's voice took on a diplomacy she could not hope to have.

Tomlinson snickered like Robert had told an insipid jest. "So that's how it is here." He wagged his thin eyebrows.

"Sir," Robert boomed. "She's a lady, and you're a wicked fiend."

Tomlinson dropped his smile and glared at Robert. "Take her away." Jaw clenching, he spun and marched into the parlor.

As Robert helped Hannah upstairs, she heard stone pieces of the chess set rain against the wall in the parlor.

On the landing, the children stood huddled together. Guards were in their bedchambers, thrusting over chests of drawers, yanking off mattresses from frames.

The boys ran to her. "What's happening, Mother?" Sam asked.

Benjamin's trembling body clung to her legs. He wiped his tears on her skirt.

"Did I do something wrong?" Joseph's red-curly hair lay askew from being in bed. "Where is Father?"

"I wasn't sure what to tell him," Janie shrugged one shoulder.

"You did naught wrong," Hannah answered. "Your father is being questioned by Church authorities. I need you all to be very brave and tell the man downstairs how good your father is. He'd never mistreat anyone and shouldn't be kept from us."

Robert took her arm. "Janie and Barbara, can you keep the boys together while I help your mother. She'd stay with you if she were well enough."

They nodded and grouped back together in each other's arms.

In her bedchamber, Thomas used the poker to shroud any evidence of pieces of paper in the hearth. The stack of papers Hannah had left on the floor were gone. The wound of burning John's writings would stay with her forever.

"Come away from there," Robert said urgently to Thomas. "Go be with your siblings."

Thomas left as a guard entered.

Robert ignored him and helped Hannah into bed—his gentleness in stark contrast to the guard rifling through the cupboard and dumping contents on the floor. He didn't glance once at the fire hearth.

But she'd not thought to search through the clothing to make sure no papers were in John's pockets. "Robert," she whispered, "Bless you for being here. Keep my children safe."

The guard threw the last of John's doublets on the floor and started his hunt through the desk.

"They'll not threaten children with me in the room." Robert tried to appear fierce, but his gentle features weren't cooperating.

"Tomlinson may ask you to leave," she whispered.

"I will not. You know how hard 'tis to get rid of me." He grinned and winked—both appeared forced.

His loyalty did give her hope, but after he stepped from the room and the guard stopped his searching and left, she couldn't relax. Worry ate at her stomach. Her ears were tuned to all sounds in the house.

The fire in the hearth roared.

Still with a fever though, she occasionally shivered. Although more than exhausted, she couldn't rest. She finally decided it did her no good to lie there if all she did was worry. She swung her legs out and had placed her feet on the floor when Janie entered.

"All is well. That evil man questioned us all and is now talking with Robert. His men are waiting outside." Janie lifted the coverlet and helped Hannah back into bed. "I've put the children to bed." She sat beside her. "No one said anything ruinous to further hurt Father." She looked at her hands. "Tomlinson interrogated me about Father's activities and if he ever came home late at night." She hesitated. "I lied, Mother. Will God forgive me?"

Hannah stroked her arm. "I've lied this night as well. Our lies were not designed to harm but to help another. I cannot believe a God who loves his children would punish us. But best to pray for forgiveness, don't you think?"

Janie nodded. "Robert says we can help Father by being tolerant of anyone who asks us questions. He said he'd go visit Father and let us know how he's doing."

"Bless Robert."

"He still extols you for saving his mother's life. Methinks that favor has brought good back to us and may continue to do so."

"I pray it will be so." Hannah pulled Janie to her. "The Lord saw fit to bestow upon me honorable children. I'm in *His* debt."

Chapter Thirty-Two

Hannah traveled with Thomas and Barbara to the trial scheduled by the High Commission at the Palace of Westminster. As they crossed over London Bridge, wafts of smoke filled the carriage. Peering about, Hannah saw large bonfires in the streets and Laud's men in black livery throwing books into the flames.

Thomas looked out too. "By Laud's decree, they're burning books, pamphlets, and news leaflets that don't pass censor or are not written by the Church."

Hannah remembered burning John's writings, and a deep sadness tugged at her. She wanted to go back to the days she lived in Egerton and raised cheerful babies and always had a song on her lips. She hungered to hold John in bed and know that he'd keep her safe and love the Church as much as she. But Bishop Laud kept John at New Prison, in Clerkenwell, on the outskirts of London. She hadn't been allowed to visit him or her siblings.

Thomas grasped her hand. "All will be well." His tone was tender.

"You sound like your father."

"Thank you, Mother." He squeezed her hand.

All her children had been trying to cheer her these last days, but 'twas a desperate attempt at the impossible. Although she felt better physically, only a cough and fatigue remained, her spiritual nature had suffered, and she feared she'd never be the same person again.

Barbara shifted on her seat. "Will Mistress Denne be at the

trial?"

Hannah had agreed to let Barbara come this day because she had been almost as distraught over her friend's arrest as much as her father's. She said she wanted to see Elizabeth and know of her welfare. Barbara blamed herself for Elizabeth's arrest as did Dorothy. But if anyone was to blame, 'twas John. He shouldn't have allowed the girls to have gone into such a dangerous situation.

"I suspect Dorothy will be there. She wrote to tell me Elizabeth's father would not pay the bond to get her released." Hannah leaned forward and laid her hand on Barbara's knee. "He has disowned her. Her association with the Separatists can ruin his reputation, and he could lose his occupation with the Church. I thought to offer our assistance and have Elizabeth live with us upon her release. Would you like that?"

Barbara cheered considerably, her dark eyes filling with tears of gratitude. "Very much. I'll treat her as my sister."

Hannah sat back, wondering how she could feed an extra person when she'd little means to feed her own on the small salary Thomas now offered. She prayed God would provide and bring John home soon.

Their carriage slowed on the street leading to Westminster. With the road packed with conveyances and people, they couldn't pass. 'Twas much like Leighton's flogging had been with vendors calling out their foods for sale and pamphlets being sold. People pressed toward the palace, dressed in both rags and fine fabrics. The blue sky of what could have been a pleasant spring day brought fair temperatures.

"We best walk from here," Thomas suggested.

They left the carriage with the driver and joined the throng of trial-goers. Who were all these people interested in those accused of schism from the Church?

Hannah looked for anyone she knew but saw only strangers. She hoped they saw her as a stranger too and not as the wife of the Separatist leader, an enemy to God and traitor to his king.

"There's Thomas Lothropp, the son of the heretical leader," someone called out.

Thomas stepped away from Hannah and Barbara, moving back into the crowd.

Hannah immediately realized he was trying to make sure they weren't associated with him. Barbara grabbed her arm. Hair lifted at the nape of her neck. Afraid to glance back, after a few moments she couldn't help herself.

Thomas strode tall, his shoulders thrown back, acting as if he weren't the object of derision. Someone pushed him, and those he fell against shoved him away. He straightened again and walked on.

"You should be rotting in prison too," a young man with a frayed hat hollered. "Only bad seeds come from rotten fruit."

Barbara pulled Hannah forward. "He's strong, don't worry."

The walking caused Hannah's cough to surface. She swallowed, trying to keep it at bay. They made their way into the palace and were directed to a large room with tiered bench-seating and a blue ceiling covered in gold-painted stars. The bishops who would judge were not yet seated at the front.

"Hannah," someone called. "Over here." Robert waved them over. He normally would have called her Mistress Lothropp in public, but he protected her as Thomas had.

Robert had saved a large space on a bench two rows back from a roped-off area of chairs.

"You're so good to us, Robert." Hannah and Barbara sat. "Thomas is with us, but I dare say won't sit near us. Dorothy Denne will be here though. Shall we save a seat for her?"

"By all means." Robert sat next to Hannah.

"How is Enid?" she asked.

"Still very sick." Distress etched Robert's face. "It no longer seems a natural sickness for a woman breeding. She no longer wants to eat, and she's near delivery." He wiped his face with his hands. "How do you fare?"

"Better."

Guards led prisoners into the room and told them to sit on the chairs in the roped-off area.

Hannah stood to see them better. Many were strangers but when Penninah and Samuel came in arm in arm, she swayed where she stood. They wore the same clothes they were arrested in even though Hannah had sent them fresh. Samuel limped and Penninah had a laceration on her cheek, but otherwise they looked well. Filthy, but well.

Penninah scanned the crowd. She locked eyes with Hannah, smiling as if they were meeting at the theatre for a night of enjoyment. Then winked.

Her ridiculousness reminded Hannah of their father. It was all a show.

Elizabeth's beautiful red hair had been chopped off.

"Other than her hair, Elizabeth looks well," Barbara whispered and waved to her.

Hannah hadn't told Barbara that Dorothy had delivered money to the prison to keep her daughter safe from rape and molestation.

"She hasn't been in prison long enough to get lice," Robert grumbled. "I'll wager someone fetched a large sum for her red hair to be used as a wig."

Hannah couldn't see John. Something was wrong. "Why isn't John with the prisoners?"

"I don't know." Robert tugged her to sit before she called attention to herself.

Dorothy made her way over. She sat next to Barbara.

Hannah reached across her daughter to grasp Dorothy's hand. She squeezed it, but Dorothy said naught, her lip trembling with emotion.

Thomas entered, inconspicuously looked her way, then sat on the floor in front of the first row of benches.

The room filled, reeking of unwashed bodies both from the prisoners and spectators. With the chamber at capacity, others congregated around windows and outside the door in the hallway.

"If this trial is like others I've been to for the Separatists, it will play out like a mockery to justice," Robert whispered to Hannah. "Prior to the High Commission questioning the accused, they'll ask them to make an *ex-officio* oath which will bind them to answer all questions on *any* subject. The oath is used as coercion to self-incriminate. It is not the typical oath of loyalty."

"I don't understand," Hannah said.

"The bishops will try to force the prisoners to testify against themselves, trap them into feeling as if they've mortally sinned by not taking the oath, and fine them with contempt of court for silence. I'll be surprised if they even talk about not using the prayer book or if churches shouldn't be ruled by bishops. There'll be no jurors or solicitors to help the accused. The High Commission is about enforcing conformity, and they answer only to the monarch. There's no longer a Parliament or—" He stopped himself and mumbled under his breath, "Or English common law."

Hannah worried at her lip. She prayed for God's protection for her family. But what if John, Samuel, and Penninah had lost God's protection because they'd left the Church? If what Robert said proved true, failure loomed certain. There would be no release from prison.

A back door opened, and six men filed in, four wore the robes of bishops. The room quieted, and all stood. Many bowed to the clergy at the far end of the room who were stepping up onto the dais.

Robert leaned in and whispered. "The judges, all bishops and ministers, act as prosecutors. Other than the king, the Court of High Commission contains the highest rulers of our kingdom. You may have seen some of these men, such as the Archbishop of Canterbury, George Abbot." He pointed to the fat man in the long and curled periwig.

Hannah had met him in Canterbury when first married. She'd considered him one of the most exalted of men at the time, never guessing he'd one day be possibly sentencing her husband to imprisonment or death.

"But also to judge this day is the Archbishop of York, Richard Neile." He pointed to a greying man with the face of a Roman conqueror, his stiff ruff so large it all but covered his ears. "And of course, you know the Bishop of London, William Laud."

John's enemy wasn't what Hannah had imagined. He was a petite man with high-arched eyebrows above striking dark eyes. He pursed his mouth as if he'd detected something foul near his presence and brought a lace handkerchief to his nose with delicate fingers. This was the man who held power over John's life?

"Just now sitting is the Bishop of Saint David's, Theophilus Field."

Bishop Field's long face with pointed mustache and beard held only an expression of boredom.

"Then there's the King's Advocate, a judge and politician, Sir Henry Marten, and lastly the court registrar, whose name I don't know."

How could John face these bishops whom he'd once revered? Her stomach rolled with unease.

The registrar rose. "All be seated."

Everyone sat, and still Hannah couldn't see John. Was he not to be tried this day?

Thomas glanced back at her with worry in his eyes.

She coughed, and Barbara rubbed her back.

The registrar held up a large paper and addressed the room. "All those who were taken in Blackfriars, who were brought to the court under the custody of the keeper of the New Prison, shall be addressed this day."

Where was John?

"Out of prison divers persons which were taken on Sunday

last at a conventicle meeting at the house of Humphrey Barnett, a brewer's clerk, dwelling in the precinct of Blackfriars." The registrar peered at those on the chairs. "By name, John Lothropp, their minister. Humphrey Barnett, Henry Dod, Samuel Eaton, William Granger, Sara Jones, Sara Jacob, Penninah Howse, Sara Barebone, Susan Wilson, and divers others there were which appear not this day."

"Mister Lothropp, the minister, does not appear to be here," Archbishop Abbot spoke up.

The registrar pivoted to Abbot. "He kept himself out of the way for a while, therefore the man of the house wherein they were first taken shall be called. Humphrey Barnett, step to the stand."

Hannah shifted. Kept himself *out of the way for a while*? What did he mean?

"When were you last at your parish church?" Laud interrogated Barnett with an edge to his voice.

Barnett held his chin up and looked at his accusers. "I was at *my church* when in *my house* at the conventicle. I used to go to the parish church but my wife will not."

The Archbishop Neile appeared surprised. "Will you suffer that in your wife?"

Before Barnett answered, the King's Advocate Marten said, "These persons were assembled on Sunday last at this man's house in Blackfriars, and there unlawfully held a conventicle, for which there are articles exhibited in this court against them. I pray that they may be put to answer upon their *oaths* to the articles, and that they set forth what exercises they used, and what were the words spoken by them."

"Here we go," Robert said near her ear.

Marten spun and pointed to Henry Dod. "And as for you, Mr Dod," He glared at him. "You might well have forborne, seeing you have been warned heretofore and passed by upon promise of amendment."

Dod stood. "Good Mister Advocate, spare that."

Laud pumped, "Do *you* go to your parish church?"

"I have come to my parish church as often as I can and used to come thither, but I endeavored to hear the most powerful minister," Dod answered.

Laud frowned. "You heard Mister Lothropp?"

By his response, he as much as admitted John the most powerful minister. Many of the bishops drew sour faces at the faux pas, and a few in court snickered.

Laud waved them off. "What ordination hath he?"

"He is a minister," said Dod.

"Did you not hear him preach and pray?" Laud swung his hand out as if he were in a theatrical. "Nay! You and the rest take upon yourselves to preach and to be ministers."

"Nay," said Dod.

Laud leaned forward. "Yes, you do, for you were heard preaching and praying."

Dod looked to Barnett, probably wondering the same thing as Hannah—why Barnett had been asked to stand and be questioned while the questioning had actually fallen on Dod. "I shall be ready in this particular to confess my fault, if I am convinced to be in any."

Laughter boomed from the audience.

Barnett and Dod were requested to be seated.

Hannah would have cowered if it was she being questioned by these God-fearing, powerful men, yet Barnett and Dod didn't speak in fear. They appeared clear in their minds as to whom they'd follow and what they believed. And she knew John would also stand firm in his own personal convictions, even if it meant being away from her and the children forever more.

The trial went on as Robert predicted with the clergy trying to put two more of the accused to oath. The accused then asked to be excused so as to have more time to consider and be informed of what the oath required, dodging an oath that would be self-incriminating.

Archbishop Abbot looked pointedly at each of the people brought into court that day. "You show yourselves most unthankful to God, to your king, and to your Church of England."

"God be praised," Archbishop Neile chimed in.

Abbot nodded. "Through his majesty's care and ours you have preaching in every church and men have liberty to join in prayer and participate of the sacrament and have catechizing, and all to enlighten you and which may serve you in the day of salvation. You! In an unthankful manner cast off all this yoke and in private unlawfully assemble yourselves together, making rents and divisions in the Church." Abbot's voice rang sermonic. "If anything be amiss, let it be known. If anything be not agreeable to the word of God, we shall be as ready to redress it as you, but whereas it is nothing but your own imaginations, and you are unlearned men that seek to make up a religion of your own heads, I doubt no persuasion will serve the turn." He spun to address the other bishops. "We must take this course. For they are called here to stand upon the bonds. And let us see what they will answer. It may be they will answer what will please us." It appeared Archbishop Abbot would rather proceed without the oath.

Hannah knew their answers would not please any of the clergy.

Laud's face reddened. "It is time to take notice of these. Nay, this is not the fourth part of them about this city." His gaze darted toward the prisoners. "You'll see," he boomed. "These came of set purpose, for they met not by chance. They are desperately heretical. They are all of different places. One of Essex, Saint Austin's, Saint Martin's Le Grand, Buttolphs, Algate, Thistleworth, and Saint Saviour's." He threw out his hand. "Let these be imprisoned. Let me make a motion. There be fewer of the ablest men of them. Let these four who have answered be the ones we proceed against. And if the rest come in, they shall be received, but if they will not, I know no reason why four or five shouldn't answer for all." His hand dropped and eyes narrowed as he peered at someone entering the room.

John stumbled forward, hardly keeping himself erect.

Many gasped, but 'twas Barbara who screamed.

Hannah felt she might swoon.

His hair, matted in blood, lay plastered to his scalp, and his shirt was dark with dried blood stains.

Love and dismay fought within Hannah.

Manacles kept his hands clasped in front of him.

Dear God, this can't be happening. Hannah wanted to take him in her arms.

Thomas sprang to his feet, but the man next to him pulled him back down.

Robert reached around Hannah and Barbara, holding them tightly. Dorothy did the same from the other side.

John didn't look up.

"By what authority do you have to preach and keep a conventicle?" Laud thundered.

John opened his mouth.

"How many women sat cross-legged upon ye bed whilst you sat on one side and preached and prayed most devoutly?" Laud shouted over whatever John tried to say.

Hannah swallowed hard, taking deep breaths to keep from vomiting. This foul-mouthed, vile Bishop of London was her ecclesiastical patriarch? A spiritual leader of her beloved church?

Had John been right when he'd told her the headship of Christ had been preempted by a hierarchy of men in robes *calling* themselves bishops? Father had often taught her that the evidence of pride was anger. Laud was a man so full of pride that his anger spewed forth as easily as breathing.

John straightened and looked to Laud. "I keep no such evil company—there were no such women."

"Are you a minister?" Laud narrowed his eyes, his face shrewd.

When John didn't readily answer, Archbishop Abbot snapped, "Are you a minister?"

"I am a minister." John finally answered.

Hannah cringed inside. That admission alone could give him a sentence of death. Why, John? Why?

Bishop Field narrowed his eyes at John. "Were not you Doctor King's—the Bishop of London's sizar in Oxford? I take it you were, and you show your thankfulness by this?"

"I am a minister," John answered with more volume.

Laud banged his fist on the raised desk in front of him. "How and by whom qualified you as a minister? Where are your Orders?"

John took a step closer to Laud. "I am a minister of the gospel of Christ, and the Lord has qualified me."

Murmurings rose throughout the courtroom.

Hannah knew him to be strong, but his admission sounded to be a statement truer than anything she thought she would hear from the archbishops. Had she been wrong all along? It did not matter, it was the clergy with the power to condemn.

The registrar called over the voices, "Will you lay your hand on the book and take your oath?"

"I will not." John stood straighter and shook his head.

Laud pointed at Dod, Barnett, and then John. "You three are the obstinate and perverse ringleaders of these folks." He flung his hand toward the others. "You have this day been assigned to answer upon your oath."

"I hope we are not so impious," Dod said. "We stand for the truth. For taking the oath, I crave your patience. I am not resolved upon it."

Barnett added, "I was at the church, but for taking the oath, I desire to be resolved."

"Mr Lothropp, has the Lord qualified *you*?" Laud dared him to answer again. "By what authority? What orders have you?"

"The Lord has qualified me," John said simply. He shifted slightly as if he were struggling to keep himself erect.

Hannah saw that one of his eyes was swollen shut. She could not bear to see his suffering. He needed her and she could do nothing. She turned her head into Barbara's neck.

Barbara wrapped her arms around Hannah. They wept quietly.

Robert and Dorothy still held to them both.

"You answered the Lord has qualified you, but is that a sufficient answer? You must give a better answer before you and I part."

"I have done naught which might cause me justly to be brought before the judgement seat of man. And for this oath, I do not know the nature of it."

Hannah took comfort that at least his voice sounded strong. She pulled herself upright, trying to be as brave as he.

King's Advocate Marten said, "The manner of the oath is that you shall answer to all that you are accused of—for schism."

"If he will not take this oath, away with him." Archbishop Neile made a shooing motion, like brushing away a fly.

Laud smirked. "Away with him!" He looked away.

John stumbled forward, standing before all the bishops. "I desire that another outcome be decided upon. I dare not take this oath."

The bishops whispered amongst each other. Laud wrote something down and handed it to the registrar, who stood and announced, "All should be kept in straight custody. Especially Lothropp."

"You have more to answer for than you know of." Laud glared at John.

A man stood and came forward without being called upon.

"That's Samuel Eaton," Robert whispered.

Hannah had never seen nor heard of the man.

Laud's eyes widened. "Why did you assemble in a conventicle when others were at church?"

"We were not assembled in contempt of the magistrate," Eaton said.

"Nay?" Laud sputtered. "It was in contempt of the Church of England."

"It was in conscience to God." Eaton addressed the other bishops. "May it please this *honorable* court." He went on to argue his cause for several minutes, explaining that those captured were honorable people who read scriptures and practiced catechisms.

Finally, Laud had enough of Eaton trying to exonerate the accused. "Will *you* take the oath?"

"I do not refuse it, though I do not take it. It is not out of obstinacy, but that I shall answer at the last day."

Laud rolled his eyes and told him to sit down.

John still stood, not offered a chair.

A couple of women were called forward but would not take the oath.

Marten looked to a paper in front of him and called out, "Samuel Howse."

Hearing her brother's name startled Hannah. Maybe the bishops were not in agreement with Laud and would provide others a chance to speak as they'd Eaton?

Samuel stood slowly.

Hannah couldn't see blood on his person, as on John, but something seemed amiss.

"You are required by your oath to answer to the articles," Marten said.

"I have served the King both by sea and by land. I would be at sea now if this restraint had not been made upon me. I thank God none can levy a charge toward my conversion."

The registrar asked Samuel, "Will you take your oath?"

"I am a young man and do not know what this oath is." Samuel straightened.

"The King desires your service in obeying his laws." Marten waved Samuel away and looked to his list. "Penninah Howse please come forward."

She stood and quickly stepped to the dais.

Hannah sent up a prayer of thanks that her sister appeared strong and well.

Archbishop Abbot adjusted his peruke and stared at her in what looked like boredom. "Come, what say you?"

"I dare not swear this oath until I am better informed of it, for which I desire time."

The oath Robert told Hannah of must have been discussed amongst the Independents in prison or even before their arrest. They all appeared aware of its ability to incriminate. To offer ignorance was perchance the best way to avoid punishment.

Laud pointed a finger at Penninah. "Will you trust Mister Lothropp and believe him rather than the Church of England?"

"I refer myself to the word of God whether I may take this oath or not."

Laud scowled and shooed her away, but Marten intervened and grilled, "Must you not be ready to give an answer of your faith?"

"Aye, I will give an answer of my faith if I be demanded but not willingly foreswear myself." Penninah curtsied and returned to her chair.

"I'm pleased to witness your sister's faith," Robert said softly.

Faith? Hannah felt as if she were in a nightmare that would never end.

Joan Ferne and Elizabeth Denne were called forward, but they also refused the oath until they were informed better as to what it was. When Elizabeth returned to her chair, she glanced up at her mother with what looked like regret.

Hannah wondered how many prisoners taken over the years were innocent like Elizabeth. Could the Church not deal justice fairly?

Sarah Barebone also would not swear. She said she didn't understand the oath. "I will tell the truth without swearing," she said.

Many more were called upon, but none would swear the oath.

Laud stood, hardly taller than the bishops that were still seated. "It is forbidden to have assemblies outside of your parish. We here enforce the Act of Supremacy and Act for the Uniformity of Common Prayer and Service within the Church. It is inexcusable for you to challenge these acts or our authority." He looked to the other bishops.

Archbishop Abbot also stood. "Take them away and commit them all to the New Prison."

An arrow of fear struck at Hannah's core. It was not a death sentence, but living in prison could mean death with its disease and lack of food.

The rest of the council stood, and the registrar read from his paper. "It is appointed that at the next court, being a fortnight after this, because of Ascension Day, the prisoners shall be brought to the Consistory at Saint Paul's. There's too much trouble and danger in bringing so many prisoners as there are over the water to Lambeth."

Many court proceedings were held at Lambeth Palace, near Hannah's home, and where Archbishop Abbot lived when in the city. But John's congregation was too large to fit within the court chambers there.

So this was not the final decree, Hannah realized. Was there still a chance of freedom?

The audience stood as the bishops paraded out, their

ecclesiastical vestments flowing around them. Hannah was no longer sure whether they wore robes of judgement or robes of vanity.

Laud could be heard giving thanks to God for overcoming His enemy, a seed of sedition. "God's power resides in the king," his words faded into the hallway.

Hannah quickly searched for John, but he was already gone. Her mouth went dry. Was he to suffer more abuse? Guards herded the rest of the prisoners away. She caught a glimpse of Penninah's uncovered red-gold hair as she was shuffled out.

Hannah coughed, but it didn't relieve the tightness in her chest.

What had the trial accomplished? 'Twould be May Eighth before they met in court again. She imagined the next court proceedings would be much the same as today. No one would take an oath that forced them to answer questions that had naught to do with going to a conventicle—questions in which answers could cause them to be imprisoned for years, lashed, or tortured. The bishops were counting on the power of the oath to manipulate the prisoners' consciences so that they might give their illicit opinions and activities. On this day, it didn't work.

But for how long could they hold out?

Chapter Thirty-Three

Already rubbed raw from the manacles, John's forearms now burned with the new pain of rough rope tied at his wrists. The rope led to the back of an oxcart tethered at Saint Paul's courtyard, where a crowd of onlookers gathered.

A large, squat man with a hood shrouding most of his face, known only as "the executioner," stepped forward and shredded John's shirt with a dagger, exposing his back.

John's rapid heartbeat overtook his thoughts. He'd known it could come to this, but there was no preparing.

Within moments, a whip ripped into his skin.

He shuddered with the flaring pain.

The oxcart lurched forward.

John tried to stay on his feet.

"Serves you right, Lothropp . . . acting as God Himself," someone called from the crowd.

"Son of sedition," "antichrist," and "heretic," also rang out from the many who lined the street.

John had heard the contemptuous chants before but never directed at him. Each insult stabbed. Another burst from the whip brought him down on one knee. He clenched his teeth to endure the fiery singe of pain, the rope straining at his wrists.

"That's only two lashings, apostate. How are you going to withstand the next one-hundred and ninety-eight?"

The crowd roared with laughter.

The oxcart dragged him, but he soon pushed himself to standing.

The Pulse of His Soul

The driver obviously not about to halt for any obstacle, never looked back.

John's throat burned from lack of water and the dust floating around him. Another blaze of the whip tore into his flesh. He gritted his teeth then quoted scripture. "'. . . be strong, dread not, nor be afraid of them: for the Lord thy God Himself doth go with thee, He shall not fail thee, nor forsake thee.'"

Onlookers huddled together, pointing and shouting obscenities.

"Please, God. Keep my family from seeing this," he begged in a quiet plea.

Another slash to his back. He grimaced and continued praying.

A bull-of-a-man stepped forward, hawked, and spit in John's face.

Trembling from pain and disgust, John puked on bull-man's boots.

The crowd guffawed uproariously.

Another crack of the whip, but John felt nothing.

Bull-man screamed like a woman, grabbing at his bleeding cheek.

"Keep away from the prisoner," the executioner yelled.

The oxcart pulled on, heading for Newgate Prison, over a mile away.

The whipping continued until John went numb. He stumbled and landed in warm manure, choking on the pungent stench. Trying to get to his feet, he slipped in the muck. The oxcart dragged him forward. Rocks dug into his belly, and his wrists burned as if they were on fire. He feared his shoulders would come apart.

When the cart slowed, John pushed himself up, only to receive another lashing—this one splitting skin on his shoulder. He floundered along, losing count of how many lacerations had been delivered.

A wash of ice-cold water splashed across his side and back, the shock turning to relief from its numbing affects.

Thomas stood at the roadside, an empty crock in hand.

"Go home!" John tried to yell but his voice was only a hoarse whisper.

Thomas kept to the speed of the cart. "I'd take the lashes for you if I could." He wiped at tears. A snap of the whip slapped near his arm.

"And I'd be happy to deliver," the executioner bellowed.

Exclamations rang out in taunting.

"Go!" John pleaded, dread building that his son would be persecuted too.

Thomas sank back into the throng, but followed along in the shadows of the crowd.

John would rather die than see Thomas go through this pain and humiliation. What had John done to his family? Would they forgive him? Could he forgive himself?

Another bite of the whip struck onto already shredded skin. Warm blood trickled down his back.

The second court hearing this morning had gone much like the first. Everyone denied understanding of an oath meant to implicate them, and they were *all* condemned to Newgate or the Clink Prisons. But only John received the punishment of two-hundred lashes, a £500 fine, and to be pilloried for public humiliation.

The whip seared John's ear, and he cried out, almost falling again. He couldn't control the contractions bursting in his stomach, and he bent to vomit.

The whip thrashed his lower back where it hadn't snapped before, singeing more agony.

The oxcart pulled on, and he didn't know how much longer he could stay conscious.

Another splash of cold water helped numb the pain. He looked for Thomas, but saw Robert quickly running away. John's chest filled with love and gratefulness for having righteous men in his life.

"Stay away from the prisoner," the executioner growled toward the throng.

What a blessing Robert hadn't been arrested with the rest. Although John hadn't been admitted visitors in prison, he was still privy to rumors and knew Robert watched out for his family. "Bless him, Lord."

Another scald from the whip stung as much as the others. His body quaked. Would it never end? How much farther to the prison?

The next slash sent John to the ground. He crawled and let the floggings strike his buttocks.

"Yah," someone shouted as if to a horse, to the amusement of many.

The oxcart stopped for cross-traffic, giving John a short reprieve from the rocks cutting into his knees and bound hands. Flies buzzed around the excrement on his face. He struggled to stand as the whip lacerated his skin. His blood splattered onto a woman's skirt.

The cart pulled him on, his legs as heavy as lead.

Over the ringing in his ears, he could no longer hear the derogatory remarks from the crowd. Another splash of water rained down, this one cleansing the manure from his face.

Praise-God Barebone handed the crock to another and saluted John with a hand over his heart.

John acknowledged him with a nod and prayed this meant Thomas had truly left.

The executioner sent the whip toward Praise-God but it didn't catch his mark. The crowd and Barebone quickly stepped back.

God, is this where you want me to be? What good can I do here? John appealed.

Within a few minutes, more water doused John, the deliverer running away. Samuel Hinckley of Kent?

John shook his head. He must be delirious. He hadn't seen Hinckley in years.

The cold water seemed to save him. Baptism by torture? He almost chuckled, but another bite of the lash sent him sprawling. He hadn't strength to rise, and darkness loomed until all went black.

Another drench of icy water brought him to. Dragged on his side, he could hardly find strength to shove himself upright. His arms and legs shook with the exertion. Every inch of skin, every muscle, every bone screamed in pain.

The oxcart finally stopped in front of a towering, stacked-stone building, the iron-spiked outer door and tall battlements ready for a dreaded war with evil. Even the air had transformed to a thick smell of rot. Death shrouded the gallows standing to either side of the towers. Decomposing bodies dangled from both and rotting heads on pikes were unrecognizable.

The cart driver lumbered down. He limped to the back of the cart and untied the rope. Throwing it over his massive shoulder, he roughly pulled John toward the prison yard pillory.

Once John's neck and arms were pinned into the holes of the wooden framework, he lost consciousness again. When he awoke, he felt as if his neck had dislocated. Pushing as far forward as he could, he relieved some of the pressure but felt like skin was peeling off his back.

"We're with you, Reverend Lothropp," a woman's kind voice called.

But many more told him what a fiend and heretic he was.

As much as he tried, he couldn't dismiss the hatred directed at him. His soul cried to God. *Am I acceptable to You?*

He needed to focus on friends and family who cared, like those who had thrown the water. He tried to see the woman who'd called out kindly, but the thick wooden pillory kept him from lifting his head. He stared at the blood-spattered earth below him. Clouds moved over the sun, and he thanked God for the small favor.

As the day wore on, more people called out sympathy, but the greater of the crowd shouted them down.

John was in and out of consciousness. Eventually shadows grew long in the small area of his eyesight, and people grew still. "Who is there?" he croaked, his throat feeling as if it were coated in dust.

"Those who love you," Robert answered from afar.

John envisioned guards keeping the people at bay.

"I'm here." Thomas sounded strangled, as if he were still crying.

"As am I," many voices chimed. He didn't recognize any as Hannah or his daughters and found that to be a great relief.

"For those who remain"—John licked his cracked lips,—"know that the charges of sedition heaped upon me are false. I love my Lord and desire only to follow Him." Clearing his throat, he longed for a drink. "God is my true judge."

"Amen" and "here-here" were shouted back.

"Stay strong, my friends." Black spots floated before John's eyes, and he pressed himself to stay conscious, blinking many times. "Do not lie to keep your freedoms. 'Tis not worth the sacrifice of one's soul."

Someone heavy-footed stepped onto the raised platform of the pillory. "Shut your gob." He stuffed a foul-stinking cloth into John's mouth, pulled tight, and tied it at the back of his head.

"Lothropp, ye 'ave a visitor." Tobias, the jailer, held a dim-lit lantern at the small barred opening, throwing shadows under his protruding eyes. The key rattled the lock, and the heavy wooden door pulled open. John heard the clink of a coin hitting another, probably in Tobias's hand.

John squinted into the darkness. "Who's here?"

"It be Master Lothropp." Tobias thrust a man into the cell and slammed the door with a clank of the lock. "Come to sing ye lullabies." He sniggered as if he'd said the most whimsical thing and then left, taking his lantern, and what little light it gave, with him.

As much as John didn't want Thomas seeing him, his presence gave John much needed comfort.

"I can't see you, Father," Thomas called out. "Give me a moment for my eyes to adjust."

John dragged himself up using the clammy stone wall. Since the lashings and pillory a sennight before, he couldn't rise without assistance, spending most of his time on his stomach, his back still burning with weeping lacerations. A smithy had added to the pain by fitting shackles at John's ankles near the festering dog bite.

"Father." Thomas's tone held worry.

"Follow my voice. I'm alone and you've naught to fall over." His face warmed with embarrassment over his uncleansed body and the bucket in the corner with the filth of his waste. The cell must reek.

With his hands outstretched, Thomas found his father and cautiously held him at the waist. "I dare not touch you. Does it still torment?"

"Aye, but holding you is enough for me. Fare you well, son?"

"I don't fare well. At night when I close my eyes, I cannot make the image leave of what they did to you."

John released Thomas and held his face in his hands. "I'd wipe that memory from you if I could. Tell me our women were not with you that day."

"Nay, Robert would not allow it. Mother wanted. . ." He frowned.

"What is it?"

"Mother wanted to come and probably would have fought him on it, but she's still . . ." Thomas looked away.

"Ill? Is she unwell, Thomas?" He'd rather live in his pain than know that to be true.

Thomas nodded.

John dropped his arms. Oh Hannah! "Don't tell her what you saw here. I sent word with Robert that none of my family was to come—including you!"

Thomas bit his lip. "Robert told me of your command, but . . ." he peered into John's eyes. "Enid Linnell died after childbirth. Robert doesn't leave his home."

John staggered. "Not sweet Enid!"

Thomas steadied him. "With Mother ill, Enid gone, Robert distressed, you and Aunt Penny and Uncle Samuel in prison, I feel I've entered purgatory." His voice was as a man in agony.

"I can see how you must. Remember Him who has given you life and, in this hard time, try to find the blessings. 'Be not afraid, for I am with thee: Melt not away as wax, for I am thy God to strengthen thee, help thee, and keep thee with the right hand of my righteousness.'" Feeling dizzy, John placed a hand on the wall. "I need to sit, do you mind?"

Thomas retrieved something by the door then sat by John's side on the cleanest straw John had left, the straw he slept on.

"Mother has sent fresh clothing, blankets, and food. He pulled from the basket a small jar. "This is salve she brewed for your back and dog bite."

John swallowed hard. "'Tis a tender thing to be cared for by a woman. Tell her so, will you." How he loved his Hannah.

"Aye."

"What do you know of the congregation?" He'd questioned the same of Robert but in so much pain during the visit, he disremembered what he'd said.

"Of the forty-two arrested, some were released on bond but still had to come to the court proceedings. As I suppose you witnessed, none of them would take the oath. Including you, twenty-six now are here or in the Clink."

"Where are your aunt and uncle?"

"In the Clink, as is Elizabeth Denne. Her father has disowned her and won't let Dorothy visit Elizabeth or Mother." Thomas clenched his fist. "Barbara cannot be consoled."

"Try to help her understand."

Thomas nodded. "You're the only one with a private cell."

"They fear I'll cause trouble, mayhap. That shows you how little they know me. But I wouldn't be here if they did, now would I? It's a punishment to not be near the others, to not be able to help them with their troubles. I've failed to keep them safe. Their sufferings haunt me as I lay here day after day."

"You cannot take on guilt for their choices. No one made them attend the conventicle. Even I followed my own conscience. Never did you make me feel I had to attend."

John draped his arm over Thomas's shoulders, and the movement pulled at the wounds on John's back. Warm blood seeped into his shirt. "A man couldn't ask for a better son. My greatest regret is leaving my family to find their own means of survival." He cleared his throat to try and shove back emotion. It might make Thomas worry more if he saw his father weep. He'd lament later. He needed to change the subject. "How is your occupation?"

"I'm blessed to work for a fellow Independent who will not release me because I'm the son of a . . . a leader. I can keep meat on the table. The girls are helping Mother sell her vegetables and herbs at market. There's much on the vines, and she expects a bounty in June and July."

"God is good. Your mother's love and skill with gardening is blessing your lives."

"And yours." Thomas held up a small berry pie.

"And mine. Although I fear it cost coin to get that to me."

"Aye."

"Don't come here often, son. You're lucky Tobias let you pass. There are others who will collect your shillings and food to deliver to me yet keep it for themselves."

"I almost forgot." Thomas dug under a blanket and brought out a candle. "I brought six of these with paper and quill, but the guard took everything but this one candle. There's flint and stone in the basket."

The key in the lock snapped.

John didn't realize Tobias had been so near. Had he been listening? Had Thomas incriminated himself by saying he'd been at the conventicle? "Help your mother by taking over the catechism for your brothers. They're young and need a man's guidance. Take them and the girls to church." He hoped Tobias heard but also wanted Thomas to do it. The family would be safer if they attended the Anglican Church, as Hannah and the young children had never stopped doing.

"Get ye gone, boy," Tobias shouted in the dark. He must have extinguished his lantern so they'd not suspect his spying.

Thomas rose and helped John to stand. "I'll be back."

"I've enjoyed our visit but keep the others away. Tell them 'tis because of my great love and concern. As I sit here daily, I need to know they're safe."

"Come now." Tobias waved Thomas to the door.

Thomas nodded and grasped John's hand one last time then hurried out.

The door slammed shut and footsteps receded.

John turned toward his unseen cellmate. "You have eyes where I don't, Lord. Keep him safe. Heal Hannah."

Chapter Thirty-Four

The summer day hot, Hannah wiped her brow and helped Janie pack up empty wooden boxes and the few turnips, beets, berries, and apricots they hadn't sold.

Just as they finished, Thomas arrived to pick them up in the old handcart he pulled to and from market once a week. Soon after John's conviction, Hannah had been forced to sell the horse and carriage to pay his £500 fine.

"There's still hours of light left," she said to both her children. "I want to pass by the Clink in case we may get a glimpse of Aunt Penny, Uncle Samuel or the others."

"I expected as much," Thomas replied.

Although Hannah detested the Southwark market area, she'd been selling there because it was nearest the Clink. It made it easier to pass by each week.

Thomas pulled the cart, and Janie walked with Hannah behind. She coughed into her handkerchief, pressure coming from deep within her chest. Recently, she'd started coughing up pink streaks of blood. She'd been using her herbs to heal herself, but naught helped.

Janie gave a slight shake of her head. "Why don't you ride, Mother? I'm sure Thomas wouldn't mind."

"Nay." Hannah wouldn't give Thomas extra weight to pull.

Her breathing hitched when she noticed the man in Laudian livery.

Since John's imprisonment, the man often hounded Thomas, creeping around like his shadow. He didn't try to keep himself hidden but neither did he approach.

Thomas kept to his work, home, and Anglican Church attendance, never giving the henchman aught to charge him with. But to Hannah, 'twas one more worry and trial her husband's decisions had created.

Near the prison, the clanging of the blacksmiths' hammers often rang out. Today that hammer clanked against a pin driven into irons placed on a fleshy man's bulging ankles. Two guards stood on either side of him.

At the street-level grates, prisoners called out to passersby. Sometimes it was the men at the grates but most often the women. Their hands beckoned at people's feet, outstretched for coins or anything anyone would bestow.

"A penny for my skirt," one woman begged with desperation as Hannah neared. 'Twas hard to tell the harlots from those who were just trying to stay alive. Prisoners were so anxious for coin to pay for food or get their irons removed they'd live naked if they had to. Assuming she was still alive come winter, that poor woman would be cold and begging for clothing and blankets.

Hannah gathered the rest of the apricots from the cart. "Thomas, guard the cart and produce." She pointed across the street, away from the prison beggars. "Pull up over there."

She gave the fruit to the woman who wanted to sell her skirt, then she and Janie crept slowly along, crouching and looking at the prisoners at the grate. A hot and pungent, malodorous stench of body odors and urine emanated from below.

"We've been doing this for months." Janie wiped perspiration from her brow. "Do you reckon the gaolers will award anyone from a conventicle a chance to street sell? All we ever see are harlots it seems." Janie stooped, peering past those with their hands outstretched.

"I'm starvin', lassie. Has you a shilling?" a woman with a deep-purple bruise on her face implored.

Janie gave her a coin.

"Bless you."

"I'm looking for my aunt. Do you know of a golden-redhead named Penninah?"

She shook her head. "Sorry love."

Hannah and Janie kept lumbering along, crouching to see into the dark chamber below ground. Hannah thought she heard her name.

"Hannah." She heard again.

"Please let me pass." Penninah pushed at some women before her. One slumped her shoulders in resignation and moved away from the grate, letting Penninah step forward.

Hannah quickly gave the woman leaving a shilling. "Oh, Penny! I'd all but given up hope we'd ever see you here."

Janie squatted beside Hannah, and Penninah grabbed both their hands and kissed them. "I had to sell my hair to get street grate privilege." She pulled back her scarf. Her once lovely hair had been cropped ragged and short. "Makes it easier for others to find and remove the lice, at any rate. And it's much easier to style." She grinned with the twinkle in her eye that had always been there.

How that twinkle remained, Hannah didn't know, but that grin loosened some of the worry in her chest.

Penninah still wore the dress she'd been captured in four months before. Now filthy and threadbare, it hung looser on her thin frame. Her normally creamy-pale complexion had become ashen, her cheeks and eye sockets receding into smudges of blue skin. When she'd pushed away her scarf, fresh bruises showed on her neck the size and length of fingers.

Hannah's stomach pulled up, and she groaned inwardly. She reached and traced a bruise. "I thought torture without royal warrant illegal?"

Penninah's brow wrinkled with perplexity. "Who's going to tell if it means death or more torture?"

"There must be someone to report it to?" Janie said.

Penninah's eyes lost some of their twinkle. "Mistreatment doesn't always leave marks anyway."

"What do you mean?" Janie asked.

"It's just that sometimes it feels like I'm in a grave, buried alive." She brushed away the words. "'Tis only my world of woe. Know that I'm well now, and Independents try to give care of each other here."

Hannah grasped her hand. "Praise God you're alive."

Looking behind her, Penninah said, "Stop shoving, I just got here." She turned back to Hannah. "I don't know how much longer they'll let me be at the grate. Hasten and avail me all you know of those we love."

"We're getting by without John. Thomas has taken on most of the expenditures, and we sell vegetables at market. Johnny has come home from Eton because we can no longer pay his tuition, and he recently found employment delivering for a butcher. Thomas visits John at Newgate. He's in solitary confinement, weak and troubling over all of you. I believe Samuel is here in the Clink. Do you ever see him?"

"Nay. They keep the men and women separated."

"Janie, gather the few vegetables we have left in the cart and bring them here."

She hurried off.

Hannah pulled her shawl loose from where it hung at her belt. Tied inside was all her day's earnings. "Take this." The coins clinked, and a barely-dressed woman next to Penninah narrowed her eyes toward the shawl.

Penninah growled at her—a sound Hannah would have never imagined coming from her refined sister.

Hannah's throat tightened at the situation, her next breath bringing on a cough that took a moment to control. "Without John's apostasy you wouldn't be in prison and neither would Samuel or Elizabeth—or all the rest." These same thoughts burned a hole in her heart each night as she lay in bed thinking of all John's mistakes. Her family persecuted because of him.

"Forgiveness of others is really about having a relationship with Jesus Christ," Penninah said gently. "Forgive John for the damage he's caused for he's done more good than bad." She rubbed Hannah's arm. "You aren't looking well. I imagine you're as thin as me. What ails you?"

"Naught," Hannah lied. "I'm just not sleeping well at night because of night sweats and my worries."

"Your cough sounds worse. Have you seen a physician?"

"I've no money for a doctor. I'm treating myself."

Penninah sighed in resignation. "Tell Dorothy I'm with Elizabeth. Our congregation keeps her safe, but don't tell Dorothy she's getting an education from harlots. We all are. They're treated much better here than us *heretics* and are usually the most cheerful. The Independents and Puritans are seen as traitorous and subversive." Penninah made a sound of disgust. "And the gaolers sometimes allow the prostitutes out at night if they'll bring back money."

"Is there no way to get you out?"

"Not unless Laud actually becomes a follower of Christ and stops pretending to be."

Hannah took in a deep breath to quell the pain in her heart. Their situation appeared hopeless.

Janie arrived with the produce in a bag. It didn't fit through the grates. They removed the turnips and beets, fit the bag of berries through, and then jammed the beets through one by one. The turnips too large, they shoved until the grates stripped some of the skins and meat from the vegetables.

The woman next to Penninah grabbed what she could off the grates and shoved it into her mouth.

Penninah added the food to the shawl.

A petite, black-haired woman in her twenties elbowed forward. "Did ya get somethin'?"

Penninah handed her the shawl of money and food.

Hannah stuck her arm through the grate, trying to grab it back. "That's for you and Elizabeth, Penny!"

"And I thank you but if I don't share with those I've made covenant with, I'd rather starve to death." She gently pushed Hannah's arm away. "They've shared with me and kept me alive. We're as family."

"I see." Shame warmed Hannah's face. Her father had taught her those same principles of generosity.

"Are ya the pastor's wife?" the woman asked.

Hannah had hidden from that fact so often, she couldn't get her mouth to acknowledge the question. Her throat grew dry, and she burned at the thoughtlessness of what she'd done—trying to keep food from the hungry.

"She is," Penninah said. "Susan, this is my sister Hannah and her daughter Janie."

Susan dipped a quick curtsey. "I envy ye your husband. I be treated miserably by mine. When 'e died, I found myself on the streets for 'e made no provision. Reverend Lothropp found a home for me where I could be a scullery maid. Made sure I knew where the conventicles be because the spirit there encouraged me so. Never 'ave I experienced such nurturin' folk. Reverend Lothropp is a true minister of God for 'e proved that the greatest of all virtues is charity. Bless ye." She curtsied and left.

Her words about John touched Hannah's heart deeper than anyone's had. She'd often wondered if John surrounded himself with his congregants because he trusted them not to leave him like his childhood family had—a kind of security—but the Spirit now told her that was incorrect. Her anger at John melted and she longed to hold him. The Independents obviously nurtured one another through Christlike charity and beyond what anyone in her parish church did.

Another woman quickly took Susan's spot. Prisoners shoved Penninah from behind, and she growled again, telling them to wait.

Janie tapped Hannah's arm. "Tell her about Mistress Linnell."

"Do tell." Penninah fidgeted with her scarf.

"Enid Linnell has died, leaving Robert with four little ones." Penninah's hand stilled.

"His mother lives but grows feeble," Hannah said.

Penninah's eyes pulled in concern. "Deliver him my sympathies. I'm truly grieved. She was a good woman, to be sure." Her chin trembled. "Poor Robert."

"He asks about you often. Even comes here sometimes, hoping to catch one of the Independents at the grate. I'm pleased I can finally tell him something."

"I'll watch for him." Penninah brushed at her ragged tufts.

A young girl of mayhap ten, pushed against Penninah from behind. "Let me have a turn."

"Thank you for everything, Hannah. Your money will pay for bedding and food."

"We'll come each market day to watch for you," Janie said.

"Bless you." Penninah smiled and waved. "I love you both." She turned and left; the space she'd occupied immediately swallowed with begging women.

Hannah had naught else to give. She and Janie joined Thomas and walked toward home past the Globe theatre, busy with customers cued up for a play, and along the river, foul smelling at low tide. Hannah's fatigue grew so great, she eventually succumbed to riding in the cart.

Thomas assured her that she felt no heavier than the produce he'd pulled to market that morning.

In the cart, she chewed at her cheek. She'd given Penninah the money meant for John this week. She'd have to eat less and use some of Thomas's earnings for John.

Chapter Thirty-Five

Chinks of soft morning light reached out from a high, small barred window but didn't quite make it to John. Sparkling ice veiled the stone walls in intricate patterns.

A shudder shook him, rattling his teeth. He'd awoken to another bone-chilling morning. He could hardly feel his fingers and toes, his nose surely frost bound. He exhaled, his foggy breath floating into the cell. Sitting up, he rubbed his nose and ears, trying to get some feeling into them.

One of the men in the cell coughed. Another broke wind.

John stood, wanting to walk about, but eighteen thin bodies sprawled onto each other on the straw-covered, damp stone floor, in a cell built for eight. Laud's crusade on the faithful who didn't attend the king's church overcrowded the jails. At least the bodies added some fraction of warmth. If warm could be a word used in this hellhole.

John had been here since October, now four months back. But he ought not complain, for six months of solitary confinement had about made him insane. At least now he could talk with others, even if a few were heathens who wanted to argue all points doctrinal and holy. He'd converted two to the gospel, one a Catholic.

Thankfully, Granger had been arrested with a Bible that they hadn't taken away, the reading of which gave John something to do during the days.

For the past sennight, Granger lay in the corner, suffering from headaches and red spots of gaol fever. He'd lost his muscles.

John no longer thought of him as the angry ox. In two months' time they'd all have been in prison a year. If bodies could not stay strong, he prayed souls could.

Kneeling, John gave his morning prayers, thanking God for his life and asking for the safe care of Hannah and the children and all those in his congregation who were in prison.

The sounds of gaol coming to life interrupted his pleas as men woke and urinated into frozen pots. Those in shackles rattled their irons. Groans of misery spread in his cell and the one above.

He finished his prayer and sat back on his heels.

Loud stomping awoke the others and hay dust floated down from cracks in the floorboards above.

John assumed someone above tried to kill another rat. His own cell had plenty of the vermin, and rat droppings ran along the floor by the walls.

"If you're on God's side, why do ya suffer 'ere in prison?" A thief named Nico grilled. An unbeliever, he sometimes wanted to know the gospel but on other occasions hoped to prove it wrong.

Facing Nico, John took a seat on the cold floor. "The Apostle Paul was certainly on God's side and held in prison multiple times, once for two years."

Another prisoner joined the conversation. "We should sing hymns to bring on a violent earthquake so the foundations of the prison will shake the prison doors open." Those who knew the Apostle Paul's story laughed, but the amusement fell short and died away, their tired, gaunt faces dejected.

"Did God save Paul?" Nico questioned.

"Nay, but from prison, the apostle spent a lot of time writing letters and teaching God's word." John wished he'd paper and quill to do the same. "He taught that Jesus the Christ will come and make all things right in the end. Through His love, He'll raise the just to abide with Him forever."

Nico grunted. "Why does God allow us to suffer if He loves us so?"

"Trials come to the sinner and sinless. Freedom to make choices is God's law for all. Because of the evil choices' others make, the righteous must suffer." For this reason, John knew he couldn't solve his problems and had to surrender them to the Lord. 'Twas a struggle to accept, one he worked on daily. He couldn't improve or mend his life, or the lives of his wife, children, and congregation. 'Twas the most heart-wrenching challenge for him to accept. He felt helpless to make anything better.

One of the Puritans in the cell turned to the thief. "You need not worry over redemption, for only the chosen will rise."

John didn't agree with predestination and believed those who did needed a lesson in humility. But he'd learned long before that it wasn't worth arguing with men who didn't want to be taught the glorious gift of repentance.

The sound of the turnkey brought the conversation to a close and most men to their feet. Two guards brandishing maces stood behind Bram the gaoler. He placed a large vessel of thin broth on the stone floor and left, locking them in the cell once again.

John scooped mugs of cold broth into two cups, then helped Granger to sit, holding one of the mugs to his lips, giving him time to slowly drink.

Neither Robert nor Thomas had visited in at least six months. When they failed to get food through, John had naught to sup but broth for two meals a day, save supper, where he also got a chunk of stale bread. The first few months of his imprisonment, he imagined food at home—the fresh smell of new peas, the tartly-sweet taste of a tomato from Hannah's garden, the crunch of an apple—but now hunger didn't plague him so much. His hollow stomach rarely growled anymore.

Later in the morning, the turnkey sounded again before its usual time, and men perked up.

Bram stepped in with his guards behind him. "Lothropp, come with me."

John felt something akin to panic. He hadn't left the cell since he'd entered four months before. Had a new sentence come through? One with more dire consequences?

"Lothropp," Bram shouted. "Now!"

John grabbed his mug and blanket, his only possessions, and followed Bram into a narrow, dark hall. Striding freely, without bodies in the way, felt surreal. Something crunched under their feet. Vermin?

They turned a corner and flickering wall sconces lit the passageway. The walls were slick with slime, like those in his cell. The smell of rotting flesh burned his nostrils.

When they came to metal double-doors, a large padlock attached to a chain linked through the handles. Bram unlocked it and shoved the doors open.

The sunshine about brought John to his knees. He threw his arm over his eyes, trying to quash the sharp pains shooting to the back of his head.

The Pulse of His Soul

Bram pushed John into a cobbled courtyard.

Someone gently grasped John's arm. "You're so thin," Robert's compassionate voice said in sadness.

"Robert!" John tried to uncover his eyes, but the sun jabbed like pokers. "How could this be?"

"I have grievous news, my friend. Hannah is dying."

John's legs collapsed beneath him and Robert caught his fall.

Bram yanked John's arm away from his eyes and his blanket and mug fell to the cobblestones with a clatter. "I don't 'ave all day. Follow me." He took them to the blacksmith's lean-to off the courtyard. A great fire burned in a forge. "Shackles," Bram instructed.

"But his son paid to have them removed." Robert still held to John, keeping him upright.

John's thoughts swam. Hannah dying?

"Dawsey," Bram barked. "After 'e's shackled, take the prisoner and be back when 'is wife is dead."

Dead. The word kicked John in the gut. He squinted to see one of Laud's men in black livery trot to where they stood.

"Stay with this man at all times. 'E's a traitor to the king and a seditious heretic." Bram shoved John onto a stool and went back into Newgate, slamming the doors, the chains clinking into place.

John slumped on a crate and cared little what anyone said or did.

Once the shackles were fitted, Dawsey called, "Raise the gate."

The massive wheel ground against metal teeth in its rotation to hoist the spiked gate.

Robert helped John stagger past the blanket and to the main gate. "We'll leave the blanket, John. I fear it might have fleas."

John stumbled away as if in a nightmare. The freedom he'd dreamed of became a straight path to hell. Hannah was dying. Life couldn't get worse. Mayhap he could save her by coming home and giving her hope? Perchance this was Robert's plan all along?

They got in Robert's carriage, Dawsey sitting silently by John. At least Dawsey had the decency for that favor.

They pulled into the bustle of London, and Robert brought from a basket some bread, cheese, and dried apple slices, handing them to John.

Surprisingly, it didn't look appealing. John's hollow belly clenched in a knot.

"You must eat for strength, John. You've misfortune ahead."

John nibbled on the food, but it gave him a stomachache. He

hoped he could keep it down.

They stopped in front of a shop with a sign that read "Barber and Tooth Puller." But when the barber smelled John, he threw a hand over his nose and refused him service. "I'll not have lice in this shop. Take him to the river."

Robert bought a small sharp knife from him, and the men got back in the carriage. "A fire burned the northern end of London Bridge a few days ago, and parts of Thames Street. We'll need to go by river and bathe you when we land."

They caught a wherry, stopping at a stone quay jutting into the river. No other boats docked there. They disembarked, Robert and Dawsey holding to John, who couldn't manage a long enough stride in his shackles to step from the boat by himself.

A few bloated, dead rats lay on the riverbank and flotsam, ice chunks, and other debris bobbed in the water. John wondered if the river were any cleaner than he.

Robert held blankets and clean clothes under an arm. A soap chunk bulged his pocket. "Apologies, brother, but I'll not have your family seeing you this way." He set down the bundle. "It'll be cold, but we must clean you before I bring you home." Speaking to Dawsey, he requested the fetters unlocked so John could remove his pants.

Dawsey stepped forward. "I trust you not to run."

"He's too weak for that," Robert said in disgust.

Unlocking the chain between the shackles, John examined the guard — a blond man of mayhap five and twenty, freckles thickly covered his small nose.

"I fear you're too frail for the currents, John, so bring yourself into the water, holding to the quay." Robert helped him.

John lowered himself in with a gasp. The icy river felt colder than the cell he'd come from. His body went numb while Robert lathered him.

People passed in boats, expressions of disgust on their faces.

John rinsed with a dunk, and then Robert pulled him out. "You weigh as much as a child," he grumbled, shaking his head. "Curse Laud for this."

"You curse the anointed? You want to return to prison with Lothropp?" Dawsey snapped.

Some men came down, wanting to rent a wherry. Robert, Dawsey, and John stepped closer to the bank to get out of their way.

Robert held up a blanket and asked John to strip. "Cast your clothes in the river."

Trembling uncontrollably, John did as requested then dressed into clean, dry clothes. Good riddance to the old.

Robert put him in a coat, wrapped him tightly in a dry blanket, pulling on stockings and shoes, and then Dawsey locked the chain between the shackles. Robert went to work on John's beard and hair, painfully scraping his face and head.

He endured without a word. Hannah dying brought him here, and he couldn't cease thinking about it.

The sun rose past the noonday hour, heating the day, and John eventually stopped trembling.

Robert looked him over thoroughly. "I don't see any lice now that I've shaved your hair. I wish I'd thought to bring a wig."

Back in a hired hackney, Robert pulled from his basket and handed John a handful of parsley. "Here, eat this to freshen your breath."

His friend had considered everything to make John presentable. 'Twas woefully wrong, returning home in emotional devastation.

When they stopped in front of the Lothropp house in Lambeth, John desired to get to Hannah quickly, yet also didn't want to see her in death's grip.

Robert placed a hand on his knee. "No one is expecting you because I didn't want to disappoint if the archbishop wouldn't allow this visit. Thomas and Johnny are at work, but the others will be shocked yet pleased to see you. If you can help it, don't let your children see you weak in spirit. They're already consumed with grief and fear over losing their mother and being left orphans."

All elation at seeing his family was overshadowed by Hannah's sickness.

Robert's brown eyes conveyed worry. "I'll make sure they're cared for when you and Hannah cannot. Others in the congregation have been coming daily to care for their needs." He turned to Dawsey and said harshly, "*No one* has come from their parish church."

Dawsey glanced away. How'd he become a Laudian henchman when he appeared kinder than the others, John did not know. He'd assumed a prerequisite for the job was to be a cold-hearted fiend. He'd keep an eye on him. Mayhap he held back for the sake of death's approach?

The men entered the house without knocking.

The boys were in the parlor, playing on the floor. They turned toward the parlor's open double doors.

Sam, almost thirteen and becoming a young man, stood slowly. "Father?" his voice caught. He ran to John and threw his arms around him. "Father." Sam slumped into John's chest.

The embrace was supernal. 'Twas the devil's will that kept him from his family and this goodness.

Joseph and Benjamin joined in, enveloping John, weeping and cheering in relief.

Janie and Barbara came from the kitchen, awe in their expressions. Janie wiped at tears. As the boys released their father, the girls took him in their own embraces.

John's heart all but broke to be welcomed in such a way and at such a sad occasion that should be joyful. "I'm here only . . . only until I'm taken back to prison." He glanced back at Dawsey.

"I know you." Janie stared at Dawsey with a show of disgust. "I've seen you following Thomas these past months."

Dawsey ducked his head. "Aye. 'Tis my job."

"Your father needs to visit your mother," Robert cut in. "Come with me to the parlor, children, and avail me the latest news."

Dawsey followed John up the stairs. 'Twas slow going with the shackle chain barely long enough to span each rise. At the closed bedchamber door, John turned to him. "Must you be privy to such a private conversation between husband and declining wife?"

Dawsey reddened. "I'll wait here at the door."

Chapter Thirty-Six

The weight of someone sitting on Hannah's bed caused it to sink.

Waking, she opened her eyes and looked directly into the face of her smiling husband—bald and gaunt. Had she slipped from life so effortlessly? She'd not realized he'd come to heaven before her.

He took her hand in his, his skin cold, fingers skeletal.

The grasp felt real. Her heart sped. She hadn't died. "Uncommon as your smile is"—she swallowed, trying to find strength to speak—"I'm happy to see it."

"I love you." He kissed her with chilled lips. "I don't want to live without you. What can I do to keep you on this earth?" The timber of his words sounded magical, but the question she'd no answer for.

She hadn't heard his voice in so long she'd almost forgotten the renewing effect it had on her. "Am I truly dying?" A cough pulled at her chest. She didn't want John to see the blood. She turned away and tried to cough lightly, but the tugging in her lungs grew stronger. She pulled a cloth from her sleeve, coughing hard into the linen. She tucked it back away, knowing the crimson stain lay inside. "How could it be that you're here?"

"Robert petitioned that I might be here for . . . for you." He wouldn't look in her eyes.

She always knew when he held back his emotions. He didn't want to say he'd come to say farewell.

"God must truly love me, for to see you again has been my

greatest wish." She swallowed, trying to keep down another cough. She felt so tired but she needed to tell him how forgiving him had quieted her heart. "Do you need to serve more prison time?"

"There's a guard outside this door." He reddened.

She wasn't sure if his reaction was in anger, frustration, or shame. Deep lines marked his thin face, the deepest between his brows. She reached to touch it and soften his furrowed forehead.

He caught her hand, kissing it gently.

"We're both waifs. How did this happen? I'm only eight and thirty, but you're an old man." She laughed lightly.

A tear squeezed from his eye, and he quickly brushed at it. "I fear 'tis my fault you're so ill. Can you forgive me for leaving you so long alone with the children?" His jaw clenched. "Can you forgive me for all . . . all those times I left you to wonder if I was safe?"

"I forgive you." And she felt in her heart that she truly had. The burden had started to leave the day the woman at the prison testified John a true minister of God. And the months since she'd spent in prayer with a true desire to forgive John. Peace had eventually come when she stopped judging him.

He slumped forward, wiping more tears.

"But I must too ask your forgiveness." She resisted the urge to sleep and pushed herself on. God had offered her this last chance to tell John her mistakes—to beg his forgiveness. "For a time, I lost my understanding that God would not steer you wrong. I forgot that you're here to serve Him." She rubbed his arm. 'Twas as frigid as his hand. "Because I couldn't teach the gospel, methinks I lived my aspirations through you and wanted you to do what *I* expected to be right." She swallowed again, wanting a drink of water, but feared she'd vomit like she'd been doing for days. "I couldn't be a minister, but you could, and you didn't do it as I wanted you to."

"I hold no bitterness for your actions. You've had much to bear."

"Forgive me for not understanding when you followed your own conscience to serve the Lord as you were called. I shouldn't have gotten in the way of that. I judged you, which is only God's right." Her disappointment in life was all her own making. "John, I'm sorry I failed you. Truly I am. I should have been at your side these many years."

He shook his head. "Faith is a difficult journey and finding unification with others, including a spouse, is a gift. A relationship with God is individual, and although I wished you were by my side, I never faulted you for your own journey." He kissed her forehead.

His tenderness warmed her as much as his words.

"We weren't there for one another." John's tears flowed unbidden now. He didn't try to wipe them away. "And if you must leave this earth before me, I beg God to allow a life together after this one. Mayhap then we'll get it right."

She couldn't bear his heartache. "Come, lay by my side."

He slipped off his shoes and opened the coverlet, stretching out next to her. His shackles clanked together.

His ice-cold body caused her to shiver.

He pulled away.

"Nay." She pulled him back to her. "The blankets will warm you." Her own body had been cold all day. She rubbed his back with weak strokes, not knowing how much longer she could stay awake. Her hands passed over raised scars. Anguish stilled her breath. "Our love has overcome our trials." She kissed his neck. "I leave this life with a full heart." She felt as if she couldn't catch her breath and waited a moment before continuing. "I leave with gratitude to God to have devised such a plan that this is not the last time we'll be together." She relaxed, feeling for the first time in a very long time that she and John had quieted their hearts in all things. No obstacles stood between them, and their love brooked eternal.

She awoke sometime in the night, the room quiet and dark. John breathed next to her, still in her arms. What a glorious blessing God had granted her to have him with her now. "John," she whispered in his ear.

He awoke instantly. "How do you fare? What do you need?"

"Take me to my garden."

"Can you walk?"

"Nay. Carry me . . . oh, your shackles. Should we awaken Thomas?"

John lay silent, playing with her hair. "I'll ask Dawsey." He arose and pulled coats from the cupboard. He slid hose on Hannah along with her coat and then wrapped her tightly in a blanket and went out the door.

She heard only murmuring in the hall before a sleepy looking young man, pulling on a black Laudian coat, entered their bedchamber. She recognized him as the man who followed Thomas about the city.

He bowed to Hannah, concern tightening his eyes. "Do you mind if I lift you?"

She shook her head.

He gathered her in his arms and took her downstairs.

John led the way to the garden and sat in a chair.

Dawsey laid Hannah in her husband's arms as gently as if she were a baby, set his own hat on John's bald head, then disappeared into the shadows of the night.

Hannah dozed, cold but content. When she awoke again, the stars had faded. "You can and will survive without me." Her breath floated in a wisp on the chilly air. "What you're doing with your ministry is right and good and will provide you strength." Speaking tired her, but she must help him live free of guilt. "Teach others the joy of following God as you have."

He sobbed. "I don't want to live without you."

"The children need you." Motherhood had been a calling to her as great as John's had been to minister. She'd loved being a mother to such remarkable children. They all had the courage and kindness of their father. She felt blessed beyond measure in that regard. *Please God, provide them the strength they need to live without me.*

A pain pulled at Hannah's chest. She needed to cough but didn't have the strength, pulling in air was arduous, frightening.

John shook her. "Stay with me, Hannah!" Tears ran down his chapped cheeks.

The velvet night faded into dawn as a soft light broke out across the lower sky. She felt connected to both earth and heaven. Life. She needed to let it go.

John looked at her with his gentle brown eyes. "Thank you for teaching me to love and be loved, to laugh at myself—and *at you*." Laughter bubbled from his chest. "You did tell the most imprudent jests sometimes. That wit, I grew to love so much." He fingered her hair. "Remember our first argument?"

"Not sure—there were so many." She lightly chuckled.

"When I told you I was ordained to judge?" He snorted. "I'd never seen a woman display so many hues of red. Young and ignorant then, I said you were the weaker vessel—a creature intellectually, physically, morally, and even spiritually inferior." He shook his head. "Wrong on all counts."

"Aye, you were." She grinned.

He sputtered another laugh, wiping the tears that fell.

He was leaving her the best gift—his laughter.

"Your father will be waiting for you." He paused and looked

about. "I feel him near," he whispered with awe.

"Aye." She did too, for days now. And she couldn't wait to see her babes, Anne and Sarah.

"I've been thinking about the women in the Bible and their importance to the Gospel," John said, giving Hannah another true gift.

She smiled and relaxed against his chest. "Go on."

"After Jesus's resurrection, there must have been a reason He appeared to Mary Magdalene first. I believe He trusted her to deliver His message to the apostles, commissioned to share her testimony—a testimony of her risen Lord—one of peace and hopefulness that in the end we'll all rise again and be together. Who better but a woman to share such news?"

She knew John took her hand because she saw it but could no longer feel her hands or feet. Her breathing became more troubled, shallow and then sporadic. She gazed at him in a silence rich with assertions of gratitude and love that she could no longer vocalize.

He appeared to understand and kissed her lips.

She was so weary. 'Twas time to sleep. "Last blessing," she said with all the strength she had left. "Release me."

John laid a hand on his beloved's head with gratitude in his heart that she saw him as a man who held authority to bless her, and he did so in the name of God. "May the Holy Father deliver you from evil, preserve you in righteousness, and bring you everlasting life through Jesus Christ our Lord. Be released from your suffering. Amen." He kissed her cold forehead. "Go to God, Hannah."

A silence descended on the garden and in his heart.

Although the sun had risen, there were no chirping birds or buzzing insects. 'Twas as if they acknowledged Hannah's passing, knowing life without her would be only half a life. Her talent to make things flourish had gone with her.

Eventually, the children came out, each saying their farewells, telling their mother how much they'd miss her and that they'd see her again one day.

She didn't answer back.

PART IV
Chapter Thirty-Seven

February 1633
Newgate Prison, London, England

Drowning in a sea of sorrow that threatened his sanity, John didn't care when Bram shoved him into a different cell than the one he'd left.

"Keep ya gob shut," Bram warned. "If ya don't preach, I'll take the shackles off."

John didn't have a problem with not preaching. He turned from his cellmates and grieved in his own dark world.

Hannah no longer waited for him. He was alone, like when his mother had died. As insignificant as the dust he slept on, no one truly knew him intimately and loved him all the same. He knew he was feeling sorry for himself, but the unending ache in his heart made him not care. Nobody needed him here.

Samuel Eaton approached John numerous times to try and get him to talk. "Your pain should be receding. You have a mission to fulfill."

"You don't have a wife and children and don't understand my pain," John grumbled.

"Do I have to have a family to know what God desires me to do?" The hurt sounded evident in his tone.

John turned away.

The Pulse of His Soul

Losing Hannah had awakened a fear in him much like that of when he'd been a boy, only now 'twas God who had left him, not his father. So vast was the void in John's soul that he couldn't see the end of it. God had shown His love for John by placing others in his life to love him. Now that God had taken Hannah away, John knew God no longer cared. He no longer saw John in his rathole on earth, in a country gone to hell.

Eaton's brother, Theophilus, had money enough to get food and letters sent in, which Eaton shared. He'd read the letters out loud, but none of the news mattered to John.

Months went by, John never received a visitor or his own letters. If Eaton hadn't shared his food, John may have died. There were days he didn't care if he did.

Thomas and Janie were near twenty, old enough to care for the family. Having a condemned father only made life harder for the children anyway. They would do better without him. They'd be fortunate and happier not to witness the immense guilt he felt over not taking care of Hannah well enough. They must blame him for their mother's death, and they were right. John could have saved her if he hadn't loved God more than his wife. Is that not what Hannah had feared all along—even before they married?

One day, months later, Eaton read aloud his brother's most recent letter about an insignificant political figure named Oliver Cromwell who had sermonized to the Independent congregation. "He wants to do something about the king's personal rule," Eaton whispered.

John rolled his eyes. There was no fighting King Charles or his alter ego Bishop Laud. And 'twas folly for Theophilus Eaton to mention names in letters that passed through Bram's hands. He hoped Cromwell could stay well away from Laud's grasping claws.

Eaton turned the page and read, "The congregation has gotten so large that we cannot easily meet together. They bicker over whether an infant should be baptized or if the ordinance should be performed once a person is old enough to judge his standing with the Lord. There are those who say their former baptism with the Church should be valid."

John lifted his head. "Read that again."

Eaton did so.

For the first time in a long time, John's heart felt unsettled over someone else. For some reason the Independents hadn't yet released him as their pastor. He still felt responsible for their care and didn't want them arguing, for the fracturing of the community would be their fall. Baptism had been a subject they'd many times discussed without coming to a conclusion. Surprised it'd come to bickering, he wanted to help. "Write your brother and have him tell the congregation to be patient. I'll pray over the matter."

Eaton's eyes grew wide and he stammered, then said no more. 'Twas obvious he'd lost faith in John.

That night when all were sleeping, John moved to his knees. He knelt for a long time before he could petition his Lord. John began his prayer by asking for forgiveness for his time away from God. He prayed for his family and his congregation. With his heart sufficiently comforted, he questioned if infants should be baptized. He didn't receive an answer.

Each night, he prayed the same prayer and he didn't receive an answer. But as he prayed, he did come again unto God, his old friend, and cried in thanksgiving. He'd not been forsaken. 'Twas John who'd pushed away, not his Lord.

One night as he lay awake, to his astonishment, the Holy Spirit filled his heart and mind, telling him not to make any declaration at present about infant baptism, and that no parish church was a true church.

The next morning, he dictated a letter to his congregation at the risk of Bram reading it.

Confirmation that the letter made it came when Eaton received word that a split had taken place. The stricter Separatists dismissed themselves from the congregation and followed John Spilsbury, their new minister, to establish a distinctive church that baptized its adult followers.

Eaton studied the letter. "Theophilus writes, 'The rest are at peace and have renewed their covenant to walk in the ways of God so far as He had made them known or should make them known. We're satisfied with infant baptism and await your and Reverend Lothropp's return, praying for you daily.'"

The letter moved John. From that day forth, his desires were for his release to once again make covenant with his congregation and lead them to freedom of worship.

In August, Archbishop of Canterbury George Abbot died, and by September, William Laud took his place. He and King Charles added to the Book of Sport countryside festivals and wakes to the list of sanctioned Sunday recreation. They then strictly enforced clergy to read it in church. 'Twas all as it had been for John. Many of the clergy refused to obey the mandate.

Rumors came to John's prison cell, one that Robert Browne

had died in a Northampton jail. John hoped the nonconformist had finally found peace.

Another rumor from the papists in the cell, claimed that the Roman Catholic Church began an inquisition of a man named Galileo, who asserted the Earth revolved around the Sun. They deemed his statements heretical.

Religious leaders all over Europe wielded ungodly power, and John felt wheels revolved faster toward a true reformation of God's church.

Laud made his influence known to all and continued publicly burning books and searching out those who didn't attend the Church of England. Ranks of Puritans and Separatists grew in opposition to him.

John agonized for his family living so close to Lambeth Palace, which now was the residence of Archbishop Laud.

On a day in November, Samuel Howse was shoved into the cell. He tripped over some men gambling on the floor.

John rose to his feet as quickly as he could with shackles. He hadn't kept his mouth shut as Bram warned, and had converted many prisoners. "I'd heard you were in the Clink." He embraced his brother-in-law, feeling guilty that he too may blame John for Hannah's death.

But Samuel gave him a hearty hug, with no reservations. "I'm not joining you here but have come to bestow news. To show his good will, the new Bishop of London, William Juxon, released all our Independents but sadly not you or Eaton. You two are deemed too dangerous to be on the other side of these bars."

John's first emotion was joy for the freedom of his family and friends and his second was fear that this cell could forever be his home. "Avail me all you know."

Within a few minutes, before Samuel could share news other than about Penninah and Elizabeth, Bram came to the cell with his two muscular guards. "That's enough, Howse. Come with me."

"But I paid you five shillings." Samuel placed his hands on his hips. "You promised a quarter hour."

"I changed my mind." Bram narrowed his eyes.

"Go, Samuel." John whispered. "Write me through Eaton's brother."

Samuel quickly said, "Penny and I are caring for the children. They're all well."

Bram yanked Samuel from the cell.

His visit and his news cheered John for weeks, all the way to

December, when Bram barked through the slit in the door that John had visitors. For some reason they were not allowed in. John stepped to the small opening and peered out. "If it isn't—"

"Your friend," Nathaniel Tilden hurriedly filled in, shaking his head imperceptibly.

John could well understand that Tilden didn't want to be recognized here.

Samuel Hinckley stepped into view. "We've missed you, Reverend Lothropp."

"And I, you two. What say ye, and how do you fare?" The door opening was so small, he couldn't see the two men at the same time—only a small portion of Tilden's immaculately-trimmed beard.

"We've come to say goodbye," Tilden lowered his voice. "For we sail with our families on the *Hercules* in March."

"To where we spoke of many years ago?" John quizzed, trying to remain confidential.

"That's right," Hinckley whispered. "I've four children now, and this man has seven. We all go together."

"Have you worries of travel?" John asked, for the voyage often meant death, especially for the young.

"The Lord is directing us to our new home. I went there in '26 and was granted fertile land of which I expect much abundance." Tilden cleared his throat. "We've been praying for your release and are hoping you might join us there."

John's breath caught in his chest. He didn't know what to say.

"The men of Kent can be together again," Hinckley's hopeful voice came from near the slit.

"And our fourth member?" John asked, hoping they'd understand he meant Fenner.

"If he be so blessed, for we've also visited him here this day."

"Here?" John was much surprised Fenner lay in a cell under the same roof.

"He too knows of our plans and doesn't reckon his family will come."

"Come along," Bram's voice shouted. "Time to leave."

"May we meet again," Tilden and Hinckley whispered and then they were gone.

On Christmas day, the talk was of how Laud opulently decorated his chapel and had been receiving extravagant gifts of horses, deer to roam his park, and all manner of foods and décor. It seems he spent his time entertaining at musical programs and gaming on his bowling green with royalist guests strolling his elaborate gardens.

John lay on his thinning blanket, hungry and filthy, thinking about how the Apostle Paul accurately described John's own day, when he wrote a letter to Timothy. 'In the last days, perilous times shall come. For men shall be lovers of their own selves . . . despisers of those that are good . . . lovers of pleasures more than lovers of God . . . Ever learning, and never able to come to the knowledge of the truth.'

Chapter Thirty-Eight

As if John had spoken his thoughts from the night before directly to Bram, he and his henchmen entered the cell before the broth delivery and grabbed John up off the floor. "I told ya to keep your gob shut." Bram dragged John as if he were a child, pulling him downstairs to the lower part of the prison, in which John had never been.

The shackles clanked together, gouging into John's boney ankles.

With Bram's accomplices holding torches, they entered a small, dank chamber with no window. Chains dangled from the wall with blood splattered across the stones.

One of the accomplices placed his torch in a sconce and helped Bram fetter John to the wall, and then they left.

The sound of the door slamming brought with it a feeling of unexpected courage. Peace washed over his heart. Those against him may shatter him physically, but he'd never let them have his soul.

In complete darkness, it seemed for hours he stood, arms aching to drop to his side. He prayed by name for each his children, that they may endure if he died. He finally fell asleep.

The rending of being pulled by his hands jolted him awake. He rose to his toes to provide his arms relief, but he couldn't keep the posture for long. His courage of only hours before gave way. *God, why are you asking so much of me? I'm but a man.*

Not knowing if it were night or day, he tried to sleep again, but oblivion was only fitful.

The Pulse of His Soul

At last the door opened, and Tomlinson strode in carrying a torch. His salient features puckered in a display of haughtiness. He held the fire near John's face, the heat of the flame licking too close. "I see you're now living in a sewer where you belong." He hovered his torch along the moldy walls, curling his lip and making noises of disgust. "Do you wish you were sailing with your friends?" He raised an eyebrow. "Instead of dying here?" Tomlinson's spies had obviously reported John's visit from Tilden and Hinckley.

Tomlinson ran his tongue over his teeth. "I saw your letter about baptism, and it made me scoff, but Archbishop Laud is not so pleased." His voice tightened. "Tell me, who are your friends who went to America?"

"I have no friends who went to America." John didn't lie. They weren't to leave until spring.

Tomlinson pulled from his pocket a small metal instrument and slid it over John's thumb. "This thumbiken will help you remember names." Tomlinson screwed down a metal plate. "It was a simple question, and I've many more. You can answer quickly, and I'll leave, or we can spend hours discussing your heretical associations." Tomlinson screwed the device tighter.

Groaning at the intense pressure, the pain consumed John's whole being. "I have no friends in America."

Tomlinson attached another thumbiken to John's other hand, twisting the thumb-screw as tight as the other. "What are the men's names who are going on a voyage?"

"You're mad," John said through clenched teeth, wanting to vomit.

"Are they part of Cromwell's group?" Tomlinson stood close enough for John to smell his rancid breath.

His stomach roiled. "Who?"

"Oliver Cromwell, you fool."

The name vaguely familiar, John had trouble concentrating over the pain pulsing down his arms.

"Reported in one of your letters, Cromwell spoke to your congregation."

"I've received no letters." Eaton had.

Tomlinson tightened the thumb-screws. "Tell me!"

"You can't get information from me . . . that I don't know." The pain in his thumbs bolted to his head. He felt like both might explode. Fear and panic overtook thought.

"I'll strap you on the rack." Tomlinson's tight-lipped, narrow-nosed face came closer.

John groaned, his stomach convulsing until he puked.

Cursing, Tomlinson skipped backward, vomit splattering on his shoes. "Tell me about Cromwell," he shrieked.

John's head and thumbs pulsed and pounded. All went black.

When he came to, the room was dark. The pressure was gone from his thumbs, but they were swollen and wouldn't bend. He rose up on his toes to try and return the feeling into his arms. It didn't work. His shoulders burned from the effort, and he blacked out again.

Sometime later, Bram's men released John's arms from the chains, and he slumped to the wet and cold stone floor.

They'd left a cup of broth. Why if they were only going to kill him?

'Twas hours before the trembling in his arms subsided enough for him to pick it up. He grabbed the cup between palms, and drank it down, his thirst still not quenched. His stomach threatened to send it back up. He leaned against the wall and concentrated on keeping it down, eventually entering the oblivion of slumber.

Always in the dark, John couldn't tell the time. Days seemed to go by between Tomlinson's visits. Using many means of torture, he demanded the names of Separatists.

John didn't provide names. He would not be the cause of any Independents spending time in gaol.

Sometimes Tomlinson questioned John about Cromwell, of whom John knew naught. Why did Tomlinson see Cromwell as a threat?

To conquer the madness of being isolated in the dark, John quoted scripture pertaining to specific topics. One time the topic was faith, whereas another, enduring to the end. His favorite of all the verses had to do with light. He'd imagine light emanating from God, filling his small cell. Light bursting a hole in the wall, and John running out to go home. Light eclipsing the earth and dispelling all evil. When he thought of Hannah, he'd try to remember the Bible stories about women. Sometimes he talked to her as if she were there beside him.

Tomlinson's visits became fewer and fewer, and then not at all. But John wasn't moved from isolation. Hours upon days, he lived in the dark, fearing he'd go mad. When they brought his broth and sometimes bread, 'twas the highlight of his day, and the only way he'd an accounting time passed. Broth in the morning. Broth and bread at night.

One day, Bram opened the door and snarled, "Come with me."

The torchlight pierced John's eyes.

It took him a few tries before he could stand. He stepped forward and collapsed. Black spots threatened to gather into a solid wall.

"Drag him." Bram directed his men.

John passed out on the stairs. When he opened his eyes again, he floated in a boat. Wearing Laud's livery, two men he'd never seen before sat on either side of him. Two others stroked oars through the water. The sun shone so brilliantly darts shot to the back of John's eyes.

A guard handed him a cup of ale, which John drank, and then another was supplied, and a slice of dried fish. 'Twas as a feast. John pulled in a deep breath of fresh air.

"I 'spose ya can't smell the reekin' river over your own putrid stench," one of the guards commented.

They floated to a long dock with an opulent, brightly painted purple and blue barge moored there. 'Twas adorned with a fringed canvas.

The guards lifted John from the boat and helped him up a slope, the smell of grass sharp and clean. Lambeth Palace, with a tower of stone, sat perched behind a glorious garden, formally manicured and in full spring color.

Spring! It took John a moment to realize he'd been in the dungeon at least three months if not more. The one-year anniversary of Hannah's death had passed without notice and Tilden and Hinckley would've already sailed.

They passed ancient fig trees. "Why have you brought me here?" John questioned.

One guard grunted, but no explanation followed. They entered the palace through a back door and were greeted by someone else in Laud's livery, a burly man with thick eyebrows. A dog sprang up and growled low, showing his fangs, eyes on John. "Stand down, Beelzy," the burly man said. He motioned to John. "Follow me."

The hallway opened to an expansive waiting room with decorative plastered ceilings adorned with crystal candelabras. Colorful carpets covered exquisitely patterned wood flooring and blue velvet draped at the long windows. A harp stood in one corner. A retinue of male servants waited near walls while others stepped in and out of doors.

"Let me try and walk," John said, feeling the ale and spring air had helped him come back amongst the living. He shuffled slowly but stayed on his feet.

Laud's burly servant knocked on a door.

After murmuring within stopped, Dawsey came out. He grinned at John and tapped his hat before leaving.

"Enter," John recognized Laud's nasally voice.

Had God really brought John before his accuser? He'd never imagined this in all his wonderings while lying on his cell floor.

Dressed in a gown of honey-colored taffeta and velvet, Laud sat behind a highly carved, gold-embossed table. He wore a white, flowing wig, giving him the appearance of a little man consumed by hair.

Laud placed a lace handkerchief to his nose and pulled a crystal bowl of pink carnations closer. "You do not bow?" His stern words were barked.

The courtesy hadn't occurred to John, and he couldn't bring himself to do it. He stared at Laud, waiting for an explanation of why he'd been brought here.

Everything around him spoke of wealth. Laud's eyes bespoke vile hatred. His pride had stolen his soul. "Are you John Lothropp, the man who led dissenters to meet at conventicles?" Laud had the power to destroy John, yet he didn't know him by sight?

John looked down. His pants hung on a skeletal frame. Was his face so much altered too? Mayhap even his closest acquaintances wouldn't recognize him. "I'm John Lothropp."

Laud looked toward the door as if he were wishing a servant would come and call him away—perchance to dinner where he'd feast on roasted lamb with gravy, warm bread, and fresh spring vegetables.

John's stomach clenched.

"You've been in prison two years. What say ye now? Are you ready to sign the oath?"

"I'll not sign an oath that can be used against me."

Laud sighed loudly, fingering a curl of his wig. "What if I told you, your children have been to see me, begging like street urchins, to allow their father his freedom?"

Who allowed his children near this man? "I cannot sign an oath that—"

"They've softened my heart."

John doubted his hard, black heart could be softened. Something must be in it for him or mayhap unknown forces manipulating Laud.

"My guardsman vouches for your children. They've not associated with the heretics you once preached to but attend their parish services regularly."

"My children are as blameless as their mother, who died because I couldn't care for her."

Laud made a sour face. "I'm willing to forego the oath if you're willing to sign a document stating you'll step down from being a Separatist minister and absent yourself from all conventicles. And that you'll not preach in a home, church, prison, establishment of any kind, or on the streets."

Could John agree to such? It would not bruise his integrity in any way. Well, unless God commanded him otherwise. "God is my king, and I serve only Him, but I'll agree to your stipulations of no meetings or sermonizing."

Laud's face reddened. "You stand before me in rags and claim holiness abides in your heart enough to hear God's word? That's the problem with you, Lothropp. You pretend to wield power you haven't had since you renounced your orders twelve years ago."

John puzzled over Laud remembering his history. Mayhap not knowing John's name earlier had been a façade to belittle him? A way for Laud to feel his own controlling power? "All men may have God's guiding spirit. 'For as many as are led by the Spirit of God, they are the sons of God.'"

"Do not quote scripture to me!" Laud darkened in silent anger and stood. "I want you out of the kingdom," he shouted. "If you do not survive a voyage away from this country, it will be God's own revenge for your wickedness. And if you're not gone by Trinity Term, I expect you to pay the court a fine of £200. If you don't do this, you'll be arrested to stand before the High Commission's Star Chamber and sign the oath."

Was Laud releasing him? Like a dove, hope perched in John's soul. "I'll sign the document and resign as minister and will not preach until I've left England."

Laud glared and sat. With quill in hand, he scratched John's freedom in a few quick sentences. "Davis," he shouted.

The burly servant opened the door.

"Take this paper to the prisoner and have him sign." He raised his handkerchief to his nose.

John signed, and Davis took the paper back to Laud, who placed his own signature upon the form. "Guards. Take the prisoner to the smithy by the old jail and remove the shackles."

John stumbled toward home, his strides unnatural after wearing chains for over a year. The day grew late, no one walked by his side to guard him. Could he be truly free or would Tomlinson be waiting for him at his home? Emotions of joy and fear played together.

He didn't want his family seeing or smelling him in such a condition, and hoped he'd be undetected if he washed in the dark at his well.

As he neared, Robert and Penninah sat under a tree in discussion that brought their heads close together. If John didn't know better, he'd imagine them lovers, discussing a happy future.

When Robert saw John, he sprang to his feet and trotted over. "I knew 'twould work. They've set you free!" Robert's nose wrinkled. "Let's agree to an embrace after you bathe."

Penninah approached. "Welcome home, brother. I concur with Robert about the embrace." Her cheerful eyes were embrace enough.

John missed these two more than he'd realized. Natural cheerful affection was a gift from God. What a blessing that Hannah had raised their own children to be good-natured. He couldn't wait to see them.

"What say ye about the stipulations given for your freedom?" Robert questioned.

"I'm to resign as pastor of the Independent Church and not preach in any home or establishment."

"Then we must go to the Colonies where they'd welcome your leadership." Robert turned to Penninah and took her hand. "Don't you agree, my love?"

John staggered.

"Whoa there. Come lounge under this tree." Robert led John to sit on the ground.

"What was it you knew would work?" John asked Robert.

"That the goodness of your fair children would crack Laud's cold heart. That, and some tears and begging. They were not play-acting, for I've heard it often enough."

Penninah stood over John. "They've missed you so, John."

Her voice so much like Hannah's caused his heart to still.

"Now that you'll be living at home, 'twould be highly inappropriate for a single woman such as Penny to live under a widower's roof."

John hadn't considered that. He looked to Penninah.

But instead of sad eyes, hers danced with mirth.

"What would you have me do?" John questioned. Why was dismissing Penninah something to be happy about?

"Let her come live with me, as my wife." Robert brought Penninah to his side.

Chapter Thirty-Nine

The breeze off the River Thames cooled John from the August sun.

The air smelled of fish from a nearby fishing vessel. Seagulls circled, squawking, and landed on its deck, only to be shooed away. Hundreds of people on the docks lugged barrels, chests, trunks, bedding, and basins to be loaded on the ship *Griffin*. Thirty-two of them were with John, Independents who believed they were bound together in faith and hardship, following him to the Massachusetts Bay Colony.

Cattle, pigs, chickens, and geese were towed in cages or prodded on board. With almost five thousand immigrants now in the Colonies, they'd much need of food.

Johnny hadn't looked John in the eyes since his return from prison. Even now, Johnny bit his lip and glanced away. "Farewell, Father."

John knew what it felt like—a son being left by a father. He took Johnny in his arms, wanting to share these things with him. "I pray you'll come to us when Uncle Robert and Aunt Penny do."

Johnny stiffened. "I cannot live amongst those who have separated themselves from the Church of England."

They'd been over this before. But John hoped a tender parting might help change his son's mind and overcome his anger at John for leading his family astray and making them suffer while he languished in prison. Johnny had sacrificed much by leaving school and gaining employment to help support his siblings.

"Mayhap Widow Linnell will live a long and generous life."

Johnny shrugged. "Uncle Robert will not leave here until she passes."

John knew as much and would miss his friend, now brother, until they came to the Colonies. "You need not wait for them. I've left you money enough for transportation to come any time. There are many ships that sail there in warm weather."

Johnny nodded noncommittally.

If the ship went down, at least John's lineage wouldn't be obliterated from the earth.

He shouldn't have thought that and quickly sent a plea to God to keep them safe. "Uncle Robert is your patron now and where you'll go on holiday. Write to me and avail me of your schooling. I've paid tuition enough to get you to graduation."

"Thank you, Father." Johnny turned to say his farewells to his siblings.

John glanced about him and over his shoulder for Laud's pursuivants, knowing they could arrest him for twice missing his court appearance and not paying bond. It was also not uncommon for Laud to keep a ship from sailing to Massachusetts. Those Independents not sailing were on the outskirts of the crowd, standing guard and ready to alert John if henchmen appeared.

As Laud had demanded, John tried to get passage for the Massachusetts Bay Colony before Trinity Term, with no success. Since June, he'd been in hiding as a fugitive avoiding arrest while recuperating enough to survive a voyage of probable seasickness. He also had to sell his property and help others plan their voyage as well. Procuring thirty-three tickets at once wasn't an easy feat.

Robert and Penninah joined them with Robert's four children at their sides. "I look forward to the day we meet again," Robert said as he embraced John.

"As do I. See if you can convince Johnny to come."

Stepping closer, Penninah said, "I'll help in that regard, but he's as stubborn as his mother." She looked to the sky. "Sorry Hannah, 'tis true." She embraced John. "I miss her so." And then she whispered, "I wish she were here to see the babe I now carry."

He pulled back and grasped her hands. "What wonderful news."

She laughed, her color high, looking as beautiful as a bride of three months should. "I'm not getting younger, and there's no time to waste."

"I hope it's not too long before I'm able to meet the babe."

"It cannot be soon enough." Penninah wiped a tear and

turned. "Come, say farewells to your Aunt Penny," she called to John's children, who by now were all tears over leaving Johnny.

Elizabeth Denne stood amongst the Lothropps, now a member of the family. She kept glancing over her shoulder, looking about, hoping for her own farewell with her kinsmen.

John had gone to Denne personally to try and get him to see reason, but his servant would not allow John entrance. As he left, a cloth dropped from an upstairs window. He picked it up and found a note and ring tied inside, Dorothy's parting gift to her daughter. John looked up.

Dorothy in tears, waved him on.

Penninah gave her woeful farewells to her brother, Samuel.

He too seemed to be fighting emotions. "Keep me informed on Mother's health and the family's interests."

A person passed carrying windows to the ship to be used on a new house in Massachusetts. It'd been fourteen years since Separatists made a settlement at Plymouth Plantation and still building materials were needed.

John checked on his Independent friends, to be sure all was as it should be, and then began the chore of loading their goods and claiming a space on the ship.

Later that morning, they pushed-away from the dock without discovery by Laud's men, and John waved farewell to his congregants, family, and young son, only seventeen and not yet a man. Robert's oldest, nine-year-old Hannah, wrapped an arm around Penninah's waist and looked up, saying something to her new mother. Life had a funny way of making itself come full circle. A mournful feeling came over John, as if he were leaving his own Hannah behind. "Don't be long in coming," he shouted to the wind.

When Penninah, Robert, and Johnny were no longer distinguishable, the children left John's side to make themselves comfortable below.

Late in the day, the *Griffin* sailed from the river's estuary and met the tides of the North Sea. John stood again on deck, watching the land of his birth grow distant, the stretch of England's coast a last connection to his life of almost fifty years. "May God care for you and bring you from unrighteous control. For you will ever be the mother—a parent who raised up children that have left with tears in their eyes to escape persecution that impersonated virtue."

John turned away and strode to the bow, looking toward the great expanse of the sea. In his heart, he felt God had provided a new path for him. He'd invest his life with meaning in America.

A few days into the voyage, many suffered from seasickness. To John's surprise, he didn't have a weak stomach and was able to help Samuel with those who did. Accustomed as Samuel was to seafaring, he cheered immensely when they'd left land.

With the endless swells of the ocean, the ship pitched and yawed. A sennight in, it was as if almost everyone onboard endured sickness. John, Samuel, and a few others worked tirelessly to alleviate misery.

That night, in the cramped and dank hold, John wanted naught more than to climb into his sleeping bunk, but he first forced himself to follow his routine of reading God's word. He opened his old Bishops' Bible, now a relic of the past—big and meant to sit upon a pulpit. Although cumbersome to carry, he felt as attached to it sentimentally as he did spiritually for its teachings and guidance.

He opened to Acts and read of the apostles' missionary endeavors and of the Lord commanding Paul to teach the Gentiles. For them, it was a time of change and trying to understand other peoples' ways. But God said to Paul and Barnabas—John held the candle closer, trying to see the words—'I have made thee a light of the Gentiles, that thou be the salvation unto the end of the world.'

John pondered on the early development of the church when there were contrasting opinions of what laws should be followed. The apostles had come from different backgrounds and were teaching Gentiles who didn't believe as they. The apostles met together to decide what changes needed to be made and, although they spoke their minds, there seemed no serious discord. 'Twas proof that under the influence of the Holy Spirit, harmony could be reached.

John startled awake to the smell of burning paper. Having fallen asleep with a candlestick in hand, a spark or the candlewax had burned holes into many of his Bible's pages. "Nay, John, you fool!" He felt heartsick.

The next morning, he glued small, new pieces of paper on the pages that had holes. From memory, he wrote in the words of the missing verses that had been burned away.

During the voyage, he came to know many who were not from his congregation. They too left England because of religious persecutions and joined together in hymns and prayers both morning and night. John desired to commune with them and find harmony as the apostles had.

That desire was tested every time a minister named Zechariah Symmes preached on deck. Upon introduction, John found him to be a graduate of Oxford and an overly priggish Puritan. Was this but a small glimpse of his neighbors in New England?

John became acquainted with William Hutchinson, a wealthy textile merchant who wore a black felt hat and the somber attire of a Puritan, but had a gentle and kind face. They spent many a day discussing religion. When his redheaded wife, Anne, wasn't caring for her many children—for she must have had a dozen—she'd join the men in their discussions. Her knowledge and passion for the scriptures appeared so great that she often reminded John of Hannah, who would have reveled in such discussions with another woman. And like Hannah, Anne Hutchinson even knew her herbs.

The nights were the loneliest. John laid on his bunk, missing his wife and wishing with all his heart she were sharing this journey with him.

One day, after a Bible discussion about Ruth and her unwavering faith, John said to Mistress Hutchinson, who held a sleeping babe in her arms, "I suspect if my wife were here, you'd be great friends. She too was well versed in theology and interpreting scripture. She suffered grievous disappointment in not being able to sermonize."

"I detect you were a devoted couple. I'm sorry for your loss and sorrow. She must have been an ardent Separatist."

"Nay. She followed her own conscience and stayed close to the Anglican Church."

Mistress Hutchinson sat up straighter, her green eyes wide. "God has seen fit to teach you tolerance in matters of acceptance."

John stared out at the brilliant blue sky and never-ending ocean. "You're so right." He'd not realized how many of his beliefs were formed because of Hannah.

He told Mistress Hutchinson some of his past troubles with the Church.

She sympathized and disclosed her father had been imprisoned multiple times. "We're leaving all that behind and must forgive those who have set this exodus upon us. Forgiveness of others is about having a relationship with Jesus Christ."

Penninah often said the same words. He'd start that day, asking for strength to forgive those who imprisoned, tortured, and abused him. 'Twould not be easy, although he had no thought of revenge. His revenge would be to live and teach others a gospel that holds to God's truths in a land where destiny is created by the individual.

On September 18th, a brisk wind swept them westward. John stood at the bow with many others, having heard the crewmember's cry of "land ahead." The land, still a smudge on the horizon, was a home of solid ground yet to be explored.

Sam, Joseph and Benjamin hooted and cheered, anxious to run and play on land. Elizabeth and Barbara held to one another, whispering something that made them smile.

During the voyage, Thomas had grown a full beard, its colors of blond and red much like Penninah's tresses. "At last the journey comes to an end."

"But has it?" John shrugged at his son.

William and Anne Hutchinson and their children stood at the rail close by. William called to John, "I hear to live amongst those in Boston, we must confess our conversion and declare an oath to the Bible's teachings."

"My congregation requires no confession of faith to a cleric. We're done with that and are not responsible to each other for our testimonies, but to God only."

Janie came beside him and wrapped an arm around his waist. "I miss mother." She laid her head against him.

"As do I." The pain of Hannah's absence was immense. It could pull him into a dark hole if he'd let it. His comfort was knowing there was always good ahead, as there had been when his mother had died. Hannah had filled that void. The steady time with his children now helped fill the loss of Hannah. "I'm sorry you've lost her guidance for your new life."

"Do you believe I'll find someone to marry here?"

He admired her for trying to look forward. Her youth would serve her well. "It will be a blessed man who takes you as wife. May you be as fortunate in a spouse as I was with your mother."

"She said almost the exact words to me of you on more than one occasion. She loved you so." Janie tightened her embrace, and his family nestled close, their excitement evident in their exclamations as the smudge of land became more distinct. He knew his children would eventually have families of their own, but he hoped they'd never be far distant.

John found courage knowing he could now do what his heart desired and for the first time understood how Hannah wanted the same thing. He could preach with no worry of being arrested.

By the time they'd entered the harbor, the sun began to fade in the west. A watchman's torch brought them safely in.

Was it coincidence that a ship named *Griffin* had brought them here? The mythical creature, a blend of lion and eagle, symbolized courage and boldness. John hoped to teach his children to walk with courage and boldness in their beliefs. Although a journey to God was individual, all must come before Him one day—John's family, Tomlinson, Laud, and John himself.

His future only God could see, his path illuminated by a light greater than the one in the distance.

The End

Author's Notes
Life in America

Currently, the Sturgis Library is partially built from John Lothropp's 1644 home in Barnstable, Massachusetts, where he once conducted his religious meetings. His 1605 Bishops' Bible is on display in the reference room. Visitors can see the burn marks sustained during his voyage on the *Griffin* in 1634.

No passenger list of the *Griffin* was preserved, but Governor John Winthrop wrote in his journal on 18 September 1634, "…the Griffin & another shippe now arivinge with about 200: passingers & 100: cattle (mr Lothrop & mr Simmes 2: godly ministers cominge in the same shippe.)" (Dunn et al., 1996). A later entry documents the Hutchinsons were also on the *Griffin*.

The Independent congregation arrived in Boston but stayed only a few days before departing to Scituate where they gathered on 27 September 1634. The names of the thirty-two congregants who came with Reverend John were not recorded, but some have been discovered through extrapolation of records and are listed on a following page. "A few were farmers and planters as they were called after their arrival, but the majority were mechanics and tradesmen. Nearly all of them were well informed, intelligent men" (Otis, 1888). The newcomers were expected and heartily welcomed in Scituate by Nathaniel Tilden, Samuel Hinckley, and other early emigrants from the county of Kent.

Other Men of Kent, who had sailed before 1634 and resided in Plymouth, left that village and came to Scituate once the Lothropp group arrived. In fact, previously in 1626, Nathaniel Tilden had traveled to New England (it is assumed without his family) and in 1628 was granted land in Scituate with the hope of settlement. He returned to England and in 1634 brought his family to live in Massachusetts.

Scituate was a small coastal village thirty miles south of Boston and twenty miles north of Plymouth. Only nine houses had been erected on what was called Kent Street. Although Scituate sat on a harbor, it also had a freshwater pond. The word "Scituate" is derived from the Native American word *satuit* meaning "cold brook."

The small congregation met in a member's home on 8 January 1635, formally establishing themselves as the First Church in

Scituate. It must have been a busy village with the newcomers building homes, fishing, hunting and—when weather permitted—breaking ground and planting crops. John had a home on Kent Street and a farm on the driftway.

His twenty-year-old daughter Jane wed soon after arriving in Massachusetts to Samuel Fuller. A former *Mayflower* passenger, Samuel had come to America in 1620 as a child with his parents, Edward and Ann Fuller. The same day as his marriage, Fuller was granted four acres in Scituate where the couple made their home. It was probably around this same time when John married for a second time and wed Anna (possibly surname of Hammond or Dimmock). On 6 June 1636, Anna gave birth to John's sixth son, Barnabas. At not quite fifty-two, John also became a grandfather that year when Jane gave birth to a daughter named Hannah.

That same year, John finished building his home on the harbor. Assuming twenty-four-year-old Thomas, Elizabeth Denne, and Reverend John's other four children from Hannah lived with him and his new wife and baby, there were nine people in the home—more if Anna was a widow with children when John married her. Samuel Howse had married Elizabeth Hammond in April and set up his own residence. John's older children would soon find spouses too. Barbara married John Emerson 19 July 1638, also establishing their home in either Scituate or Duxbury.

Finally, Robert and Penninah Linnell sailed the ocean to join their family. They brought Robert's four children by his first wife and a son by Penninah named Shubael. In John Lothropp's hand, he wrote in the church records, "My Brother Robert Linnell and his wife having a letter of dismission from the Church in London joyned to us Septemb. 16, 1637" (Loomis, 2011).

The years were prosperous. Although John's new wife lost an infant daughter, she found herself pregnant again when disagreements over religious matters and a shortage of cultivable land sent John's congregation looking for a new place to settle. They petitioned the General Court of Plymouth Colony for a location and were granted Barnstable, over fifty miles south on Cape Cod Bay, in the Great Marshes of Mattakeese.

Leaving fewer than sixty people in Scituate, John moved with twenty-five families to Barnstable 20 October 1639. They came by land and sea. Driving livestock and hauling the household goods over land proved the most difficult because of the many hills. It's not known how Anna at nine-months-pregnant traveled, but these are things less thought of when history is recorded. She survived and gave birth to a daughter, Abigail, twelve days later.

There were fewer houses in Barnstable than there had been in Scituate. Two groups had already failed to settle the area. But some of John's contingency had come in July and prepared a few structures and food for the newcomers. It is written that they were comfortably clothed and lodged and had an abundance of food—pork, poultry, venison, fish, rye, barley, wheat, and Indian corn.

With no meetinghouse, they performed an act of thanksgiving by holding their first meeting on a large rock situated on high ground near Coggins Pond. They took communion there and have left a legacy of what is now called "Sacrament Rock." Later, on a very cold winter's day in December, the congregation's first recorded meeting to praise God took place at the home of Mister Hulls. It would be seven years before they'd build a meetinghouse, but they were accustomed to meeting in homes, for it's what they had done (secretly) in England.

Thomas Lothropp became a land surveyor and at the age of twenty-seven married a widow, Sarah Ewer (surname Larnett or Larned) on 11 December 1639, establishing their home in Barnstable and raising five children.

By 1640, forty-one family names were recorded in the records of Barnstable. John and Anna had two more children over the years, Bathsheba and John. It seems this is the second time Reverend John named a son John. Perhaps the first was after his father-in-law John Howse? The first son John was still alive in England at this time.

John initially built a small, "cold" (his word) house. But by 1644, his second, larger, warmer home was completed in the early American colonial style of a fairly symmetrical rectangle with two stories and a steep roof. The congregation met in this house; the same building that presently stands as part of the Sturgis Library, the oldest library building in America, where Reverend John's Bible is left open to scorched pages in Acts.

Here he became known as the minister of the Congregational Church. The church—now known as West Parish Church in the village of West Barnstable—survives in customs and worship to this day. The Independent Church in England had been a congregational church. And just as they had in London, they covenanted together "to walk together in all God's ways and ordinances, according as He had revealed in His word, or should further make known to them" (Dale, 2015). They believed that each church was to control its own affairs. The town prospered under the spiritual guidance of John and for seventy-eight years was the only church in Barnstable.

Reverend John's five younger sons grew to marry and have successful lives. All were founders of New England families—Samuel Lothropp settling in Connecticut with a wife and nine children, Joseph in Barnstable with a brood of thirteen, Benjamin in Charlestown with nine, Barnabus also helping populate Barnstable with fourteen children, and the youngest John (the 2nd) marrying twice and having thirteen children in Barnstable. Abigail married James Clark and raised seven children in Plymouth, and Bathsheba married Benjamin Bale and settled with five children in Dorchester.

Nathaniel Tilden did not make the move to Barnstable, perhaps because of poor health, and died at Scituate in July 1641. He's buried in the Men of Kent Cemetery there. Samuel Hinckley's family came to Barnstable, and his children married and spread south to Hyannis Port where his descendants can still be found to this day. Robert and Penninah Linnell had a daughter named Bethia born in Barnstable. They lived a long life with their children and are buried on Lothrop Hill in Barnstable.

Amos Otis was a historian who lived in Barnstable two-hundred years after John. He studied the lives of John and his contemporaries. Otis wrote, "Mr. Lothrop was as distinguished for his worldly wisdom as for his piety. He was a good businessman, and so were all his sons. Where every one of the family pitched his tent, that spot became the center of business, and land in its vicinity appreciated in value. It is men that make a place, and to Mr. Lothrop in early times, Barnstable was more indebted than to any other family" (Otis, 1888).

As the Separatists found their new way of living in the Plymouth Bay Colony, those left in England continued to struggle, but conditions were soon to improve. Eight years after the Lothropps left, an Irish insurrection instigated what came to be known as the English Civil War. The first conflict was settled when Oliver Cromwell claimed a victory for Parliamentary forces at the Battle of Naseby in 1645, but warring continued over the manner of England's governance and military, pitting the supporters of King Charles I against the Parliamentarians. On 30 January 1649, King Charles I was beheaded after the parliamentarian court declared him guilty of attempting to "uphold in himself an unlimited and tyrannical power to rule according to his will, and to overthrow the rights and liberties of the people." Chief Judge John Bradshaw

The Pulse of His Soul

proclaimed the judgement of the court: "he, the said Charles Stuart, as a tyrant, traitor, murderer and public enemy to the good of this nation, shall be put to death by severing of his head from his body." Before his execution, the king stood on the scaffold in front of the Banqueting House in London and declared himself as a "martyr of the people."

With the execution of King Charles I and the exile of his son, King Charles II, the forced worship by the Church of England ended at last. The Commonwealth ruled England until 1653, and then the Protectorate under the personal rule of Oliver Cromwell ruled until 1658. Although the reinstallation of a king did eventually happen when King Charles II was restored to the throne in 1660, the wars established that an English monarch could not govern without Parliament's consent.

Archbishop William Laud's position of influence under King Charles I suffered when Parliament ended the personal reign of his king. Laud was brought before the Long Parliament in 1640 and accused of treason. He was imprisoned in the Tower of London and beheaded on Tower Hill on 10 January 1645. Laud is believed to have been "the greatest calamity ever visited upon the English Church" (Collinson, 1984).

John Lothropp lived to hear news of England's wars, beheadings, and church politics, and witnessed more Independents coming to New England. At almost 69 years of age, he died in 1653. His will left real property in Barnstable and money valued at 72 pounds, 16 shillings, and 5 pence. But that was not the true inheritance John left behind. He was a man who'd lived hardships most could not fathom. He journeyed through doubt, disbelief, impoverishment, death of his most beloved, torture, imprisonment, losing his home and country, and through it all still grew a testimony of Christ that could not be shaken. In America, he found a place to rest and keep his commitment to walk in all of God's ways.

Following are quotes of those extolling the Reverend John Lothropp:

> "He was a man of a humble and broke heart and spirit, lively in dispensation of the Word of God, studious of peace, furnished with godly contentment, willing to spend and be spent for the cause of the Church of Christ." (The Secretary of the Court for the Jurisdiction of New-Plimouth, Nathaniel Morton, 1669.)

He is described in Governor John Winthrop's journal as "rejoicing in having found for himself and his followers a church without a Bishop... and a state without a King" (Dunn, 1996).

"[Lothropp] was an independent thinker. He received no doctrines on the faith of others, he examined for himself, decided for himself. Though bold and decided in his denunciations of the arbitrary acts of the bishops, he was as meek as the lamb in reproving the faults of his brethren, and the children of his church. Creeds and confessions of faith he rejected. The Bible was his creed . . . Whatever exceptions we may make to Mr. Lothrop's theological opinions, all must admit that he was a good and true man, an independent thinker, and a man who held opinions in advance of his times" (Otis, 1888).

"...he was endowed with a competent measure of gifts and earnestly endowed with a great measure of brokenness of heart and humility of spirit" (Goehring, 1959).

"Mr. Lathrop was a man of deep piety, great zeal and large ability" (Pope, 1900).

"A man of a tender heart and a humble and meek spirit" (Champlin, 1912).

In the *New England Memorial* by Nathaniel Morton, John Lothropp was considered to be one of the five most important ministers to arrive in New England during the Great Migration (Morton, 1669).

Factual Notes of Historical Figures

During the time of this novel, England followed the Julian Calendar, also called "Old Style." The beginning of the legal new year started March 25. If an event was recorded as occurring 6 January 1588, as in the death of John Lothropp's mother, in our calendar today—the Gregorian Calendar or "New Style"—it would be 6 January 1589. Dates used below and in this novel are changed to the Gregorian calendar.

Also Note that "c." below represents "circa" and is used when a date is approximated.

Barebone, Unless-Jesus-Christ-Had-Died-For-Thee-Thou-Hadst-Been-Damned "Praise-God" (c.1598-1679) Praise-God Barebone, one of the first proponents of the free market, was a lay preacher and leather-seller on lower Fleet Street in London. In 1630, he married Sarah and had at least one son named Nicholas. In 1641, Barebone was known to have preached to audiences as large as one hundred and fifty at the Lock and Key, his home and place of business. At a sermon against bishops and *The Book of Common Prayer*, hostile apprentices gathered outside his home and broke windows and his business sign. He and many of the Separatists attending were arrested and imprisoned for an unknown time.

Barebone was active in London politics, becoming part of the Puritan sect The Fifth Monarchists (sect active from 1649 to 1660). From July to December 1653, the Parliament assembly nominated by Oliver Cromwell during the English Commonwealth was called Barebone Parliament (also known as the Little Parliament), acquiring its name from its nominee. Through speeches and published tracts, he endeavored to prevent the restoration of the English monarchy. In 1661, he was arrested, charged with treason, and imprisoned in the Tower of London. After a petition from his wife, Sarah, he was released in 1662. The Great Fire of London engulfed his place of business in 1666.

Bellamy, John (c.1596-1653) A native of Oundle, Northamptonshire, England, John Bellamy apprenticed with Nicholas Bourne, a London stationer. Bellamy became a bookseller and printer in 1622 at the Two Greyhounds and later Three Golden Lyons, both in Cornhill near the Royal Exchange.

It is assumed he became acquainted with Edward Winslow, a Separatist (later *Mayflower* Pilgrim), who apprenticed under John Beale whose bookshop Bourne stocked the titles Beale had printed. Bellamy was described as a young man of "a most pious . . . quiet and tender conscience" (Rostenberg, 1956).

Known as a publisher of Americana, having connections with both the Leiden community and the *Mayflower* passengers, Bellamy published one of the most important narratives relating to New England called the "Relation or Journal of the beginning and proceedings of the English Plantation settled at Plimoth in New England." The narratives of Edward Winslow and William Bradford were edited by G. Mourt and generally called Mourt's *Relation*. In 1624, Bellamy published "Good Newes from New England" by Winslow. For the next two decades, he went on to publish numerous works of the Separatist and Puritan leaders, explorers, historians, and New England Colonists.

Bellamy considered himself a semi-separatist. At about twenty years old, he attended meetings with Henry Jacob's Independent congregation. He called the congregation a "true Church of Christ, the Ministry thereof as received by the people, a true Ministry," and also said of John Lothropp, he was a "learned, holy, humble and painful preacher" (Rostenberg, 1956). Around 1626, John Bellamy severed his association with the congregation over matters of ordination rites and administration. Nevertheless, he claimed his feelings for the congregation were of love and respect.

Bellamy took an active part in religious and political controversies. During the Civil War, he took up arms for Parliament and was given the rank of colonel. He retired about 1650 in Cotterstock, Northamptonshire. It is believed he did not marry as he left the bulk of his property, a house and two shops in Saint Paul's Churchyard in London, to his siblings and their children. He bequeathed books to form a standing library for the ministers of Cotterstock. At the time of his death, he'd published 237 works.

Browne, Robert (c.1550-1633) Born in Little Casterton, a few miles south of Stamford, England, Robert Browne descended from a family of aldermen, public servants, and members of Parliament. He graduated with a degree from Corpus Christi College, Cambridge in 1572 and became a lecturer at Saint Mary's Church in Islington. His dissident preaching against the doctrines and disciplines of the Church of England attracted attention. Eventually seceding from the Church, he founded his own church on Congregational principles.

Sometimes called the father of Congregationalism, he wrote fiery religious tracts in the early 1580s and was considered a radical. "Brownist" became known as a frightening term for disorderly sectarianism. William Shakespeare mentions Brownists in *Twelfth Night* Act 3, Scene 2 when Sir Andrew says: "An't be any way, it must be with valor, for policy I hate. I had as lief be a Brownist as a politician."

Browne's first arrest in 1581 led to his release soon after on the advice of William Cecil, his kinsman. He left England for Middelburg in the Netherlands later that year where his most important works were published. Two men were hanged in 1583 for circulating Browne's tracts. He returned to England in 1585, supposedly giving up his Separatist ideals, and was employed as a schoolmaster and eventually a priest. His wife, Alice, gave him nine children.

Some of Browne's ideals from "A Treatise Upon the 23 of Matthewe" (1582) were used in this novel as Browne fictionally attacks rhetoric and debates with John Lothropp on his style of preaching. Many of the years between 1616 and 1632 have Browne's activities unaccounted for. Historians speculate he traveled to teach his doctrine. Always engaged in controversy, Browne was looked upon as a renegade but self-styled himself as a nonconformist. He was imprisoned thirty-two times for his beliefs. The last time, imprisoned for hitting a constable, Browne died in jail at Northampton in 1633.

Cushman, Robert (1577–1625) Robert Cushman was born in Rolvenden, county of Kent, and his stepfather was Thomas Tilden. It is uncertain how closely related Thomas was to Nathaniel Tilden, but they lived within a few miles of one another. Cushman apprenticed as a grocer in Saint George Parish. In 1604, he was prosecuted for illegally distributing derogatory religious libels against the Church of England in Canterbury.

Around 1611, he moved to Leiden, Holland, where his wife and two children died. For the Separatists there, he was a Chief Agent and organizer of the *Mayflower* voyage of 1620. To procure supplies for the voyage, he traveled to England from Holland many times from 1617 to 1619. In 1619, he and John Carver secured a patent from the Virginia Company for the Separatist congregation led by John Robinson. Cushman wrote the booklet "Cry of a Stone" about the Pilgrim's lives in Leiden, but it wasn't published until 1642 after his death.

While Robert Cushman was not a character in this novel, he is mentioned as gathering supplies in Kent and meeting with John Bellamy with letters and historical documents meant to be disseminated to others. Historically, he did both of those things. Bellamy published Cushman's "Sermon Preached at Plimmouth in New-England Dec 9th 1621" shortly after Cushman returned from a visit to New England.

Denne, Dorothy Tanfield (1593-1637) Daughter of John Tanfield of Copfold Hall in Margaretting, Essex, England, Dorothy Tanfield married Thomas Denne c.1610. She was thought to have given birth to ten or eleven children, Elizabeth Denne being her fourth. It is apparent she lived in both Canterbury and London with her husband.

Denne, Elizabeth (1619-1659) Thomas and Dorothy Denne's daughter, Elizabeth Denne, was imprisoned with members of John Lothropp's Independent congregation when she was approximately thirteen years old. It is not known how she became a member of the London Independent Separatist congregation so young or why she would travel to America at fifteen without apparent family members. It is the author's assumption that she had connections to the Lothropp family. She was the same age as Barbara Lothropp, and moved in the same circles as John and Hannah Lothropp in Kent. In Ipswich, Massachusetts, she married Daniel Warner in 1641, had five sons and three daughters and died soon after the birth of her eighth child.

Denne, Thomas (1577-1656) Thomas is known as "Denne" in this novel so as to not create confusion among the other men named "Thomas." He was born the eldest of five sons to Robert, a prosperous yeoman at Denne Hill, five miles from Canterbury. The Denne family had settled the area in the 13th Century. Denne underwent legal training at the Inner Temple, culminating in his admission to the bar in 1607. He lived in Canterbury by 1612. In 1617, he was retained as counsel. In the 1620s, he defended Canterbury's charter at Westminster. He was elected to Parliament in 1624. Throughout the 1630s and 1640s, he quarreled with his brother and only living son over the ancestral Denne estate and consequently gave his whole estate to his daughter Mary and her husband. A painting of Thomas Denne can be found at: http://www.nzgrantfamilygenealogy.com/getperson.php?personID=I1209&tree=Grant

Eaton, Samuel (c.1596-1665) The third son of Richard (vicar of Great Budworth, Cheshire, England), Samuel Eaton was born in the hamlet of Crowley. Educated at Cambridge, he graduated with a BA in 1624 and an M.A. in 1628. Thought to have joined John Lothropp's Independent congregation soon after, Eaton was imprisoned in Newgate with that congregation in April 1632. Some reports show he spent two years in prison with Lothropp, whereas others show Lothropp with William Granger and Ralfe Grafton. It is possible Lothropp was with all three. Based on an order given by the High Commission court for both John Lothropp and Samuel Eaton to appear on 9 October 1634, which they did not, it seems Eaton was released from prison soon after Lothropp. On 19 February 1635, Lothropp and Eaton were ordered to be committed for contempt. Lothropp was in New England by this time, but it appears Eaton may have stayed in England until 1637 when he went with his brother, Theophilus Eaton, to New England.

Up until 1637, it is conjectured Eaton served as a leader to those left behind in Lothropp's flock. In 1637, Henry Jessey became pastor. That may have been when Eaton left for America. However, he did not stay in New England and returned to England in 1640. He preached in Boston, England, but didn't settle there permanently. Instead, he spent most of his time preaching in Cheshire. In 1662, he moved to Denton, near Manchester, where he died at age sixty-eight. At his funeral, it was said that he had a grievous bodily affliction and had been dying many years. It is believed he never married or had children.

Fenner, John (1596-?) - John Fenner's baptismal record from Pluckley, Kent, England, shows Edward Fenner as father and has no listing for mother. Other than a document dated 16 February 1626 that a John Fenner of Egerton was teaching Separatist theology at the home of John Bax in the parish of Ash, few records can be found about this man. John Bax appeared in the Archdeacon's Court to make an accounting of the meeting. There is also record of a John Fenner of Appledore in Kent marrying Thomsin Sutton 1 June 1626 in Ashford.

The documents found for the *Hercules* ship, in which Tilden and Hinckley sailed to New England, do not show John Fenner onboard, but the list is not all inclusive. Because his name cannot be found in Scituate or Barnstable records, it is not believed he sailed to New England with John Lothropp on the *Griffin*. A John Fenner of East Grinstead, Sussex, England, appears in the High Commission Court records on 9 October 1634, his "appearance respited till next court day." It was also on this court day that Samuel Eaton and John Lothropp were recorded as "to be attached for non-appearance, and bonds to be certified," but they were already in New England. Fenner is found in the London Independent Church records as joining in 1636.

Granger, William (1596-?) William Granger was born in Elham, Kent, England. Although he is listed as imprisoned with John Lothropp, there is no existing record of him in New England. Granger's probable brother Thomas married Grace Hasell 26 September 1620 in Eastwell. They may have been the parents of John Granger, who bought land in Scituate in 1640. Thomas and Grace lived in Scituate also, and Thomas died there before 3 January 1642. It's probable William Granger never left England. He appeared in court on 12 June 1634. After refusing to take the oath or to answer articles, he was imprisoned again in the Gatehouse with William Batty, another Independent. It is not known how long Granger spent in prison. But in 1644, he was still in England and recorded as the administrator to the will of Thomas Howse (brother to Hannah, Penninah, and Samuel) in London. Another administrator was Praise-God Barebone, so it appears Thomas Howse *also* became friendly with the Independents in London. Considering William Granger grew up in Eastwell, as did Thomas Howse, they probably knew each other most of their lives.

Hinckley, Samuel (1589-1662) Born in Harrietsham (but from Tenterden), Kent, England, Samuel Hinckley was the son of Robert and Katherine Leese Hinckley. He married Sarah Soole 17 May 1617 in Hawkhurst and emigrated to New England on the *Hercules* with four children, sailing from Sandwich 14 March 1634. In the book *Genealogical Notes of Barnstable Families* by Amos Otis, Hinckley is recorded as "honest, industrious and prudent." Upon arriving in New England, he built a house next to Nathaniel Tilden in Scituate on what they named Kent Street. In July 1640, Hinckley sold his house, farm, and meadows and built a new home in Barnstable to maintain his closeness to John Lothropp's congregation. One of the oldest houses on Cape Cod, it still stands and is called Mulberry Cottage because of the mulberry tree in the front yard. After Hinckley's first wife passed away in 1656, he married Bridget Bodfish. He and Sarah's son Thomas, born 1618 in Kent, England, became the sixth and last governor of Plymouth Colony.

Howse, Hannah (1594-1633) The eldest daughter of John and Alice Lloyd Howse, Hannah Howse was born in Egerton while her father served as curate from 1592-1596. She married John Lothropp 10 October 1610 at Saint Mary's in Eastwell, Kent, England. With Lothropp she had at least eight or nine children. The youngest, Sarah, cannot be confirmed and did not live to adulthood. No records show that Hannah left the Church of England to attend the Independent Church as her husband did. She continued to have her babies baptized into the Church of England by her father, Vicar John Howse, in Eastwell. Living in Southwark at the time, she would have had to travel with the child to do so. She was not arrested with the Independent congregation in April 1632. Although the illness which caused her death is not recorded, it seems to have lingered. As in the novel, her husband was granted a temporary release from prison to offer his farewell, and she died 16 February 1633 in Lambeth Marsh.

Howse, John (c.1569-1630) After matriculating Saint John's College, Cambridge, John Howse served as curate from 1592 to 1596 in Egerton and vicar from 1603 to 1630 in Eastwell, Kent. His ancestral lines are unclear, but the Howse family was probably from somewhere near the county of Suffolk where he married Alice Lloyd 30 August 1593 at Lavenham. There is a documented minor noble Howse family with estates in nearby Norfolk. He and Alice had nine children. He died 30 August 1630 in Eastwell. Alice died 8 November 1653 in Kent. Saint Mary's Church in Eastwell dates from the 15th century and now stands in partial ruins by Eastwell Lake. The church monuments were removed and reside in the care of the Victoria and Albert Museum.

Howse, Penninah (1596-c.1670) The second child of John and Alice Lloyd Howse, Penninah Howse was born in Egerton, Kent, England. At the age of about thirty-eight, around 1634, she married Robert Linnell. Linnell was a widower with three daughters and one son. They sailed to Massachusetts in 1638 and settled in Scituate but soon moved to Barnstable with Reverend Lothropp's congregation. They had at least two children together. Shubael Linnell was most likely born in England around 1635. Bethia Linnell was born in Barnstable in 1640. Penninah and Robert remained in John Lothropp's congregation and are buried on Lothrop Hill in Barnstable.

Howse, Samuel (1610-1661) The seventh child of John and Alice Lloyd Howse, Samuel Howse was born in Eastwell, Kent, England. Early in life, he probably worked on trade ships. There is no record of him participating in the military, although it's not out of the question that he did. At twenty-two, he was arrested with the Independent congregation and testified in trial, "I have served the King both by sea and by land. I would be at sea now if this restraint had not been made upon me" (Burrage, 1912).

Howse traveled to Massachusetts, likely on the *Griffin,* and built a house next to John Lothropp in Scituate. There he was known as a ship carpenter. He married Elizabeth Hammond April 1636, and they had four children. Sometime around 1639, Howse moved to Barnstable with Reverend Lothropp. But records show he also resided in Cambridge by 1642 and moved back to Scituate in 1646. His moves may have been due to his profession as a ship carpenter. His shipyard was near Hobart's Landing, Scituate.

Howse's children and descendants used the surname spelling House. Some Colonial New England documents record the spelling as Howes. Samuel Howse may be the ancestor of the author, whose House family can be traced to North Carolina in the late seventeen-hundreds but has not as yet been connected to the Massachusetts Howse families.

Hutchinson, Anne Marbury (1591-1643) The daughter of Francis and Bridget Dryden Marbury, Anne was baptized on 20 July 1591 in Alford, Lincolnshire, England, and grew up to become a charismatic scholar. Her father, an Anglican cleric, schoolmaster, and playwright encouraged education for his sons and daughters. Anne's father served two short jail terms and a two-year prison term for coming into conflict with clergy about their need to be better educated and for criticizing Church of England doctrine.

In 1612, Anne married fabric merchant William Hutchinson, a Puritan from Alford. They had fifteen children. She and her family traveled to New England on the *Griffin* in 1634 and likely didn't know John Lothropp until that trip.

In Boston, William Hutchinson prospered in his cloth trade and made many land purchases and investments. Anne routinely served those in need and became a midwife but also organized weekly meetings of mostly women to discuss Bible passages and sermons to give expression to her own scriptural views. Anne's popular teachings and theology of "absolute grace" were shaped by Reverend John Cotton, an influential minister in both England and the Massachusetts Bay Colony. Her friendship with Cotton was not enough to save her from the displeasure of Governor John Winthrop, who had strong beliefs against women preaching doctrine. Governor Winthrop described Anne as "a woman of ready wit and bold spirit," an insult in that day. She believed the Holy Spirit to be her guide and sometimes disagreed with ministers. In 1637, the General Court convicted Anne of "traducing the ministers" and sentenced her to banishment from the Massachusetts Bay Colony.

When the First Church in Boston then excommunicated her, she and her family along with some supporters founded a settlement on the island of Aquidneck in 1638, which is now Portsmouth, Rhode Island. William Hutchinson died in 1642. When the Massachusetts Bay Colony made serious threats to take over Rhode Island, Anne moved to Long Island Sound (near present Pelham Bay, New York), into the jurisdiction of the Dutch. In August 1643, Indians massacred Anne, her servants, and seven young members of her family, save one nine-year-old daughter who they captured and much later traded to the English.

Jacob, Henry (1563–1624) Born to John Jacob, yeoman, of Cheriton, Kent, England, Henry Jacob inherited his father's property at Godmersham, near Canterbury. He attended Saint Mary Hall, Oxford from 1581 to 1586, graduating with an M.A. For a time, he was precentor of Corpus Christi College, Oxford. He received orders with the Church of England and served in a parish church in Kent. It may have been about this time that he married Sarah (no surname known). They had several children. Jacob found interest with the Brownists and lived in Holland from 1593 to 1597. Believing there were many true Christians in the Church of England, he formed a non-separatist independent faction of former members.

Jacob returned to England for a short time. After he opposed doctrine in a pamphlet, writing that bishops had no authority to rule over pastors, he was imprisoned. When released, he fled to Middelburg, Netherlands, where English exiles formed a congregation. They called themselves the "Jacobites" and included famous Separatists such as William Bradshaw, William Ames, Robert Parker, and Paul Barnes. They believed a church was gathered by a free and mutual consent of believers who covenanted to live as a holy society. They also believed Christ and his Apostles instituted and practiced the gospel in the same way.

In 1610, Jacob went to Leiden to confer with John Robinson. There he was influenced by Robinson's theological views and his church government. They believed in the election of ministers, spiritual correction of sinners, and that salvation came from Christ, rather than from bishops. He wanted to reform the Church of England in this way and appears to have been a moderate on infant baptism.

Jacob returned to England and formed a congregational church in Southwark in 1616. They called themselves the Independent Church. He was a passionate and deeply committed man who tried to help others worship the way their conscience dictated. He called for toleration for politically loyal nonconforming Protestants and differed from other Separatists, believing he and his congregants could keep open channels with the parish churches and partake of communion. However, he did draw up a Confession of Faith with twenty-eight particulars in which he dissented from the Church of England. For a short time in 1622, he went to the Virginia Colony to teach his ideals there. Later that year, John Lothropp moved to Southwark and attended conventicles with the Independents.

By 1624, records differ on whether Jacob traveled to Virginia again or simply made plans to travel there before he became ill. He died in April or May 1624 in the parish of Saint Andrew Hubbard, London. He was sixty-one years old. At this time, John Lothropp was sustained as the pastor for the Independent Church.

Laud, William (1573-1645) Baptized 7 October 1573 in Reading, Berkshire, England, William Laud was the only son of William (a clothier) and Lucy Webbe Laud. Educated at Saint John's College, Oxford, Laud became president of Saint John's after a patronage struggle. King James swept aside irregularities in the election, showing preference to Laud. He served Bishop of Rochester Richard Neile, with whose help he secured a succession of ecclesiastical appointments until he became the chaplain and confidant of George Villiers, 1st Duke of Buckingham. Charles I started his personal reign in 1629. Having dissolved Parliament three times since 1625, he found Laud to be a man he could use to further his purposes. Laud advocated the Divine Right of Kings, arguing that Charles I had been chosen to rule by God. Starting in 1626, Laud ascended to positions of influence. In July 1628, he became Bishop of London, and those who served him became known as "Laudians" or "Lauders."

Laud was unmarried, humorless, short, and known to be sensitive about his diminutive stature. His private diary contained evidence of erotic dreams about Buckingham and other men, and he is thought to have had homosexual leanings. During the 1632 trial of John Lothropp, it was Laud who asked, "How many women sat cross-legged upon ye bed whilst you sat on one side and preached and prayed most devoutly?" With this grossly inappropriate comment, especially for one of such high ecclesiastical standing, he displayed his tactlessness, not for the first or last time. An official court jester is recorded as having said, "Give great praise to the Lord, and little Laud to the devil."

Laud yielded his power over the Separatists, hunting them down and trying them before the Court of High Commission. He saw the Separatist movement as a threat to the episcopacy and ordered the burning of books, bringing in his Laudians as censors. He controlled the printing presses and prohibited discussion of predestination and many other controversial topics of the time. He enforced strict accordance to *The Book of Common Prayer* and felt it his duty to impose uniformity in the Church of England. He started a reform movement with an emphasis on liturgical ceremony and clerical hierarchy—the exact opposite of what the Separatists desired.

In 1633, Archbishop of Canterbury George Abbot died, and Bishop of London William Laud was ordained to the position of archbishop in September. Using his severe strength in the royal prerogative courts of the High Commission and Star Chamber, he'd already been extending his authority over the kingdom. He was almost sixty when he became the religious spokesman for King Charles I's regime and had made significant changes by moving the communion tables altar-wise at the east end of chancels as they had been when Catholicism was in practice. Within a few years, some bishops wanted confession to take place before receiving communion and called for such ceremonies as bowing at the mention of the name of Jesus, practices eliminated during the Reformation. The acts directly contradicted the Calvinist doctrine of salvation through faith alone. The tension between the Church of England and Puritans and Separatists grew to a breaking point, yet Laud never had a conflict with royal and ecclesiastical powers.

Records show that John Lothropp's children went to Archbishop Laud in April 1634 and asked for their father's release. Yet the reasoning behind Laud's agreement is uncertain. It had been over a year since Hannah Lothropp's death. Why had he not released Lothropp then when his children became orphans? Laud's rationale is lost to time.

After the Lothropps left England, the war on Separatism continued without abatement and caused what is now called The Great Migration. Separatists and Puritans fled England by the thousands.

When Laud persecuted Puritans with popular support, a tide turned. King Charles I's non-parliamentary levies and extended demands on ship money caused resistance by the gentry. And the Scottish Presbyterian Church fiercely opposed Laud's attempts at getting them to use the Anglican *The Book of Common Prayer*. By 1639, the Bishops' Wars began, and Puritans gained power in Parliament after an eleven-year hiatus, abolishing the Star Chamber Proceedings and ordering the Book of Sports to be publicly burned. Mass demonstrations and petitions displayed a prominent hatred of Laud. In 1640, he was accused of treason and imprisoned in the Tower of London. By 1642, an Irish insurrection instigated what came to be known as the English Civil War.

Due to Laud's advanced age, many Parliamentarians hoped he'd die in prison so they wouldn't have to execute an anointed archbishop. But Laud survived and went to trial in the midst of the Civil War. He was found guilty of high treason and beheaded at Tower Hill 10 January 1645.

Leighton, Alexander (1568- c.1643) Born in Scotland and educated at Saint Andrews University, Alexander Leighton received a Doctor of Divinity and became a minister for the Church of Scotland. He later attended medical school in Leiden, Holland, and practiced medicine in Utrecht. It was here that he wrote his first book against the rule of bishops. He moved to London in the 1620s and taught aspiring doctors.

In 1628, Puritans convinced him to write another book decrying episcopacy. He wrote it specifically for Parliament in hopes that they would save the kingdom from the tyranny of King Charles and the abuse of power by bishops. Although Leighton wrote the book in London, he traveled to Holland to have it printed. While he was there, King Charles dissolved Parliament. Leighton returned to England without his book. Merchants smuggled copies in which came to the attention of Bishop Laud. Leighton was arrested by a troop of armed henchmen as he left Blackfriars Church in London. He was brought before the Star Chamber because of his publication "An Appeal to Parliament; or Zion's Plea Against Prelacy." Leighton's flogging and his son being held at gunpoint after his arrest as written in the novel are true events. When Edward Wright, the sheriff of London, came to Leighton's home, he and his men also roughly manhandled Leighton's wife and stole apparel, household goods, and furnishings. Before the flogging at Westminster 29 February 1629, Leighton was taken to Newgate Prison courtyard, put into irons, and thrown into what was called a "dog hole"—an open pit overrun with rats. Exposed to the winter elements, he was left there for three days without food, drink, or covering. He was then kept in solitary confinement at Fleet Prison for fifteen weeks without charges brought against him. Physician friends visited him in prison and reported that he suffered from poisoning and that his hair was falling out and his skin shedding. Eventually tried and convicted of ten charges without making a defense, even though his book was printed abroad and never circulated, he was fined ten thousand pounds that could not be paid. With the help of friends, Leighton escaped, but was apprehended in Bedfordshire and brought back to prison. It was at this time that Laud made sure Leighton was punished publicly with a flogging at Winchester.

After twelve years of incarceration, Leighton could not walk, see, or hear. The Long Parliament met and heard Leighton's case in 1641, determining that the warrant, fine, flogging, and perpetual imprisonment passed by the High Commission was illegal as was the taking of Leighton's papers and household goods. One of the resolutions passed for Leighton was "That the archbishop of Canterbury [Laud], then bishop of London, ought to give satisfaction to Dr. Leighton for his damages sustained, by fifteen weeks imprisonment in Newgate upon the said bishop's warrant" ("Alexander Leighton D.D. (1568- ca1643)" The Reformation website). Although there is no record that Laud was held in Newgate, he was kept in the Tower of London.

Linnell, Robert (1584-1662/63) Although Robert Linnell's birthplace is unknown, some have speculated it to have been London, England. The name of Linnell's first wife is also unknown, but recent research suggests it may have been Susan. She gave Robert four children (Hannah, David, Mary, and Abigail) and she probably died in connection to the birth of Abigail around 1633. Linnell married Penninah Howse around 1634, and they had a son, Shubael, probably born in London. They traveled to New England and are recorded for the first time in the church records of Scituate 16 September 1638. They moved with the Scituate congregation to Barnstable. Linnell held land holdings of ten acres in town, bounded northerly by the harbor, and three acres in the Common Field for planting as well as other lands, his largest land holding being sixty acres. He and Penninah had a daughter, Bethia, 7 February 1640 in Barnstable. In New England records, the Linnell name is sometimes spelled Linnet(t).

Lothropp, Anne (1616-1617) Daughter of John and Hannah Howse Lothropp, Anne Lothropp was baptized on 12 May 1616 in Egerton, Kent, England. She lived about one year, dying 30 April 1617. Her death record can be seen in the Saint James Church registrar, written in the hand of her father.

Lothropp, Barbara (1619-?) Daughter of John and Hannah Howse Lothropp, Barbara Lothropp was baptized 19 October 1619 in Egerton, Kent, England. In 1634, at the age of almost sixteen, she traveled to America on the *Griffin* with her father. Four years later, 19 July 1638, she was married by Captain Myles Standish to John Emerson, a planter, in Duxbury, Massachusetts. She was believed to have established a home with her husband in Scituate and to have moved to Barnstable with her father's congregation. Some records show her death 19 July 1638 (marriage date), and tracing her line seems unlikely.

Lothropp, Benjamin (1626-1691) Son of John and Hannah Howse Lothropp, Benjamin Lothropp was baptized in Eastwell, Kent by his grandfather, John Howse, 24 December 1626. He is believed to have been born in Southwark. At the age of seven, in 1634, he sailed on the *Griffin* to New England. He married Martha (possible last name Cotton) 11 December 1650 in Barnstable and settled in Charlestown, north of Boston, where they raised nine children. He died there 3 July 1691.

Lothropp, Jane (1601-c.1659) Half-Sister of John Lothropp and daughter of Thomas and Jane Carter (or Brennen) Lothropp, Jane Lothropp was baptized 14 March 1601 in Etton, Yorkshire, England. Little is known of Jane's history. She was around five when her father and mother died. It is not known who cared for her and her siblings—nine orphaned children—for the oldest was sixteen and the youngest two. It is also not known if Jane lived with John and Hannah Lothropp, but she likely did live with a relative. It is not known if she married, but she died about 1659.

Lothropp, Jane "Janie" (1614-1683) Daughter of John and Hannah Howse Lothropp, Jane Lothropp was baptized by her father in Egerton, Kent, England, 29 September 1614. She traveled on the *Griffin* to Massachusetts, landing 18 September 1634. Seven months later, 8 April 1635, she married Samuel Fuller, son of Edward and Ann Fuller. Samuel Fuller came over on the *Mayflower* when he was eleven. They were wed by Captain Myles Standish in the home of James Cudworth. On that same day, Fuller was granted four acres on Greenfield Street in Scituate. The couple had four children there and later moved to Barnstable where they had five more children. She died in Barnstable 31 October 1683. She is the ancestress that ties the author's husband and children to the Lothropp family.

Lothropp, John "Johnny" (1617-c.1653) Son of John and Hannah Howse Lothropp, John Lothropp, Jr. was baptized by his father in Egerton, Kent, England, 22 February 1617. It is not known if John Lothropp, Jr. was aboard the *Griffin* in 1634 and later sailed back to England, or if he simply did not sail to Massachusetts. The reason he would have stayed in England is also unknown. It is believed he married Mary Heily of Wandsworth, Surrey, England. He is mentioned in his father's will in 1653 as living in England.

Lothropp, Joseph (1624-1702) Son of John and Hannah Howse Lothropp, Joseph Lothropp was baptized by his grandfather, John Howse, in Eastwell, Kent, 11 April 1624. He is believed to have been born in Southwark. At the age of ten, he sailed on the *Griffin* to Massachusetts in 1634. Sixteen years later in Barnstable, he married Mary Ansell 11 December 1650. They raised thirteen children. He supported his family as a conveyancer of property and a clerk in Barnstable. For eleven years, starting in 1667, he was a representative of the Council of War and served as a lieutenant and then captain in the Indian Wars. He died about April 1702 and is buried on Lothrop Hill in Barnstable, Massachusetts.

Lothropp, Mary (c.1578-1628) Sister of John Lothropp, Mary Lothropp was the second born to Thomas and Maude Howell Lothropp. At thirty-three, she married John Gallant (or Gallande) 13 October 1611, who probably had children from a previous marriage. Mary died 20 October 1628. She had no known children.

Lothropp, Robert (c.1561-1632) Half-brother of John Lothropp, Robert Lothropp was the eldest son of Thomas and Elizabeth Wood Lothropp, which made him the oldest of twenty-two siblings. He was probably born about 1561 in Cherry Burton or Etton, Yorkshire, England. There is little information about his life, but he is thought to have died 28 March 1632 in Yorkshire.

Lothropp, Samuel (c.1622-1699) Son of John and Hannah Howse Lothropp, Samuel Lothropp was probably born in Southwark, but no record has been found of birth or baptism. He came to Massachusetts on the *Griffin* at age of about twelve. In 1643, when he was about twenty-one, and still single, he became a judge in Barnstable. He married Elizabeth Scudder 28 November 1644. They had nine children and lived in various towns in Connecticut.

In 1648, they were in New London (then called Pequot) where Lothropp built a church and served as a judge for the area. He served in Major Williard's expedition against the Ninigret in 1654 and also with Lieutenant Avery in the expedition for the relief of Uncas (a sachem of the Mohegans) around 1659. In 1668, he removed to Norwich, Connecticut, where he worked as a constable. After Elizabeth died about 1690, he married Abigail Doane in the early 1690s. He died 29 February 1700 and is buried at Old Norwichtown Cemetery, Norwich, Connecticut.

Lothropp, Sarah (c.1628) The probable, but unproven, daughter of John and Hannah Howse Lothropp, Sarah Lothropp is the female child made mention of in this novel as having been born early and living only two days. However, there is no birth or baptismal record for her. She is found on some Lothropp genealogical family group records but not others. It is not a known fact that her name was Sarah.

Lothropp, Thomas (1612-1707) Eldest son of John and

Hannah Howse Lothropp, Thomas Lothropp was baptized by his grandfather, John Howse, 21 February 1612 in Eastwell, Kent, England, but was probably born in Egerton. He sailed on the *Griffin* at the age of twenty-two and became a surveyor in Barnstable, Massachusetts. He married Thomas Ewer's widow, Sarah Larnett/Larned, 11 December 1639 when Lothropp was twenty-seven. At a town meeting in 1641, he was appointed a "measurer of land" and further laid out the town of Barnstable. Lothropp and his wife raised five children in Barnstable. He died 21 February 1707 at ninety-five and is buried on Lothrop Hill Cemetery. Lothropp's youngest daughter, Bethia, married John Hinckley, Samuel's son, bringing the Lothropps and Hinckleys together as family.

Lothropp, William (1587-1628) Brother of John Lothropp, William was the fifth and last child of Thomas and Maude Howell Lothropp. He was baptized 24 May 1587 in Etton, Yorkshire, England. Little is known of his life and the author went off the assumption that he joined the military because of the common dogma of the first-born being the heir, second-born for the church, and third-born an active interest in the wellbeing of the kingdom, that being a military obligation. Some online ancestral charts show him as marrying and having a son named John in 1613 and making his home in Yorkshire.

Lothropp, Thomas (1582-1629) Brother of John Lothropp, Thom Lothropp was the third-born of Thomas and Maude Howell Lothropp. He was baptized 24 October 1582 in Etton, Yorkshire, England. He gained his master's degree in 1608 from Cambridge and was a rector in Dengie, Essex, from 1613 to 1629. He married Elizabeth (surname unknown) about 1615 and had six daughters by her, four living to adulthood. Elizabeth was pregnant when Lothropp died in January 1629, but he might not have known. His will had been written 20 October 1628, and there is no mention of the child "to be born." He left his four daughters properties throughout Essex. His wife gave birth to an only son, Thomas Lothropp, who was baptized 21 June 1629 in Dengie—a son never to know his father.

Robinson, John (c.1575-1625) Born in Sturton-le-Steeple, Nottinghamshire, England, John Robinson became a curate for the Church of England in 1602. In 1604, he refused to conform to anti-Puritan decrees given by the Church and joined a Separatist congregation at Scrooby. By 1609, the approximately three-hundred-member Scrooby congregation, including Jonathan Brewster and William Bradford, was in Leiden, South Holland, hoping to worship as they felt God required.

Although only mentioned briefly in this novel, Robinson was of great importance to the success of the Pilgrims leaving Holland and England. As the Separatist minister of the Leiden congregation, he had association with Henry Jacob when Jacob visited Holland. Jacob's London Independent Church was modeled after Robinson's. It is possible Jacob acted as the agent for Robinson's *Essays*, a collection of sixty-two essays on ethical and spiritual topics published by John Bellamy in England. Jacob's congregation most likely distributed these essays amongst themselves and followed their precepts.

When the Pilgrims left for the Colonies, Robinson elected to remain in Holland with the majority of his congregation, assuming he would go later, but he died in 1625. In a sermon to those leaving in 1620, he said, "For I am very confident the Lord hath more truth and light yet to break forth out of His holy Word" ("John Robinson" Encyclopædia Britannica, 2020).

Robinson's son Isaac traveled with the *Mayflower* Pilgrims as their pastor. He lived in Scituate by 1634 and attended Reverend Lothropp's congregation, marrying another member, Margaret Hanford. He removed to Barnstable with the congregation in 1639.

Tilden, Joseph (1585-1642) Baptized 28 November 1585 in Tenterden, Kent, England, Joseph Tilden was the son of Thomas and Alice Bigge Tilden and the younger brother of Nathaniel. He was a "girdler of London," which may mean he was in the industry of making belts and girdles (a product of a livery company) worn by an official or someone of rank. He was one of the merchant adventurers (guild of overseas merchants) of London who fitted out the *Mayflower*, hoping to make a profit from the fur trade in the Colonies. Tilden also furnished capital to maintain the infant settlement at Plymouth. Although he helped finance the Pilgrims, there are no records of him being a Separatist or a part of John Lothropp's congregation in Southwark or Scituate.

There is a record of a Joseph Tilden owning land in Scituate after the congregation had moved to Barnstable, but this may have been Nathaniel Tilden's son Joseph, not his brother. That Joseph Tilden witnessed the will of Thomas Prior in June 1639 in Scituate.

If it was Nathaniel's brother, then he returned to England. There is record of his death in London 1 February 1642. He made his nephew, Joseph Tilden of Scituate, his residuary legatee and much of his property was shipped to Plymouth Bay Colony.

Tilden, Nathaniel (1583-1641) Baptized 28 July 1583 in Tenterden, Kent, England, Nathaniel Tilden was the son of Thomas and Alice Bigge Tilden. He came from a family of wealth with a history of aristocrats who'd served monarchs. He likewise served his community as mayor of Tenterden. Tilden married Lydia Hucksteppe, who bore him twelve children, seven living to adulthood. He came to Boston on the *Hercules,* landing May 1634 with seven children and seven servants, settling in Scituate near Plymouth. But records show he also came to New England in 1626 and was granted land in Scituate in 1628. It is assumed he came without his family during his first visit(s).

It appears Tilden was the first of the Men of Kent to colonize Scituate, and he very well could have instigated getting his friends and family to settle there. He's recorded in Scituate records as a town officer, leading citizen, and appointed ruling elder of the First Church in Scituate, of which John Lothropp was pastor. He died in 1641 and is buried in Men of Kent Cemetery, Scituate. A year after his death, his widow married Timothy Hatherly, a man of wealth and influence.

Tomlinson - (birth and death dates unknown) Tomlinson, William Laud's warrant officer, was supposedly the leading henchman who arrested John Lothropp at Humphrey Barnett's home in April 1632. He appears in records about John Lothropp but is otherwise hard to find in historical documents.

Independents Arrested

Below is a partial list (thirty-two of forty-two) of those arrested with John Lothropp on April 29, 1632 at the home of Humphrey Barnett in Blackfriars, London. Ten others, the names of which have not been found, were released on bond. It is said eighteen escaped from the meeting, which would mean there were sixty in attendance.

Mrs Allen	Samuel Howse
Thomas Arundell	Sara Jacob
William Attwood	Sarah Jones
Sarah Barebone (escaped)	John Ireland
Humphrey Barnett	Marke Luker
Mrs Barnett (released)	Elizabeth Melborne
Abigail Delamer	John Melborne
Elizabeth Denne	Mabel Milbourne
Henry Dod	Henry Packer
Sam Eaton	W. Parker
John Egge	William Pickering
Joan Ferne	Robert Reignolds
Ralfe Grafton	Elizabeth Sargeant
William Granger	Toby Talbot
Amy Holland	Susan Wilson
Penninah Howse	John Woodwyne

Trial and Imprisonment

The transcript of John Lothropp's trial in the Court of High Commission was printed in Chapter Thirty-Two of this novel as written in historical records other than modernizing spelling. The author was not able to find the criminal sentencing of John Lothropp so instead used the sentencing punishments of another Separatist, John Lilburne, aka "Freeborn John," who in December 1637 was arrested for disseminating literature that was not licensed. The manuscript he dispersed claimed that bishops of the Church of England were servants of Satan. When Lilburne went before the same judges as John Lothropp, he too refused to take the *ex officio* oath, saying, "I am unwilling to answer any impertinent questions, for fear that with my answer, I may do myself hurt. This is not the way to get to liberty" (Dorn, 2013). The court fined him £500, sentenced him with 200 lashings which took place while tied to the back of a moving oxcart traveling to the prison yard, and then sent him to be pilloried and imprisoned.

Records could not be found documenting which prison John Lothropp served his two-year prison sentence—Newgate or the Clink. It appears many of the Independent congregants were sentenced to the Clink, but Samuel Eaton and others were at Newgate Prison, and historians conjecture Lothropp was with Eaton.

Renowned for appalling conditions, both Newgate and the Clink were known for cruelty and violence. All criminals were imprisoned together whether they committed petty crime, highway robbery, rape, murder, or were heretical and enemies against the Church of England. Upon arrival, the prisoner was shackled and led to a cell. In Newgate, those sentenced to death were kept in a cellar beneath the keeper's house. Prisoners could expect brutal treatment and harsh conditions from the gaol keepers who were offered incentives to perform cruelty. They'd exact payment from the inmates for any favor, their incomes depending upon extortion of their wards. The gaolers charged for having shackles released or lightened, bedding, candles, fuel, visitors, and whatever other modest comforts the prisoners beseeched. Food and drink were typically charged at twice the outside price.

Although Newgate stood for almost 800 years and was demolished in 1902, some of the Clink walls still stand as a museum. Built in Southwark in the 12th century, the prison had grates at street level. For a fee, prisoners would be allowed to stand at the grate and beg passersby or sell anything they had with them, including their clothing.

It is a fact that John Lothropp was released from prison for a time to visit his dying wife. To achieve this short liberation, it is assumed that someone petitioned the king or archbishop. It is not known who succeeded in attaining such a favor.

The Griffin

A full manifest is not in known existence for 1634. What we do know about the ship's passengers and cargo is from Governor Winthrop's journal and an extrapolation of other records. The ship weighed in at 300 tons and brought religious dissidents to Massachusetts Bay in 1633 and 1634. In the 1633 voyage, she transported John Cotton, Samuel Stone, Thomas Hooker, and Anne Hutchinson's eldest son, Edward, amongst approximately 200 other passengers. Seaborn Cotton, the son of Reverend John Cotton, was born on the ship.

The 1634 voyage, in which John Lothropp and his family and congregation were passengers, was thought to have carried 150-200 people. This included the William and Anne Hutchinson family, minus Edward who came the year before, along with 100 cows and many pigs, chickens, geese, barrels of food, and a large amount of home building materials. William Hutchinson brought house windows and probably an abundance of fabrics, considering he was a fabric merchant and continued the trade in New England.

Men of Kent

Besides those mentioned in this story, John Lothropp associated with other Separatists in Kent, England, who later traveled to America. When he settled in Scituate, there were those who settled near him known as the Men of Kent. Besides Nathaniel Tilden, Samuel Hinckley, and Samuel Howse, there was John Lewis, William Hatch, James Austin, and certainly others. More than half of the 102 passengers who came to New England in the *Hercules* were afterwards inhabitants of Scituate. Whether or not they were part of John Lothropp's congregation or simply from Kent, it's hard to say. Many Men of Kent lived on Kent Street in Scituate. When John Lothropp moved to Barnstable in 1639, most followed.

John Lothropp's Compatriots

Below is a list of people known to have gone to Massachusetts before, with, and after Lothropp.

Anthony Annable (by 1633 "Men of Kent")
James Austin (probably *Griffin* or *Hercules*)
Thomas Besbeech/Besbedge (1634 *Hercules* "Men of Kent")
Thomas Chittenden/Chittingden (1635 *Increase* "Men of Kent")
Henry Cobb (by 1633 "Men of Kent")
James Cudworth (assumed 1634 *Griffin* but possibly earlier)
Elizabeth Denne (assumed 1634 *Griffin*)
Henry Ewell (1634 *Hercules* "Men of Kent")
Edward Foster (by 1633 "Men of Kent")
Richard Foxwell (by 1633)
William Gilson (by April 1633 "Men of Kent")
Thomas Granger (assumed 1634 *Griffin*)
Jane Harris (by June 1635)
William Hatch (1634 *Hercules* "Men of Kent")
Samuel Hinckley (1634 *Hercules* "Men of Kent")
Samuel Howse (assumed 1634 *Griffin*)
John Lewis (1634 *Hercules*)
Robert and Penninah Howse Linnell (by September 1638)
Manassah Kempton (1623 *Anne*)
Ephraim Kempton (possibly 1623 *Anne*)
Widow Norton (assumed 1634 *Griffin*)
Henry Rowley (by 1633 "Men of Kent")
Nathaniel Tilden (1634 *Hercules* "Men of Kent")
Alice, Elizabeth, and Rebecca Wincopp (assumed 1634 *Griffin*)
John and Goodwife Woodwyne (assumed 1634 *Griffin*)

Timothy Hatherly was an early merchant adventurer who helped finance the Pilgrims and may have come to New England to scout out the possibilities for the Independent congregants to later follow. He came in 1623, 1631, 1632, and met with Lothropp's congregation when they arrived in 1634. He is known as the "father of Scituate." He married Nathaniel Tilden's widow, Lydia, in 1642.

Humphrey Turner was one of the seventeen organizers of the First Church in Scituate in 1634, under Reverend Lothropp. He may have come from the Independent Church in England.

End Note

Sadly, when writing a novel, not every person involved in someone's life can be mentioned, even when some of those people may have been very important to the character of John Lothropp. Through my research, I noted names of his congregants in both London and New England (see also: "The Roots of the Ancient Congregational Church in London, Scituate, and Barnstable, Rev. John Lothropp Minister" by Dan McConnell, *Cape Cod Genealogical Society Bulletin*, Fall 2008.) I'm sure I'm missing many important individuals. If you descend from John Lothropp or any of his contemporaries, please tell us your ancestor's story at www.orasmith.com

Famous Decendents of John Lothropp

John Lothropp's integrity and goodwill have been emulated by his descendants. Many of them influenced America's government, religion, economy, the arts, and more. Below are listed some of the most famous.

United States Presidents
Ulysses Simpson Grant (1822-1885)
William Howard Taft (1857-1930)
Franklin Delano Roosevelt (1882-1945)
George Herbert Walker Bush (1924-2018)
George Walker Bush (1946-)

United States Government
John Lathrop (1699-1752) Representative in Connecticut Legislature
Samuel Huntington (1731-1796) Signer of the Declaration of Independence
Samuel H. Huntington (1765-1817) Governor of Ohio
Milledge Luke Bonham (1813-1890) Governor of South Carolina, Confederate General
Melville Weston Fuller (1833-1910) Supreme Court Chief Justice
Adlai Ewing Stevenson I (1835-1914) Vice President, Representative from Illinois
Oliver Wendell Holmes, Jr (1841-1935) Supreme Court Justice
Julia Clifford Lathrop (1858-1932) Children's Bureau, Social Reformer
Eugene Foss (1858-1939) Governor of Massachusetts
Robert Bacon (1860-1919) Secretary of State, Ambassador to France
Robert L Bacon (1884-1938) Congressman
Gaspar G Bacon (1886-1947) Lt Governor of Massachusetts, President of Massachusetts State Senate, Army Veteran, and Chief of Staff to General Patton.
John Foster Dulles (1888-1959) Secretary of State
Henry A. Wallace (1888-1965) Vice President, Secretary of Agriculture and Commerce
Allen Dulles (1893-1969) Director of CIA
Prescott Sheldon Bush (1895-1972) Senator
Wayne Lyman Morse (1900-1974) Senator
Adlai Ewing Stevenson II (1900-1965) Politician and Diplomat
Thomas Edmund Dewey (1902-1971) Two-time Governor of New York
George Frost Kennan (1904-2005) Diplomat and Historian
George W. Romney (1907-1995) Governor of Michigan, President of American Motors
Thomas H Eliot (1907-1991) Congressman
Kingman Brewster (1919-1988) Ambassador to Great Britain, President of Yale University
Terrel Bell (1921-1996) Secretary of Education

Theodore L. Eliot (1928-2019) Ambassador to Afghanistan, Secretary General
Adlai Ewing Stevenson III (1930-) Senator
Orrin Hatch (1934-) Senator (longest serving Republican senator)
David Daniel Marriott (1939-) Congressman
Mitt Romney (1947-) Senator, Governor of Massachusetts
Jeb Bush (1953-) Governor of Florida
Jon Meade Huntsman, Jr (1960-) Governor of Utah, Ambassador to Russia, Singapore & China
Sarah Palin (1964-) Governor of Alaska

Royalty
Sylvia Leonora Brett (1885-1971) Ränee of Sarawak
Diana Frances Spencer (1961-1997) Princess of Wales
Serena Alleyne Stanhope Armstrong-Jones (1970-) Countess of Snowdon

University Leadership
John Hiram Lathrop (1799-1866) President of Univ. of Missouri, Univ. of Wisconsin, Indiana Univ.
Frederick Augustus Porter Barnard (1809-1889) President of Columbia University
Amasa Leland Stanford (1824-1893) Founder of Stanford University, Governor of California
Jane Lathrop (1828-1905) Co-Founder of Stanford University (wife of Amasa Stanford)
Daniel Coit Gilman (1831-1908) President of U.C. Berkley and John Hopkins University
Francis Edward Hinckley (1834-1900) Co-Founder of the University of Chicago
Charles Seymour (1884-1963) President of Yale University
Kingman Brewster, Jr (1919-1988) President of Yale University, Ambassador to Great Britain

Religious Leadership
Pastor Joseph Lathrop (1731-1820) 1st Congregational Church, West Springfield, Massachusetts for 62 years
Reverend John Lathrop (1740-1816) Congregationalist in Boston, Massachusetts
Joshua Huntington (1786-1819) Clergyman, Founder American Educational Society
Ephraim Peabody, III (1804-1856) Pastor of King's Chapel Unitarian Church in Boston
Reverend Donald Lathrop
Reverend Ivan Lathrop
Samuel A. Eliot II (1862-1950) President of the American Unitarian Association
Reverend John Howland Lathrop (1880-1967) Unitarian Church of Brooklyn

Religious Leadership of the Church of Jesus Christ of Latter-day Saints
(The LDS Church has found interest in John Lothropp because he was the ancestor to a large number of the original Church members, including Joseph Smith. Members of the Church did much of the genealogical research on the Lothropp/Lathrop descendants here displayed.)
Frederick G. Williams (1787-1842) Counselor to the President, Joseph Smith
W.W. Phelps (1792-1872) Composer of Hymns
Edward Partridge (1793-1840) First Presiding Bishop

Joseph Smith (1805-1844) Founder of the Church of Jesus Christ of Latter-day Saints
Oliver Cowdery (1806-1850) Counselor to the President, Joseph Smith
Parley P. Pratt (1807-1857) Apostle
Wilford Woodruff (1807-1898) President of the Church
Orson Pratt (1811-1881) Apostle
John Losee Van Cott (1814-1883) Missionary to Scandinavia
Joseph F. Smith (1838-1918) President of the Church
Joseph Fielding Smith (1876-1972) President of the Church
David A. Smith (1879-1952) 1st President of the Mormon Tabernacle Choir
Spencer W. Kimball (1895-1985) President of the Church
Marion G. Romney (1897-1988) Apostle
Nathan Eldon Tanner (1898-1982) Apostle
Harold Bingham Lee (1899-1973) President of the Church
Gordon B. Hinckley (1910-2008) President of the Church (also descendant of Samuel Hinckley)
James E. Faust (1920-2007) Apostle
Bruce R. McConkie (1915-1985) Apostle
Boyd Kenneth Packer (1924-2015) Apostle
M. Russell Ballard (1928-) acting Apostle
Gary E Stevenson (1955-) acting Apostle

Writers, Actors, and the Arts
John Lathrop (1772-1820) Lawyer, Poet
Henry Wadsworth Longfellow (1807-1882) Poet
Oliver Wendell Holmes (1809-1894) Physician, Essayist, Poet, Humorist
John Lathrop Motley (1814-1877) Author, Diplomat, Historian
Charlotte Saunders Cushman (1816-1876) Actress
Frederick Law Olmsted (1822-1903) Landscape architect, Journalist
Ina Coolbrith (1841-1928) 1st Poet Laurette of California
Ernest W Longfellow (1845-1921) Artist, Art Collector donating to Boston Museum of Art
Lewis Comfort Tiffany (1848-1933) Artist, Philanthropist
James Ford Rhodes (1848-1927) Industrialist, Author, Pulitzer Prize for History
Francis Augustus Lathrop (1849-1909) Artist
Octave Thanet (Alice French) (1850–1934) Author
George Parsons Lathrop (1851-1898) Author, Newspaper Editor
Charles Eliot (1859-1897) Landscape Architect, Pioneer of Regional Planning
William Lyon Phelps (1865-1943) Literary Critic, Teacher, Scholar
Charles Edward Ives (1874-1954) Composer
Georgia O'Keeffe (1887-1986) Artist
Samuel A. Eliot, Jr (1893-1984) Author
Harold Hart Crane (1899-1932) Essayist
Walt Disney (1901-1966) Animator, Film Producer, Entrepreneur
George A. Smith, Jr (1905-1969) Professor at Harvard Business School, Author

Ora Smith

Robert Penn Warren (1905-1989) Author
Oren Lathrop Brown (1909-2004) Vocal Pedagogue at Julliard
David Bacon (1914-1943) Actor
Louis Staunton Auchincloss (1917-2010) Lawyer, Author, Historian
Dina Merrill (1923-2017) Actress, Philanthropist
Shirley Temple (1928-2014) Actress
Dick Clark (1929-2012) Radio and TV Host
Clint Eastwood (1930-) Actor, Filmmaker, Musician, Politician
Anthony Perkins (1932-1992) Actor
Tuesday Weld (1943-) Actress
John Arthur Lithgow (1945-) Actor, Author, Poet, Musician
Linda Hunt (1945-) Actress, Narrator
Orson Scott Card (1951-) Author
Treat Williams (1951-) Actor, Writer, Aviator
Mark Isham (1951-) Musician, Film Composer
Alec Baldwin (1958-) Actor (as are brothers Daniel, William, Stephen)
Kyra Sedgwick (1965-) Actress, Film Producer, Director
Paget Brewster (1969-) Actress, Voice Actor, Singer
Ethan Hawke (1970-) Actor, Director, Screenwriter, Novelist
Maggie Gyllenhaal (1977-) Actress, Film Producer
Jake Gyllenhaal (1980-) Actor, Film Producer
Jordana Brewster (1980-) Actress

Others

Jabez Huntington (1719-1786) American Revolution Major General of Connecticut Militia
Benedict Arnold (1741-1801) Traitor of the American Revolution
Jedediah Huntington (1743-1818) American Revolution General
Eli Whitney (1765-1825) Inventor of the Cotton Gin
A.S. Wadsworth (1790-1851) Commodore with over 40 years duty in US Navy
Samuel Morse (1791-1872) Inventor Single-wire Telegraph, Co-Developer Morse Code
Charles Goodyear (1800-1860) Discoverer of the Vulcanization Process for Rubber
Sylvester Hulet (1800-1885) California Gold Miner, Helped Establish Las Vegas
James Bonham (1807-1836) Hero and Messenger of the Battle of the Alamo
Robert Breck Brigham (1826-1900) Philanthropist
Simon Newcomb (1835-1909) Astronomer, Applied Mathematician
Albert Milton Lathrop (1841-1943) Pioneer and Chronicler
Alice M Longfellow (1850-1928) Historical Preservationist, Philanthropist
C.W. Post (1854-1914) Founder of Post Cereals
Sir Robert Laird Borden (1854-1937) Prime Minister of Canada
Franklin Henry Giddings (1855-1931) Sociologist
John Pierpont Morgan (1867-1943) Financier, Philanthropist
Harvey Fletcher (1884-1981) Father of Stereophonic Sound, Physicist

The Pulse of His Soul

Alfred Carl Fuller (1885-1973) Founder of Fuller Brush Company
Marjorie Meriwether Post (1887-1973) Founder of General Foods
Donald Lines Jacobus (1887-1970) Genealogist regarded as the Dean of American Genealogy
Charles Scribner III (1890-1952) Publisher (and son)
Marshall Field III (1893–1956) Publisher of Chicago Sun, Bankrolled Saul Alinsky
Dickinson Woodruff Richards (1895-1973) Nobel Prize in Physiology
Amelia Earhart (1897-1937) Aviation Pioneer
Henry Sturgis Morgan (1900-1982) Co-Founder of Morgan Stanley
Benjamin Spock (1903-1998) Physician, Educator, Writer
Julia Child (1912-2004) Celebrity Chef
James Fletcher (1919-1991) Administrator of NASA for Space Shuttle Program
William Wrigley (1933-1999) Chewing Gum Manufacturer, Owner of Chicago Cubs
Jon Meade Huntsman, Sr (1937-2018) Businessman and Philanthropist
Aaron Wells Peirsol (1983-) Olympic Medalist Swimmer

Sources:

"Famous Kin of John Lathrop" website FamousKin.com, https://famouskin.com/famous-kin-menu.php?name=16312+-john+lathrop

"Famous Kin of John Lathrop: Colonial Immigrant Ancestor" website FamousKin.com, https://famouskin.com/famous-kin-menu.php?name=6855+john+lathrop

Holt, Helene. *Exiled: The Story of John Lathrop 1584-1653 Forefather of Presidents, Church Leaders and Statesmen.* Utah: Maasai Publishing, 2002.

-------- *John Lathrop 1584-1653: Reformer, Sufferer, Pilgrim, Man of God.* Utah: Institute of Family Research, Inc., 1979.

"John Lathrop List of Famous Descendants" website Familypedia, https://familypedia.wikia.org/wiki/John_Lathrop_List_of_Famous_Descendants

"Lathrop Genealogy" website, http://users.erols.com/jlathrop/genealogy.html

"Lathrop Notables: Descendants and In-laws of John Lathrop" website, http://ntgen.tripod.com/bw/lath_ntble.html

Price, Richard Woodruff. *John Lothropp: 1584-1653 A Puritan Biography & Genealogy.* Utah: Price and Associates, 2004.

"Rev John Lothrop" Geni.com Project, https://www.geni.com/people/Rev-John-Lothrop/6000000000908380315

"Sarah Palin Related to Princess Diana and Franklin D Roosevelt." *The Telegraph*, October 9, 2008. website Telegraph.co.uk, https://www.telegraph.co.uk/news/worldnews/sarah-palin/3161998/Sarah-Palin-related-to-Princess-Diana-and-Franklin-D-Roosevelt.html

*Special thanks to Gary Boyd Roberts and his initial genealogical research tracing the descendants of John Lothropp.

The Pulse of His Soul

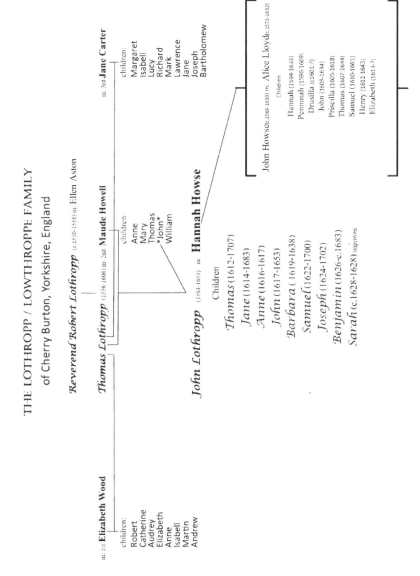

THE LOTHROPP / LOWTHROPPE FAMILY
of Cherry Burton, Yorkshire, England

Reverend Robert Lothropp (c.1510-1558) m. Ellen Aston

Thomas Lothropp (1536-1606) m. 2nd Maude Howell   m. 3rd Jane Carter

m. 1st Elizabeth Wood

children:
Robert
Catherine
Audrey
Elizabeth
Anne
Isabell
Martin
Andrew

children:
Anne
Mary
*Thomas
John
William

children:
Margaret
Isabell
Lucy
Richard
Mark
Lawrence
Jane
Joseph
Bartholomew

John Lothropp (1584-1653) m Hannah Howse

John Howse (c.1569-1630) m: Alice Lloyde (1572-1652)

Children

Hannah (1594-1633)
Penninah (1596-1669)
Drusilla (c1601-?)
John (1603-1634)
Priscilla (1605-1618)
Thomas (1607-1644)
Samuel (1610-1661)
Henry (1612-1643)
Elizabeth (1613-?)

Children

Thomas (1612-1707)
Jane (1614-1683)
Anne (1616-1617)
John (1617-1653)
Barbara (1619-1638)
Samuel (1622-1700)
Joseph (1624-1702)
Benjamin (1626-c.1683)
Sarah (c.1628-1628) unproven

Glossary of Terms

Below are helpful definitions to understand England's religious fervor in the 16th and 17th centuries. Although the many religious factions during the Reformation could not agree on what was doctrinally correct, most did see the need for change.

Church of England (also known as the Anglican Church):
The only church legally functioning in England at the time of this story (1588-1634). It was ruled by the monarch as the "supreme governor" first, then two archbishops assigned by him; one in Canterbury, the other in York, with the Archbishop of Canterbury the most senior cleric. From there the clerical hierarchy fell to the ordained clergy orders of bishops, priests and deacons.

King Henry VIII renounced papal authority when he failed to secure an annulment of his marriage to Catherine of Aragon in 1534. He then passed the Act of Succession and the Act of Supremacy, which recognized that the King was "the only supreme head of the Church of England called Anglicana Ecclesia." The Church was organized with a framework of doctrines, in particular in the Thirty-Nine Articles of Religion and *The Book of Common Prayer*. The Church of England considered itself reformed in that it was shaped by some of the doctrinal principles of the 16th Century Protestant Reformation. Many people in the 1600s felt it still held too closely to the Catholic ceremonies, vestments, and ornaments. The Church emphasized the teachings of the early papal church as formalized in the Nicene and Athanasian creeds. During the Reformation, cathedrals and church buildings in England, which were once Roman Catholic, came under the governance of the Church of England.

The reformation of the Roman Catholic Church is considered to have started with the publication of the *Ninety-five Theses* by Martin Luther in 1517, ending in 1648 with the Treaty of Westphalia, which also ended the Thirty Years' War in England. The Church of England is based on a belief that the Bible contains the core of all Christian faith and thought. *The Book of Common Prayer* was used as a way of worship. Instructions for worship were learned by every person (starting in childhood) through catechisms. Anglicans rehearsed the articles of their beliefs found in *The Book of Common Prayer*. Anglicans also held to holy communion and infant baptism being ordained by Jesus Christ.

During the time period of this novel, every British citizen was expected to attend the Church of England. To not worship as a member of the Church was treasonous and those who did not were punished by persecution, fines, loss of home and livelihood, imprisonment, and torture. Those labeled as "heretics" or enemies to the Church may have gone before the Court of High Commission for trial and sentencing.

Court of High Commission:

Supreme ecclesiastic court in England during the 16th and 17th centuries founded by Queen Elizabeth to give the Crown power to try offenses against the Church and to subjugate any who would resist the supremacy of the Crown. Canterbury Archbishop John Whitgift obtained increased powers for the Court in the 1580s, giving it nearly unlimited power over civil and church matters. The Court of High Commission exercised control over the people of England by licensing plays for publication (Shakespeare was producing during this time), and by 1624 requesting all books on religion to be licensed.

Many felt the court was used as an instrument of repression against those who refused to acknowledge the authority of the Church of England. It used its near-unlimited powers to visit, investigate, correct, and discipline Anglicans and their clergy. During John Lothropp's time in London, its membership was probably over one hundred men, mainly archbishops, bishops, ministers, the kings advocate, and canon lawyers. The most controversial instrument of the court was the *oath ex officio*, which was often forced upon the prisoners. Defendants were to swear before God to answer truthfully any question on any topic that was put before them and the judges could withhold details about the charges. If the oath was refused, the case was sometimes turned over to the much-feared Court of Star Chamber, or the person could be tortured or imprisoned. Those who submitted to the oath, could be forced to incriminate themselves, providing grounds for their own conviction.

Diocese:

An ecclesiastical territory under the jurisdiction of a bishop. There were thirty-four diocese of the Church of England in the early 17th century. John Lothropp lived in the Canterbury Diocese while he resided in Egerton, county of Kent. Canterbury is the oldest diocese in England, founded in 597. Each diocese had a cathedral that was the "seat" of the bishop but was run independently of him. Diocese practices were decided by a general synod.

Parish:

An ecclesiastical district in which everyone in a certain area was assigned to the Church of England. Each parish often consisted of one church building and community, submitting to the oversight of the larger church hierarchy. Parish priests in the church were divided into vicars, rectors, and perpetual curates. Sometimes they were assisted by a curate, deacon, or a lay parish clerk or worker. Ideally, every Englishman had a parish priest to whom they could turn. Both in this novel and historically, John Lothropp was a perpetual curate of Egerton Parish, his brother Thom was a rector of Dengie Parish, and his father-in-law John Howse was a vicar of Eastwell Parish.

Rector:

Rectors were Anglican parish priests who were responsible for the operation of an ecclesiastical institution such as a university, church, cathedral, or parish. Rectors received both greater and lesser tithes. Anglican parish priests were divided into rectors, vicars, and perpetual curates. These were distinguished according to the way in which they were appointed and remunerated.

Vicar:

Ordained priest assigned to a particular parish. Vicars' responsibilities may have included religious services such as worship, marriages, funerals, and baptisms, and also the care and wellbeing of their parishioners. Lay property owners, known as impropriators, had the right to nominate a vicar. Vicars received the lesser tithes only.

Perpetual Curate:

A type of Anglican parish priest who may have had all the same duties as a vicar if there was not a vicar present in the parish, as seemed to be the case with the perpetual curacy of John Lothropp. In the 17th century, a perpetual curate's title would have been reverend or parson. He would have answered to the bishop directly over the diocese. "Perpetual" meant they could not be removed by their nominating patron. They could only be removed through an ecclesiastical court, or make the personal choice to renounce their clerical orders. "Curates" were licensed by the bishop to cure the souls of those in a parish.

Protestant:
By the middle of the 16th century, after a thousand years of Roman Catholic domination, people began complaining that the Church was not teaching people to grow spiritually and live better lives, but instead it was helping itself to the people's monies. Many rejected Papal corruption, supremacy, and the sacraments, disagreeing about the real presence of Christ in the Eucharist, among other things. Those who rejected the Catholic Church were called Protestants (or "protestors" of the faith). The Council of Trent clarified the doctrines contested by the Protestants and provided the leaders of the Reformation with the ammunition to incite followers.

Conformist:
English Protestant who accepted the newly created Church of England as similar to Catholicism, but instead of the Pope carrying divine authority, it was the British Crown. Conformity sometimes depended on enforcement from church wardens and local citizens.

Non-conformist:
English Protestant who does not conform to the doctrines or practices of the Church of England. A non-conformist advocates religious liberty and equality, and opposes compulsion and coercion. In the early 17th century, dissenters did not necessarily remove themselves from church attendance (as a Separatist would), but did voice their displeasure through moral sensibilities.

Separatist:
English Protestant who denied the Church of England altogether. They separated themselves from the perceived corruption of the Church and formed their own congregations. They felt true Christian believers should seek out other Christians and together form churches that could determine their own affairs without having to submit to the judgment of any higher human authority, such as a king. Some believed the Church of England failed to promote faith because of lascivious living and greed of the hierarchy. Because Separatist congregations were

illegal in the early-mid 17th century, many of its adherents were persecuted by the High Commission. They were generally labeled as traitors and heretics, and many left England. Separatists were often Calvinists, but not always. The American Pilgrims were considered Separatists.

Non-Separatist:
Person who sought to reform the Church from within, as did the Puritans, but didn't hold to the Puritan's strict beliefs. There were many Non-separatists who joined the Independent Church under Henry Jacobs and John Lothropp and still attended their parish churches and held to ceremonies such as the baptism of infants. They believed churches should not be ruled by bishops. Some called themselves Semi-separatists.

Puritan:
Person who held the belief that the Bible—and not traditions—should be the sole source of spiritual authority, holding that the pattern for organization of the church was laid down by the New Testament. They were also at the forefront of the campaign for reform. The key ideas of the Reformation in England were a call to "purify" the Church of England from its Catholic practices—thus the believers called themselves "Puritans." They insisted on significant changes in *The Book of Common Prayer* but were reasonably satisfied with the Church's Calvinist teachings on predestination and the Eucharist. Although they didn't leave the Church, they maintained that the Church of England was only partially reformed. They called for ethical and moral purity, believing true reformers should remain in the church, working for this purification. They adopted a literal reading of the Sabbath commandment (Sabbatarianism) that called for both worship and rest on the seventh day of the week. They believed Paradise would occur on Earth prior to the final judgment (millennialism). Because their ministers made it their purpose to interpret scripture for the people, ministers took a central role in their society. The primary difference between the Separatists (Pilgrims falling into this group) and the Puritans was the Puritans believed they did not need to abandon the larger Church of England.

The Puritan's culture of thrift and industry fostered prosperity for themselves and their community. Puritans were known to wear simple clothing that was black or dark brown. They felt it ungodly to laugh or have fun and considered gifts, parties, and decorations to be idolatry. Puritans preferred to call themselves "the godly." After the Pilgrims, the Puritans developed a colony in America that they wanted to be a model to the world. In 1630, a famous Puritan, John Winthrop, wrote of settling the Massachusetts Bay Colony: "We shall be as a city upon a hill, the eyes of all people are upon us."

Brownist:

Those who followed the writings and teachings of Robert Browne, even after he recanted those writings himself. Browne was at the forefront of religious dissent and at the beginnings of the English Separatist movement, advocating religious separation from the Church of England. He was an active Separatist from 1579-1585 and became a self-styled preacher without a preaching license. After multiple imprisonments, abuses, and warnings by the Church, he was excommunicated. He later facilitated a reconciliation with the Church of England and said he would conform to their teachings. It appears he did not, but was still actively criticized for recanting his principles to gain his own personal liberty. Browne may have reverted back to some of his earlier beliefs and activities during the latter period of his life. Throughout much of the years 1616-1632, his activities are unaccounted for. It is suspected he traveled during this time to teach his doctrine. He called himself a nonconformist.

Pilgrim:

Those who were on a pilgrimage, looking for the promised land. The Pilgrims who first fled England to find religious refuge in the Netherlands and then settled at Plymouth Colony in 1620, considered themselves Separatists from the Church of England. Some have called them Brownists, after the nonconformist Robert Browne, but most of these Pilgrims asked not to be called Brownists. But Brownists, Independents, and Separatists were all terms used somewhat interchangeably for those who broke with the Church of England and went to the Colonies. The Pilgrims were *not* Puritans, as some have mistakenly stated. They sailed on the *Mayflower*, originally headed for Virginia, but storms sent them off course to Massachusetts where they built and settled Plymouth Plantation. The Puritans came to America after the Pilgrims and were associated with the judgements upon Anne Hutchinson, the Salem Witch Trials, and other harsh resolutions. Massachusetts Puritans and Pilgrims/Separatists were distinct groups of people in that the Puritan's had not separated themselves from the Church of England. The Pilgrims believed in religious freedom, the Puritans did not. The Pilgrims believed in freedom of conscience and the Plymouth churches were overwhelmingly Congregationalist and Separatist in form. It is believed that the Pilgrims did not call themselves by the name of Pilgrim, but that it came into being as a moniker given them by others around 1800. And contrary to popular belief, it's likely they wore colorful clothing of blues, greens, and oranges.

Independent Church:
Founded by Henry Jacob in 1616, the Independent Church was an illegally (and usually secretly) run religious congregation in Southwark and London, England made up of Separatists and Semi-separatists. Members believed the parish churches ought to be independent from one another and they advocated local congregational control of religious and church matters. They were against the bishops, but not the Church of England. Both Separatists and Semi-separatists believed bishops should not run the Church and believed in freedom of conscience. As a whole, the Independents refused to take a stand against the Church of England, hoping God would eventually manifest to them the way they should walk in the ways of righteousness. Their biggest strength may have been that they covenanted together to take care of one another. Many of the Independent Church members in London who went to America became members of the Congregational Church in Massachusetts.

Note: In 1633 there was a break in the London Independent Church when a disagreement arose regarding infant baptism. Those who did not believe in infant baptism left the Independent congregation and are considered part of the foundational Baptist Church.

Papist
A Roman Catholic. As *popery* would refer to the Roman Catholic doctrines, ceremonies, and system of government.

Conventicle
A secret or unauthorized meeting concerning religious worship for congregants to hear unlicensed preachers.

Sermongatting
The practice of an individual traveling out of their parish boundaries to listen to a preacher other than their own.

Schism
Separation of an individual or sect from a church over doctrinal differences.

Sizar
An undergraduate who receives maintenance aid from a university or sponsor.

Ora Smith

Reformation Timeline
in John Lothropp's Lifetime

1584 John Lothropp born to Thomas and Maude Howell Lothropp in Etton, Yorkshire, England
1584 Jesuit and seminary priests banned in England
1584 Remedial bill introduced into Parliament on behalf of Puritans defeated
1585 England established the Roanoke Colony in North America (re-established deserted colony 1587)
1585 Queen Elizabeth ordered bishops to deal harshly with Puritans
1585 Catholic priests ordered to leave England or suffer death
1587 Mary, Queen of Scots is beheaded for her complicity in a plot to murder Queen Elizabeth
1588 Spanish Armada defeated by English fleet
1589 John Lothropp's mother died in January
1589 Fulke's Refutation showed Catholic Rheims Bible as a corrupt compromise to Bishops' Bible
1590 Shakespeare's first play Henry VI, Part 1 depicts the collapse of England's role in France
1593 Separatist Henry Barrowe hanged for advocating congregational independency
1593 Anyone over the age of 16 who did not attend church in the month was to be imprisoned
1593 Those who didn't attend church within a three-month period were exiled or killed
1597 Irish Rebellion (Nine Years' War) led by Hugh O'Neill and fought over English rule in Ireland
1602 John Lothropp entered Oxford
1603 Queen Elizabeth died and James VI of Scotland crowned King of Great Britain
1603 750 Puritans presented King James the Millenary Petition but he was not sympathetic to their cause
1604 Henry Jacob imprisoned for beliefs that individual churches should be self-governing
1604 Non-conforming Anglican clergymen compelled by severe restrictions to obey the Crown
1605 Gunpowder Plot devised as an effort to end the persecution of Roman Catholics, but failed
1605 300+ clergymen ejected, silenced, or suspended; some imprisoned, others driven into exile
1606 John Lothropp at Cambridge when his father died
1607 Jamestown, Virginia established as the first permanent English settlement in North America
1607 John Lothropp ordained deacon and began ministry as curate in Bennington
1608 Anglican clergyman John Robinson became Separatist and went to Holland with followers
1610 John Lothropp became perpetual curate in Egerton and married Hannah Howse
1610 Henry Jacob exiled and joined John Robinson in Leiden, Holland
1611 John King, well-known Calvinist and anti-Catholic preacher, consecrated the Bishop of London
1611 King James Bible published and used throughout the English-speaking world
1612 John Smyth, exiled to Holland, penned a daring declaration for religious freedom
1616 Henry Jacob established the unlawful Independent Church at Southwark/London
1616 King James released 4,000 Catholics from prisons against Parliaments complaints
1618 Thirty Years War began over territorial and dynastic problems
1618 Thirty Years War widely regarded as a contest between Protestants and Catholics
1618 *Book of Sports* introduced
1618 16 Catholics are executed for opposition to the Church of England
1619 Initiated by rise of Arminianism, the international Synod of Dort resisted by English bishops
1620 Separatist Pilgrims sailed to America on the *Mayflower*
1621 Remedial bills introduced into Parliament on behalf of Puritans are defeated
1621 Lord Chancellor Francis Bacon convicted of corruption

The Pulse of His Soul

1622 John Donne preached to enormous crowd at Saint Paul's in favor of Church of England policies

1622 King James exerted a nuptial treaty for his son and a Catholic Spanish princess

1622 King James released Catholics from prison to appease the Pope to agree to nuptials

1622 John Lothropp renounced his orders with the Church of England

1623 The Spanish match of a proposed marriage for Prince Charles broke down completely

1623 King James reissued the strict printing injunctions of Queen Elizabeth

1624 Henry Jacob died and John Lothropp sustained as the minister of Independent Church

1625 King James died and his son, Charles I, crowned King of England, Scotland and Ireland

1625 King Charles married Henrietta Maria of France, a Roman Catholic princess

1625 War on Spain is declared, a fiasco with many dying from disease and starvation

1628 A disgruntled soldier, John Felton, assassinated the Duke of Buckingham, George Villiers

1628 William Laud became Bishop of London

1629 King Charles I dissolved Parliament for final time and started his personal reign

1629 Great Migration to New England begins with people leaving England by the hundreds

1630 Alexander Leighton flogged and mutilated

1632 *Histriomastix* published, attacking English theatre and Christmas celebrations, among other things

1632 John Lothropp and congregation imprisoned

1633 William Laud ordained Archbishop of Canterbury

1633 New *Book of Sports*, adding wakes and countryside festivals to the list of sanctioned recreations

1633 Ministers who refused to read the *Book of Sports* to congregation were deprived of positions

1633 Robert Browne died in a prison in Northampton

1634 Puritan William Prynne arrested, pilloried, and mutilated for publishing *Histriomastix*

1634 John Lothropp with family and congregation sailed to America

1637 John Lilburne imprisoned for disseminating literature claiming that bishops were servants of Satan

1639 Bishops' Wars began, originating over control and governance of the Church of Scotland

1640 Puritans gained power in new Parliament

1640 High Commission Star Chamber abolished

1640 Parliament ordered Book of Sports publicly burned

1640 Mass demonstrations and petitions displayed a prominent hatred of William Laud

1640 William Laud arrested and held in the Tower of London

1642 English Civil War broke out

1645 Parliamentary forces claim victory at the Battle of Naseby

1647 William Laud beheaded

1649 Parliament held King Charles under house arrest at Holdenby House in Northamptonshire

1649 King Charles beheaded

1649 Charles II exiled and forced worship by the Church of England ended

1649 Commonwealth ruled England

1653 Protectorate under the personal rule of Oliver Cromwell ruled England (by 1660 Charles II restored to the throne, establishing that an English monarch could not govern without Parliament's consent)

1653 John Lothropp died in Barnstable, Massachusetts, Plymouth Bay Colony

Bibliography

-------- "Alexander Leighton D.D. (1568- ca1643)." The Reformation website. https://www.thereformation.info/alexander_leighton/

-------- *Bishops Transcripts, Eastwell, St Mary*. Diocese of Canterbury, Parish Registers, Kent County, England. doc. Dcb/BT1/82/3, Baptism of Thomas Lothropp by John Howse. Canterbury Cathedral Library and Archives. 11 March 2019.

-------- *Bishops Transcripts, Eastwell, St Mary*. Diocese of Canterbury, Parish Registers, Kent County, England. doc. Dcb/BT1/82/11, Baptism of Joseph Lothropp by John Howse. Canterbury Cathedral Library and Archives. 11 March 2019.

-------- *Bishops Transcripts, Eastwell, St Mary*. Diocese of Canterbury, Parish Registers, Kent County, England. doc. Dcb/BT1/82/16, Burial of John Howse. Canterbury Cathedral Library and Archives. 11 March 2019.

-------- *Bishops Transcripts, Egerton, St James*. Diocese of Canterbury, Parish Registers, Kent County, England. doc. Dcb/BT1/84/14, Baptism of Anne Lothropp by John Lothropp. Canterbury Cathedral Library and Archives. 11 March 2019.

-------- *Bishops Transcripts, Egerton, St James*. Diocese of Canterbury, Parish Registers, Kent County, England. doc. Dcb/BT1/84/17, Baptism of Jane Lothropp by John Lothropp. Canterbury Cathedral Library and Archives. 11 March 2019.

-------- *Bishops Transcripts, Egerton, St James*. Diocese of Canterbury, Parish Registers, Kent County, England. doc. Dcb/BT1/84/18, Baptism of John Lothropp by John Lothropp. Canterbury Cathedral Library and Archives. 11 March 2019.

-------- *Bishops Transcripts, Egerton, St James*. Diocese of Canterbury, Parish Registers, Kent County, England. doc. Dcb/BT1/84/18, Burial of Anne Lothropp by John Lothropp. Canterbury Cathedral Library and Archives. 11 March 2019.

-------- *Bishops Transcripts, Egerton, St James*. Diocese of Canterbury, Parish Registers, Kent County, England. doc. Dcb/BT1/84/18b, Baptism of Barbara Lothropp by John Lothropp. Canterbury Cathedral Library and Archives. 11 March 2019.

Bond, Francis. *An Introduction to English Church Architecture from the Eleventh to the Sixteenth Century*. London: Oxford University Press, 1913.

-------- *The Book of Common Prayer: King James Anno 1604*. London: William Pickering, 1844. Google Book, https://www.google.com/books/edition/The_Book_of_Common_Prayer/tGBNAAAAYAAJ?hl=en&gbpv=1&dq=Book+of+Common+Prayer,+1604+edition&printsec=frontcover

Browner, Jessica A. "Wrong Side of the River: London's Disreputable South Bank in the Sixteenth and Seventeenth Century." *The Annual Journal, Vol 36*. University of Virginia: Corcoran Department of History, 1994.

Bruce, John. *Calendar of State Papers, Domestic Series, of the Reign of Charles I, 1633-1634*. The High Commission Court Records preserved in Her Majesty's Public Record Office. London: Longman, Green, and Roberts, 1863.

Bunker, Nick. *Making Haste from Babylon: The Mayflower Pilgrims and Their World*. New York: Vintage Books, 2010.

Burrage, Champlin. *The Early English Dissenters in the Light of Recent Research 1550-1641, Vol 1* and *Vol 2*. Cambridge: University Press, 1912.

-------- *Canterbury General Licence Register*. Diocese of Canterbury. doc. DCb/L/R/7 folio 52, cure of souls licence to John Lothropp 10 January 1609/10. Kent Archives and History, Maidstone.

-------- *Canterbury General Licence Register*. Diocese of Canterbury. doc. DCb/L/R/7 folio 66, cure of souls licence to John Lothropp 15 August 1610. Kent Archives and History, Maidstone.

-------- *Canterbury Marriage Licence Register*. Diocese of Canterbury. doc. DCb/L/R/7 folio 69v, marriage licence of John Lothropp and Hannah Howse. Kent Archives and History, Maidstone.

Chamberlin, Russell. *The English Parish Church*. London: Hodder & Stroughton, 1993.

-------- "Clergy of Church of England (in England)." FamilySearch online, Wiki Article, 2 February 2015, https://www.familysearch.org/wiki/en/Clergy_of_Church_of_England_(in_England)?fbclid=IwAR14DlezIcO-

QrgntBEcgJxw2otut68FmNU4B2kRLAQ4KWtxtyq9aRyAPBsw

-------- Clergy of the Church of England Database (searchable), https://theclergydatabase.org.uk/jsp/search/index.jsp Collinson, Patrick. *The Religion of Protestants: The Church in English Society 1559–1625*.USA: Oxford University Press, 1984.

-------- "Congregationalism" *Encyclopædia Britannica*, Vol 6, 1911. Wikisource.org, https://en.wikisource.org/wiki/1911_Encyclop%C3%A6dia_Britannica/Congregationalism

-------- "Court of High Commission: English Ecclesiastical Court." Encyclopedia Britannica online, Jul 20, 1998, https://www.britannica.com/topic/Court-of-High-Commission

Dale, R.W. *History of English Congregationalism*. New York: A.C Armstrong and Son, 1907.Google Book, https://www.google.com/books/edition/History_of_English_Congregationalism/s-20mAgY6y8C?hl=en&gbpv=1&dq=Dale,+R.W.+History+of+English+Congregationalism&printsec=frontcover

de Sandwich, Peter. "Some East Kent Parish History." *The Home Counties Magazine, Vols 1-14*, https://sites.rootsweb.com/~mrawson/ekent.html

-------- "Definitions of Puritanism." Wikipedia webpage, https://en.wikipedia.org/wiki/Definitions_of_Puritanism

Dewey, Richard Lloyd. *John Lathrop: Arrival in America and Family Tree*. Utah: Apocalypse Books, 1988.

Dorn, Nathan. "John Lilburne, Oaths and the Cruel Trilemma." In Custodia Legis, Law Libraries of Congress: Library of Congress website, art. April 25, 2013, https://blogs.loc.gov/law/2013/04/john-lilburne-oaths-and-the-cruel-trilemma/

Dunn, Richard S., James Savage, and Laetitia Yeandle, eds. *The Journal of John Winthrop, 1630-1649*. Massachusetts: Harvard University Press, 1996. Google Book, https://www.google.com/books/edition/The_Journal_of_John_Winthrop_1630_1649/mHNorpMOvWkC?hl=en&gbpv=1&dq=Winthrop,+John.+The+Journal+of+John+Winthrop,+1630-1649&printsec=frontcover

-------- "Early Families of Scituate." The Scituate Historical Society website, http://scituatehistoricalsociety.org/early-scituate-families

-------- "Early Families of Scituate, Massachusetts." Geni.com Project, https://www.geni.com/projects/Early-Families-of-Scituate-Massachusetts/7203

-------- *Eastwell Inventories*. Diocese of Canterbury, Kent County, England. film PRC 28/18/29, Inventory of John Howse. Canterbury Cathedral Library and Archives. 11 March 2019

-------- *Eastwell Wills*. Diocese of Canterbury, Kent County, England. film PRC 32/49/306c, Will of John Howse. Canterbury Cathedral Library and Archives. 11 March 2019

-------- *Eastwell Wills*. Diocese of Canterbury, Kent County, England. film PRC 16/195/H4, Will of John Howse. Canterbury Cathedral Library and Archives. 11 March 2019

-------- The Editors of Encyclopaedia Britannica. "John Robinson" Encyclopædia Britannica Publisher: Encyclopædia Britannica, inc., February 26, 2020. Website,https://www.britannica.com/biography/John-Robinson-English-minister

-------- Encyclopedia Britannica biographies (searchable), https://www.britannica.com/biography/

Evans, David R. "John Howse, Rev." Evans Family Webpage: Portland State University, http://web.pdx.edu/~davide/gene/Howse_John.htm

Gipps, Bryan. *Egerton Church and Village*. (1995) Pamphlet 7/6, Canterbury Cathedral Library and Archives. 11 March 2019.

Goehring, Walter R. *The West Parish Church*. West Barnstable, MA: Memorial Foundation, 1959.

Griswold, Barbara Stone. "Congregational Dynamics in the Early Tradition of Independency" PhD diss. Waco, Texas: Baylor University, 2006.

Hannula, Richard. *For Christ's Crown and Covenant: Sketches of Puritans and Covenanters*. Idaho: Canon Press, 2014. Google Book, https://www.google.com/books/edition/For_Christ_s_Crown_and_Covenant_Sketches/Nq6tDwAAQBAJ?hl=en&gbpv=1&dq=Hannula,+Richard.+-For+Christ%27s+Crown+and+Covenant:+Sketches+of+Puritans+and+Covenanters,&printsec=frontcover

-------- "History of St Augustine's Abbey." History and Stories, *English Heritage* online magazine, https://www.english-heritage.org.uk/visit/places/st-augustines-abbey/history-and-stories/history/

Holt, Helene. *Exiled: The Story of John Lathrop 1584-1653 Forefather of Presidents, Church Leaders and Statesmen.* Utah: Maasai Publishing, 2002.

-------- Bishops Bible ed. 1604, https://studybible.info/Bishops/

Huntington, Elijah Baldwin. *A Genealogical Memoir of the Lo-Lathrop Family in this County.* Connecticut: Julia M. Huntington, 1884.

James, Leonie. *The Household Accounts of William Laud, Archbishop of Canterbury, 1635-1642.* New York: The Boydell Press, 2019.

-------- *John Lathrop 1584-1653: Reformer, Sufferer, Pilgrim, Man of God.* Utah: Institute of Family Research, 1979.

-------- "John Lothrop Biography." Sacramento: The Northwestern California University Law School, https://nwculaw.edu/john-lothrop-biography

LaPlante, Eve. *American Jezebel: The Uncommon Life of Anne Hutchinson, the Woman Who Defied the Puritans.* San Francisco: Harper Collins, 2005. Ebook

-------- *List of Eastwell Incumbents.* doc. U108/3/36, John Howse 29 April 1603. Diocese of Canterbury. Canterbury Cathedral Library and Archives. 11 March 2019.

-------- *List of Egerton Incumbents.* doc. U108/3/37, John Lothropp 15 August 1610. Diocese of Canterbury. Canterbury Cathedral Library and Archives. 11 March 2019.

Loomis, Lucy (compiled). *John Lothrop in Barnstable.* 2nd ed. Massachusetts: Sturgis Library, 2011.

Mackenzie, K.D., and Claude Jenkins. *Episcopacy Ancient and Modern.* New York: Society for Promoting Christian Knowledge, 1930.

Marshall, Peter and Manuel, David. *The Light and The Glory 1492-1793*. Michigan: Revell, 2009.

McConnell, Dan R. "The Roots of the Ancient Congregational Church in London, Scituate, and Barnstable, Rev. John Lothropp Minister." *Cape Cod Genealogical Society Bulletin*, Fall 2008.

McDayter, Mark. "London ca. 1676: London Prisons." Restoration & 18th Century Studies in English at Western, https://instruct.uwo.ca/english/234e/site/bckgrnds/maps/lndnmpprsns.html

Moorman, John. *The History of the Church in England*. Pennsylvania: Morehouse Publishing, 1980.

Morton, Nathaniel. *New England's Memorial*. Massachusetts: Allen and Farnham, 1669. Internet Archive, https://archive.org/details/newenglandsmemor00m/page/n10/mode/2up

Mortimer, Ian. *The Time Traveler's Guide to Elizabethan England*. New York: Penguin Books, 2012.

Needham, Albert. *How to Study an Old Church*. London: B.T. Batsford, 1957.

O'Day, Rosemary. *The Family and Family Relationships, 1500-1900: England, France and the United States of America*. London: Red Globe Press, 1994.

Otis, Amos. *Genealogical Notes of Barnstable Families*. Barnstable, Massachusetts: F.B. & F.P. Goss, 1888.

Parkin-Speer, Diane. "Robert Browne: Rhetorical Iconoclast." *The Sixteenth Century Journal*, vol. 18, no. 4, 1987, pp. 519–529. JSTOR, www.jstor.org/stable/2540867. Accessed 16 Feb. 2020.

Philbrick, Nathaniel. *Mayflower: A Story of Courage, Community, and War*. New York: Penguin Group, 2006.

Plomer, Henry Robert. "A Dictionary of the Booksellers and Printers who Were at Work in England, Scotland and Ireland from 1641 to 1667." Wikisource.org, https://en.wikisource.org/wiki/A_Dictionary_of_the_Booksellers_and_Printers_who_Were_at_Work_in_England,_Scotland_and_Ireland_from_1641_to_1667/Bellamy,_or_Bellamie_(John)

Pope, Charles Henry. *The Pioneers of Massachusetts: A Descriptive List, Drawn from Records of the Colonies, Towns, and Churches, and Other Contemporaneous Documents*. Maryland: Genealogical Publishing Company, 1900. Google books, https://www.google.com/books/edition/The_Pioneers_of_Massachusetts/ur2OJjh5ZLgC?hl=en&gbpv=1&bsq=lathrop

Price, Richard Woodruff. *John Lothropp: 1584-1653 A Puritan Biography & Genealogy*. Utah: Price and Associates, 2004.

-------- "Queen Bertha: A Historical Enigma." Women in History, *English Heritage* online magazine, https://www.english-heritage.org.uk/learn/histories/women-in-history/queen-bertha-historical-enigma/

Quinton, Rebecca. *Glasgow Museums Seventeenth-Century Costume*. London: Unicorn Press Ltd., 2013.

-------- *Register Abbot III*. folio 190v & 191. Abstract from Latin: 20 October 1630, death of John Howse. Diocese of Canterbury. Archbishop's Registers at Lambeth Palace Library.

-------- *Register Whitgift III*. folio 275v. Abstract from Latin: 29 April 1603, John Howse instituted to the parish of Eastwell. Diocese of Canterbury. Archbishop's Registers at Lambeth Palace Library.

Riddle, Samuel H. "Quarterly Register and Journal of the American Education Society." *The American Quarterly Register*, vol 15, p 62. American Education Society, 1843.

Rostenberg, Leona. "John Bellamy: 'Pilgrim' Publisher of London." *The Papers of the Bibliographical Society of America*, vol. 50, no. 4, 1956, pp. 342–369. JSTOR, www.jstor.org/stable/24299559

Savage, James. *A Genealogical Dictionary of the First Settlers of New England*. Vol. 3: Surnames K-R. Germany: Jazzybee Verlag, 2016.

-------- *The Seven Villages of Barnstable*. Town of Barnstable: Vail-Ballou Press, 1976.

Sparkes, Abigail. "The Life and Death of William Laud." Historic UK: The History and Heritage Accommodation Guide online magazine, https://www.historic-uk.com/HistoryUK/HistoryofEngland/The-Life-and-

The Pulse of His Soul

Death-Of-Wiliam-Laud/

Strong, Roy. *A Little History of the English Country Church*. London: Jonathan Cape, 2007.

Strong, Roy. *Visions of England*. London: The Bodley Head, 2011.

-------- "Styles of Belief, Devotion, and Culture." *The Norton Anthology of English Literature*, Norton Topics online (ref Book of Sport), https://web.archive.org/web/20041204142451/http://www.wwnorton.com/nael/17century/topic_3/sports.htm

Taber, Helen Lathrop. *A New Home in Mattakeese: A Guide to Reverend John Lothropp's Barnstable*. Massachusetts: Rock Village Publishing, 2013.

Thrush, Andrew, and John P. Ferris. "Denne, Thomas (1577-1656), of St Alphege, Canterbury, Kent and the Inner Temple, London; later of Denne Hill, Kingston, Kent." *The History of Parliament: The House of Commons 1604-1629*, ed. 2010, https://www.historyofparliamentonline.org/volume/1604-1629/member/denne-thomas-1577-1656

-------- "The Trial and Execution of Charles I." The History Learning Site, 2020. United Kingdom website, https://www.historylearningsite.co.uk/stuart-england/the-trial-and-execution-of-charles-i/

Waters, H. F. *The New England Historical and Genealogical Register, Vols. 37-52*. Boston: New England Historic Genealogical Society, 1913. Google Books, https://books.google.com/books/about/The_New_England_Historical_and_Genealogi.html?id=hkjQ90cX71oC

White, Gail M. *Etton: A Village of the East Riding*. East Yorkshire: Hutton Press, 1992.

Wood, Margaret. *The English Mediaeval House*. London: Bracken Books, 1985.

Acknowledgements

I am beyond grateful for the advice of my good and kind advanced readers who combed the early versions of The Pulse of His Soul. Namely, author Evelyn Tidman in England, Richard Price of Price Genealogy and a Lothropp descendant, Marla Vincent of the John Lothropp Foundation and a Lothropp and Hinckley descendant, Rene Allen and Jo Ellen Guthrie who were there with me from the story's conception, Brent and Sarah Hinze who emphasized *it has to be a movie!*, Deanne Richardson, Joan Sowards, Candy Hunt, Patti Hulet, Gwen Rogers, Sandra Sorenson-Kindt, Cindy Higginson, Angelique Conger, Gail Porter, Jill Hydrick, and Carter Hydrick.

Thank you Peter Fagg for making my research tour in England an enjoyable outing that felt more fun than academic. I'm now not only well educated on Queen Bertha, but also on mushy peas. The drive through Kent added pleasure and a stop at the beach made the trip memorable.

Thank you Anne Law for your calligraphy map skills.

And, although we've never met, I'd like to give a special thanks to Barbara Stone Griswold for her PhD dissertation "Congregational Dynamics in the Early Tradition of Independency." It was through her clear and precise research and writing that I came to finally understand the differences between a Separatist, a Nonconformist, and a Puritan. I also learned that the Independent Church in Southwark was a sister church to the John Robinson congregation in Holland where the American Pilgrims originated.

Editors are never in the spotlight and really should be. They make the writing shine! My wonderful editor, Lori Freeland, has become my friend. She is a good and gracious person who teaches with patience and wisdom of the craft. Thank you, Lori, for also encouraging me along the way.

Thank you Adrienne Quintana for having patience with me. The Lord blessed me with access to your talents. I will always appreciate your honesty and direction.

Also by the Author

Children's Picture Book
A Christmas Story of Light

Heritage Fiction
The Cry of Her Heart
A companion novella to
The Pulse of His Soul:
The Story of John Lothropp, a Forgotten Forefather
Get it free at www.orasmith.com

White Oak River: A Story of Slavery's Secrets
Soon to be released in 2021

Ora Smith, a genealogist who writes Heritage Fiction, creates fascinating stories about her ancestors based on true events. She loves nothing better than to be whisked off to past eras to meet those whose lives are worth sharing.

The Cry of Her Heart
A companion novella to The Pulse of His Soul

Punished for her choice to leave the Church of England and meet illegally with the secret Separatist community, genteel Penninah Howse is thrown into Clink Prison with little chance of release. To survive prison under the evil of Bishop William Laud's tyranny, she must evade the advances of a malicious jailer, learn to live with a cruel cellmate, and battle the enemies of hunger, filth, vermin, and self-doubt. When Robert Linnell finally succeeds in buying visitation rights, her old and dear friend not only brings food, he brings hope. Is there a chance he'll find a way to secure her release? Or will this be her life forever?

Get the novella free for a limited time and sign up for Ora's newsletter at www.orasmith.com

Watch for another **Heritage Fiction** about Ora Smith's ancestors in *White Oak River* to be released early 2021.

White Oak River: A Story of Slavery's Secrets

To marry John Mattocks, Caroline Gibson leaves behind her genteel life, which she finds much easier than leaving behind her bigotry. While she's content being served, John lives to serve others. Following his heart to become an abolitionist preacher, he turns his back on his family's wealth and their long-held institution of slavery. But when Caroline discovers her own hidden ancestry, the Civil War's failure to create a changed society begins to mirror their marriage, not only leaving the nation in despair but their relationship as well. Can their love stay strong and find deeper roots in forgiveness and acceptance?

This dramatic story of love, faith, family bonds, and discrimination is based on true events of the author's great-great-great-grandparents in North Carolina.

The Lothropp Family Foundation was founded by Helen Lathrop Taber in 1989 in Barnstable, Massachusetts, the final home of Reverend John Lothropp. The mission of the nonprofit foundation is to preserve and memorialize the historical lives of Reverend John Lothropp and Mark Lothrop. It is a membership-oriented foundation which encourages gatherings of descendants to learn about their ancestors and one another. The Lothropp Family Foundation holds a biennial reunion in various locations around the country. Grants are made annually to nonprofit organizations who are restoring or preserving historical buildings or artifacts related to Reverend John Lothropp and his descendants. www.lothropp.org

Made in the USA
Monee, IL
22 September 2021